# As The World Dies

*A Zombie Trilogy*

# Fighting to Survive

Book Two

Rhiannon Frater

ISBN/EAN13: 1440424764/9781440424762

# Author's Note

*"The best-laid plans of mice and men often go awry."*

This popular quote sums up the last six months of work on this novel.

The entire trilogy was first published online and there are over 1,600 pages of manuscript pages. We knew that we would have to revise and edit the manuscript into three novels, but felt the work was fairly complete and this should not be a big issue. Originally, my husband and I thought we could have the book ready to publish in Fall of 2008.

We were wrong.

The second book, originally titled **Struggling to Survive**, ended up missing a lot of scenes that I could have sworn were in the original manuscript. After much investigation and reflection, I realized that what was so clear in my head never made it onto paper. Entire scenes, huge chunks of plot lines, and important moments of characterization were missing. Since the original was written piecemeal, often when I was traveling for work, I didn't always know where I had left off when I wrote the next chapter. This resulted in the second book not being nearly as ready as we thought.

So I ended up writing about Jenni and Katie once again and was able to weave the missing scenes back into the manuscript. By the time I finished, over one hundred new pages were injected into the story. All the vital missing scenes are now present in this version.

As I revisited the world of the fort, I realized something I had not before. The title was wrong. Katie and Jenni and the others were not struggling to survive: they were fighting. Fighting zombies, bandits and, in some cases, each other. Thus a new title was born.

I hope you enjoy *As The World Dies: Fighting to Survive.*

*--Rhiannon Frater*

*Dedicated to my loyal fans. Your encouragement keeps me writing!*

*Thanks to George A. Romero for your movies, and all the wonderful nightmares you've inspired. Those nightmares ended up in this trilogy.*

*Special thanks to Mom for your constant support of my writing and your dedication to helping me achieve my dreams. You are the greatest!*

*And to my husband for your technical expertise, encouragement, and patience when I spend long hours writing.*

Somewhere in Texas...

The fort...

# Chapter 1

## 1. Terror in the Darkness

The hallway was barely illuminated by the blue light shimmering up the stairs from the TV in the living room. The light flickered along the walls and ceiling, providing just enough light to make out her path. Groggily, Jenni walked toward her youngest son's bedroom, which was located near the top of the stairs. She shoved her long dark hair out of her face and glanced down the staircase. Through the railing slats, she could see her husband, Lloyd, in the living room, where he spent most of his time at home staring at a plasma-screen TV. She could just make out the black silhouette of his head against the brightly-lit screen.

Warily, wanting to avoid alerting him to her presence, she hurried into Benji's room.

The Mickey Mouse night-light illuminated the room just enough for her to make out the form of her sleeping three-year old son. Resting in his racing car-shaped bed, his little hand was thrown over his dark blond curls, his lips parted as he softly snored. Smiling, Jenni knelt down and tucked in his Winnie the Pooh blankets around his body. He was just recovering from a cold. She wanted to make sure he didn't get chilled. Her fingers gently caressed his soft, full cheek then smoothed his curls back from his face. He resembled his father in coloring and facial features. She prayed every day that he did not have his father's violent temper or cruel streak. She wanted him to grow up and be a good, strong man who would love his family and protect them: not brutalize them and make them fear him.

A noise from downstairs startled her. She tensed, waiting for the sounds of Lloyd's footsteps on the stairs. Instead, only the distant hum of voices on the TV wafted up to the room.

Lloyd hated for her to "coddle" the boys. He grew annoyed with her checking on them at night and accused her of spying on his late night habits downstairs. Frankly, she preferred it when he remained down there watching his porn, calling his girlfriends, and leaving her to sleep alone in their bed.

"I want you to not be like him," she whispered to Benji as he slept. "Don't be like him."

She kissed Benji's forehead and breathed in his sweet baby smell. She loved him so.

Drawing back, she looked over at the side table. There was an oatmeal cookie still on his plate, but the milk was gone. Both the boys enjoyed a nighttime snack before bed. She didn't see the harm in it. She used all natural ingredients in the cookies and they were delicious. Feeling a little hungry, she grabbed up the cookie and began to nibble on it.

*Don't grow up to be like him,* she wished.

*He won't grow up,* a voice answered her.

She frowned as she chewed the cookie. That was a horrible thought to think.

*He doesn't live past tonight. You know that. Remember?*

"No," Jenni whispered, pressing her hand to her forehead. "No." She didn't want to remember.

Images flashed in her mind: bloody, chaotic, and terrible.

"No," she moaned. She closed her eyes and she stuffed the cookie in her mouth and chewed vigorously. It had lost all its flavor and gave her no comfort.

"What the hell are you doing?"

Lloyd's sharp voice startled her.

She looked up at him, trying to chew the cookie fast and swallow before he could see she was eating outside of the strictly-regimented diet he had created to keep her thin and beautiful.

"What the hell are you eating?" Lloyd's voice was terrible and his darkened form in the doorway terrified her.

She finished chewing and swallowed hard. "Nothing...I-"

"What did you do to Benji? Oh, God, Jenni, what the hell is wrong with you?"

Jenni looked toward her son to see his tender belly torn out and his intestines strung across the bed. One of her hands clutched the flesh tightly. Slowly, she raised her other hand to her mouth and felt that her lips were slick with blood.

"Jenni, what did you do?"

She began to scream...

Jenni woke and sat up sharply. Her heart thundered in her chest. In the dim light leaking in around the edges of the makeshift tent she shared with Juan, she could see that her hands were not covered in blood. Pressing her fingertips to her lips, she felt their soft, dry fullness and sighed with relief. Laying her forehead against her drawn up knees, she took deep breaths and tried to calm her wildly beating heart.

Juan's hand gently touched her back then withdrew. Jenni knew he was used to her nightmares and knew not to coddle her. She didn't want to be touched or calmed down after the nightmares. It often took her several minutes to gain full control of her senses and convince herself she was truly safe and far away from her dead family.

The blue tarp that made up the tiny tent rippled around her in the night breeze. A light from outside peeked through a tear in the top of the tent and cast a soft beam across her hands. They were clean. There was no blood on them. All around her, outside the tent, she could hear people softly talking, snoring, coughing, and sneezing, as they, too, dealt with the night terrors that came with sleeping and dreaming.

Shoving her thick black hair back from her face, she took another deep breath. She slowly accepted the moment as her reality. Why her brain tried to convince her that she had not escaped the morning the dead took over she could not fathom. It was Lloyd who had taken Benji's tender flesh. It was Lloyd who had become one of the undead and destroyed their family and home forever. None of it had been her doing. She had barely escaped the house. Had it not been for Katie saving her, she probably would have joined the ranks of the zombie hordes. Katie had heard her screaming and driven up in that battered white truck to rescue her. Together they had escaped into the Texas Hill Country and found safety with a group of survivors holed up in a construction site in a small town.

She had survived. She was alive. She had rescued her stepson from the camp he had been attending, she had found love with one of the construction workers named Juan, and now, free from her dead husband's reign, she was strong and living her own life.

Taking a deep breath, that did not feel forced or ragged, she slowly relaxed. Letting herself fall back onto the cot, she curled up on her side, facing away from Juan. It was uncomfortable sleeping on the twin cots that were bound together, but she liked feeling him near her. In the gloom, he slid his arm around her waist and she smiled.

In silence, they lay side by side and waited for sleep to come again.

Sleep hopefully free of the past and the terror that came with it.

## 2. A Moment of Peace

Juan listened to Jenni's breathing become deeper and deeper until he knew she was asleep once more. He didn't move despite his arm falling asleep. She was holding onto his wrist tightly. He didn't draw it away for he wanted to make sure she felt his presence even in her slumber. It was hard to see her struggling with the nightmares about what had happened to her children. It was especially hard knowing that he could not give her any real comfort.

But Jenni kept the dreams to herself, mourning in ways he could not understand. He was convinced that her evolution into a woman who could dispatch zombies with eerie efficiency was her way of coping with her children dying. As far as he knew, she didn't even talk to Katie, her very best friend, about the death of her children. In Jenni's waking moments, she was loving, outgoing, and funny. But in her dreams, she was afraid and shattered emotionally. It broke his heart.

His long body pressed up against hers, he could feel the softness of her black hair against his chest. His body was sore and tired from all the work he was doing on the "fort." The construction site the survivors were living in was quickly becoming too cramped. As more survivors found their way to the fort, it was increasingly more difficult to keep things safe and sanitary. There was one shower and one bathroom in city hall for everyone in the fort.

The survivors had to get into the old fashioned hotel that loomed over the construction site. There was a side entrance to the hotel and a front entrance, but no way into the hotel from the construction site without risking being out in the open. And the zombies did tend to appear out of nowhere.

Juan's first major task had been to make a secure way into the fort for the vehicles they were sending out to salvage supplies and find survivors. Finally, the "Panama Canal" was done and it was basically two gated enclosures leading into a walled off area where they could keep the vehicles in an old newspaper building delivery truck garage. The old newspaper building was completely uninhabitable and would take months to clean out and repair. With the heat of the summer just around the corner as well as the thunderstorm season, the survivors just didn't have the time to repair the building. They had to get into the hotel.

Jenni's grip on his arm lessened as sleep took her completely. He kissed her shoulder hoping and praying that her dreams would not be ones of terror. Closing his eyes, he tried to block out the aching of his body and capture what little sleep he could before tomorrow came and a whole new day of hard work would consume him.

He was so tired in both body and mind. Jenni brought him happiness, but he wanted a rest from the daily terror they all experienced since the zombie apocalypse had started. He wanted to sleep in a real bed with Jenni and not feel afraid. Was it wrong to hope for a little peace for both of them? He hoped not, because that is what he prayed for every night.

Beyond the walls of their little fort, the world was still dying and the dead were walking, but all Juan wanted was a moment when all would feel alive and good. Maybe it was too much to hope for. Perhaps this moment, listening to Jenni breathing as she slept peacefully, was all he could truly wish for.

With a long sigh, he tightened his deadened arm around her waist and held onto her tightly.

# 3. The Lurking Past

Katie sat on top of the city hall roof in a plastic chair with her arms folded over her breasts and her head tilted back to stare at the stars. She was done with sleep for the night. One more nightmare about her dead wife and she would start screaming and never stop. The ache in her chest hurt so bad; she didn't want to see her loved one's mutilated form rushing her with clawed hands anymore.

The cigarette dangling from her fingers was burning down slowly. Raising it to her lips, she took another long drag, then exhaled slowly. She watched the smoke unfurl against the backdrop of the stunning black sky with pinpricks of stars. She had quit smoking when she had met Lydia. Lydia had hated smoking with a passion. Her fiancé at the time had been a chain smoker and she had never even thought about quitting until she had met Lydia. After one look into Lydia's amazing eyes, Katie would have done anything for her.

A tear slipped free from her eye and traced down her temple as she stared up at the sky. Sniffling loudly, she took another drag on the cigarette, desperately seeking some sort of satisfaction in the process.

Lydia was still out there, one of the many undead hordes. Katie had barely escaped with her own life while on the way to work. Thankfully, she had been rescued by a man who had been dragged down by the zombies. She had raced home in his old battered white truck only to see her beautiful wife gorging on the body of a fallen postman.

Her life with Lydia had ended in that terrible, brutal moment. She would never hold Lydia's soft, delicate hand, kiss her sweet lips, or feel her gentle caress ever again. It had ended just like that.

Another tear slipped free and she blinked hard.

How could she love Lydia so much and yet feel drawn to Travis? How could she betray Lydia's memory like that?

Nearby, the guard on the roof coughed and stretched. It was Bill, the cop from a little town where she and Jenni had taken refuge. He was watching the street for any sign of the zombies. They had cleared out a majority of them from the town, but many still lurked out there. Caught in bushes, trapped in buildings, wandering through the hills...

Who would have ever imagined that the dead would walk the earth outside of a George A. Romero film? She never did. Ever. She had dealt in a real world. She had worked hard as a prosecutor, doing her best to bring justice to the world while living a simple life with Lydia.

And then it had all ended.

This new world confused her. It was full of the walking hungry dead. Surviving from one day to the next was everyone's top priority. But beyond that, there seemed so little time to mourn before making new connections, new friends, and even new loves. She saw it all around her. Families torn apart by the first day of the zombie rising were forever gone, but new families were being born all around her. Strangers were becoming brothers, sisters, aunts and uncles to each other. The elderly in the fort were now everyone's grandparents. At the thought of the elderly, Old Man Watson came to mind, bringing a smile to her face. Although he could barely hear, he was everyone's great grandpa now, one who hugged and kissed, who always smiled, always happy to be part of the survivors.

Jenni was her new sister. Jenni's stepson Jason felt like a nephew, Juan was her annoying new brother in law, and Travis...

She rubbed her nose with irritation and sighed.

Travis was the man everyone loved. Everyone listened to him. Everyone believed in him. He was calm strength in the midst of chaos. He was handsome, but didn't know it. And, sometimes, he was a bit of a nerd. Despite herself, she smiled at the thought of him.

From the moment she had met him, she knew he was important to her life. To the lives of all the survivors. She had believed in him instantly. And as they grew to know each other, it had become more than apparent that he had fallen in love with her.

But as far as Travis knew, it was a lost cause. Katie had a wife in her old life and he saw her as unattainable. And she had encouraged that belief. She was afraid if he realized she was actually bisexual, he would immediately pursue her.

Despite herself, she knew in her heart that she would not resist him for long. She hated this new world where everyone seemed to be living at an accelerated pace. Life seemed so precious and short now that there was no real time to mourn the world they had lost. They had to survive and find their own small moments of happiness, or else the life they had now was meaningless.

"Oh, God, Lydia," she whispered, wiping tears away.

"Huh?" Bill looked toward her.

"Nothing, Bill. Just talking to myself," she answered with a forced smile and sat up. She put out her cigarette on the roof and sat with her elbows resting on her knees.

"Gotcha. I find myself doing that, too." Bill's big round face grinned at her, then he returned his gaze to the street.

Katie stared down at the hunting boots she wore. They had been given to her by the sweet old man who had run the hunting shop were they had taken refuge in that first terrible night. Clad in jeans and a tank top, she felt far away from the tailored and perfectly-coifed prosecutor persona she had worn for years. But, she had to admit, the jeans and tank top fit who she really was; a no-fuss girl with wavy blond hair and big green eyes who liked to wear comfortable shoes and casual T-shirts.

Standing up, she pulled the tank top down over her belly and walked toward the edge of the roof. The hotel loomed over the construction site that was full of makeshift blue tarp tents. The elderly and the few surviving women with children were asleep in the city hall, but the younger people were tucked into tents. The nights were growing warmer and warmer as the summer unfurled.

"Got one down on the far corner, but I can't get a bead on it," Bill said to her.

She looked to where he pointed and caught sight of a figure swaying back and forth near an empty building on the far side of the fort walls. A lamppost and tree partially blocked it from view.

"I think it got its foot caught in the sidewalk cracks. It's really uneven there." Bill sighed and stared at the zombie sadly.

Katie didn't say anything. There wasn't much to say. A lone zombie was usually a pretty sad sight from a distance. The mutilated form always spoke of a terrible ending to a human life. But the second it saw you, it was the most horrible thing you had ever seen. Its eyes would flash wide and its mouth would open to reveal terrible teeth as it reached toward you and let out a horrible shriek.

"Hey," Travis' voice said from behind them.

She turned to see him walking from the stairway. He was wearing a dark T-shirt and jeans. She felt an inward pang of desire that she tried hard to ignore. She couldn't help herself, but his broad shoulders and curly hair made her want to touch him. Setting her lips tightly together, she looked away from him. She couldn't betray Lydia's memory.

"Hey, Travis. What's up?" Bill stood up and tugged his shirt down over his beer belly.

"I think we're going to go ahead and take the street next to us tomorrow. It's getting hotter and with June hitting soon, it's only going to get worse. We need to get into the hotel, but we need our people safe and out of the way."

"Taking the Dollar Store over?" Bill waved toward the side street that they had yet to claim into the fort.

"Yeah. Can't put it off anymore. 'Sides, with the Panama Canal working, we can risk closing off that street."

Katie could feel Travis glance toward her. She folded her arms over her breasts to try to steady herself. She felt so lonely tonight. She wanted him to hold her, but she feared what that may lead to.

"I figure you'll wanna go in, so if you want to go get some sleep, I can take over," Travis said to Bill.

Bill thought this over. "Did you get sleep?"

"Yeah. I'm good. We'll head in around nine or ten."

Bill glanced at his watch. "I could use about four hours of sleep." He handed the rifle to Travis.

Travis took it awkwardly. He wasn't very comfortable with guns, but he was trying.

"Catch you later, Katie," Bill said, patting her arm as he headed off.

"Sleep well, Bill!" Katie called after him.

Then she was alone with Travis.

"Did you sleep?"

She finally looked toward him and nodded. "Did you? Or did you lie?"

"I slept enough," he answered, and shrugged. He took Bill's place and immediately saw the tangled up zombie. He frowned when he realized he didn't have a clear shot. "Is everything okay with you?"

"I'm fine," Katie assured him.

"Ralph dying and Nerit coming here seems to have shook you up," he said. He looked at her worriedly.

The two elderly people who had taken her and Jenni into their home above the hunting store that first night had come up against ruthless men that had killed Ralph before Nerit, his wife and former sniper for the Israeli army, took them out.

"I'm fine. Really," Katie stepped away from him, deciding it was time to go. She wanted to cry again and she wanted him to comfort her.

"Katie," he said softly, reaching toward her.

"I'll catch you later," she said, and briskly walked away.

When she reached the stairs, she hurried down the steps and put as much distance between her and Travis as she could. Once down in the hallway of city hall, she leaned against the wall and felt tears fall down her face as she gave into her pain and wept.

## 4. The Lonely Guard

Travis wanted to follow Katie, but he couldn't. Guard duty was a serious thing. The zombies were sparse of late, but they all knew how quickly that could change. Every time they felt they had secured their area, more of the walking dead would come wandering out of the landscape to screech and moan at the walls.

Rubbing his face with one hand, Travis let out a long breath. He had seen the torment on Katie's face, had wanted to comfort her, but knew she wouldn't let him. Perhaps things had gone too far when they had shared that kiss not too long ago. Immediately, she had withdrawn from him and there was nothing he could do but wait and let her work things out.

What he could do was make sure that the small haven they were carving out in the world of the dead stayed safe. Tomorrow they would secure the road next to the fort and take over the Dollar Store. The shops next to it were empty and in disrepair, but they might be able to use them as well. To enter the hotel, they had to make sure the survivors were in a safe place. There was a risk with breaking into the hotel. If there were zombies inside, they could swarm out into the fort and that would be the end of everything. They had built a small walled in area up against the back of the hotel to use as an entrance, but there were no real assurances that the wrought iron gate would hold if a horde of zombies were inside the fort. As a secondary precaution, they planned to create a temporary shelter in the Dollar Store after blocking off the street.

Travis narrowed his eyes as the zombie staggered free from where it had been temporarily trapped. Raising the rifle, he fumbled with the safety. Using the sight, he aimed for the zombie's head. He felt uncomfortable using the weapon, but they needed to keep the area as zombie free as possible for tomorrow.

The zombie stopped walking and he could see a skirt flowing in the breeze around its crooked legs. It slowly began to raise its hand. Before it could issue its horrifying screech, he pulled the trigger.

It collapsed onto the sidewalk as the echoes of the shot faded away.

With a sigh, Travis lowered the rifle.

Tomorrow was a new day.

A new beginning.

And that was all any of them could hope for anymore.

# Chapter 2

## 1. Taking Risks

Beads of sweat slid down Juan's spine as he stood on the wall ready to direct the operator of the huge crane. The side street that ran alongside the fort had been left open until today, as it had been regarded as an escape route. Now, though, they needed the room to continue the expansion of the fort. The huge crane was lowering the long storage containers into place to block off the sides of the street. Once that was done, they would send a team in to clear the buildings of any possible zombies.

By tomorrow, new walls would be in place to hold off the zombie hordes and the fort would gain the use of four more buildings. Luckily, the downtown area was so old that the buildings were flush up against each other. They only had to worry about the two ends of the street and securing the back entrances into the buildings.

The breeze was still cool despite the sun's rays. He wiped his forehead beneath the brim of his cowboy hat. Looking over his shoulder, he could see the survivors watching from the safety of the fort. Excitement was already building. It was going to be an intense day and they all knew it. If their luck held out, it would be a good one, too.

Travis joined him on the wall, where he looked down at the front windows of the Dollar Store. They were covered in huge paper posters announcing the latest items for sale. The posters were mostly of Easter baskets and Easter treats. Juan frowned as he realized the holiday had passed without anyone even noticing it.

It was hard to see into the building. No one had seen any movement inside the store, but that did not mean that there wasn't anything inside.

"Think someone is in there?"

Juan shrugged. "We did try to get everyone into the construction site once it started going to shit. I know someone went over and knocked on the door, but they weren't open yet."

Travis yawned, rubbing his face.

"No sleep?"

"Not a lot. You?"

"Once we're in the hotel, I think I'll sleep a lot better," Juan answered.

"Yeah. I can't argue there."

"Hey, guys," a voice called out.

Juan and Travis both looked down to see one of the newest members of the fort climbing up the stairs to the wall. It was Eric, an engineer from Austin. He and his girlfriend, Stacey, had been rescued a week ago from a water tower on the outskirts of town where zombies had trapped them for nearly a month. Eric was still far too thin for his height, but he looked better than he had. He hesitated at the top of the ladder and looked up at them worriedly.

"Whazzup?" Juan cocked his head curiously.

"Hey, I know you guys said I can't go into the store, but I really do feel I need to inspect the store and the other shops once they are clear. You know, before we move people over the wall. All these buildings are really old and we can't be too sure if they are sound structurally."

Juan almost laughed. He was pretty sure most of the old buildings were better built than the newer ones, but Eric looked very sincere.

"Yeah, man, that's cool," Juan said.

"I don't see that as an issue after we're sure its clear," Travis agreed.

Eric climbed onto the wall and cautiously stood up. He gained his balance and folded his arms over his chest. "What you guys did with the construction site to make it into a fort is outstanding, but-"

"Eh, I understand." Juan shrugged. "We're taking risks all the time."

"But we can't risk too much or we lose everything." Eric pushed his glasses up on his nose.

Juan couldn't blame him for looking nervous. He had heard Eric's story and knew that he and his girlfriend had barely survived out there on their own.

Travis looked down the street toward the corner where he had killed the zombie the night before. "We've already lost too much to risk the loss of everything. That's why we need a safe, secure location outside the main construction site for when we break into the hotel. So if there are zombies in there and they manage to get into the construction site, we can contain them."

Eric nodded. "I know. I do. I understand. We're all just-" He motioned to all the people watching them from below. "-scared to be on the other side of this wall."

Juan and Travis looked back toward the line of stores. Juan knew they were both thinking the same thing.

They had no choice.

"I know that they sent you up here for reassurance. I can promise you, and everyone down there, that we will not move anyone over into the new area until we're absolutely sure its clear of zombies. We'll also make sure the zombies won't be able to get in," Travis said in a very firm voice. "We have no choice. With the summer storm season just around the corner and the temperatures sure to start hitting in the hundreds, we need to have a good sound shelter for everyone."

"Yeah, one fierce storm and we're flooded out down there. City Hall can't be a permanent home for everyone. It wouldn't be sanitary for long," Juan added.

"I guess the way things are set up right now just feels so safe. Risking anything is just scary. I'm not dissing what you guys are saying or insinuating that you don't know what you're doing, just some of us..." Eric faltered as he gestured down into the construction site.

Juan looked down as well. A good-sized group of people huddled together. Eric's still emaciated girlfriend was holding her Jack Russell Terrier, Pepe, and looking up at Eric with a worried expression. Juan thought she was a pretty little thing. She had long tanned limbs and pale blond hair, but her cheeks were hollow and her shoulders bony. He could understand Eric's desire to protect her. The people gathered around her were also looking worried. Juan realized Eric was a spokesman for more than his own fears.

"Man, we got loved ones, too. We're not going to risk them. Okay?" Juan tried to give the man a reassuring look.

Eric looked toward Travis. The man gave him a firm nod before Eric turned to look at the Dollar Store. He seemed to come to some sort of peace about the situation and sighed. "I'll let them know," he said, and climbed down the ladder.

"You can't blame them," Juan said once Eric was down below and talking to the group. "They weren't here to see this construction site get made into a walled-in fort. They weren't here, man."

Travis looked calm, but Juan could tell he was upset by the set of his jaw. "We're just doing our best to keep them all safe and in sanitary conditions. We're damn lucky the power is still on."

"It's that new hydroelectric power station they built a few years back. I betcha anything."

"But for how long will it stay operational?" Travis lifted his sunglasses, rubbing his eyes before setting them back into place. "I guess it doesn't matter. Right now, we get a secure location for them while we go into the hotel, then we claim it, and go on from there."

"And hope the bandits don't show up," Juan added.

"Let's not even talk about those bastards right now."

Juan shrugged. He supposed now wasn't the time to talk about the marauders who killed Nerit's husband. There was fear that they were still more out there. It probably wasn't time to bring up the vigilante in the fort, the one who had thrown someone over the wall, bound and gagged with duct tape, to feed the zombies. Yeah, the victim was the local drug dealer and the scum of the earth, but someone had taken justice into their own hands. That fact put everyone on edge.

"Just another day in zombie land," Juan said with a wide grin. "Gotta love it."

Travis chucked. "Yeah, ain't it grand?"

## 2. Waiting

Despite herself, Katie slept a few more hours in the small room she shared with Nerit. When she awakened, Nerit was gone. Yawning, she pulled on her shoes and headed to the community dining room.

Katie poured more milk onto her cereal, staring at the watery milk filling in around the flakes. She was slowly getting used to the powdered milk. It didn't taste bad; it just looked off. Picking up her spoon, she dug into the corn flakes, wishing there were a banana to add.

The salvage team from the grocery store had brought back tons of food in cardboard boxes, cans, and bags, but the fruit had all gone bad. Rosie, Juan's mother, had salvaged seeds from the rotten fruit to be planted in a garden she was planning with Peggy, the city secretary. Katie hoped it was successful; she missed fruit desperately.

With a sigh, she reached out and picked up her small paper cup of vitamins that everyone was required to take in the morning. She downed it with orange juice made from a powdered mix.

Jenni crashed into the chair across from her. "We're heading in!"

"Huh?"

Jenni gulped down her vitamins dry. "Dollar Store. We're heading in." Jenni poured Fruit Loops into a bowl and reached for the pitcher of milk. "Travis says I can go in with Ed, Bill, and Felix."

Katie tried not to frown, but it came automatically.

"Oh, c'mon. You volunteered to go into the hotel. You and I have more experience with zombies than most of these guys. You know, from when we were out on the road. You so cannot get into my face for volunteering for this. It's probably empty!"

"I just worry," Katie admitted.

Jenni snorted. "You're such a mom."

"I just had a bad night last night. I worry about the ones I love."

"You love someone other than me?" Jenni widened her eyes playfully. "Oh, wow. I have competition for best friend? I'll cut 'em!"

Despite herself, Katie laughed. "Yeah, I'm so sure you can take Nerit down. Or Jason. Or Old Man Watson. Or..." She faltered at Travis.

Jenni crunched her cereal. "You're such a dork."

"Thanks, I needed that." Katie shoveled more cereal into her mouth.

"I had a rough night, too. Fucking nightmares."

Katie waited for Jenni to go on, but, as usual, she didn't.

"So, I'm going to take this ax in that Ed got from the grocery store. I've been practicing using it and I like it so much better than the spears. It has this really great energy when you swing it." Jenni added more cereal to her bowl. "I'm going to have such a great sugar high off this stuff."

"Pure carbs. We seriously need more protein in our diets," Katie said in a serious tone. The salvaged meat from the grocery store freezer wouldn't last much longer. It was part of dinner only. Lunch was usually stuff from cans.

Jenni wrinkled her nose. "Whatever. So, the new ax-"

Katie listened to Jenni prattle on about her newest weapon with amusement. It was a very Jenni thing to do. As of late, her friend avoided talking about the past or anything to do with the life she had lost. Katie marveled at Jenni's ability to move on, but at the same time wondered if all the things she was ignoring would one day catch up with her.

Jason, Jenni's stepson, and Jack, his ever-faithful German Shepherd companion, joined them. Katie and Jenni both hugged the teenager and showered the dog with attention before they settled down at their table. Jason's bangs were long. He tended to stare at the world through the brown, straggly strands, but he was a smart kid, a good kid. Katie was glad they had been able to rescue him from the camp he had been attending during the first days of the outbreak.

"I was talking to Roger, that science teacher, and he says my plans for a catapult are really good. Think if I talk to Juan he could get me the stuff to make it?" Jason picked out Grape Nuts from the boxes on the table, which impressed Katie, until he drowned the little nuggets in sugar and milk.

"Yeah. He would totally do that. But probably not until we get the hotel under our control. He's all obsessed with getting us in." Jenni slurped down the sugary milk in her bowl.

Jason frowned, then shrugged. "I'm just trying to help out."

"Don't take it personal. The guys are all obsessed with getting us into the hotel. The City Hall's air conditioner is not that great and some of the older people will suffer if the heat gets any worse." Katie rubbed the boy's back to reassure him.

"Yeah, but we're not building enough defenses. What if a bunch of them show up? Or the bandit guys? Or..." He shrugged. "Whatever. I'm just a kid."

"And a moody one," Jenni teased.

"Mom!"

Jenni leaned over the table to hug and kiss him relentlessly. Jason tried to fight her off at first, then started laughing. Satisfied, Jenni slid back into her chair.

"Gawd, Mom," Jason said, his cheeks flushed.

Katie grinned and tucked back into her breakfast. Suddenly, she didn't feel so down or so alone. It was a good feeling.

## 3. Going In

"Go in, secure the front. Jenni and Bill, you take right. Me and Felix, we'll take left. Do not fire your weapon unless you have to and only if you are sure everyone else is clear. We don't need friendly fire in there," Ed said firmly. He was a scrawny, grizzled guy in his late fifties. A local, he was a tough Texan who had run a small farm on the outskirts of town. His peach groves were the only fruit they had any hope of bringing into the fort, but the salvage team had yet to get out that far. There were plans to head out there in a week's time.

Felix, a good-looking young man from the Houston area, stood with his makeshift spear in one hand. He had modified it to have two deadly ends and he often practiced with it. Jenni thought his skin was amazing. He was so black, his skin gleamed purple in the sunlight. He dressed like a thug, but when he spoke, you quickly realized he was much more than he appeared to be. He was the son of white parents who had adopted him from Africa and had been raised in an affluent part of Houston. He had been a student at the University of Texas when things had all gone to hell. He had barely made it out of Austin alive. Felix didn't talk about it, but Jenni got the impression he was torn between many different worlds.

Bill looked toward the store from their perch on the wall. "I can't see there being anyone in there if they haven't shown up at the front door." He hitched his belt a little higher and looked somber.

Ed shrugged. "In this world, can't be too sure about nothing."

"Amen," Jenni agreed, and lifted her ax up. "And I'm ready to choppy, choppy."

"You're one crazy bitch," Felix chided with a grin.

"Uh huh. Your point is?"

Felix held up one hand and twirled a finger around to indicate she was loopy.

Jenni grinned.

The road was blocked off on both ends by the huge storage containers and cement bags. Snipers, including Nerit, stood on the corners of the fort wall ready to shoot any approaching zombies. What the small team had to worry about was inside the Dollar Store and abandoned shops.

"We all know Jenni is batshit crazy, but it's okay. She's good at killing the gawddamn zombies," Ed said with a wry grin. "So let's go in and see how things are cooking in there."

Jenni looked down into the fort and saw all the people staring up at them. She waved to Katie and Jason. Juan was up on the far wall and she blew him a kiss. He caught it and pretended to smack it onto his ass. She laughed.

Ed headed down the ladder first, followed by Felix, then Bill, and finally Jenni. She jumped down the last few rungs and landed on the hot road. The entire downtown area was paved in red bricks. A few blades of grass were sticking up around the edges, but otherwise it was in good condition.

Despite the heat, they were all in jeans, boots, gloves and jackets. Jenni's hair was braided and pinned up on her head to avoid giving the zombies anything to grab onto. Her work gloves were lightweight, but would be a bitch for any zombie to bite through. She was overheated already, but they had to stay safe.

They slowly approached the Dollar Store. It was hard to see inside past the advertisements taped to the windows. The lights were off; the gloom was unwelcoming. Bill went down on his knees before the door and started to pick the lock. Busting the door open would be the last resort.

"Ha. I bet everyone thought the black man would be doing that," Felix remarked with a grin.

"You learn things on the job being a cop," Bill said somberly.

"Don't care if you're black or white or brown or whatever," Ed said, "just as long as you don't turn green and bite me."

Jenni laughed and Felix smiled.

Bill's brow furrowed as he concentrated. After a moment, he smiled. With a twist of his wrist, the lock spun, and the door opened slightly.

They all gagged at once. The smell coming out of the store was putrid.

"Fucking shit," Felix gasped.

"We got a dead one in there all right," Ed said grimly.

Bill crawled away from the door, his eyes watering, trying to get a clean breath of air.

Jenni pulled her bandana up over her nose. "Gawd, that is awful."

"Enclosed space and rotting dead stuff; not a good combo. Let's do this, people," Ed said, pushing the door all the way open with one foot. He stared into the gloom, his rifle with the makeshift bayonet at the end at the ready. "Hey!"

His voice filled the store. A low growl answered.

"It's dead and talking," Ed said somberly, and walked in.

Felix moved in right behind him as Bill climbed to his feet and joined Jenni. He wiped his eyes and cheeks with a bandana, then nodded to her. His eyes were still smarting, but he looked ready. Jenni slid into the darkened interior slowly.

## 4. The Store

The front of the store was empty except for a line of small shopping carts. Both checkout stands stood empty. Jenni walked cautiously toward the first aisle to the right as Ed and Felix moved to check out the left side of the store.

Bill peered behind the checkout stands just to make sure they were truly empty. He held his machete at the ready, but with a swift motion of his head, indicated nothing lingered there.

Jenni lifted the ax a little higher as she headed down the first aisle. It was loaded up with makeup and all sorts of lotions. A lone bottle of shampoo lay in the middle of the aisle. She scooted it out of her way with the tip of her boot. Bill moved up alongside her, close enough for Jenni to hear his steady breathing. It was comforting. Slowly, she edged around the corner, looking into the aisle that cut down the side of the store. It was empty.

Together, they advance slowly to the next aisle.

Ed and Felix were obviously not finding anything as well, but the stench and low moans told them all quite clearly something was dead in the store and still moving. The aisle packed with baby supplies made Jenni's head swim for a moment, but she shoved any thoughts of Benji out of her mind and set her jaw determinedly.

The aisle was clear.

Bill moved up toward the next aisle.

Another low moan reverberated through the store.

"Is anyone alive in here?" Felix's voice called out.

Another low moan, not a screech, but a moan, answered.

"If you're human and hurt, say something," Felix went on.

Somewhere, the moan grew into a hungry growl.

"Yep, zombie," Ed said.

"For sure," Felix agreed.

Bill froze for a second as they reached the aisle full of photo books and frames. A lot of merchandise lay on the floor, broken and smashed. Slowly, Jenni lifted her eyes upwards. An arm dangled off the shelf over the display of cheap, but cute frames. It was savagely bitten in several places. A low moan came from the shelf.

"Found one," Bill called out.

The zombie moaned. Its arm twitched.

"I bet he crawled up there to get away," Jenni whispered.

The zombie, wedged tightly between two metal shelves, wiggled anxiously, knowing human flesh was nearby.

"How do we do this?" Bill looked perplexed.

Jenni motioned to the zombie's foot. "Drag it down and deal with it?"

Bill frowned deeply. "Could go wrong on the way down. Could twist around and land on us or something."

The zombie thrashed around still unable to free itself.

"Let's go to the other side," Jenni suggested.

Bill and Jenni crept around to the other aisle, this one loaded down with all sorts of household supplies. The zombie's other leg and arm were hanging out on this side. It was a young man, probably in his late teens. If he hadn't such a slim build, he may have never wedged himself between the two metal shelves. He saw them and thrashed even more, growling. Jenni looked around her and spotted a small stepladder used to stock the higher shelves. It was toppled over on its side and she bet the kid had used it to climb up out of the way of a zombie. Grabbing it, she dragged it over in front of the zombie. Out of the corner of her eye, she could see its decaying hand reaching out desperately to get her, but she was out of reach.

"Hold me," Jenni ordered Bill, then stepped up to the top step.

Bill's big hands grabbed her hips and held her tightly. Jenni was now face to face with the zombie. Its hand waved in front of her eyes, straining desperately to reach her. The kid's face was stained with his tears and blood. She felt sorry for him. He didn't look that much older than Jason. But, regardless of his youth, his time was done on this earth. She was ready to send him on.

She swung her ax as hard as she could into the face of the zombie. He grabbed her wrist just as the ax head buried itself into his skull. Almost as soon as his fingers gripped her, they went slack. Jenni wrenched the ax out of his dead features. Bill tightened his grip on her hips.

"One more whack to be sure," she said.

She swung the ax again and felt it cleave the zombie head in half. Now she was sure it was over. Black goo slid out over the edge of the shelf.

"It's done!"

Her voice echoed.

A low moan from the back of the store answered.

"Sounds like we got another one," Ed called out.

"I figured that. This one climbed up on a shelf to escape something," Bill answered back.

A more desperate moan answered.

Jenni dropped off the stepladder and held her dripping ax tightly in her hands. She felt a little sick about the death of the kid. The first death, not the one she had given him. The world was just fucked and awful.

The next area was full of hanging clothes and bedding supplies. Jenni and Bill made sure to study any shelving above eye level. The moans they kept hearing were from the back of the store, but they were very cautious as they moved on. They had to be. It was far too dangerous to let their guard down.

"Found her," Felix called out. "She's on your side. And you won't believe this."

Bill and Jenni finally reached the back of the store and turned the corner.

A female zombie was reaching toward Felix and Ed who were approaching her from the opposite side of the store.

"You have to be fucking kidding me," Jenni said and almost laughed.

The ground was covered in overturned trash bins of all sizes, plastic clothesbaskets, and plastic storage containers. They were splashed with blood and it was obvious a struggle had happened here. At some point, the female zombie had stepped into a bucket and caught her foot in it. As she had tried to pass between the metal shelves and a support column, her foot in the bucket had become wedged. Unable to move her foot, she was simply standing there moaning. Jenni couldn't see her face, but her body looked slim and young. She wondered if this was the one who had bitten the boy.

"Kinda dumb, ain't they?" Ed smirked.

Jenni heaved the ax over her head and brought it down hard onto the zombie's head. It wedged halfway into the thing's skull. The zombie slowly collapsed down to the floor and Jenni yanked the blade out of the dead girl.

Bill leaned down and looked at the zombie thoughtfully. "There is a bite on her hand. Only mark other than her head being split apart."

"So, she gets bit, dies, attacks the boy here, he gets bit up, she gets caught, he goes and climbs onto a shelf." Felix nodded his head. "And he dies. Makes sense."

Jenni frowned down at the body. "But who bit her?"

"They're both wearing vests and name tags. Boxes are open in the aisles. They were early morning stockers. Do you think she came in bit?" Bill looked thoughtful.

Slowly, they all looked toward the door to the storeroom.

"Great," Felix moaned.

"We do this right and careful," Ed said firmly.

The four of them slowly moved toward the swinging metal doors.

The battered metal doors swung open into a long narrow room filled with boxes piled along one wall almost to the ceiling. At the far end was the open door to a narrow bathroom.

"Hello?" Jenni called out cautiously.

They all jumped when the metal doors that opened to the loading dock outside began to shake as something on the other side beat on them. Snarls and growls that set their hair on end emanated from beyond the closed doors.

"Okay. We got one outside. Those doors are locked and holding. Check the storage room," Ed ordered.

It took ten long minutes to scour the narrow room. They moved slowly and purposefully. They checked the shelves, the boxes, the small bathroom, and the small manager's office. Nothing appeared. Nothing was hidden. They made as much noise as possible to try to get something to come out. Nothing.

"One more sweep through the store," Ed ordered.

In twenty minutes they stood outside in the street.

"Got the empty stores now," Ed said.

Jenni nodded and hoisted her ax up. "Let's do it."

# Chapter 3

## 1. Army of One

**N**erit climbed down the ladder slowly. Juan looked down at her with concern as she lowered herself into the blocked off street.

"Be careful, Nerit."

"I'm not that old." Though her voice was stern, she winked at him. She ignored Bill's attempt to help her off the ladder, but he still took hold of her arm as she lowered her booted feet to the redbrick road.

"Stores are all clear, but we got one or two dead guys trying to bust in a back door. Making an awful fuss now that they know we're here," Ed said.

Nerit nodded. They had called her over when no one could get a clear shot at the zombie or zombies. They had seen her in action and knew she was a deadly shot. All the survivors were fascinated by her past as an Israeli Army sniper. It amused Nerit, but at the same time it gave her a sense of purpose in her new home.

Nerit had brought her old Galil sniper rifle with her from the hunting store she had shared with Ralph. Over the years it had developed a few issues, but Ralph had carefully restored it. Her ammunition for the weapon was limited, but she had shunned several hunting rifles offered to her. It was a good weapon, but also it was a reminder of her deceased husband's thoughtfulness and appreciation for her skills.

"I can get him," Nerit assured Ed.

"You ain't seen him yet," Ed answered.

"I can get him or them," she repeated.

Ed looked at her for a long moment, a thoughtful expression on his grizzled face then shrugged. "We'll get you up on the roof."

Nerit smiled warmly at Jenni as she passed the much younger woman. The brunette was holding an ax smeared in foul, congealed zombie blood and looking at the older woman worriedly. Nerit knew Jenni had confidence in her abilities and did not doubt her. The look of concern was because Nerit had lost her husband to the bandits. What Jenni didn't understand was Nerit had accepted that loss. It was not easy to let Ralph go, but he was gone. She was part of a new family: she was determined to help them survive.

"Good luck, Nerit," Jenni said.

"Thank you, Jenni," she answered with a warm smile.

They entered a darkened store and Ed lead the way to a staircase near the back. The store smelled of mold and mildew, the wood floor creaked as they walked. Motes of dust swirled around in the few shafts of sunlight that managed to puncture through the grime covering the large plate glass windows in the front. The stairs moaned as she ascended them. She was careful with her footing, as it was obvious that the store had stood empty for nearly a decade. Rat droppings and dead insects littered the wood floor of the second floor.

"Got windows here, but the view is blocked out by the Dollar Store. It's a newer building and comes out further than the rest of the stores in the back. Probably built out a bit for storage and loading," Ed explained.

Nerit glanced out a broken window. A spider had taken great pains to fill in the gap between the glass and the wood frame with an intricate web. Nerit could see into the back alley that opened up behind the Dollar Store into an empty dirt lot. She could hear the zombie or zombies howling and slamming up against the loading doors of the Dollar Store, but she could not see the undead.

"Roof is this way," Ed said, and guided her up another set of very rickety steps.

Nerit was rather worried about Bill and his weight, but he followed them, treading very carefully. Ed pushed open a rickety door and they stepped out into the sunshine. The roof was not in the best condition, but seemed sturdier than the stairway.

The town spread out around them in a panorama. The red brick buildings of downtown looked quite lovely against the scenic green hills surrounding the town. The large hotel hovered behind them, untouched, waiting for them to invade. It actually was quite beautiful until you took in the cement brick walls closing off the construction site, the long abandoned storefronts, and a few zombies wandering around in the distance.

Nerit walked to the edge of the building as the warm air buffeted her yellowed silver hair from her face. The zombie was hidden from view by the side of the building. Only one leg was slightly visible as it braced itself and shoved hard against the back doors.

"See? Can't get to 'em," Ed pointed out.

"I can," Nerit assured him, and unslung her sniper rifle from her shoulder. As usual, the sniper rifle felt good and comforting in her arms. It was like an extension of her. She closed one eye and focused through the sight. Her senses narrowed down to just her vision and she removed herself from the world around her.

She pulled the trigger.

A gout of black blood erupted from the shattered ankle of the zombie. It lost its balance and tumbled. When its body fell into view, Nerit quickly adjusted her aim and fired. A plume of blood and gore erupted from its head, then it lay still.

Lowering her gun, she listened.

The pounding and growling had ceased.

"You got him," Bill said in an awed voice.

"Yes." Nerit shrugged. She watched the shadows dwelling behind the Dollar Store. "He was it."

Ed gazed down at the body, then looked toward the small field where a bike was laying on its side. "Looks like the Ramirez boy. I heard he was in trouble for dating some girl in town. His Dad worked on my farm."

Bill sighed. "Betcha he is the one who bit the girl and they managed to lock him out."

"And then it went to hell from there," Ed agreed.

Nerit looked back toward the fort and the people gathered to watch what they could of the proceedings. "Let's get some sentries up here to watch for anymore approaching this way."

"Yeah. And get the Dollar Store stock cleared out." Ed shook his head and headed back toward the stairs.

Bill looked down at the remains of the young man. "I bet he only wanted to see her and he ended up killing her instead."

Nerit could hear the sorrow in Bill's voice and knew it had nothing to do with the boy, but everything to do with his own loss.

It was an emotion they were too well acquainted with in this new world.

## 2. Packing Up and Moving On

"It still smells like zombie in here," Stacey muttered under her breath. The too-slim younger woman made a face and rubbed her pert nose.

"Zombie and bleach," Katie amended with a wry grin.

"Sounds like a drink almost." Stacey laughed and puffed air up at her flyaway bangs. She was busy packing up the contents of a shelf laden with boxed dinners and cans of soup.

"In some freaky bar down on 6th Street in good ol' Austin, Texas." Katie grinned at the thought and continued clearing the shelf. Sweat was trickling down her back and beaded her forehead. The store had been without air conditioning for weeks. At some point the breaker had been tripped. Now the air conditioner was humming loudly as it worked hard to cool the store down.

Stacey smiled ruefully. "The good ol' days."

Katie's smile faded. "Yeah. The days of yore."

"In the B.Z."

"Before Zombie?" Katie arched an eyebrow.

"Yeah," Stacey answered. She taped the box shut and scrounged around for the black marker they were using to mark the contents of the boxes on the outside flap.

Katie laughed slightly and shook her head. She was dressed in shorts and a tank top, trying not to let the heat get to her. Stacey was dressed similarly and her toothpick legs made Katie wince. Stacey and Eric had almost starved to death as they took refuge on the water tower. Though they had been on the edge of town, they had not been able to brave the zombie hordes to make it to the fort. Jenni, Bill, Felix and Ed had saved them from certain death.

It was nearly two in the afternoon and they had been working since the area had been declared clear. Katie's legs were aching and her arms felt bruised, but they needed to get the area clear. The faster they were done, the sooner they could make the area safe. Once it was secure, they could seriously consider going into the hotel.

"Sometimes it doesn't feel real. Sometimes it feels like just yesterday I was a coach at an elementary school refereeing dodge ball and hoping the bullies didn't kill the nerds," Stacey said in a soft voice.

"I know the feeling," Katie answered as she taped her box closed. "It just...changed so fast. One second the world was normal and the next it was all wrong."

"And one second people you loved were alive and the next..." Stacey shook her head, as if to shake the bad thoughts from her mind. "At least here we're safe, or at least as safe as it gets."

Katie shoved her box onto the pallet behind her and exhaled slowly. She felt winded and her face was flushed. Nearby she could hear Eric and Travis talking in low voices about the security of the back doors. Already any window to the abandoned buildings were being bricked up. She understood the fears Travis and Juan had about the small gate built to enter the hotel holding back any large amount of zombies. Part of her thought they were overly paranoid, yet she knew in this world that no one could truly be careful enough.

Stacey glanced toward Eric and Travis as they walked by them. The men were talking earnestly and gesturing around them. Stacey looked at Katie and Katie quirked her eyebrow upward.

"When they talk shop, I have no idea what they are saying," Stacey confessed.

"You and me both," Katie agreed. She wiped more sweat from her face. She was wearing gloves to prevent cutting her hands. They felt obscenely warm.

Stacey sighed and looked back at Katie. "Don't get me wrong. I'm glad Eric is involved with fort business, but sometimes I just wish..." She let out another long sigh. "You know, sometimes I wish we could just relax, for a moment, and be glad we're with each other and safe. But it's always about scrambling to be safer, scrambling to survive, scrambling to anticipate every little thing that could go wrong."

"I've been thinking about that lately," Katie confessed. "That maybe we'll never know real peace ever again. You know that feeling that the world is safe and sane. That we can get up in the morning and there will be food on the table, a job to go to, a loved one to curl up with at night. That the world humanity has created is secure." She was thinking of Lydia and their beautiful home again. She blinked her eyes hard to fight back tears.

"I guess if that's true, then any little bit of happiness we find, we should just hold onto it." Stacey looked toward Eric. Katie knew from what Stacey had told her that they had fallen slowly in love with each other as they struggled to survive. "I guess, maybe, just being here with him alive is enough."

Katie found herself looking toward Travis. "Maybe," she said at last. "Maybe." She quickly began to fill the next box, shoving cans into neat stacks inside.

Stacey lifted her box onto the pallet behind them and reached for another box stacked nearby.

"Hey," Travis said from behind them.

Katie turned around and looked up into his face as he leaned over them. Stacey sat back on her butt and let out a long, tired breath.

"You two have been in here long enough. Why don't you finish up your boxes then take a break?"

Katie nodded her head. Stacey looked relieved.

"Thanks, Travis," Stacey said and swept as much of the remaining casserole boxes into the box with one stroke of her arm. "Done!"

Travis laughed and helped her tape up the box and heave it onto the pallet. Katie quickly stacked as much of the cans as she could into her box, anxious to get out of the smelly store and take a break.

"I'll see you on the next shift," Stacey said to Katie, and jogged out of the store into the bright sunlight.

Katie hurriedly packed her box and waited for Travis to move on. But he didn't. He squatted down next to her and helped her pack the box. She didn't know what to say, but it felt awkward not to talk to him. She searched for words, but all the ones that felt ready to slip off her tongue where not ones she was ready to say.

"It looks like we'll be able to get this area secure by tonight," Travis finally said. "So we can go into the hotel tomorrow or the following day."

"It will feel good to get into it and spread out. I adore Nerit, but I need my own space," Katie confessed.

"It is hard to find actual alone time around here, isn't it?" Travis smiled at her warmly. "But it's kinda lonely at the same time."

She finally looked up at him and saw his hazel eyes were staring at her flushed face. "I'm sorry." It was all she could think to say.

"I miss you," he said. "We rarely talk."

"I have a lot on my mind," she answered lamely.

Travis started to say one thing, then visibly changed his mind. He closed his mouth, thought for a second, then said, "I just want to be your friend."

"No, you don't," Katie corrected him in a soft voice. She was painfully aware of all the people in the store, packing boxes, breaking down shelves, and cleaning up. This was not a conversation she wanted overheard and repeated around the fort. She was scandalous enough with the whispers going about that she was a lesbian.

He winced, but nodded his head in agreement. "But I can settle for being your friend." He folded the box flaps over and reached for the tape.

Katie rested her hands on the box and leaned toward him. "I need time to think."

"Being friends with me is not a threat to your memory of your wife," Travis whispered.

She couldn't answer him without giving herself away, so she busied herself by grabbing the marker and writing in bold letters on the side. She could feel Travis' gaze searching her expression for clues, seeking to understand. It made her nervous. She wanted him to walk away before he figured it out.

"Or is it?"

Her green eyes flicked upwards and she saw that he was suspicious of her silence. Maybe something in her gaze gave her away, because he took her gloved hand in his. She started to yank away, but only managed to pull her hand out of the glove. Travis caught her fingers gently in his and held her hand. He didn't seem to mind that they were sweaty.

"Katie, I'm not a threat to the memory of your wife, am I?" Travis asked in a whisper.

She could feel tears in her eyes and it was hard to speak. At last she was able to say, "Please..."

The word could mean many different things, but, surprisingly, Travis seemed to understand. "Okay."

There was a spark of hope in his gaze now and she averted her eyes quickly. She knew she had opened up the door to her heart. It may have been just a crack, but she was terrified.

"I better go check on how things are going," Travis said finally. He let go of her hand. He pulled out a bag of M & Ms from his shirt pocket and handed it to her. "It's a bit mushy still. I have a feeling there will be a run on the chocolate soon, so have this."

Katie couldn't help but smile despite herself. "Giving me chocolates now, huh?"

"I'm just a romantic kinda guy." He winked.

Her gaze followed him as he walked away. She looked down at the bag of candy and allowed herself a small smile.

## 3. Safety In Twos

Juan handed Jenni the bag of Doritos. Seated on the wall, side by side, they could see the final shift mopping the floor of the Dollar Store. Night had come and the air was cool as it ruffled their hair and dried the sweat on their tanned limbs.

"Are we really ready?" Jenni yanked the top of the bag open and pulled a chip out. The smell was amazing and she breathed it in deeply.

"Yep. Eric gave the okay on the bricked up windows and the reinforced doors. And it doesn't smell so much like zombie in there anymore," Juan said, and grinned.

"Yum. The smell of Doritos is so much better." Jenni pulled a chip out and munched it down with relish.

Juan laughed and shook his head. "Ah, the simple things in life."

"Are we going in tomorrow morning?" Jenni looked over her shoulder at the dark countenance of the hotel. "Or what?"

"Travis is going to make the call after inspecting the new area one more time. He's really nervous about all this. He hates the idea of putting anyone at risk. He even put himself on one of the teams to go into the hotel."

"Travis hates guns," Jenni said in disbelief.

"Yeah, but he's doing that whole thing where the leader won't ask his people to do what he won't do." Juan shrugged. "Since I've known him he's been like that. He is annoyingly good at times."

"Not a bad boy like you, huh?" Jenni elbowed her boyfriend and stuffed another chip in her mouth.

Juan pulled off his cowboy hat and smoothed out his hair with one hand. "Yeah, he can't stand up to my cool factor."

With a smirk, Jenni leaned her head on his shoulder and continued to watch as the last crew mopped the floors inside. One of the women, a red head named Katarina, stood watch at the sentry post nearby. Jenni didn't know her too well, but knew she was a good shot. As more people came into the fort, the dynamic was changing. It wasn't just the townies anymore that made up the fort's population. People from other towns had joined them. Each new person contributed in some way where it benefited everyone. Jenni thought it was good to have diversity.

Of course, Jenni's contribution was as the loca zombie killer and she was fine with that. She ate another chip and crunched it loudly. It felt good to be on the brink of something new and big. The fort was about to grow in a dynamic way. Taking the hotel would change everything. Unless they failed. But then again, that would change everything.

"You be careful in there," Juan said softly beside her. He was staring at her face as she chewed her chips. His finger lightly slid down the bridge of her nose. "Nothing crazy okay. I know you're loca, but try to curb your natural loca tendencies."

Jenni grinned at him. "I'll come back out alive. I've got too much to live for. Like giving you hell and eating Doritos." She popped another chip.

He laughed and slid an arm around her waist.

Jenni savored the flavor of the chip she was eating and the feel of Juan's arm around her. She had no intention of dying. There was no way in hell she was going to let a zombie get her. She had not survived this long to die. She now had Juan in her life and she wanted to be with him forever. She had a new family and a new life. That was worth fighting for. Looking toward the swarthy man with the dark green eyes, she grinned.

"Let's go have sex," she said to Juan, and shoved the bag into his hand. She swung her legs down onto the ladder leading into the construction site.

"Uh, what? Okay!" Juan scrambled down after her.

At the bottom, he caught her up in his arms and threw her over his shoulders. Both of them laughing, he carried her to their makeshift tent.

# Chapter 4

## 1. The New Season

The sun was barely peeking over the edge of the fort's walls when Katie set out on her daily jog. Her hair was up in a ponytail and she wore a T-shirt and jogging shorts. For the first time, she was wearing her brand new jogging shoes. After Peggy and the Mayor had inventoried everything brought into the fort during the scavenging expeditions, they had meticulously laid out everything in large boxes or any other bin they could find, and opened up a sort of store for everyone in the basement. No currency was exchanged, but you had to sign out anything that was taken. Katie had been surprised to find a box full of jogging shoes and had managed to find a pair that fit.

Katie started on her trek around the fort, enjoying the brisk morning air, feeling it nipping her checks bright red. She was trying to enjoy the cool morning air as much as she could before summer was in full swing and the mornings would be balmy.

She was on her second rotation when Jenni dropped in beside her. She was dressed in jeans, a red tank top and her boots. Glowing with something other than the cool morning air, Jenni grinned at her.

"Gawd, I think I hate you," Katie said with a laugh. "Every freakin' night?"

Jenni laughed and easily matched her pace. "Yeah, so?"

"I almost feel bad for Juan," Katie decided.

"Yeah, I am pretty brutal. I don't know how he puts up with me."

"You're loca. And he loves loca," Katie reminded her.

Jenni lightly pumped her arms as they ran and her grin said it all. She was wonderfully in love and it made Katie happy for her.

"You know, you kinda have options," Jenni started cautiously.

35

Katie shrugged. She debated opening up to Jenni or not. Her best friend could be terribly blunt and loud at times. If she confided in her, there was a good chance that everyone in the fort would know her business fairly quickly.

Jenni frowned as they took another corner. "Haven't you ever kissed a boy?"

That made Katie laugh out loud. "Lots, actually." There it was out. She had said it.

"Before you realized you were a lesbian?" Jenni raised her eyebrow.

"I'm not a lesbian," Katie said with a smile, deciding to fess up.

Jenni arched her eyebrows even higher. "Huh?"

"I'm bi," Katie answered.

"Huh?" Jenni looked utterly confused and almost ran into a pile of concrete bricks. Katie yanked her out of the way just in time. "You had a wife."

Katie nodded as they made the turn. "Yeah, but I'm bisexual. That means I find both men and women attractive. I just happened to end up with a really fabulous gay woman instead of a really fabulous straight man. The odds usually work against that, but Lydia snatched me up."

Jenni's eyes widened, her mouth dropped open, and she made an "oh" sound that lasted for a few seconds. She smacked Katie on the arm. "Then you do have options, you bitch! Travis!"

Katie smacked her back. "Shut up!"

"No, seriously! If you like both guys and girls, you have options!" Jenni had the mad gleam of a matchmaker in her eyes.

"I don't want him to know I'm bi or that I have some feelings for him," Katie said firmly. She almost regretted telling her, but it felt good to say it out loud. "At least, not now."

"You have feelings for him?" Jenni grabbed Katie's arm and dragged her to a stop. "Oh, my gawd! You have feelings for Travis!"

"But he can't know, so keep it down!"

Jenni twisted up her face, confused. "Why not? I mean, I'm relieved. I was afraid you'd be alone for the rest of your life unless some hot lesbian came along."

Katie sighed. "Just because you put two lesbians in a room that does not mean they'll hook up. Well, unless you go with the second date Uhaul theory...

"What's that?"

"What does a lesbian bring to a second date?"

"A Uhaul. That's funny!" Jenni giggled. "So lesbians move fast."

"That's not what we're talking about!"

"Okay, but I mean, well, you have options! You can have Travis!" Jenni was almost jumping up and down with excitement. "Katie, I'm so happy!"

Katie felt her stomach tighten nervously. "I don't want options right now. I just..." She trailed off.

"She's gone, Katie."

"I know. But I just can't forget her and move on. Even if I do...." Katie wiped a tear from her eye "...even if I do have feelings for Travis. I don't want to talk about this."

Jenni sighed. She reached out and touched Katie's shoulder gently. "I just want you happy. Is it wrong for you to be happy?"

Katie shook her head. "I don't know if I can be without her. I loved her so much, Jenni. When I met her I just knew she was the one and when I met Travis-" She closed her eyes and shook her head.

"What, Katie? Tell me."

"It felt...similar. Not exactly the same. But like he was important to me. To my future. Maybe I'm just admitting it to myself now, but-" She couldn't continue. Her emotions swirled up and she tried to focus herself.

Jenni saw the tears in her eyes and threw her arms around Katie, nearly crashing them both into the ground. Katie grabbed hold of her and they hugged each other tightly.

"It's okay! It's okay. At least you know that you're not alone and that people do love you. And he'll wait until you're ready. You know that."

"I'm so grateful I have you," Katie whispered. She kissed Jenni's cheek and clung to her. "You're a good friend."

Jenni stroked her hair and looked at her intently. "I love you, but I don't want you hurting so we'll drop this for now."

Katie nodded, smiling. "Okay. For now."

Travis walked up, looking a little grim, his hands in the pockets of his lightweight jacket. Katie couldn't help but notice the bags under his eyes or his slightly mussed hair. He was carrying so much on his shoulders and she wanted to hug him. "We're going in today. According to what's left of the Internet there is a bad storm heading this way. Some survivors in a school several counties away are reporting that it's very, very bad. They lost power and had to go to their backup generator."

The women looked toward the row of generators, that up to this point they hadn't had to use, and winced.

"So, we're going in. Get ready." His gaze lingered on Katie.

"I'll change and get Nerit," Katie answered. She had this deep desire to hug him and let him know it was okay. That they would both be okay, but she couldn't let herself. Not yet.

He nodded and walked on to inform the others.

Jenni smacked Katie's shoulder. "He is so into you. Don't keep him waiting too long!"

Katie turned and glared at her. "You said-"

"Gawd, yes, but-" Jenni threw up her hands. "He's so hot!"

Katie laughed despite herself and smacked Jenni's shoulder. "Lay off. Okay? For now. For me."

"Fine, but we will talk about this later." She kissed Katie hard on her cheek and strode off.

Katie stood alone, her hands resting on her hips, and exhaled slowly. She glanced over at Travis and caught him looking at her. She gave him a soft smile and his face lit up as he smiled back at her.

Sighing, she walked into the city hall building, trying hard not to think of anything but the task ahead.

## 2. Shelter From the Storm

Stacey held the squirming Jack Russell terrier firmly in her arms as Bill and Ed helped her over the wall. Eric climbed up behind her and she could feel him reaching out to steady her with one hand. Pepe was not happy with being taken over the wall and she didn't blame him. Despite the new area being cordoned off by high new walls, she felt vulnerable being outside of the construction site.

A big black girl reached up to help her with Pepe as she climbed down the second ladder into the new area. The girl's name was Lenore and Stacey had met her the day she and Eric had been rescued from the water tower. Lenore's best friend and constant companion, Ken, stood near Lenore, clutching his cat carrier. Inside, his cat, Cher, was mightily ticked off. Stacey didn't blame her.

Other survivors were descending ladders and a special elevator had been rigged up for the elderly and disabled. The big crane from the construction site was lifting a pallet over the wall with the elderly tied securely on to it. Old Man Watson looked befuddled, but he gave Stacey the thumbs up when he saw her looking at him.

The Dollar Store was already filling up and Stacey could see people trying to find a place to camp out during the long wait for the hotel to be taken. She hoped the terrible combination of zombie and bleach was gone now.

Peggy, the city secretary, and her little boy, Cody, reached the street just as Stacey did. Cody was crying softly and the sound of his whimpering made Stacey feel even more nervous.

"It's going to be fine, honey," Eric assured her as he reached the ground. He pressed a soft kiss to her cheek. Pushing his glasses up on his nose, he looked around warily. "We made damn sure this area is secure. We'll be fine."

"You can't blame me for being nervous," Stacey answered. She slid her arms around his waist and leaned against him. The love she felt for him pulsed hard inside of her and she felt a lump in her throat.

His laid his arm over her shoulders, his fingers stroking her skin. "No, I can't. But we'll be okay. I promise."

"I cannot wait until this is over," Ken said, and pouted slightly. His cat seemed to yowl in agreement.

Lenore set Pepe down and held tightly to his leash. Pepe zigzagged back and forth in front of her. "It'll be done soon enough and we'll have a nice bed to sleep in tonight."

"We can be roommates!" Ken clapped his hands excitedly.

"Oh, no! I am so not putting up with listening to you talk in your sleep about how hot Daniel Craig is." Lenore gave him a fierce look. "Besides, aren't you supposed to be back inside the fort helping out Juan? Gimme Cher and get to work."

Ken handed over his cat, giving her a fake, disdainful look. "You're so mean."

"Move it," Lenore ordered.

Eric stepped out of Ken's way as the younger man made his way back up over the wall.

"Good luck, Ken!" Eric called out.

Ken posed cutely on the ladder. "I will stun and amaze all with my mad skills!"

"He's a gopher for Juan," Lenore explained. "Like that's hard."

"Bitch," Ken sniffed and hurried over the wall.

Lenore grinned.

Stacey laid her head on Eric's shoulder. Her stomach was in knots.

"We'll be okay," Eric repeated, but she could see fear clearly in his eyes. They had barely survived coming to the fort. They had hoped their days fearing for their safety were over, but obviously they were not.

"Zombies don't got a chance against this crew. We're tough," Lenore said in her usual gruff tone. "We're mean. We're nasty. Plus, Ken could talk them to death."

Stacey laughed and took Pepe's leash when Lenore held it out to her. Pepe danced around her feet, looking up at her anxious.

Together, they walked toward the Dollar Store.

Overhead, the skies opened up.

It began to rain.

# 3. Check In Time

Nerit took a deep breath and strode up onto the platform overlooking the hotel's designated point of entry. Clad in her old jeans, a button down shirt, and Ralph's hunting jacket, she was warm, despite the cool, damp wind gusting through the small fort. With her yellowish-white hair tied back from her face, her eyes looked keen and intense.

This was something she was good at. She felt like killing.

In Israel, things had been rough when the nation had first arisen. She had fought bravely and with pride. Her almost eerie ability to nail any target from a great distance had given her an illustrious career. It had helped that she had the cool detachment needed to do the job of a sniper. Some had called her one of the most calculating and aloof women they had ever met. In reality, she was just good at her job. There were moments when she was haunted and the nightmares came, but she had always kept herself focused on the greater good. Defending Israel had been her priority. She had done her job well.

But now it was much more personal. She could still kill with skill and cold detachment, but it did not give her nightmares anymore. She was living in a nightmare. What she killed now were not terrorists or enemies of her homeland, but the undead citizens of her adopted country. The country had fallen. The fort was home; the zombies were the enemy.

If the bandits ever came to the fort and tried to do there what they had done to Ralph....

Pressing away thoughts of Ralph, she lit a cigarette and exhaled slowly. She was already in that calm cool place where the world was gray and devoid of anything other than her pulse and breath.

She was elevated above the construction site so she could see easily into the brick pen they had built around the old entrance to the hotel. It was high enough to keep any zombies out, and they had made the old wrought iron gate the doorway into the tiny courtyard. The pen was, essentially, as safe as it could be.

The dark gray clouds continued to sprinkle drops down on their heads, but the almost-black clouds in the distance spoke of a violent storm.

Slipping into position, she enjoyed the feel of the cold metal of her sniper rifle in her hands. Closing one eye, she became one with the gun; the sight became their mutual eye, harsh and unblinking. She could easily see everyone gathering to go in. She could see the bricked up entrance.

She was ready.

\*\*\*

Travis was not ready for this. He was certain of it. His stomach was in knots and his hands wouldn't stop sweating. Looking around at the people gathered in small tight groups around him, he felt his panic building.

They were finally going into the hotel. The small walled-in courtyard with the wrought iron gate suddenly seemed so flimsy to him.

What if hundreds of those things had somehow gotten into the hotel? What hope would they have of holding them off? Thank God they had created the new secure area. It now seemed foolish that they had ever considered going into the hotel without making sure that the survivors were safely tucked away first.

He glanced over his shoulder at Nerit. She looked calm, deadly, and ready. His gaze flicked to Juan, who was talking intently to Jenni. Travis knew Juan was very worried about Jenni going in to help clear out the building. He really couldn't blame him. Jenni was a good shot, but the situation was fraught with danger. Travis was also worried about the woman he cared about.

He glanced toward Katie, who was standing nearby. He was worried sick about her going in. He knew she was a good shot and had more experience dealing with zombies up close than just about anyone. He had confidence in her abilities, but still he felt a sense of dread. Too many times before, he had come close to losing her.

The last few weeks had been hard. After their surprising kiss, Katie had drawn far away from him. It stung him, but he could understand to some degree. Yesterday she had given him hope. Maybe it was misplaced, but when she had whispered 'please' to him, he took it as a sign she wanted time to deal with feelings she had for him. He had seen something in her eyes that had been surprising and encouraging. He was willing to give her time, but now that they were both going into a dangerous situation, he craved one last significant moment with her.

Mike, the man in charge, moved to the center of his carefully chosen groups. A former military man, he had grouped people into teams and trained them to work together for the last few weeks. His dark skin was beaded with sweat and rain. He looked strong and unafraid.

"We're about to go in. Remember to stay with your group. Stick to your predetermined route. If you meet with a large amount of zombies, do not return to the fort, but call for backup and fall back to the main lobby. You are not to return to the fort until the hotel is clear. If something goes wrong, start climbing and go to a higher floor."

His voice droned on, firm, intent and commanding. Travis watched people gazing at the tall man with deep respect and fear. There was a sense of terror building in the fort. It was inevitable. Things had been so calm, so safe, for weeks now. It had given all of them a false sense of security. And now it could all end. Yet, they needed to get into the hotel with summer heat coming. Plus, people were short-tempered and moody over the lack of privacy and the long lines into the bathrooms and shower. They had to expand the fort now, not later, when things were much rougher.

Mike finished. Everyone stepped back to let two construction workers through to unlock the wrought iron gate that opened up into the small courtyard. Travis watched anxiously, feeling sweat starting to trickle from his brow down his cheeks.

The two construction workers gave the thumbs up to Mike and entered the small area. Taking turns with sledgehammers, the two men began to chip away the brick to form a small hole about shoulder high in the wall. The sound of the sledgehammers cracking apart the bricks and the destroyed fragments slamming into the ground filled the hushed silence of the fort. Swinging one last time, the huge construction worker named Jimmy punched through the bricks and cement. As the hard little bits of the wall crumbled away and the dust cleared, the hole stood stark and black against the red wall.

"We're through," Jimmy said with a smile.

His partner , Roger, cautiously leaned forward attempting to peer in.

A hand lashed out of the hole. Roger yelled and fell back.

A torn, gray, black mottled face appeared, teeth gnashing, as a zombie tried to push his body through the hole.

People screamed and the construction workers scrambled back.

Terror gripped everyone.

The zombie's head jerked back as a nice neat hole in the center of its forehead oozed black blood down over its now limp features.

People were shocked, then realized what had happened. A few looked up to where Nerit still was poised for another shot.

The zombie hung awkwardly in the hole, then a skinless hand appeared desperately reaching toward the humans. Struggling to get past the other zombie, the new one grunted and growled until finally the limp body fell away. It thrust its head through the hole.

Again, a nice little round hole appeared on its forehead and it dropped out of sight.

Another face appeared, this one feminine. blond hair clung to the dried blood on its face. Someone screamed in horror, "Natalie!" then the zombie's head snapped back and she, too, was gone.

They all waited and watched. Travis could feel sweat and rain trickling down the sides of his face.

The hole remained empty.

Bill entered the tiny courtyard, rifle in hand. He flicked on a flashlight, shone it into the room beyond the hole, and gingerly peered in.

"Check the floor," someone shouted out.

Bill nodded and looked down. "Clear! Inside door appears to be locked."

Travis took a breath and started walking toward Katie. She looked toward him and gripped her gun even more tightly in her hands.

Jenni glanced at him as he passed, then back at the hole the construction workers were now widening for them to pass through.

Walking up to Katie, Travis gazed down at her intently. "If anything happens to me..."

"I know," Katie answered. "And you'll do the same for me."

He nodded and stood there awkwardly.

Katie stood up on her toes and kissed his rough cheek. Her lips lingered near his ear. "We'll be okay."

He breathed in the scent of her hair and skin and looked into her eyes. "We will?"

"Yeah," she answered, and smiled.

He almost kissed her, but the moment was shattered when Nerit strode past them, smoking her cigarette.

"Let's go clear it out, children. Time is running out."

## 4. Breakfast is Served

"Let's go zombie killing," Jenni said with a wild grin of delight. Throwing her arm around Juan's neck, she drew him down for a long intense kiss. She let go of him to hug the very surly Jason.

"Loca, be careful," Juan said softly. His fingers trailed along the nape of her neck lovingly. "Please, don't be too loca."

"No worries. Seriously, I'll be fine." She gave him a reassuring smile and turned toward her son.

"Mom," Jason said, his voice cracking. Juan had enlisted Jason as one of his helpers for the day. Jack was on guard duty. The dog's rabid hatred of zombies would come in handy if any got too close to the courtyard.

"It's okay," Jenni assured him with a kiss on his forehead. "Just do your job and we'll swap war stories later."

"Mom, just don't be loca. You know, like Juan said."

"Have a little faith here," Jenni ordered. "I'm good at this."

"Maybe a little too good," Juan teased her.

She rolled her eyes. Leaning over, she kissed Jack on top of his head. "Be a good dog. Take care of the boys."

Jack whined a little and pawed at her knee.

Jenni's smiled grew wider as she felt their love pouring over her. She felt needed, wanted, desired, and important. All the things she had never been before. She wouldn't let them down.

With a wink, she walked to her two partners in crime. Ashley was a former waitress. She was a frail little thing, but had a determined look on her face. Ned was a former school bus driver. He was tall and a little awkward with his height. Now both were armed to the teeth, looking nervous as hell. Though everyone had been undergoing training, it was Jenni who was in charge. She was the best shot and had the most experience with the zombies. It was hard to know how good a shot some of these people were considering ammunition was used very sparingly, but she was hoping the training sessions with Mike would paid off.

Mike's group, consisting of Felix and a short man named Charles, was the first into the room beyond the jagged hole in the wall. Nerit's group followed. She had two construction workers with her, Jimmy and Shane. Shane was someone Jenni hated with a passion. He had attacked Katie when she had shot and killed his brother during one battle with the zombies. Shane's brother had been bitten, but Shane had gone wild. Jenni hated that he was going along.

Jenni's group moved into the small courtyard to wait. She pushed up on her tip toes to see what was up in the room beyond the hole in the wall. She could see the first groups moving slowly toward the door that would let them into the hotel.

Mike reached out and touched the doorknob. It was covered in dried blood. Gore, dried and black, was splashed on the walls.

"They probably came in here to hide and one of them was bit and turned," Mike decided.

Cautiously, he swung the door open. Nothing stirred in the hallway beyond. His group moved slowly out the doorway and disappeared.

Nerit's group advanced across the room, then they too slipped out into the hall.

Jenni lead her group into the small courtyard. The stench from the small room assailed her senses and she sneezed. Drawing up all the bravery she could muster, she stepped into broken doorway into the hotel.

"Shit," Ned whispered, looking at the dead zombies and the remains of their feeding frenzy weeks ago.

"Don't let it get to you," Jenni ordered.

She moved across the room, her eyes feeling wide and crazed in their sockets. The gloom was stifling and the stench overwhelming.

The storm was drawing closer and loud booms of thunder filled the room. What a perfect development for this day. Lightening, thunder, hard wind, and rain. It was like a horror movie. She shivered at the thought.

Jenni's long hair was tied up on top of her head and under a cap. No one was allowed to leave their hair down. It would be too easy for a zombie to snag it. The cap felt itchy and heavy on her head, and she scratched at it awkwardly. Behind her, Ashley held the high-powered flashlight high and illuminated their path.

Stepping into the hallway, Jenni walked slowly, her feet silent on the plush carpet. With a carpet this thick would they hear anything creeping up on them? She didn't want to think about that too much. She had a job to do and she didn't need to freak herself out. It was bad enough just knowing that zombies were in the building. Following the route she had memorized during the many briefings, she headed around a corner and down the hall that would lead into main dining room.

Glancing over her shoulder, she made sure that Ashley and Ned were behind her. She caught sight of Katie and Travis entering the hallway with Roger. She liked Roger. He had playfully put on a red T-shirt and dubbed himself "the red shirt on the away party" in homage to the Classic Star Trek show. It had cracked up everyone at breakfast, but now she was worried. Maybe you shouldn't joke about death.

"It is a good day to die," she heard Roger mutter in his best Worf imitation.

Jenni suppressed a smile and continued down the hallway. There were no doors off this hallway. Just pretty gilded mirrors and fancy artwork. An occasional table or chair rested against the wall. It was a fancy way to decorate a very boring hall.

Reaching the dining room, she swung the rifle from side to side, looking all around. The pretty round tables were decorated with a spray of now dead flowers. The china and silverware were laid out meticulously with napkins twisted into the shapes of swans resting on top of the plate. There was no sign of disturbance here. Jenni was rather overwhelmed by the old-fashioned opulence of the room. The hotel had obviously been carefully restored with the hope of luring in high-end clientele.

Moving determinedly toward the kitchen, Jenni took a deep breath and caught the faint whiff of decay.

"Shit!" Jenni exclaimed. "They're here!"

Abruptly, the door to the kitchen was flung open and the wait staff flooded into the room ready for their breakfast.

# Chapter 5

## 1. The Away Party

Katie took point with her group since she was more experienced with weapons. It didn't escape her how ironic it was that she was finally doing what her father had always hoped for. Being a good solider. She had considered following his footsteps into the Marines, but had opted for college and law school instead. Now she was wondering if she should have gone into the Marines. Maybe if she had she wouldn't be scared shitless.

Travis tripped and fell over a chair in the hallway.

They all froze.

Katie turned to give him a dark look and whispered, "Shhhh" at him.

"Sorry," Travis muttered.

Their destination was the first floor lobby. The idea was to clear out the center of the first floor first and work outwards. The lobby was quite large, so they were taking the left-hand side. Another group was taking the right. Two halls lead to the lobby.

Katie walked slowly, her steps measured, cautious. Nearing the archway leading into the lobby, she took a deep breath. If the front door was open, they were most likely fucked. Sunlight was very visible on the far wall, illuminating their way. Something was open.

Travis and Roger behind her, she moved slowly along the wall, and out onto the tiled floor, her boots making soft tapping sounds. The enormous oak staircase cut the lobby in half and they slipped along its side. Katie glanced upwards, toward the railing and the second floor.

Nothing.

Slowly, one of the large windows came into view. Light was pouring in through it, but the front doors were closed. Chained, in fact.

She sighed with relief and turned to see a zombie staring at her. It was a maid, standing on the stairs. Her head was hanging by sinews and flopped sideways on her chest. She would have appeared headless from the behind. But from her angle, she could clearly see the barely attached head and its crazed eyes. It was obviously too confused by its condition to know what to do. It scuttled one way then the other, uncoordinated.

"Damn," Roger whispered.

Katie drew her bowie knife from her belt and approached the creature slowly. It blinked at her, its mouth open, trying to scream at her, and started snapping its jaws at her. Again it swayed back and forth, obviously not sure how to move toward its prey.

With a grunt, Katie shoved the creature over and it landed hard on the stairs. Its head flopped to one side, its teeth snapping. Lifting the knife over her shoulder, Katie narrowed her eyes, aimed, and struck the zombie through the eye as hard as she could. The knife hit bone and she twisted, pushing further in. The jaws stopped snapping. Katie braced her foot on the head and drew out her knife. Cleaning the blade on the dead maid's dress, she looked up to see Roger and Travis looking at her in shock.

"What?"

"Damn," Roger said.

Katie looked around and saw the other team lead by Katarina entering the far side of the room. They signaled that they were clear and Katie nodded. The walkie-talkie sputtered, "Dining room! Now! Fuck Fuck! Fuck!" Jenni's voice was frantic.

The gun shots began.

## 2. Nothing Ever Goes As Planned

In some ways it was just like a video game. You fired until the gun clicked empty, reloaded, fired again, reloaded...

There just needed to be an annoying male voice telling you when to reload and it would be perfect. But there wasn't and the zombies rushing them weren't carbon copies of each other and wouldn't vanish when hit. They were dressed alike in their waiter costume, but very different. Some were almost sprinting toward them. Others were struggling just to walk. The more whole "I obviously died by my throat being bit out" were fast and the "I got swarmed by a bunch of them and obviously got really eaten up" staggered.

The runners went down fast, since they were the front of the pack, but they were so quick they closed the gap between the living and the undead with startling swiftness.

Luckily, Ashley and Ned did exactly what they were supposed to do. Mike had taught them to divide up the zombies into, as he put it, "Pie slices" with everyone taking one slice to concentrate on. Jenni fired right down the center. Ashley fired at anything to the left of them as Ned took care of those on the right.

The swarming zombies fell quickly as the shots hit them true. Some even tripped over their comrades, landing hard on their faces, before having their heads blown off.

The three humans backed up slowly, all trying not to panic as the gush of zombies faded out to a trickle. As the last shot echoed through the room and the last zombie toppled forward, they all three let out the breaths they had been holding.

"We did it!" Ashley beamed happily.

Jenni nodded grimly, and said, "But listen."

From the distance was the sound of running feet, grunts and growls.

"Shit, they're coming," Ned muttered.

They ran across the dining room, jumping over the dead bodies, moving to the far side. Jenni began to shove over the heavy tables, making a barrier as fast as she could. The other two joined her.

Mike, Nerit, and the rest of their teams ran in the door. Seeing the upturned tables and all the dead bodies, they quickly understood what was happening.

"Check the kitchen," Mike ordered.

Nerit moved faster than any woman her age should be able to and motioned to Shane to heave her up onto the bar behind the upturned tables. She immediately aimed toward the main doors.

The grunting, moaning, screaming zombies were drawing closer.

"Kitchen is clear with only a back door into the side street," Felix said.

"If we have to, that's the way we'll fall back," Mike answered.

The dining room doors busted open and Travis, Katie and Roger ran in. Katie sprinted across the room, evading the tables and bodies, with Travis close behind. Roger huffed, as his huge girth swayed as he moved, but he managed to reach the overturned tables just as the doors swung open again.

Katarina's team ran in. They rushed headlong through the tables, knocking over chairs, and tripping in their panicked state. The reason for their desperation became quickly clear. The doors never closed for they caught on the mangled, mutilated bodies of the dead right behind the last team.

Katarina fell in her haste to get around a table. The first zombie in the mob reached down to grab her and Nerit put a hole through his head.

There was hesitation to fire from the people huddled behind the tables. With three people running in desperate haste toward them and blocking their view, Nerit took a majority of the shots.

Jenni aimed for the zombies furthest from the running humans and fired off a few shots. She could feel the tension growing steadily as the room slowly filled.

Katarina managed to get up and run again, but four more zombies grabbed hold of her denim jacket. She twisted, yanked, and squirmed her way out of the jacket and broke free, running again.

Jenni heard a man's scream and barely saw one of the men, whose name she did not remember, go down. Gunshots rang out steadily, but the man kept screaming.

"Nerit!" Mike's voice was an order.

Another shot, then the man stopped screaming.

Katarina reached the tables and squirmed behind them. She quickly turned to fire at a zombie in hot pursuit.

There was no sign of the other man. He had gone down so silently, no one had noticed. The room was now clogged with the undead. They were tripping over their dead comrades and falling over chairs and tables. The most agile had pursued Katarina, but as they had drawn near the barricade, they had gone down in a hail of bullets.

Jenni kept firing, aiming as much as she could, but she was terrified and that terror made some of her shots go wide.

Her gun clicked empty, and Mike shouted at her, "Reload."

She almost burst out laughing.

## 3. The Madness of War

Katie found herself wedged behind a table with her back against the wall with Travis beside her and Nerit standing on the bar behind them. She hated being stuck in the corner.

The gun kept jerking in her hands. Her fingers ached as she tried to aim true and take the heads off as many of the zombies as possible. There had been estimates that only twenty people were in the hotel. That estimate had been seriously low. At least a dozen lay dead on the ground and maybe thirty were still moving around and trying to get to the living flesh.

A zombie pushed his way past a nearby table and charged at the barricade. He hit the table Katie was behind and it started to tip. Pressing her back against the wall and bracing the table with one foot, she aimed at his head as he snarled, reaching for her. Pulling the trigger, she was already flinching, knowing blood and gore would splatter her.

"Gross," she muttered as wiped brains off her face, and aimed at the next one rushing toward them.

Next to her, Travis was busy reloading someone else's gun for them. Jenni was screaming at the zombies as she fired. Nerit was cold and calculating above them as she systematically eliminated the quickest of the undead, leaving the slower, more mutilated ones staggering toward the tables.

"Gawddammit! Why are there so many?" Felix exclaimed.

Beside him, Shane didn't answer as he shoved the end of his rifle into a snarling zombie mouth and fired.

Four zombies hit the barricade at the same time and some people had to stop firing so they could brace it. Nerit was in the midst of reloading so Travis picked up a heavy candlestick and brought it down hard on the head of one of the female zombies snarling at them.

Katie screamed as something grabbed her leg. She looked down to see the hand of a zombie gripping her ankle. It had reached through the gap between the table and wall. Its growling face was barely visible. With surprising strength, it tugged on her, sending her tumbling backward into the bar.

Travis brought the candlestick down hard on the head of another zombie as more hit the barricades. Now only a few people were firing into the crowd of zombies. The others tried to keep the tables from toppling over and allowing the zombies through. The room was filled with the screams of the humans and the growls of the zombies.

It seemed everyone was shouting at once: Mike ordering people to hold the tables in place, Katarina screaming that her table was slipping, Nerit telling everyone to be calm, Felix and Shane were shouting as several zombies were trying to topple their table, Katie screaming because the zombie was dragging her leg out into the open. It was chaos.

Travis continued to slam the candlestick downward, blood and gore flying everywhere. One of the zombies grabbed his arm and, for a horrible moment, everyone panicked. Nerit put a bullet through the zombie's head, but more were grabbing at Travis's arm.

"Jacket off!" It was Katarina's voice.

Travis yanked his arm through the sleeve as fast as he could, Katarina helping him pull the jacket off. It was ripped off him and dragged into the mouths of the hungry zombies on the other side of the barricade. Jenni grabbed Travis' arm and saw that he had escaped without a bite.

"Shit! That was close! You're fine!" she said, and went back to firing at the very frustrated looking zombies.

Katie, meanwhile, was on the floor and trying to pull her leg away from the zombie. She had trouble getting leverage to yank her leg back.

"Some help here!" Katie tried to aim at the zombie's head, but it was out of view behind her captured foot.

"Keep the tables in place!" Shane roared.

Beside him, Charles and Ned struggled with a table.

Mike's voice was fierce over the shots and screams. "Hold the line! Don't let them through!"

Nerit kicked Mike in the shoulder. "Katie's in trouble!"

Mike looked over to see what was happening. "Shit! Travis! A zombie has Katie!"

Travis turned to see what was going on and went very white. He grabbed the first thing he saw on the bar. Falling to his knees, he began to stab the dead hand as hard as he could with the corkscrew.

"Fuck!" Roger was beginning to lose his fight to keep one of the heavy tables up as four zombies growled and reached for him.

Jenni turned and fired as the table was righted. She and Roger ended up staring over the table at the zombies.

Katie struggled to find anything to grip onto as the zombie kept pulling on her foot and drawing her leg closer to the gap that would bring it into the open.

Katarina picked up a chair and hurled it at one of the zombies trying to climb over the tabletop toward Jenni and Roger. It was hit square in the face. It rolled off the table and tried to crawl under it. Roger shoved the table back over and pinned the zombie under it. Jenni fired point blank into its head, then aimed over the edge of the table at the remaining ones, firing a little wildly, but managing to kill them.

"Someone shoot this sonofabitch!" Travis kept stabbing the grayish dead hand as hard as he could, breaking bones and tendons. Still, it pulled Katie's foot. It almost had her whole booted foot in the open now and was obviously aiming to get to the more tender calf.

"I can't get a clear shot," Nerit responded.

More shots, more growls, more people swearing.

Katie grabbed hold of Travis, trying to pull herself free from the unrelenting grasp of the zombie.

Suddenly, there was silence.

"That's it," Katarina whispered in awe.

"Gawddamn, fuckin' zombies!" Shane cursed and threw his table over onto the dead creatures.

"We have this fucker left," Travis shouted.

The zombie's other hand slid through the gap, grabbed Katie's ankle, and yanked her leg out into the open with one swift pull.

"Fuck!"

"Travis!"

Travis shoved the table over onto the zombie. Mike and Roger grabbed Katie and yanked her free.

An enormous zombie was growling, still after its prey as it reached for Katie desperately. It wiggled back and forth under the table.

Jenni ran over and jumped on top of the table and began hopping up and down on it. Roger laughed and joined her, the table seesawing dangerously. Katarina got on the table, braced herself on the wall and jumped up and down as hard as she could.

Mike added his weight as well, grinning.

The others joined in, almost hysterical smiles on their faces, as the adrenaline rush in the veins spurred them on. As they slowly crushed the zombie beneath the table into mush, its bones cracking under their weight, they did a jovial little dance of death.

Nerit let herself down from the bar slowly, cursing in Hebrew, while Travis helped Katie to her feet.

Looking across the room, Katie was overcome by the stench of death and the gore that was splattered everywhere.

There was a loud, sickening popping noise from under the table, and the zombie's growls ended.

Katie ran into the kitchen and threw up in the sink. She was shaking hard, her hands trembling, her stomach recoiling at what had just happened, and her near death.

"Well," Jenni's voice said from the other room, "I'm glad I'm not cleaning up this mess."

## 4. Words are Dangerous

Juan helplessly stood outside along with everyone else that was not part of the original entry teams. There was an utter sense of horror and desperation that gripped them as they listened to the gunfire within the hotel and the unholy sounds that accompanied it.

Like the others, he could not take his eyes off the closed door into the janitor's closet. Through the padlocked gate, the painted bluish-gray door, splashed with dried blood, seemed ominous. What if it cracked open and those things poured through into the small courtyard? Suddenly, the wrought iron gate seemed inconsequential.

His grip tightened on his gun as he lifted his walkie-talkie to his mouth. He hesitated, realizing that in the midst of battle the last thing they needed was him yelling for them to report in.

Then, as quickly as the gunshots had erupted, there was silence.

He immediately pressed the button, "What the fuck happened?"

There was a long pause, static, laughter, and then, finally, Mike's voice came through the static. "We got swarmed, but we're okay now. I have a feeling that every zombie outside of a locked door headed our way."

Juan was about to ask about Jenni when he heard her voice plainly. He felt the tight knots in his back release. "Did we lose anyone?"

"Yeah, Mark and Wallace."

"Damn."

"We're going to need to start room to room now. Send in the backup teams and have them meet me in the lobby. Still use caution, there could be stragglers," Mike's voice said through the static.

Juan heard Jenni yell, "Love you, babe" and he smiled slightly.

"Okay, sending them in. Take care of yourselves."

Turning, he motioned to Bill and Curtis to head in with their teams. Glancing toward Jason, he gave the boy a slight smile.

"Your Mom's okay."

"I know," the teenager said in a quiet, distrustful tone.

Juan hesitated, then shrugged. The kid hated him and he knew it, but at least the boy still had his Mom and he still had his loca.

He watched Bill and Curtis' team disappear into the building and felt the knots in his back return.

Ashley stood quietly to one side as everyone flipped the tables back over and began the process of making sure the zombies were truly dead. Caution was the key word, and everyone was very careful. But their aim had been true and the many dead were finally at peace. During the fracas, Ashley and Ned had been constantly reloading guns. It wasn't until toward the end, she had ended up helping brace a table. Now she stood looking at her fingers and the long scrape across them.

Nearby, Jenni used a broken chair leg to bash in the last zombie's head as a precaution.

Meanwhile, Ashley just stared at her hand.

It was just a scrape. That's all it was. Just a scrape.

***

Katie rinsed her mouth out with water from the faucet. It tasted odd, but Juan had explained the hotel used well water. Watching the water swirl down the drain, she ran her wet fingers over her brow and took a steadying breath.

Of course, the kitchen reeked of death, so she threw up again.

Finally, she was done. She wiped her mouth again and looked around. There were buffet bins filled with decayed food laid out for what was probably going to be a brunch. A large menu was tacked up on a board. Next to it was an easel with a large placard on it. "The Daughters of Texas present The Restoration of Historical Ashley Oaks." it read at the top and listed the guest speakers.

Katie staggered out into the main room and looked around. It was as she suspected. Most of the zombies were women. In the fray, she hadn't even noticed. Most were wearing neat little matching outfits and expensive shoes. Other zombies were the waiters and kitchen staff. That meant maids and janitors could still be around. Walking around, studying the bodies, she identified the front desk receptionist and a doorman.

"Shouldn't be too many left," Mike was saying.

"Actually, these are mostly brunch guests. There was a meeting here during the first days," Katie said. "And the lobby and kitchen crew. The maids and the janitors are probably around."

Mike looked around, truly seeing the zombies for the first time and what they were wearing. "Oh. Yeah. We killed two janitors in that room and a maid."

"But how many were on shift?"

Jenni nodded. "I worked in a hotel. There should be a work schedule up at the front desk!"

She started heading out the door and Mike immediately motioned Ned and Ashley to follow. "Stay with her."

Ashley nodded, still looking pale from the battle and Ned swaggered with more confidence than he should have considering the situation.

Katie sighed and looked around. "I'm thinking that the maids may have barricaded themselves into bedrooms like that one zombie that took a header out of the window when we first arrived."

Travis stood nearby looking at his slimed up jacket and tossed it away with disgust. "Which means every room we enter could be full of really hungry zombies."

"Nothing about this is easy," Roger said, and kicked a pink Ferragamo high heel across the room.

"Just gotta find them and shoot them in the head," Shane said from where he was straddling a chair and looking bored.

"Unless they eat your ass first," Felix grumbled.

Mike patted Felix on the back. "The trick is to shoot them in the head before they get that chance."

Bill and Curtis entered the room, followed by a guy named Davey. They all three looked impressed with the scene.

"Been busy, I see," Bill said.

"Nothing we can't handle," Shane retorted. "Despite the lesbos, fatsos, and old people."

Everyone chose to ignore him.

Jenni ran back in, waving a clipboard. "Okay, I got the roster."

She handed it automatically to Katie though Mike had been reaching for it.

"Okay, gimme a second..." Katie looked around, counting the kitchen staff and the wait staff. She looked at the list. "All the kitchen people are accounted for and so is the wait staff. Both front desk people are here as is the doorman. We are missing four maids..." She flipped a page and studied it for a moment. "And two plumbers. They were called in to look at the showers on the sixth floor."

"So the sixth floor is a potential hotspot," Mike said thoughtfully.

"And the maids could be anywhere," Travis said with a sigh.

"Six zombies," Katie said. "And the manager of the hotel."

"Not so many compared to this," Bill pointed out.

"Yeah, but they could be anywhere, upstairs, in closets, under the beds-anywhere," Travis answered.

Everyone stood in a circle, pondering this.

Jenni looked around, then up at Katie. "Well, it can't be that hard, can it?"

Katie arched an eyebrow at her.

Jenni smiled at her. "I mean, what could go wrong?"

Nearby, Ashley looked pale and a little unsure on her feet. Putting her head down, she took a deep breath.

Katarina looked toward Nerit and said, "Can I tag along with you?"

Katie still felt unsteady and a little nauseous, but there was so much to do. Travis gave her a weak smile and she reached out to him. He took her hand and squeezed it.

"We stand here any longer and we're going to end up freaking ourselves out and giving up," Mike said after a beat. "We survived this. We survived all that shit that went down the first days. We'll survive this."

Katie nodded her head, as did the others. Mike was right. They had to keep going. Standing here freaking themselves out was doing none of them a bit of good.

"So, let's get going and get this done. What more can go wrong?" Mike said with a laugh.

It was then that Ashley looked up, growled, and bit into Mike's throat.

# 5. What Should Have Been

*He's not supposed to die*, was Jenni's first thought. *He's the black hero of this tale. He's supposed to survive, isn't he? At least until the end...*

But Mike was struggling, his throat caught in the angry bite of the tiny blond woman. Her bony arms were around him, crushing him as she tore at him. Everyone was frozen in disbelief.

It wasn't real. It couldn't be.

But it was.

"Get her off! Get her off," Mike gasped.

Travis grabbed Ashley's long blond hair and yanked her back. Blood sprayed everywhere, hot and red with life.

Katie moved fast, a hunting knife in her hand. The others were moving too slow, the shock of the attack dulling their reactions.

The thing that had been Ashley was now turning toward Travis, chewing the flesh she had torn from Mike's neck. Hissing, she was about to strike again and Travis tried to duck away.

Holding the knife over her head with both hands, Katie brought it down hard. With a disgusting sound, the knife plunged through the zombie's check, shattering teeth and wedging into her jaw. They both fell to the ground, the zombie beneath, Katie on top.

Jenni ran forward, her hand holding her gun, flipping the safety off.

Katie pinned the small zombie to the ground and hacked at its head with her knife. The skull cracked beneath the blade and she kept slamming it down until the thing that had been Ashley shuddered and was silent.

Mike lay on the ground nearby, shivering violently, his hands pressed to his throat. Blood was bubbling up between his fingers and spreading on the floor around his head like a red halo. Jenni fell to her knees beside him. Feeling impotent to do anything, she laid her gloved hand on his cheek and he looked toward her.

"I didn't...see...her..." he said, looking regretful and sad.

"I know. I didn't either," Jenni answered.

"I'm sorry, but keep...going..." Mike whispered, and was gone.

Jenni drew her hand back. Tears streamed down her face.

Travis drew his gun and aimed it at Mike's head.

"Do it," Katie said softly, standing slowly, wiping off her knife on her jeans.

Travis narrowed his eyes, his hand trembling.

"Do it before he comes back," Nerit said sternly.

Travis struggled to pull the trigger. Jenni could see the agony in his eyes. "Can't," Travis sighed, beginning to lower the gun. "Someone else-"

Mike's eyes flashed open and he growled.

Blood erupted between his eyes and he was truly gone. A delicate little hole, bubbled with blood as Nerit stepped over Mike's body.

"If you hesitate again, I will shoot you. I will not lose anyone else because you could not pull the trigger," she said coldly, and brushed past Travis to stand guard at the door.

"This isn't right, man. This isn't right," Felix exclaimed, falling to his knees beside of Mike.

"What do we do?" Katarina asked softly. Her shock was mirrored in the faces of those around her.

Jenni looked back at Mike, so peaceful in his final death. "We keep going."

Bill leaned down and grabbed up Mike's walkie-talkie. "We go on. We finish this. Easy as that."

Curtis shook his head and grabbed a tablecloth to cover Mike with.

Jenni looked down at Mike and sighed.

*You were supposed to make it to the end. Mike, does this mean this is the end?*

Even Shane was solemn as Curtis laid the white tablecloth over Mike's still features.

# Chapter 6

## 1. Pieces of Hell

**W**e keep going," Bill said for emphasis. "We get this job done."

"How could she turn so fast?" Katarina asked.

Katie looked up at her, holding the dead woman's hand. "She was bitten. Looks like one of them got her hand and she yanked it back. It's not a distinct bite mark, more like a scrape, but it was enough."

"Ashley's been anorexic for years and has all sorts of health issues. Probably took her down fast," Curtis said softly. "Poor thing."

"So you have to kill whoever is bit immediately or we'll lose more people," Nerit said in a cold voice. "We can't be sure how long it will take before they turn."

Katie shivered at her tone and glanced at Travis. His head was down and he obviously knew the comment had been directed at him. He was staring at the gun in his hand in a strange, almost angry way.

"That's bullshit. What if they don't change? What if the bite don't take? We can't just shoot everyone like that lesbo bitch shot my brother!" Shane's voice was fierce and he glared at Katie.

"And what if we let one person with a bite live long enough to change and began spreading it through the fort? Then that is the end of us all. Do you want to be one of those things? Do you? Do you want to be the reason all the survivors of this fort die? Tell me. Do you want that on your hands?" Nerit gave Shane a cold, fierce look.

Shane didn't answer. He just looked away.

Bill began reorganizing the teams, trying to keep them evened out with skill level. Everyone was emotionally and physically exhausted, but they had to go on. This is what Mike had trained them for and even though he was no longer with them, they had a job to do.

Katie looked at all the bodies again and looked down at Mike's covered body. Jenni was standing nearby, her expression a little distant and disturbing. Katie reached out and took her hand and Jenni turned to look at her. Her eyes had a glazed look Katie hadn't seen since the first day they had met.

"Jenni?"

Jenni frowned a little, and said softly, "He wasn't supposed to die."

Katie hugged her tightly. "None of us are. Not like this."

Jenni nodded mutely, drew away, and clutched her gun tightly. "I just don't want it to be the end."

"It's not," Katie said firmly. "We just have to keep going. Fighting. For everyone's sake, Jenni, we gotta get this done."

Jenni looked up and her gaze seemed a little more focused. "Yeah, for everyone still alive."

Bill looked toward Nerit, who was standing near the doorway watching the hall. "Nerit, we clear?"

"No movement. I think the rooms are what we need to worry about now," Nerit answered.

"But be cautious anyway," Bill reminded everyone.

There were nods and people visibly pulled on their inner strength as they prepared to go on.

Bill raised the walkie-talkie to his mouth and pressed the button. "Juan, we're continuing on."

"We heard gunshots," Juan's voice cackled through the receiver.

"Yeah, we lost some people. Mike and Ashley."

"Shit," Juan's voice answered.

"We'll be in touch." Bill motioned to Nerit.

The older woman started down the hall followed by her new team of Katarina, Shane and Jimmy. The other teams followed as Bill pointed to them. They were back on schedule and heading to their assignments.

Katie looked toward Roger and Travis. They were talking softly. Roger nodded slightly, but obviously looked ill at ease. As she neared them, Travis sighed and looked toward her.

"I'm sorry, Katie. I won't fuck up again," he said.

She shrugged and looked toward Roger. "No one thinks it's easy killing what used to be your friend, Travis." Forcing herself to look at him, she could see the pained expression in his eyes.

Travis said softly, "Just a living nightmare, isn't it?"

Katie blinked, realizing what had happened. Travis had once confided in her that he had been struggling with his bizarre visions since the first day. He often saw his friends transformed into zombies for quick flashes. Now he was seeing those nightmares become reality. No wonder he had hesitated shooting Mike.

She reached out and touched his cheek. He nuzzled her fingers, comforting himself, then he straightened.

"Let's do this."

***

Room after room was empty. Offices, closets, bathrooms, empty...

Each time a door swung open, Nerit's gut clenched and her finger prepared to squeeze the trigger. Nerit rarely flinched in the face of danger. In fact, she rarely felt afraid. Her calmness was something she was used to, but now, she felt fear struggling to gain a hold of her.

Each large piece of furniture could be hiding danger, every partially opened door a potential for death...

There were signs of violence. Behind the front desk there was an enormous pool of dried blood and pieces of intestine and organs. The manager's office had all the furniture knocked over and the heavy desk shoved aside, but no blood. Maybe he had escaped.

Walking quietly down the narrow hall, opening closed doors, the four of them moved with silent efficiency. The remains of the life that existed before the undead rose danced before their eyes as tombstones of days gone by. TVs and computers sat silently, screens blank. A newspaper laid on the floor in a bathroom declaring, "The Dead Walk".  A reminder of the first days, of what had happened, and of what now existed in the world.

In a supply closet, banners for the grand opening of the hotel were folded up, waiting to be hung up. But that Grand Opening would never happen or at least not the way the investors had thought it would.

As they opened the very last door, it swung open into a small office. Inside were three bodies. None moved.

It was a woman and two children. The woman had evidently smothered the kids and drove an ice pick through their skulls. They were carefully arranged on the floor, their arms around each other. She had then clutched the ice pick in one hand and had fallen sideways onto it. She was lying next to the children, her eyes wide and staring, but they were all most definitely dead.

Making sure the room was clear, Nerit approached the door  and studied it. There were no claw marks on it or any sign of distress. The woman had hidden back here, terrified, until she had made a desperate choice. Nerit returned to the manger's office and found a framed photo. It showed a young man, the dead woman and three children.

"What do you think happened?" Katarina asked.

"I think he told her to hide with the kids. Maybe he tried to go for help," Nerit answered.

"And never came back," Jimmy finished.  "And she stayed here."

"She may have been too terrified to try to go for help or try to escape," Shane said.

"And yet the construction site was so close, safety so close," Katarina whispered.

Nerit nodded and lifted her walkie-talkie to her mouth. "Juan, first floor is clear. We're joining the teams on the second.  But we may have one more zombie. I think the manager's family was visiting on the first day.  One of his kids is not accounted for."

"Shit," Juan's voice said.

"Zombie kids.  I hate them," Shane muttered.

Nerit motioned for the group to follow her. They moved down the hallway in silence, leaving behind the mother and her two small children to rest in peace a little longer.

***

Jenni's revised group of Ned, Felix and Charles moved down the second floor hallway, guns at the ready, alert, and fearful. Ned held a large flashlight up, illuminating their way. The power grid was still up for the town had power, but a breaker had been tripped inside the hotel and it was dark, musty, and terrifying.

Despite the renovations, it seemed the hotel had been determined to keep its old world charm. The doors were not unlocked by card keys, but with regular keys. Master keys had been found behind the front desk and passed around to the various teams. Charles carried their set in his meaty hand. He looked very nervous as sweat poured down his face.

They had figured out a method for clearing out the rooms. Jenni and Felix would keep watch while Ned held the flashlight up so Charles could unlock the door. Then Charles would fling open the door while Jenni and Felix aimed straight into the room, ready to fire at anything that stirred. If nothing immediately popped out, they would move slowly into the room and check the bathroom the same way. The beds were old fashioned and so they had to check under them. This was accomplished by Felix ripping the comforter off and Jenni squatting down to make sure it was clear.

It was definitely a good plan and it worked through four rooms, but the stress level was growing. They were all struggling with a growing sense of dread. Maybe it was the darkness that dwelled in the hallway, the cloying stench of death that seemed to hang in the musty air, or the way the world outside seemed so far away as the storm boomed overhead.

The fifth door loomed before them and Charles wiped his brow with his hand and looked toward Jenni. "Ever feel this was a bad idea?"

Jenni laughed. "Ever since we came in."

Charles leaned over and unlocked the door.

Felix made a little noise in his throat.

"What is it?" Charles looked at him nervously.

"The stench," Felix answered.

Jenni let herself sniff the air and flinched. "Shit."

They all steadied themselves and Charles flung open the door.

Nothing stirred in the room.

Cautiously, they moved into the room, doing exactly what they had done before. The space under the bed was clear. The wardrobe was empty. The bathroom door loomed before them, taunting and terrifying.

The stench was so bad, their eyes were watering.

"I hope I don't get this room," Charles muttered, and flung the bathroom door open.

Nothing stood before them, but the toilet with a tidy little white strip of paper across it and an empty clawed tub.

"Where the fuck is it coming from?" Ned exclaimed.

Jenni looked back toward the open door that led to the hallway, then back into the bathroom. "We're missing something."

The zombie stepped out from behind the door and bit into Ned's shoulder before anyone could even react. Ned screamed in horror and pain and staggered under the dead woman's grip. Jenni raised her gun immediately and shot both of them in quick succession.

"No," Charles gasped.

"That was fucked up," Felix said and wiped his brow. "Shit!"

Jenni was breathing hard, staring at the bodies. Lifting her walkie-talkie, she said, "Make sure to check *behind* the fucking doors. One was behind a door when we opened it. It got Ned."

There was silence, then Nerit's voice said, "Understood."

Jenni wiped a tear away and looked at Charles and Felix. "Let's go."

As they walked out, she leaned down and picked up the flashlight from Ned's slack fingers.

"Second floor clear," came the announcement over the walkie-talkie. "Advance to third floor."

Katie stood near the stairwell. Her body was shivering. They had been in view of the other teams on occasion throughout the inspection of the second floor, but it had been nerve-wracking. They had found nothing in their rooms. Just pristine rooms ready for guests. There had been one loss on the floor and it had been on Jenni's team. That terrified her.

Jenni's team now drew near, with Nerit's behind them. Jenni looked very pale and she stared up the stairwell with a dark expression on her face.

"You okay?" Katie asked.

"No," Jenni answered. "This isn't fun."

It seemed like a strange answer, but again Jenni tended to enjoy killing zombies. The losses had been high today and it was taking them all back to the insanity and fear of the first days of the zombie plague. Katie was sure that Jenni was thinking of her lost children. She knew she was thinking of Lydia.

Travis stood nearby. His face had deep lines in it. Katie was sure she looked just as stressed as everyone else.

"Let's go," Nerit said, and lead the way.

The other teams would be going up the other stairwell on the other side of the hotel.

Nerit moved easily up the stairs, no signs of her age showing. Katie felt immense affection and respect for the woman. She seemed so in control of herself and the situation compared to the rest of them.

The long stairwell that lead steadily upwards was sterile and painted boring white. The banisters and steps were made of heavy wood and vases of dead flowers adorned tiny tables on the landings. Their footsteps echoed as they moved upwards, making them all cringe inwardly.

"This is scary as shit," Charles muttered. He was dragging along behind everyone else, his bland features looking more doughy and pale now that he was scared shitless.

Jenni looked back at him. "Don't be such a wimp." Her voice was annoyed and sharp.

"Look, we have no fucking clue what is going to happen next," Charles started.

"Bad thing to say," Roger told him quickly. "In horror movies bad shit always happens after someone says something like that."

"Like what?" Charles snapped back.

It was then the zombie dropped down from above, hit the banister, and managed to grab Charles' shirt. Katie had the impression it was missing most of its lower half and the stench was awful. The zombie hit the banister sideways. His body caught for only a moment before it fell over into the stairwell below. Its grip on Charles shirt was firm. Charles hit the rail and toppled over before anyone could grab him. Jenni managed to grab his sneaker and it came off in her hand as he tumbled over without even a gasp.

"Fuck!"

Katie and Jenni were the first ones down the stairs, the rest of the groups behind them.

As they rounded the last landing, they came across the zombie and Charles. The zombie had landed headfirst and its skull was split open, spilling curdled brains. Charles lay near him, head twisted about in an unnatural angle. Both were completely stone cold dead.

"I told him," Roger grumbled.

"Fucking stupid way to go out," Shane decided.

"I think we found one of the plumbers," Travis said ,and pointed to the name of the plumbing company on the zombie's tattered shirt.

Jenni stood staring down at Charles' body and slowly blinked. "I hate today."

***

They kept going. They had to. Despite their shocking losses, they had to keep going. Too much of an investment of time and energy and lives had been given to taking the hotel and they were determined to finish. Perhaps now they were more cautious, more terrified, and more determined, but they were still in hell.

"I feel like I'm next," Jenni muttered as she joined Curtis' group. She felt wobbly inside. Seeing three of her teammates go down so quickly had made her feel very vulnerable. Felix joined Katie's group and she missed his presence.

The process continued. Rooms were searched diligently by almost overly cautious people, then the doors were closed and large checkmarks left on the wood with blue chalk. Room by room was cleared. Then floor by floor was cleared. Jenni moved with graceful ease behind Curtis and his team, watching every shadow. They were now on the fourth floor and there had been no sign of zombies since the one that had killed Charles.

She was feeling claustrophobic and hemmed in by the building and the cap on her head was hot and heavy. With all her heart, she wanted to abandon this endeavor. It was eating at her, making her feel weak and helpless. Their tiny little world had felt so safe until now. The walls around the construction site and city hall had given them a sense of security. Their fort barely took up a one-block radius and it was cramped, but at least livable. Maybe they needed the hotel, but right now she hated it.

Anger was starting to creep up within her. She had actually felt safe and happy the last few weeks. Her relationship with Juan was still evolving, but it was good. He was not quite the knight in shining armor she imagined, but he was sweet and made her laugh. She wanted to bask in it and forget the past. Forget Lloyd, forget the dead children she had failed, forget the beatings, forget the pain...She just wanted peace in this tiny little fortified construction site in this tiny little town.

God, she hated this opulent hotel and its apparent false dreams.

"Fifth floor clear," Bill's voice said over the walkie-talkie. He was on the other side of the hotel.

Jenni and Curtis looked at each other, and then down the hallway with all its blue checkmarks on the doors.

"It would be nice if it kept going this way," Curtis said.

Jenni smacked him. "Don't say shit like that!"

"Jinx," said Jimmy, rubbing his bald head. "Don't jinx us."

"Shit, sorry," Curtis mumbled.

---

Katie, Travis, Felix and Roger came around the corner. All four looked just as harried as she felt.

Katie gave Jenni a little smile and squeezed her arm affectionately and it made Jenni smile.

It was good to at least have friends in this world.

"Sixth floor may be a hotspot," Bill's voice said over the static.

"Roger that," Curtis answered as the two teams started upwards.

The last person in Curtis group, a short skinny man named Davey, took off his hat and ran a hand over his blond hair. "Anyone else thinking this was a bad idea."

Jenni, aware of the origins of the plans to take the hotel, glanced back at Travis. "Nah, we need this building. Right, Travis?"

"With one hundred and twenty-five..." he hesitated as it dawned on him the number was now lower "...now inside the site, we need room. Especially because there are people still out there running low on supplies and needing shelter as summer hits."

Katie nodded in agreement and looked up the stairwell. "We're expanding our little world."

Davey frowned. "Well, dammit, this new world is a pain in my ass."

And with that, they started upwards.

The clatter of their heels against the stairs made everyone wince and they all pressed up as close to the wall as they could as they climbed. Eyes set upwards, their lesson had been learned with Charlies' demise.

Jenni hesitated at a window and glanced down. She looked out over the rooftops of the town toward the green hills soaked with the torrential rains. It was beautiful and her breath caught. Looking down, she could see into the construction site quite clearly. From above it looked smaller and being able to see over the walls and security perimeter made it seem vulnerable. There were still undead out there. She could see them.

"Jenni?"

"Coming, Katie."

The teams split up again, taking separate paths. Moving toward the first door, Jenni felt her stomach tightening. Just four more floors and it would be over.

"Same routine as before," Curtis said.

Jenni nodded and leaned over and unlocked the door. "Ready?" When the responses were positive, she flung open the door.

The curtains were opened and pale sunlight streamed in illuminating the room. Jenni cautiously stepped in. Davey followed directly behind her. He kicked the door hard and was rewarded with a sharp thud as the door hit the wall with a resounding smack.

Nothing behind it.

Jenni advanced slowly toward the bed and squatted down. Davey took a breath and drew the comforter sharply off of it.

Nothing below the bed.

Behind them, Curtis and Jimmy entered the room.

Jenni moved very cautiously toward the open door to the bathroom and peered in. This room was much bigger and opulent than those below. Everything gleamed and sparkled inside the bathroom, but there was no sign of anything dead.

"Clear?" Curtis looked nervously around the room.

"Wardrobe," Jenni answered.

Taking a quivering breath, Davey drew near the wardrobe. His tiny frame crouched slightly as he reached out and took hold of the handle. Jenni moved closer, her gun aimed toward the wardrobe, standing across from Davey and near the bed.

"I don't think you should--" Jimmy started.

Davey looked back as his hand rested on the lever just enough for there to be a click. "What?"

The doors exploded outward, knocking Davey to the floor, and tossing Jenni backwards onto the bed. Her gun flew out of her hand, hit the floor and skittered under a chair in the corner. The largest zombie Jenni had ever seen rushed out, stepped on Davey, and rushed toward Jimmy and Curtis at a fast clip.

Jenni rolled as fast as she could over the bed to the other side as the as the zombie ran across the room toward Curtis and Jimmy.

Another form, mostly eaten, barely resembling what had been a human female, slithered out of the wardrobe.

"Davey!" Jenni screamed.

He climbed to his knees only to be confronted by the grisly creature with strips of flesh hanging off its bones. It lunged forward and bit deep into his cheek.

Meanwhile, Curtis shot the enormous zombie in the head, but it just kept barreling forward.

"It's Bubba Wilkins! He has a metal plate in his head," Jimmy shouted.

"Shit," Curtis shouted.

Jimmy turned and tackled Curtis out of the hotel room door and slammed the door shut behind them.

Jenni stood in shock, breathing heavily. Only the bed stood between her and the two zombies.

# Chapter 7

## 1. Dance With Death

*T*his is how you die, she heard Lloyd's voice in her head. *I may not have gotten you, but he will.*

Jenni stood, breathing heavily, and watched the enormous zombie bang on the door. It hadn't noticed her yet and was desperate to get to Jimmy and Curtis.

The munching and slurping noises of the female zombie eating Davey's face and his painful sobs filled the room. She wanted to scream at Davey to shoot the creature, but she couldn't speak, didn't dare speak.

Slowly, she started to squat down so she could reach under the chair for her gun. Her breath sounded so loud and harsh in her ears, she was sure the zombie could hear her, but he kept pounding on the door. Her heart seemed to thud in time to the meaty fists banging against the door. Her skin felt slick and cold.

She began to feel along the floor under the chair, trying to find the weapon, all the while keeping her eyes on the zombie in the plumber's outfit banging on the door. Her knees were creaking in protest as she tried to keep her balance and not move too quickly. The last she wanted to do was attract the huge zombie's attention.

Davey wasn't even making a sound now and she knew what that meant. Soon there would be three of these things to deal with.

Her mind was playing tricks with her now. Memories overlapping with reality. For a moment it was Lloyd at the door and Benji on the other side of the bed. She forced those thoughts out of her mind.

*You don't understand, Jenni. You're a stupid, crazy bitch. And it's time for you to die. To turn into what we are and eat the face off your spic boyfriend,* Lloyd's voice taunted her.

Jenni grimaced as her body ached for her to move faster, but she didn't dare take her eyes off the zombie or the other side of the bed.

*You always were such a stupid little Mexican't. Can't do a damn thing right. Guess your mother's blood fucked you up more than I thought. I never should have married a half-breed,* Lloyd's voice mocked her.

Gawdammit, why did he have to haunt her now?

Her fingers were almost to the gun when the enormous zombie turned around. The flesh from its forehead had torn free and a metal plate was visible under his lank black hair. His glazed gaze rested on her. He howled and surged forward.

"Shit!"

In her haste, she knocked the gun further away and realized she had to give it up. Rising to her feet, she saw the zombie stumble on the far side of the bed. Probably over the other zombie and Davey.

Jenni backed up and felt something hard hit her hip. Looking behind her, she realized she was up against a door to a balcony. Ripping it open, she stepped out into the rain. Looking back, she saw the zombie was coming. She slammed the door shut and backed away from the French doors.

The zombie growled in fury and stumbled over the edge of the bed.

Jenni spun around trying to figure out what the hell to do. The white metal furniture was a possibility for a weapon, but he was so big.

He hit the door with a resounding crash and began to beat hard on the glass.

Jenni backed up against the stone railing and looked around once more. Her heart was beating so fast it literally hurt. Gulping down breaths of air, she tried to steady her nerves. To the left was another balcony, maybe six to eight feet from the one she was on.

The zombie's fist busted through one of the panes and it reached for her.

With determination, Jenni moved to the far end of the balcony and slid carefully onto the wide railing. Looking across the gap, she saw that she didn't have any room for error. She would have to fling herself across to the other balcony and hope she could catch onto the railing. The wind buffeted her body and she tried hard not to look down and see how far she was from the ground.

*Mexican'ts can't fly. Just swim across the river,* Lloyd's voice laughed in her head.

"Lloyd, shut the fuck up," Jenni said through gritted teeth.

Another loud crash. Glass shattered behind her.

Near tears, she lowered her feet until her heels were resting on the floor of the balcony between the ornate stone slats that held up the railing. Her butt rested on the edge of the rail and her hands held tightly to the slick stone.

This was not how she had planned to die. Falling to her death trying to escape a zombie was just not acceptable to her. Hell, dying period was not acceptable to her. Things were finally changing for her. Yes, the world was dead, but she was alive.

*Not for long,* Lloyd reminded her.

The zombie was breaking apart the door behind her.

Looking over toward the other balcony, she whispered a silent prayer and flung herself forward as hard as she could.

Her chest impacted with the stone rail and her arms grabbed hold of it. The pain of impact ripped through her as she managed to knock most of the air out of her lungs. Struggling to breathe, she pulled herself up and over the railing. Falling onto a metal chair, she gasped at the pain, and rolled off it onto her feet. She looked back to where she had come from.

The zombie stood on the balcony looking confused. It gazed straight ahead, as if searching for her in the clouds. Slow, it turned and saw her. With a raging growl, it ran straight toward the rail. To her horror, the zombie leaped onto it and through the air toward the balcony she was on.

He was much heavier and did not quite make it. His chest also hit the rail and he fell back, his torn hands gripping the cold stone.

"Gawdammit," Jenni screamed at him as he managed to hold on.

Picking up one of the heavy metal chairs, she struggled forward toward the monster. She began to bash his hands as hard as she could. She was screaming as loud as he was growling. As he struggled to pull himself up, she hit his huge hands with the leg of the metal chair. It was heavy and it was hard to wield, but she used it the best she could to batter the damn thing.

"I'm gonna fucking bash your gawddamn skull in," she hissed at him.

Lloyd's voice was quiet inside of her head now.

"I choose when to die," she screamed at the top of her lungs. "And it's not now!"

The zombie kept trying to pull himself up, but she kept smashing him as hard as she could.

Davey appeared on the balcony. His face was completely stripped away and his bloodied, fleshless face stared toward her. Only his eyes remained and, comically, his ears and a flap of his skull. With a desperate hiss, he ran toward her as well.

"Bring it on, fucker," Jenni shouted at him, and kept bashing the other zombie.

Davey flung himself over the rail and didn't get very far at all. He managed to grab onto the other zombie and they both hung suspended over the street far below. Davey began to rip at the other zombie's arms as he tried to pull himself upwards. The assault from above and below was too much. With a hungry growl of rage, the large zombie lost his hold and slipped out of sight.

Holding the chair tight in her hands, Jenni stood with her chest heaving, listening intently, and didn't relax until she heard the impact of their fall. Looking over the edge, she saw both of them on the pavement below. Davey was trying to crawl away with only one good arm. The other zombie was impaled on an old fashioned street light, its arms and legs pumping in vain to escape it.

It was the other zombies gathering before the hotel that gave Jenni pause. They were looking around, as if sensing that there was flesh to consume nearby. One of them looked up and reached toward her. About ten of them began to screech at her. Backing away, she looked toward the doors behind her. She had no gun and no idea if anything lay beyond that door.

Taking a deep breath, she began to reach out to open the door when the doors began to shake under the pounding of fists on the other side.

Jenni looked back at the other balcony she had come from. Her gun lay that way as did the other zombie.

Looking back at the door quivering before her, she made a choice.

## 2. Nightmares Realized

Katie came running down the hall with Travis and Felix close behind. They had heard the screams and had immediately charged down the hall. Roger huffed and puffed behind them as they rounded the corner.

Curtis and Jimmy stood out in the hall shouting at each other as screams came from beyond the door.

"Where is Jenni?" Katie shouted at them.

Jimmy desperately checked his pockets as Curtis cursed at him.

"Jimmy flipped out and shoved me out of the room and shut the gawddamn door. Jenni is in there. She has a set of keys and Jimmy can't find his," Curtis responded, his face red with anger.

Jimmy continued desperately checking his pockets as Katie whirled on him. "Jenni is in there? Screaming? What the fuck were you thinking leaving her alone?"

"I got it." Roger unlocked the door with their set of keys.

Next to Roger, Travis steadied himself, ready to fire.

"That fucking zombie had a metal plate in his head," Jimmy screamed at Katie. "Our shots didn't even phase him!"

"You don't leave people behind," Katie shouted angrily. For a moment, Lydia flickered in her mind. She fought back the image. "We don't leave people behind."

"Ready?" Roger asked.

Katie nodded collected herself and readied herself.

Roger flung the door open.

Something that had been human was on the floor crawling toward the balcony. When the door banged opened, it slid around, opened its mouth and hissed. Katie felt her stomach flip-flop but managed to keep it under control as she raised her gun and shot the thing in the head.

"Jenni," she called out cautiously. That thing on the floor could not be Jenni. Jenni had to still be in here, somewhere, alive.

But if she wasn't...

Entering first, Travis right behind her, Katie held her gun up and ready.

If Jenni were turned, she would have to kill her. Jenni was her friend and she loved her. It would be only right for her to be the one. But it was a task she didn't want.

Jenni couldn't be gone...

A shape loomed in the doorway.

It took a second for her to take in the long black hair. The form limped into the room and raised its head. Blood poured out of its mouth.

It was Jenni.

Katie felt like screaming.

Travis raised his gun higher. "I'll do it."

"Fuck no," Jenni choked out.

Katie hit Travis' arm and the gun went off, the bullet hitting the chandelier over the bed and sending it swinging.

"Gawddamn." Jenni spit blood out of her mouth.

Katie moved slowly toward her.

"I thought-" Travis started.

"Are you bit?" Katie had tears burning her eyes. Jenni looked bad. She could feel chills sliding up and down her spine and her stomach getting tighter.

"No," Jenni spat again. "I busted my lip jumping to the balcony. Twisted my ankle climbing over." She shoved her hair back from her face and licked her lips with a bloodied tongue. "Bit my tongue, too. Juan is so not going to like that."

Katie couldn't help but laugh. She lowered her gun slowly.

"Shit, girl. We thought you were dead," Felix exclaimed from the doorway.

"I'm not that easy to kill." Jenni grinned, then got down on the floor and climbed under a chair to retrieve her gun.

"You're fucking lucky she's still alive," Curtis hissed at Jimmy.

"Look, my bullet bounced off the fucker's metal plate," Jimmy protested.

Katie walked onto the balcony and looked around. Slowly, it dawned on her what Jenni had done. Looking down she saw a zombie impaled on a street lamp and another crawling slowly up the stairs to the front doors of the hotel.

"Travis," she said.

He walked out next to her and looked down. "Shit." Lifting his walkie-talkie, he pressed the button. "Juan, get a crew inside the hotel and secure the front door and windows. We've got a crowd gathering."

"Gotcha," Juan said. There was a pause, then, "How is it going?"

"We lost Davey. Almost lost Jenni. She's fine now. We're going continue on."

Jenni appeared in the shattered doorway and looked out at them. "There are some in the room next to us, too."

"How do you know?"

"I was over there, Katie," Jenni answered, pointing to the other balcony, "and they started banging on the door," Jenni pushed her hair back from her face. "Damn, when did I lose my hat?"

Katie reached out and touched Jenni's cheek lightly. "I'm glad you're okay."

Jenni sighed. "Well, I just don't think I'd make a good zombie. I'd try to hump Juan, not eat him."

Katie laughed and Travis chortled.

"You are crazy," Travis said to her.

Jenni nodded. "Yeah, probably. But it's probably what keeps me alive."

"I wouldn't doubt that one bit," Travis answered.

Curtis came onto the balcony and looked around. "I say we move on together as a group. Might be slower, but probably safer now that my group is down to two."

Roger and Felix stood in the room looking down at the skeletal creature on the ground.

"You know, I really don't want to be wearing a red shirt anymore."

"Just keep it together, Roger," Felix said.

Jimmy stood near the doorway, looking pissed, and sheepish at the same time. "It bounced off his fucking metal plate!"

Katie could feel her anger against him building up. He had left Jenni to die and she couldn't forgive that anytime soon. "Just shut up, Jimmy."

Jenni limped across the room and looked at Jimmy in the eye. "Yeah, shut up."

Katie followed Jenni out into the hallway and they looked warily at the next door. "So there are some in that room, huh?"

"Yeah," Jenni said as she pulled her hair up out of her face and wound it around into a bun. "Banging on the window. I didn't see how many. Could be one or more."

Katie nodded and tilted her head. "You know, for a moment, I thought you were gone."

Jenni sighed. "Yeah, me, too. But I was very determined not to go out like that. If I go, I'm going down for something big. Very heroic. Not just...not like that. I've really made up my mind on this."

Katie laughed. "Yeah, I can tell."

Travis and Curtis joined them as Roger finally looked away from the dead female zombie. Jimmy sulked behind them, but at least had shut up.

"Let's get this done," Curtis said in a dark tone and moved ahead of them.

Katie felt her stomach tense and she readied herself once more.

Jenni unlocked the door.

Curtis flung it open.

Katie shot the zombie banging on the window.

It was that easy.

Katie entered the room and they systematically checked it. She looked down at the dead maid for a moment. The woman had been untouched except for what looked like a bite on her forearm.

"Why did you tell Davey not to open the wardrobe?" Jenni asked of Jimmy suddenly.

"I saw the blood. Dried, but it had dripped down under the doors," he answered.

Jenni nodded and looked around the room. "You got him killed," she said softly. "You distracted him."

Katie could feel the tension building. "Let's keep moving. There is time for this later."

They pushed on. Door by door, room by room. Chalk checkmark after chalk checkmark. With the second plumber dead, they were feeling a bit better. Of course, there could be others they did not know about in the hotel, but the number of possible zombies was falling steadily.

"Sixth floor clear," Bill finally declared.

Jenni was walking with a limp and Katie stayed near her. She could see that Travis was stressing over Jenni's injury and was keeping his anger at Jimmy in check. Curtis was so red with anger, Katie was afraid he was going to have a heart attack. But they kept going and Roger trudged along mumbling to Felix about his red shirt being a bad idea.

## 3. Friends in High Places

Juan stood impatiently while the gate into the hotel was unchained. As soon as it was opened, he hurried through with several construction workers and a small force of armed men in tow. Stepping into the janitor's room, he looked back into the fort and saw Jason standing with a walkie-talkie clutched in one hand and his faithful dog companion at his side. He gave Juan the thumbs up. Juan smiled slightly and turned back into the hotel.

Maybe the boy and he would get along one day.

The stench in the janitor's room was pretty intense and his eyes began to water. He kicked the dead zombie bodies out of the way so the equipment could get through and grimaced as bits of gore clung to his boots.

Stepping up to the door, Juan felt his palms sweating and he took a deep breath. They were just going to have to trust that the teams had done their job and that no more zombies were roaming around downstairs.

"Let's do this," he said.

Swinging the door open, he stepped into the darkened hallway. Flicking on a flashlight, he shone the beam down the hallway. Nothing stirred.

"Scary, huh?" Ken said from behind him.

"When is it ever not scary?"

They moved swiftly down the hall and into the corridor that would lead them into the lobby. As they drew nearer, they heard the loud banging on the doors and windows.

Juan broke into a swift run. The sound of their pounding feet against the tile, the tools jangling on their belts and the humming of the wheelbarrow wheels echoed through the lobby to mix with the moans and screeches of the zombies. The heavy oak doors were shuddering under the impact of many fists being banged against it and the dim outlines of the zombie bodies could be seen through the heavy, frosted lead windows in the door and on either side of the entry.

"Let's make this fast," Juan ordered.

Immediately, the wheelbarrow full of fresh cement was wheeled into position and the pallets loaded with bricks were rolled into the room. Men and women began to quickly brick up the leaded glass windows and the doorway. An assembly line was created and people passed on the bricks to those wielding trowels. Layers of wet cement and brick were swiftly coming into being as they worked in the humid heat of the hotel lobby.

Juan turned and saw the nearly decapitated zombie body on the steps. Walking over, he looked down at it, and grimaced. "Damn." Taking out the walkie-talkie, he pressed the button. "How is your progress up there, Nerit?"

"Moving along. We're on the seventh floor," she answered.

"Curtis? How about you?"

"Also on the seventh floor. Making some progress. Jenni's hurt so we're moving slower," Curtis answered, then added quickly, "Nothing major, just knocked up a bit."

Juan felt his chest tighten. He said a little shortly, "I thought you said she was okay?"

"Yeah, but, she's limping," Curtis said blandly.

"Tell him not to worry," Jenni's voice said through the static.

"She says not--"

"I heard her," Juan answered. He took off his hat, ran his fingers through his curls, and took a breath. "Let me know how you are doing up there. We're busy down here blocking these fuckers off."

There was a loud crash against one of the windows and Juan whirled around to see the dim outline of a zombie with something quite large in its hand banging against the leaded window.

"Shit!"

The front doors were set down at street level. Stairs inlaid with marble rose up to the lobby floor from the entrance. The only windows Juan had any concerns about were the ones framing the doorway. The windows on the first floor were at least eight feet above the street. More of the zombies were picking up items to bang against the windows and doors. It was as if they understood that living flesh was just within their reach if only they could break through.

The assembly line was working faster now. Four people were working fast with their trowels, spreading fresh layers of cement, laying the brick, and then spreading more cement. Other people kept refreshing the bins of cement while others  handed down the bricks.

"Juan, we have cracks in this window," one of the men said.

Juan motioned to those standing nearby with guns to take up positions. "Keep them covered."

Lifting the walkie-talkie, he said, "We need something to brace up the new walls ASAP."

There was a pause, and then Ken, one of his assistants said, "I'm on my way."

"Faster, faster," people were saying to each other as they worked.

Juan wiped the sweat off his brow and looked at the right window. He could see long cracks in the glass.  The shady figures behind the frosted window were banging on it with large, heavy objects.

"Concentrate on that window," Juan ordered.

Overlapping each other in their haste, the four people struggled to wall in the window. It was almost five feet high when the first chunk of glass fell out of the window frame.

The workers hesitated, then resumed what they were doing.

The guards looked nervous. "We can't get good shots with people in the way," one of them told Juan.

Juan thought over the scenario realizing it would take some sharp shooting to deal with the increasingly dangerous situation.

"Nerit, I think we need you down here," Juan said into the walkie-talkie. "We're going to have trouble hitting them."

"On my way," she answered.

Another chunk of glass fell from the frame. He could hear it, but not see it.

"They're pushing on the wall," said Linda, his cousin, one of the people laying the brick. "I can feel it."

"Shit!" Juan ran down the stairs and put his hands on the wall. "Shit, they are."

Another chunk of glass fell out and a hand pushed through the gap between the broken window and the new wall.

"Watch out!"

Juan ducked away just in time, but the zombie grabbed his hat and yanked it back out of sight.

"That was my lucky hat!"

Linda slammed two more bricks into place, her heavy gloves giving her protection.

In their desperation to get into the hotel, the zombies were struggling with each other to reach in through the tiny opening in the window.

Ken, followed by more people, ran in with wood planks and large pieces of sheet metal. "To brace it," he said to Juan.

More glass fell out of the window, making the zombies more crazed and desperate. Decaying hands were appeared over the heads of those working on the wall. No one dared lay more bricks now and Linda stabbed at one hand as it dislodged a brick and pulled it away.

"Let's do it," Juan said.

"Do what?" Ken answered. "They're coming in!"

"Not yet," Juan answered, and picked a trowel. "They're reaching upwards. None of them can bite us that high. They'll just try to grab our hands. We have gloves. Keep going."

The workers hesitated and then acknowledged that he was right. Again the wall came under construction. The bricks were laid out as quick as possible as the dead on the other side tried to grab the trowels or the gloved hands of the workers.

The other window began to crack.

"Hurry it up," Juan ordered. He lifted the walkie-talkie. "Nerit, where are you?"

"Eliminating your problem one by one," Nerit answered after a beat.

"What?" Juan answered confused.

Linda was laying another brick when a hand grabbed her wrist firmly. Yanking hard, it had her pinned against the freshly made wall. Screaming, she struggled to get free.

"Taking care of your problem," Nerit answered coolly.

Suddenly, Linda drew back, the zombie hand still attached to her arm, but now severed right below the wrist.

"Now leave me alone. I have a dozen to take out," Nerit said.

Juan laughed and ran a hand over his curly hair. He had a vision of Nerit in a window high above systematically killing the zombies gathered at the windows.

And that was exactly what she was doing.

The moans dissipated and, finally, ceased. The hands disappeared from the windows and suddenly the room was eerily silent.

"All done now," Nerit's voice cackled over the static.

Juan looked down at the walkie-talkie, then looked at Ken. "She's a tough old lady."

Ken nodded. "She scares me."

"Good thing she's on our side. Now, let's get this wall done," Juan ordered.

# 4. Upwards

Nerit leaned over the balcony railing and made sure that there were no zombies moving below. Bodies littered the street and were bunched up around the front door. It had taken time to take all of them down, but she felt a sense of satisfaction at their demise. Only one zombie remained moving. It was a huge zombie stuck on a lamppost. She was leaving him alive for a reason.

Turning, she moved back into the hotel room. Much to her surprise, she saw an old woman gazing back at her with an intense expression on her face. Nerit realized she was looking into a mirror. Her hand flew up to her face as she stared at the image, startled to see her worn countenance. She had slipped so thoroughly into her role as sniper she had felt young and powerful again. It was a slap of reality to not see the young, blond woman she used to be when in the Israeli army, but instead, the older, stern woman she had become. The eyes still glinted with the same fierceness, but there were fine wrinkles around them now.

Well, enough of vanity. Ralph had found her quite lovely in her old age and that was all that had mattered.

There was killing to be done and she was quite efficient at it.

She dismissed the old woman in the mirror and walked out into the hallway. This floor was cleared and chalk checkmarks adorned all the doors. Moving at a quick pace, she felt comfortable in her role. Her gun was a cold, comforting presence in her arms.

As a young child growing up in Israel, she had been acutely aware of a world that was not always kind. Her mother was a survivor of the concentration camps where most of that side of the family had died. Her father often said that he felt Nerit had inherited her mother's finely tuned senses and fighting spirit. At a young age he had taught her and her brothers to shoot and had been thrilled when his tiny daughter immediately showed an uncanny ability to hit the bull's-eye every time. Soon he had her enrolled in competitions and many of the photos of her childhood were of her and her father standing proudly beside a shooting trophy.

Ah, her father...how she missed him. He had raised her to be strong and confident. Not once did he dissuade her from pursuing her dreams. Her marksmanship had thrilled him. When she had been awarded a medal for her valor in the Six Day War, he had crafted a fine little display case for it.

His only disappointment had been her decision to marry instead of pursuing riflery and attempting to make the Israeli Olympic team. She wondered now how he would feel about her role in this bizarre afterlife of the once thriving planet. Her medals now were the shattered heads of the walking dead. Her accolades the thanks of those she saved. There was no real victory now, just the heavy burden of doing what must be done.

Thoughtfully, she turned and headed up the stairs. How vividly her Father's face came to mind. She knew he would be proud of her and her bitter responsibility. Had he not raised her to defend her people and do what was right?

And the people in this tiny fort were her people. Through a strange string of events, she had ended up here in her twilight years. Her first husband had moved them to America in the mid-seventies and then passed away leaving her a single mother. She had remained in the country to build a life for her and the children before marrying her second husband. He had moved them out of New York to Texas where they had settled in Fort Worth. When he had divorced her for a much younger woman, she had decided to go on a hunting trip with some good friends and had ended up meeting the love of her life, Ralph. He had brought her to that wonderful hunting store in the hills while her children said their good-byes and returned to their homeland. She had firmly believed she would live there until she had left this world, but instead, Ralph had gone on without her. Now she was fighting for her life and the life of others in a tiny, makeshift fort in the middle of nowhere.

Sometimes, she thought wryly, it was if they were playing some terrible game of cowboys and Indians and hiding in their makeshift fort made of odds and ends. Of course, in this case, the Indians would eat the cowboys alive.

Entering the ninth floor, she began following the blue checkmarks on the doors. Things were moving more swiftly now that the end was in sight. She hoped they were not being rash in their actions.

Coming around a corner, she saw all of them at the end of the hall. They were clearing another room and Katie and Travis were hanging back slightly, covering the ominous looking double doors that lead upwards to the last floor and its opulent ballroom. One of the double doors was slightly ajar and Nerit could see only darkness beyond it.

"How are we doing?" she called out.

Katie turned toward her and smiled slightly. "Okay. Nothing up here. I don't think anyone got this far."

Nerit strode down the hallway, ignoring the pain in her hip and the numbness in her toes. She hated getting old. "We still need to be careful."

"Room is clear," Jenni said exiting the hotel room they had been searching.

Jenni was still hobbling, but trying not to look like she was. The poor girl was really beat up, but she was a scrappy fighter. Nerit had not been too sure about her when she had first met her. Jenni had been on the edge of a breakdown, but had somehow pulled away from it. Yes, she was still a bit on the edge of crazy at times, but Nerit had a feeling it was what kept her going.

"We're heading upstairs," Curtis said as he drew the checkmark on the door. "We're almost done. I sent Katarina, Felix, and Shane down to help the others. Juan is heading down into the basement to get the power on."

Jimmy just grunted.

Nerit gazed at him intently. She did not trust him. He was too afraid despite his bravado. Fear was normal, but you had to control it. Jimmy did not have that control.

Katie headed toward the double doors, her pistol held firmly in one hand. "I just want to get this over with."

Travis walked directly behind her. "I hear you there."

Jenni favored her leg as she began to follow and Curtis took her arm to help her.

Nerit raised her rifle as Katie neared the door to open it all the way. The pricking on the back of her neck had automatically triggered her reflexes. She trusted her instincts.

Before Katie could even open the door all the way, the maid fell through the gap in the doors and right into Katie. Flinging up her arm to protect herself, Katie fell back. Travis launched into motion to pull the zombie off of Katie.

It was all in slow motion to Nerit. Each movement distinct and vivid to her. She could see the female zombie shaking her head, trying to rend flesh from Katie's arm as Katie screamed and Travis lurched forward.

Nerit became one with her rifle as she had so many times before and through its eagle eye, saw the top of the zombie's head. She fired and watched a blossom of blood explode into view then dissipate.

Travis kicked the dead zombie away as Katie stumbled backwards, staring at her arm.

"She bit her! She bit her!" Jimmy's voice, near hysteria.

"No!" Jenni rushed forward.

Nerit swung the rifle toward Katie and Katie's beautiful eyes danced before her. Like jewels, lovely, sparkling with life.

Then Travis' back was blocking her. He had stepped between her and Katie.

"Travis, back away," Nerit ordered.

Travis paid her no heed and shouted, "You can't! You can't!"

Nerit took a step to one side and Katie came back into view. She was such a lovely girl. Nerit adored her, but she had a job to do. Katie would not want to become one of the undead. It would be a great injustice to such a strong woman.

"Nerit, no!" Travis shouted at her, blocking Katie once more from view.

Jenni sobbed uncontrollably, one hand pressed over her mouth.

Nerit could hear Katie whispering Travis' name softly, a sob in her voice.

"Travis," Nerit said firmly. "Step aside and do what is right."

"It didn't go through!" Travis whirled around. "The bite! It didn't go through." He was holding Katie's arm out for Nerit to see. The pressure from the zombie's mouth and hands had made enormous bruises, but there was no sign of the skin being broken. The heavy denim jacket Katie had been wearing had not torn.

"Thank God," Jenni exclaimed and flung her arms around Katie.

Katie looked dazed and held tightly to Jenni.

Nerit lowered her rifle and walked slowly toward them. She felt hope rising within her, but she could not give it purchase of her emotions just yet. At times she hated this coldness within her. That enormous cold splinter that sliced through her soul. The place she could go when she needed to not feel and not care. It had always been there. Even as a child. It was cold and bitter and her burden to carry. She was the woman who did what must be done.

Taking Katie's arm in her hand lightly, she turned it this way and that. Her keen eyes examined the brutal purple and green bruising. No puncture. No broken skin. No wound.

Stepping back, she nodded.

For a second, she let herself feel the pure joy that that came from knowing that she would not have to release Katie from this nightmare world, but then she shoved it away.

For there was work to be done...

"Let's move on," Nerit said firmly and turned on her heel and started up the stairs to the ballroom.

## 5. The Top of the World

Travis wasn't sure he could even breathe anymore. Seeing the zombie lurch out of the darkness to fasten itself on Katie had been one of the worst moments of his entire life. In fact, he was pretty sure this day was responsible for all the worst moments of his life.

From the dining room massacre to Jenni's appearance on the balcony and everything in between, he had felt his hold on his emotions slipping. He had not experienced the sheer horror of the first days as Katie and Jenni had until today. The zombies had always seemed so far away and impersonal. But today, there was no denying their absolute power to terrify and destroy when there were no barriers between the living and the dead.

Moving slowly up the stairs after Nerit, he struggled not to hate her. She walked in silence, her head up, her gaze sweeping back and forth, shoulders relaxed, but ready. He resented how she was so hyper-aware of all around her and how coldly she dealt with situations that made him feel ready to shit his pants. And he hated how easily she killed those they called friends once the worst has happened and they were on their way out of this world.

Yes, he had offered to kill Jenni when they had all thought she was a zombie, but that had been to spare Katie. Even now, he wasn't quite sure he would have pulled the trigger. Well, if she had lurched toward them to kill Katie, he probably would have. But all this death and killing was far removed from how he was raised. It did not come naturally to him like it did to Nerit or the others.

Frustration ate at him as he looked back toward Katie. She was walking with Jenni. Both of them were favoring injured limbs and wore bruises on their faces. He desperately wanted this to be over. This day was made all the worse because of his feelings for Katie. He not only lived in terror for his own life, but for hers. Every moment that passed that they both survived, was nerve-wracking. He felt he could not relax. Could not enjoy that they had made it this far. If he lost her, it would devastate him. His was madly in love with her and he knew it made him a bit crazy, but he couldn't help it.

Stepping up off the stairs into an enormous foyer, he was startled by the sunlight pouring through high windows. The storm had moved on and was now receding over the hills. The marble floors shone beneath a fine layer of dust and the ornate gold-gilded metal ceiling with all its fancy designs gleamed overhead. An enormous chandelier sparkled and threw diamonds of light all around.

"It's beautiful," Jenni sighed.

Roman goddesses were tucked into alcoves and plush red velvet couches adorned a few walls. Bouquets of dead flowers adorned a few small tables. The foyer stretched out to French doors that lead out onto a patio that encircled the entire top floor. To their right were two doors marked as restrooms.

They did quick, efficient sweep of the gleaming bathrooms. Empty.

"When we are done, I'm so using the ladies room," Jenni said firmly.

Nerit motioned to the ballroom.

The doors to the ballroom were open. The old fashioned, short-legged chairs with the plush velvet seats were neatly stacked against one wall.

Nerit lead them into the enormous room with its ornate fireplace and high vaulted ceilings. Chandeliers sparkled overhead. Heavy red curtains were drawn back from the windows to let the sun pour through gauzy white organza sheer curtains.

"Perfect for a wedding," Jenni sighed.

"It's what it was used for in the old days," Curtis said.

Jimmy just grunted and trailed along behind them.

Travis looked back at Katie. Even bruised and looking exhausted, she was beautiful. Standing in this huge room with her, he wondered what it would feel like to take her in his arms and dance with her.

"Let's check the patio," Nerit said.

Travis looked around at all the opulence of the room and felt slightly overwhelmed by its elegance. It was almost too much.

Nerit opened the doors to the patio and stepped out slowly.

A beautiful Roman gazebo stood over a glittering pool of blue water. An enormous patio stretched out to the stone railing that surrounded it. Travis walked slowly over to the rail and looked down to see a maintenance walkway tucked down out of view with a safety net extending outward around five feet.

*To stop suicides*, he decided.

Katie leaned over the rail to look down, then looked out toward the fading storm. "It's really beautiful up here."

He smiled. "I was thinking the same thing." He loved the way the sun was glinting off her curls. He wanted to touch them, but refrained.

"Keep alert," Nerit barked.

He frowned. Katie poked him. "She's just good at her job."

"Yeah," he said, almost resentfully.

They spread out and looked around. There really wasn't a place to hide up here.

"The elevators will be our last concern once the power is back on," Nerit said as they walked around the building.

"How about the roof?" Travis asked. He pointed up to the roof of the ballroom.

Nerit looked up. "Good point."

They all started to look for a way up. Travis began to walk along the side of the ballroom. He was more in the shadows on this side. The wind was quite fierce. Katie walked along behind him, followed by Jenni.

"That smell," Jenni started.

Travis immediately began to look around, but saw nothing. He felt panic rising up within him.

Katie looked up and whispered, "Oh, shit."

Travis looked up to see a zombie struggling to her feet at the very edge of the roof. She had been very young. Travis recognized her as a waitress from the diner. She had always smiled at him when he came in for breakfast. Brenda had been her name. She must have managed to get a second job at the hotel.

What was most heart-breaking about her was that her face was still tear-stained with dry tears and she seemed to have no injury but a bite on her arm. After lying on the roof for so long, the zombie was finding it hard to stand.

"Oh, God," Katie whispered. "She must have crawled up there and died."

The zombie snarled in frustration and finally managed to get to her feet. Then she lurched forward and made a desperate leap.

Travis and the two women ducked. The zombie sailed over their heads to be caught by the hard wind and knocked over the edge.

Looking over the rail, Travis saw her struggling on the anti-suicide net.

"Sorry, Brenda," he said. He aimed for the back of her head. For a moment, he saw her in his mind as she had been, a pretty blond girl with a big smile and rosy cheeks. Then he fired and the thing she had become fell silent on the netting.

Katie touched his arm, but didn't say a word.

"That sucked," Jenni decided.

Travis stood in silence, looking down at the body, then sighed. He had actually considered asking Brenda out at one point. It was a missed opportunity never realized; one of many. He looked toward Katie and felt a pang of regret. How had they grown so distant so fast after their kiss? Was there truly hope for them? He had to believe there was, for he could see it in her eyes.

"Good job," Nerit said from above.

Travis looked up to see her standing on the roof.

"There is a ladder over on the far side," she said, his unspoken question answered.

Curtis appeared beside Nerit and looked around. "Damn pretty up here. Almost looks like nothing bad is happening."

Travis wondered if Curtis even saw the girl lying dead on the net.

Jenni hobbled past Travis, working her way back to an entrance. "Almost done."

"Yeah. The basement is left," Curtis said.

"I hate basements," Jimmy said.

"Monsters are always in the basement," Roger decided. He had been eerily quiet and to himself for awhile now. Travis had a feeling that Roger had stopped thinking this was fun long ago and now recognized the desperateness of the situation. Of course, jokingly wearing a red shirt wasn't the best idea.

"We'll hold position here and rest until Juan calls for backup," Nerit decided.

Travis looked over the beauty of the hills. "It almost looks normal."

"Almost," Katie agreed, staring at Brenda's dead body.

The others drifted away, relaxing now that they had reached their primary objective.

Travis remained where he was, staring out over the hills. Katie stayed at his side, rubbing her wounded arm, and looking very tired. She was beautiful, not only without, but within. She was strong and smart and he adored her. In that moment, he made up his mind.

Travis turned to look at her and she tilted her head quizzically.

"Tonight," was all he said. He knew she would understand what he meant and from the look in her eyes, she did.

She raised her hand to touch his cheek, then nodded.

Turning his head, he kissed her palm, then held her hand against his face. Together, they walked back to join the others.

## 6. All Clear

"I fucking hate basements," Juan said for the fifth time.

The flashlight beams slit the darkness and illuminated the monstrous machinery that was the internal organs of the hotel. Enormous laundry machines stood silent along one wall and Juan looked at them warily. In horror movies washing machines always had bad things in them.

Around him, eight armed people began to systematically work their way around the basement, while he moved over to the fuse box. Katarina walked with him as his guard.

"I hate basements," he said again.

Standing before the biggest fuse box he had ever seen in his life, he exhaled, then began to check all the fuses.

There was the sharp bark of a gun. Someone said, "Clear."

"I hate zombies," Katarina sighed.

Juan looked around nervously then nodded. "Yes, me, too. Basements with zombies...much worse."

Flashing the light around, he caught sight of what he was looking for. "Supply room. I need fuses." He pointed.

Katarina frowned a little. "Great. Closed doors."

Juan walked over and knocked on the door.

"What are you doing?"

"If there is one in there, it should flip out and start banging back, right?"

Katarina raised an eyebrow. "You gotta point."

Juan knocked again and waited. There was no response.

"I guess it's clear," he said, and opened the door.

Immediately, a zombie, lying on the floor, lurched forward and bit into the pointed toe of one of his shitkickers.

Juan jerked back with a startled yelp and Katarina shot it in the head.

She pointed at the zombie's arms. It was a woman dressed up in a flowered dress and highheels. "No hands. Couldn't knock back."

"Well, there goes that theory," Juan said with a frown. He flashed the beam of light around the small supply room, saw that it was clear, stepped in and located the fuses.

In the darkness behind him, he kept hearing people calling out, "Clear" as they moved methodically through the basement.

Juan returned to the fuse box and began replacing the burnt out ones. He worked quickly, safely and efficiently. "That power surge the first day really fucked things up. I wonder what caused it."

Katarina continued to watch the darkness, her flashlight making long sweeps and occasionally illuminating the other people in the basement.

"I got it," Juan exclaimed.

Suddenly, the basement filled with light as the overhead fluorescent tubes lit up. Machinery began to growl to life. Everyone let out a gasp.

"Clear," someone's voice called out. "All clear."

*** 

In the lobby, Linda turned as the lights came to life, illuminating the rich dark wood and fancy furniture.

"Wow," she said in awe.

The elevator on the right side of the lobby chimed and the doors opened. A little girl staggered out, looked around, and rushed toward the nearest person.

"Freaky zombie kid," Ken shouted.

Panic swept the room as they realized the armed guards were in the basement. Around Linda, people picked up bricks. Linda picked one up and hurled it at the girl. It hit her in the chin and knocked her back. Linda smiled as her softball years paid off.

Another brick went careening toward the zombie and knocked her back.

There was a flurry of excitement as people continued to pelt the child with bricks, until she fell backwards onto the ground. Linda ran up and stared down at the growling face of what had been a child, then slammed the brick in her hands down on the girls head, shattering it into bloody chunks.

"Clear!" she shouted with satisfaction.

In the foyer to the ballroom, the last elevator opened. Travis stood ready, his gun aimed. Nerit stood beside him, also ready.

Inside was just a body, a truly dead body. It was the hotel manager. His emaciated form and the condition of the elevator let them know he had either starved to death or died of dehydration. He was curled into a tiny ball, clutching his wallet. Pictures of his family spilled out from between his fingers in clear plastic sheets.

Travis leaned over and looked at the pictures, then up at Nerit.

"I guess we're done."

Nerit nodded.

Just like that, the day from hell was over.

# Chapter 8

## 1. Beginnings...

There seemed to be very little time to sit back and enjoy their victory. Almost immediately, the clean up crews came in and began the messy job of removing the bodies. Anyone, who was strong and able enough to help was drafted into some part of preparing their new home for occupancy. Katie was exhausted, but knew it was necessary. She reported in for her next assignment and joined the rest of the survivors in the hard work.

First, the bodies were removed and discarded out the loading dock behind the kitchen into a large truck. Wearing kerchiefs over their noses and mouths as masks, the hardiest of the survivors set about dragging the bodies out using hooks specially crafted for the job. Sheets of plastic were used to wrap the corpses up then they were dragged out.

Nerit and a few of her trainees covered the disposal of the bodies from above. Tucked into the windows and balconies, they took out any zombie trying to get too close. So far there hadn't been any major incidents. A few zombies made runs at the truck only to be taken down by the snipers.

Jason was part of the crew that was sent in to rip up the rug in the dining room. They cut it into long swaths that were then rolled up, put into plastic bags, then hauled out after the bodies. Some of the women and younger girls were given gloves and large buckets of water with bleach to clean up the blood splatter. Not a nice job, but a necessary one. Anything that was contaminated by the blood and innards of the zombies was removed.

Katie helped Stacey scrub down the kitchen floor and walls. They had to literally scrape up some of the gunk. Gretchen, the librarian, and a girl with red hair whose name Katie could never remember, also came in after awhile to scrub up the blood and gore.

"You know," Stacey said after awhile, her light hair hanging in her eyes. "I really hate zombies."

"That does seem to be the general consensus," Gretchen said with a laugh.

Katie scraped up what looked to be an intestine and chunked it into a bag. "Is it just me or is this getting easier to deal with?"

"I think I've stopped noticing the smell unless it's really fresh," Stacey answered scrubbing away at the floor with a bristle brush.

Jason walked through, lugging a heavy bag of carpet. His hair was in his face, as usual, with only his eyes visible between his bangs and his mask. Behind him was his possible new girlfriend, Shelley. She was a cute teenage girl Jenni had saved a few weeks earlier. Katie caught Shelley sneaking a peak at him and smiled to herself. Life did go on whether you wanted it to or not.

Because of Jenni's leg being twisted, she was reduced to sitting in the elevator scrubbing up what little blood had been in there. Juan supervised the finishing of the walling off of the doors and windows. Jenni was convinced he had her stuck in the elevator just so he could keep an eye on her.

Katie knew this was exactly the case. Jenni's determination to keep going had resulted in her sprain being worse. Juan was too frazzled by the wounds on her face and her body to let her out of his sight for too long. Katie thought it was sweet.

Travis came through the kitchen a few times. He was helping lug bodies down from the higher floors. They exchanged awkward glances. An unspoken promise had passed between them, Katie still was unsure if she would fulfill it.

A sense of relief permeated the atmosphere of the hotel. With so many people working, things were taken care of rather quickly. All the doors into the hotel were double-checked to make sure they were secure. Any windows close to street level were blocked off. Katie knew that a few crews would be working deep into the night bricking up all street level doorways. Only the loading dock was going to be left operational, but only because the doors were thick metal and very secure.

As the sun set, the hotel came alive with lights. People that weren't directly involved in the cleanup, such as the sick, disabled, elderly and the children, were brought into the hotel. The smell of bleach had wiped out the reek of death and the up stairs windows were letting in cool, fresh evening air.

Manny and Peggy took up a place at the front desk with a clipboard and a map of the hotel interior. Katie, feeling lightheaded from all the bleach fumes, walked into the lobby to join the growing number of people gathered there.

"Okay. What we're going to do is call out names. You will come up and get your room assignment and key," Peggy announced to the group assembled.

Katie favored her bruised arm as she leaned against a pillar and listened to the names being shouted out. She felt very tired. Her hands were bright red, despite the gloves she had worn during clean up. They reeked of bleach. She couldn't wait to take a shower and get rid of that smell.

Jenni was curled up with Juan on a sofa. Juan had his arms wrapped protectively around her. Jenni glowed with pleasure. Katie noted that Jason and Shelley were hanging out together with Shelley's kid brother. It seemed to be the night for pairing up.

There was a soft nudge of her hand and she looked down to see Jack giving her a wide, toothy doggy grin. She smiled and stroked his ears, making him a happy boy.

Things were moving along smoothly with the room assignments until Steven Mann and his wife went up to the desk. It didn't take long for there to be raised voices. Mr. Mann had been *the man* around town as the primary investor in the hotel. He had been rescued from his very swanky mansion only two weeks before with his wife. Katie had heard stories of how the rescuers had staunchly refused to carry out massive trunks of clothes and shoes for them. Finally, the Manns had come with one suitcase each, but were very bitter about the situation. They both refused to do much work around the site. Resentment against them was growing.

"We are used to a certain quality of life and we have been forced to rough it here. I demand that we be placed in the finest suite. That is what we are used to and based on our former lifestyle, it is only right," Steven said.

Katie shook her head.

"The bigger suites are for families that are still together. We have you on the fourth floor in a very nice room with a king size bed. It's all about fitting the needs of the people," Peggy answered firmly, and held out the key.

"Well," said his wife, "if we are forced to live this way I demand room service now that there is an actual working kitchen and hotel."

That brought outright guffaws from those gathered around.

Peggy looked up and said shortly, "You'll get room service if you get off your ass and come down to the kitchen and help out."

"Steven, speak to the woman. I do not converse with the help," the woman, Blanche—Katie thought that was the woman's name—said to her husband.

"I demand a larger room more suited to our previous lifestyle," Steven repeated. He looked adamant and quite fierce.

"So those of us who lived in trailers should just get the shit rooms?" someone asked.

Manny looked at the list. The Manns had heavily funded his last campaign and he was often seen talking to them. Old habits die hard. "Peggy, maybe we could..."

"No, it was agreed upon." Peggy held out the keys to Steven Mann with a insistent look on her face. "By vote. Rooms are granted according to need. A married couple only needs a king-sized bed, unless maybe the married couple would rather have two beds?" Peggy smiled sweetly, but her eyes were poisonous.

"Well, I do have a rather bad ba—" Blanche started to say.

"Just what are you insinuating?" Steven looked ready to blow his temper.

Travis appeared out of the crowd looking tired and annoyed. "Steven, take your keys and go to your room. The world that you loved so much is gone now. You're now just one of us. A survivor. You hardly carry your weight so I think you're damn lucky we don't just make you sleep on a cot in the hallway."

There were murmurs of agreement.

Steven grabbed the key and fastened his gaze on the Mayor. "I will remember this."

"You do realize," Peggy said with a snarky smile, "there are no more elections to fund anymore."

"For now," Steven snapped back. He grabbed his wife's arm and dragged her off.

"I don't understand why you let them treat us this way," Blanche said as she was lead through the decidedly hostile crowd. "They're just common people."

Travis shook his head.

Katie looked down at Jack. "People are silly."

The German Shepherd thumped his tail in response and nudged her hand for more scratching. She obliged.

Mike's girlfriend, Belinda, sobbed when her name was called. Katarina helped her claim her key. The young Hispanic woman was Juan's life long crush until Jenni had claimed his heart. Belinda looked frail and shell-shocked as Katarina lead her away. Losing Mike had been devastating to all of them, but Belinda was shattered.

Jenni's name was called a few minutes later and she came up to claim her key. Jason tagged along behind her looking surly. Katie realized why. Juan's name had been called with theirs. It was their first public acknowledgment of what everyone already knew. Juan was absolutely beaming.

"C'mere, Jack," Jason called out. The dog gave Katie an apologetic look, then trotted off.

"The Four J's," Travis said with a weary smile as he joined her.

"Uh huh," Katie answered.

Jenni did look happy and taken care of. Juan helped her walk and Jason trudged along behind them, looking annoyed. Since they were considered a "family," they had ended up with a small suite with two rooms.

Eric and Stacey claimed their key together. Pepe danced around at their feet as the young couple kissed happily. Stacey had complained to Katie about the lack of privacy that haunted all the couples in the fort. Only Jenni and Juan seemed comfortable with everyone overhearing their business, or maybe they just didn't think about it.

When Nerit's name was called, she walked forward, her dog in tow, and claimed her key. She looked very weary, like she wanted nothing more than to sleep. The older woman forced a smile as she passed them on her way to claim her things.

"We're finally inside," Katie said to Travis in a low voice. "How does it feel?"

Travis looked around at all the people gathered around them, then back at Katie. "Like the cost was high, but the right thing to do."

She nodded, then heard her name called. Moving forward, she smiled at Peggy. "I'm wanting to check in."

Peggy grinned. "I have your reservation. Room 718."

Katie lifted an eyebrow. "Kinda nice for just little ol' me."

Peggy had a wicked gleam in her eye. "Uh, is it just you?"

Katie gave her a look and dared not look at Travis. "Yes, it is. Thanks, Peggy."

Peggy just smiled and called out the next name.

Moving through what remained of the crowd, Katie smiled at all the weary, stressed faces. She walked back into the construction site through the now cleaned up janitor's room. Making her way up to the small room in the city hall, she ran into Nerit carrying her suitcase. She had her rifle over one arm and her dog leash in the other hand.

"Nerit," Katie said softly. "You were so amazing."

"I'm so tired," Nerit answered truthfully. "I did my job. Now I want a bath and a nice bit of reading before bed."

Katie smiled. "You deserve a nice rest."

Nerit gave her a little hug and a kiss on the cheek. "I will see you in the morning."

"Night, Nerit," Katie answered.

Moving up the stairs and toward the small room she had once shared with Jenni, Katie found Juan picking up Jenni's bag that she kept in Katie's room, even though she slept in Juan's tent.

"We just decided today," he explained. "Life is so short. We just don't' want to waste time. We've been sleeping together in my tent. Might as well make it official and be a family."

Nodding, Katie smiled. "I get it. I understand and I think its great. I knew she would never move back in with me. Our time to be roomies is long gone."

Juan heaved the bag over his shoulder and picked up a smaller bag of items. "I really love her, Katie. She's loca, but she's my loca. I know her life was shitty before, I want to take care of her."

"I know, Juan. You don't have to tell me this."

"Yeah, but I do. You're her best friend, her sister. Other than Jason, you are her family. I just wanted you to know how I feel," Juan said. "That I really love her."

Katie gave him a gentle hug. "And that makes me so very happy."

Juan looked almost embarrassed. "I'm glad. I know you like the chicas, but Travis—"

Katie rolled her eyes and pointed at the door. "Out!"

Juan hesitated. "Seriously, maybe with a little lipstick-"

"Out!" Katie pushed him out the door.

Juan turned and tried one last time. "Maybe a wig-"

Katie rolled her eyes, then shut the door.

After packing up her meager belongings, she carried her bag to the hotel and entered the brightly-lit interior. The lobby was now pretty much empty except for a few men propping sheets of metal up against the newly walled in windows and doors for added security.

Taking the elevator that still reeked of bleach, she was relieved to not have to climb the stairs again today. Her legs were aching horribly.

Her new room was nice, spacious, and welcoming. The four poster bed and heavy Victorian furniture were not her cup of tea, but there was something very homey about it all. She pushed back the heavy dark pink curtains covering the tall, narrow windows and looked down into the street. A few figures staggered out there. They were zombies too mutilated to run and pose much of a threat. Closing the curtains, she set about putting away her things.

It was sad how quickly everything was tucked away into its proper place. In this new world, she barely owned anything. Maybe that was good, less to be attached to.

She turned down the bed and flipped on the TV.  It was on a closed circuit. Someone had put in a bunch of movies to run through the night. Terminator 2 was on and she briefly compared her arms to Linda Hamilton's. All this hard work had her looking pretty buff.

With a sigh, she headed into the bathroom for a long bath.  She undressed, her body protesting every movement.  Looking into the mirror, she saw why.  There were bruises all over her body.

As she sat in the tub in the hot clear water, she studied each one with disgust. The ones on her arm were the most terrifying, but they were a lesson learned.  A zombie could not bite through thick cloth; that was something to keep in mind.

Using the hotel's rose soap, she scrubbed herself clean and was relieved to finally not smell of death and bleach.

After her bath, dressed in a tank top and pajama bottom she had claimed from the WalMart shipment down in the city hall basement, she started moving things around the hotel room. The bed was far too heavy to move, but she rearranged the chairs, desk and vanity. Little decorative knickknacks were either tossed or put into a new area of the room. She moved the paintings around and fussed with one of the mirrors until it was set at a good height on the wall.

Finally, feeling the room was hers, she sank into a chair and began to read a book she had borrowed from the makeshift library Peggy was keeping in city hall.

When the knock on the door came, she wasn't surprised. Laying the book aside, she slid to her bare feet and walked to the door taking in deep breaths. Another knock came, quieter now. She knew Travis was giving her time to change her mind, to ignore his knocks and pretend to be asleep.

But today she had learned a valuable lesson. Time was short. Too short to worry about what had been.

Opening the door, she gazed out at Travis. His hands were resting on either side of the doorway. He was scrubbed clean and his hair was still damp. He looked tired and anxious. She realized he was waiting for her to send him away.

Reaching out, she tangled one hand in his hair and drew him down and kissed him deeply. With her other arm, she drew him into her embrace and into her room. He almost stumbled, he was so startled. Then he came easily and willingly into her arms.

Together, they shut the door behind them.

## 2. Letting go and Moving Forward

Travis has been more than a nervous wreck when he had knocked on Katie's door. His stomach had been twisted into knots and his throat dry from nerves. He had been pretty sure she was going to turn him away.

In the aftermath of the clearing of the hotel, he had begun to second-guess his short conversation with her up on the patio of the ballroom. He had slowly concluded that he had not been clear in his intentions and she had not understood what he meant.

From the moment he realized he had feelings for Katie, he was sure he was doomed to heartbreak. But he couldn't help himself from hoping. Their kiss, well two kisses, had been enough to stoke the fires of hope within him.

When she had opened the door, his heart had skipped a beat. She had looked so beautiful, so ethereal, with the light behind her illuminating her blond locks. Her sparkling green eyes had regarded him beneath the fringe of her eyelashes and he had braced himself to be sent away. Hell, he had a bottle of Jack Daniels back in his room waiting for him to keep him company after her rejection.

Instead, she had reached out and kissed him in a way that made his knees weak and the butterflies in his stomach turn into a tornado. He had almost fallen into the room in surprise, but had managed to recover and helped her close the door.

The kiss that followed was everything he had hoped for. It was sweet yet passionate, loving yet lustful, soothing yet exciting. He had wrapped his arms tightly around her and dragged her closer to him and-

"Ouch!"

"Sorry," he answered, and quickly let go of her.

"Bruises," she said with a wince.

"Oh, yeah, I forgot."

Again they kissed deeply, her hands trailed down his back and-

"Shit," Travis muttered against her lips.

"Oh, sorry," she said.

"I kinda have a bruise there."

She laughed and pulled away from him, holding out her arms. They were covered in bruises. Then she turned around and her back was a nice patchwork of purple, green, and black.

Travis grinned and showed her his arms and the enormous bruise on his side.

"Well, we match," she laughed.

Travis looped his hand around her neck and drew her close and pressed his lips to hers. They lost themselves in a kiss that felt quite like no other. He was completely enraptured with her. To his great surprise and delight; she seemed just as enamored with him.

"I love you," Travis whispered, stroking her curls, gazing into her eyes.

"Yeah, I kinda figured that out."

"Do you-" he started to say, then just opted to kiss her forehead.

She nestled into his arms, tucked against his chest, and whispered, "Yes."

Closing his eyes, he held her tightly and sighed with relief. "I was hoping, but I wasn't sure since you are a lesbian."

"Actually, I'm not," Katie said much to his amazement. Drawing back, she grabbed his hand and guided him to sit with her on the edge of the bed.

"You had a wife," he pointed out.

Katie nodded as her expression grew sorrowful. "And I love her with all my heart. I would have gladly and happily spent the rest of my life with her. But, before Lydia, I was engaged to a man. And before him, I dated both men and women. I'm technically bisexual. I find no issue loving either sex. I just happened to fall madly in love with a spectacular woman and lived a very happy existence with her until this happened."

Travis tried to take this in. Processing it was a little harder than it probably should be. "So you've been with men before?"

Katie nodded.

"Oh, thank God," Travis said. "I was worried sick about being with you and not knowing how the hell to please you."

Katie began to laugh and wrapped her arms around him. "You're really silly sometimes."

"You have no idea about the performance anxiety I was having. Hell, I was afraid you'd take one look at," he looked down at his lap, "you know...and run screaming."

Her eyes widened, then she really began to laugh. "No, no, I promise I won't. It's been awhile, but I am pretty sure I remember how it all works. Not that you're getting any soon-"

Travis blinked and immediately realized how presumptuous he had been. "No, I mean, no, Katie, of course not, I didn't mean-"

"I'm just giving you a hard time, Travis," Katie said with a soft kiss to his cheek. "But honestly, all this is not as easy for me as you may think. I'm..." She sighed and looked lost for words.

Travis gently stroked her hair and kissed her cheek. "You don't have to say or do anything you don't want to, Katie."

"I'm just dealing with a lot of guilt," Katie said after a long pause. "I lived my life in the gay community for almost a decade. Lydia and I had to fight many battles against people who wanted to punish us for loving each other. We worked tirelessly to make sure we were both covered legally should either one of us die. We worked hard for gay rights after we decided to live openly as a lesbian couple. We were well known in our community and I dealt with a lot of flack from my superiors. Even my own mother and father had trouble with the choice I had made. When I broke up with my male fiancé and moved in with Lydia, my Mother told me to never speak to her again, that I had crushed her hopes and dreams."

Travis listened quietly, trying to understand and feeling he might have a slight idea of what she went through. Of course, his only frame of reference was when he had dated a black woman for a short period and her family had been staunchly opposed to it. He had been determined to keep the relationship going, but she had opted to end it when the pressure became too great. When he had informed his parents they had broken up, he was surprised that his very liberal parents had sighed with relief. He knew it wasn't the same, but he felt that maybe he had an inkling of what she was talking about.

"So, the point of all this is, I became very used to living in the LGBT community. And trust me that wasn't always easy. If I identified myself as bisexual, I was sometimes told I just hadn't fully accepted being a lesbian. Lydia would defend me, but I eventually stopped telling anyone that identified as bi. In fact, this one woman we knew congratulated me on accepting myself as a lesbian and not being in denial. Lydia understood, even though she was never with a man nor was she attracted to them, that I had made a choice to be with her because of who she was, not her gender. I need you to understand that too."

Travis nodded. "I do get that, Katie. I do. And I don't expect you to not love Lydia anymore or think badly of your old lifestyle. All I ask is that you let what we have grow and be what it wants to be. Give me a chance to love you."

Katie took a deep breath. "I wasn't sure I wanted to do that, but I am now. Life is far too short. I can't let my nightmares or my guilt keep me from enjoying what life I have left. I realized that today. In all the insanity, death and violence, I realized that in the end I just wanted you to hold me."

Travis felt the heaviness that had been on his heart and his fears dissipate with her words. Her took her face gently between his hands and kissed her very softly. "I want to hold you."

Smiling, she kissed him back, and then slid away from him.

In silence, he slipped off his boots and his jacket and lay back on the pile of pillows on the bed. She came into his arms and lay her head on his chest. With infinite gentleness, he stroked her bruised flesh and kissed the top of her head.

It was deliciously good.

***

Eric emerged from the sparkling tub that was tucked into the bathroom of the new comfortable hotel room that he now shared with Stacey and Pepe. It was a relief, not to have to stand in line to use the restroom or sign in to take a shower. The shower had been a wonderful experience. He grinned as he wrapped a fresh towel around his hips.

The hotel room was high above the streets outside the walls of the fort where the dead roamed and moaned. There was a delightful silence to the night.

He vigorously scrubbed his wet hair with the towel, trying to dry it as he entered the bedroom. Pepe was lying in his new doggie bed nearby, wagging his tail despite his sleepy expression.

"Hey, is Pepe going to sleep with us?" Eric asked. He was used to the little guy snuggling down with them.

"Absolutely, not," Stacey answered.

Eric finally looked toward the bed. Stacey was laying across it naked and beautiful. She had insisted in showering first and now he understood why. She was smiling with the sweetest, yet most sultry smile he had ever seen on her lovely face.

"Sorry, Pepe. You're out of luck," Eric stammered. He dropped his towels and walked transfixed to the bed.

Stacey laughed with delight and held out her arms to him. "At last, we can make this official!"

"And no one will hear us!" Eric answered as he slid naked over her form.

She plucked his glasses off and tossed them onto a chair nearby. "Tell me you love me."

"I love you," Eric whispered.


***

Lenore opened up her hotel room door and stared out at Ken with her most grumpy expression. He was dressed in his new pajamas and held Cher's cat carrier in one hand and a bottle of champagne in the other.

112

"Slumber party!" He exclaimed with a grin.

"No," Lenore answered, and shut the door.

She knew it wouldn't deter him and waited for the knock she knew was coming.

"Lenore, let me in. I'm your best girlfriend."

Lenore harrumphed at this.

"You love me. Please, Lenore. Let me in. I'm afraid of zombies and I can't sleep alone. Please! I know you have two queens in there."

Lenore looked over her shoulder at the two beds.

"Another one won't hurt," his voice pleaded through the door.

Finally, she opened it and stared out at him. "One word about Daniel Craig, Clive Owen or Hugh Jackman, and I'm throwing you out!"

Ken grinned and hurried past her. "Yay!"

Lenore shut the door, grumbling, but a small smile managed to creep onto her lips. At least she had her best friend in this stupid world even if he was annoying sometimes.

\*\*\*

Peggy tucked Cody into his bed along with his stuffed bear. Her son looked up at her anxiously, his hands gripping her sleeve.

"I don't want to sleep alone in here, Mommy," he whispered.

"Cody, the zombies can't get in here. We're safe. The zombies are far away, I promise," Peggy kissed his forehead.

She was looking forward to her first night of real sleep without him clinging or waking her up with his nightmares.

"Promise?"

"Yes, Cody, I promise," Peggy answered, and felt for the first time in a long time, she wasn't lying.

Sighing, her little boy settled down in his new bed and held tightly to his bear. "Okay, cause Teddy doesn't like zombies."

"I know, honey. I know." She kissed his cheek and tucked in his covers.

As she left his room, she looked back at him one more time and felt a wonderful sense of relief that at last they were truly safe.

"Shit," Juan exclaimed as Jenni almost slipped and fell head first into the tub.

She had been trying to maneuver on her sprained leg while grabbing the bottle of champagne off the counter that Ken had stolen before she nearly fell.

Juan grabbed hold of her naked hips with his sudsy hands and held her steady as she finally managed to get into the tub without killing both of them. Lowering herself into the mountains of white bubbles, so she was straddling his lap, she grinned.

"See, nothing to it?" She took a long swallow of champagne and handed him the bottle.

Juan laughed and gulped down some of the warm champagne. "Shit, that's nasty."

Jenni giggled and pressed her bare breasts against his chest. "Almost as nasty as me?"

"Shit, girl." Juan grinned. "No one is as nasty as you."

Laughing, she kissed him and they both nearly went under the bubbles before Juan managed to grab the edge of the tub.

"You're trying to drown us!"

"Oh, shut up and kiss me."

Juan obliged. The champagne bottle fell off the edge of the tub and onto the floor.

Neither one of them noticed.

***

Katie awoke a few hours later to gentle snoring. She felt a little disoriented by the sound and the body she felt in her arms. Lydia had always snored, but the body pressed against hers was not one bit female.

It was Travis.

He was sound asleep. His arms were around her body with his body spooned up against hers. The lamp next to the bed was still lit. When she turned her head she suppressed a giggle. He was so deeply asleep his mouth was hanging open.

Stretching a little, she managed to turn in his arms and readjust herself. Her body was really aching and her bruises felt even more painful. Looking at Travis' arm draped over her waist, she could see where the zombies had grabbed onto it. Their distinct hand prints were pressed into his flesh.

They had both been immensely lucky today.

Stirring, Travis turned onto his back, his arm slung over his forehead, looking quite serene.

She had really grown to love his face. It was so strong and yet kind. Propping herself up, she stared at him and slid her hand under his T-shirt along the length of his chest. He was so very manly and muscular it was almost intimidating. But she enjoyed the feel of his skin under her hand and felt the surprising pulse of desire inside of her.

"Travis," she whispered.

One eye slowly opened. "Um."

Rising up, she slid herself up his chest and kissed him deeply.

Now she knew he was fully awake and very aware of her body against his. Through her pajamas and his jeans, she could feel him stirring in all ways.

"I promise I won't run screaming," she said very softly.

"I thought we were just going to sleep," he muttered cautiously.

"Well, if you want to," she answered, feeling a slight pang of disappointment.

Travis instantly flipped her onto her back and grinned. "Sleep can wait."

Responding hungrily to his kisses, Katie felt her reservations fading. He was gentle and tender. His kisses passionate, but loving. Any awkwardness they had both felt began to fade away as their desire for each other grew.

When she finally felt his skin against hers, she luxuriated in the feel of it. Simple things like the width of his shoulders and the narrowness of his waist and hips enthralled her. His cheek was scraggly against her skin, but she enjoyed the sensation.

Travis did not have to worry about performance anxiety. He soon had her gasping and moaning and their bruises were forgotten. She buried her face in his neck and wrapped her legs tightly around him as her body shuddered beneath him. He kissed and nuzzled her neck, stroking her hair as she trembled with pleasure.

"Love you," he whispered.

"Love you," she answered, and to her joy, she meant it.

They held each other in the drowsy aftermath of their lovemaking. He stroked her skin with infinite gentleness. She ran her hand down his side to rest on his hip. They shared little kisses and whispers of endearment. It felt good and wonderful. When they finally fell asleep, they were both smiling.

When Lydia's zombified ghost came into her dreams, Katie was waiting for her. In her dream, the specter rose over her and Travis, angry and fierce.

"How could you do this to me?" the zombie version of Lydia demanded.

"If you were really Lydia, you would be happy for me," Katie answered bluntly. In her dream, she sat up and faced the creature boldly.

The zombified Lydia hesitated. "You left me."

"You were already gone. All that is left now is the shell of who you were," Katie said in a firm, yet quavering voice. "You're not Lydia. You're my guilt that I didn't save her. I'll always love her essence. She is the love of my life. But I need to move on. I need to be happy. And if you were truly Lydia, you would understand that. You would understand that because you would love me from beyond the grave. You're not her, I'm not giving you power over me anymore."

The zombie staggered back, lost its form, and disappeared. The true Lydia stepped out of the darkness and drew near the bed. She looked whole and beautiful, her smile as wonderful as always. This spirit was different from the other. It was full of Lydia's wonderful essence. Katie could feel love radiating out of her.

"You finally let go of your guilt," Lydia whispered.

"I wish I could have saved you," Katie said in a voice that was ragged with emotion.

Lydia swept Katie's curls back from her face with a delicate hand. "It was not meant to be. I died minutes after you left. I was in the driveway when they rushed me."

Katie whimpered and clutched Lydia's hand tightly. Drawing it to her lips, she kissed it. "I'm so sorry, babe."

"My thoughts were of you, Katie. I prayed you would escape. I prayed you would live. I passed over to this side wanting you to go on. You know I'm happy, baby. I never would want you to be alone. We were so happy together. No one can ever take that from us," Lydia said in her soothing tones as she held Katie's hand.

"I love you, I never wanted to be without you," Katie said, tears in her eyes.

"And I love you," Lydia answered with the gentlest of smiles. "Be happy, Katie. Be happy and live your life."

"Lydia," she sobbed, desperately missing her.

Lydia kissed her lips, then drew back and disappeared.

Katie awoke with a start, her hand flying to her mouth. She could almost feel the softness of Lydia's lips on her own. The sun was higher in the sky. Light was pouring through the slit in the curtains.

Beside her, Travis was on his elbow looking down at her. He looked worried and he slid his hand over her hair tenderly. "Are you okay?"

"I dreamed of Lydia," she answered truthfully.

Travis nodded, his brow furrowed. "I know. You said her name."

Katie rubbed her brow and took a deep breath. "It was odd. It was like she was really here. Not like my other dreams. I really felt her here, with me. It's so odd."

Travis stroked her arm. "She's a part of you, Katie. Of course she's going to haunt you in some way."

She could see the tension in him, his worry and his fear she would push him away. "You don't have to compete with her ghost," Katie assured him.

"I don't?" Travis' voice was strained. "Are you sure?"

Katie smiled and took his face between her hands. "I'm sure. I'm very, very sure. If for no other reason than I know she would want me to be happy, to live my life, to not be afraid or sad."

Sighing with relief, Travis wrapped his arms around her. She nestled into them, and for the first time in a very long time, felt at peace.

# Chapter 9

## 1. Shuffling the Deck

Nerit's morning started as simply as her night had ended. Sliding off the bed, she opened up the curtains to take in the first rays of dawn and check the street for zombies. She noted a few wandering around and mentally made a note to deal with them later. Then she took a long hot shower that helped loosen up her stiff joints and spent all of five minutes combing and braiding her long hair, applying a bit of mascara to her lashes and some lip gloss to her lips. It was the only makeup she ever felt she needed.

Dressed in olive green jeans, hunting boots and a green T-shirt under Ralph's jacket, she made her way down to the dining room for an early breakfast. The room looked nothing like the scene of bloody chaos of the day before. Under the ornate rug had been a very pretty but faded tile floor that a few volunteers had spent all night moping and polishing. Now it gleamed under the chandelier lights.

Old Man Watson and several of the other elderly people were gathered at one table, eating their oatmeal and toast. He smiled at her warmly as she passed and gave her a little wave. His hearing aid had stopped working soon after the zombies first appeared and she suspected he had no clue what was going on most of the time. He just seemed happy to sit and watch people talk and read the old newspapers out under a tarp on the construction site that had been raised up to give people shade.

As Tucker, her old dog, wandered in behind her for his breakfast, the old man reached out to pat his head and call him a good dog.

The early morning breakfast crew laid out breakfast on a buffet table. Oatmeal, toast, eggs from a mix, and dry cereal with large chilled mugs of powdered milk greeted her. She served herself a bit of oatmeal and eggs and sighed as she poured out the thin milk. She missed whole milk and fresh eggs. A glass of orange juice topped off her breakfast. She sat down at a nearby table.

Her old dog went over to one of several food bowls put out for the dogs and started to eat, looking just as weary in his bones as she did.

"Can I sit here?" a voice asked.

Nerit looked up to see Jason and smiled warmly. "Of course!"

Jason sat down, a cloud of sullen teenager angst, and stabbed his spoon at his enormous bowl of cold cereal.

Jack strolled over to join Nerit's dog at the doggy bowls, Jason sighed.

"Juan lives with us now," he said out of the blue.

"Yes, I know. I heard," Nerit answered.  She spooned some oatmeal into her mouth.

Jason sighed a little more dramatically. "I don't understand why."

"Well, your Mother is doing what many people are doing right now, living her life in a kind of desperate rush. Death could come at any time. When you know that, you want to grab life and enjoy it before it ends," Nerit explained. "I think you will be seeing many people doing just that. Especially now that we have what feels like a safe and comfortable home."

Jason frowned a bit as he chewed his cereal. "I guess. It just feels weird. They talk in Spanish to each other a lot and I feel left out."

"Ah," Nerit said, understanding. "Well, why don't you ask them to teach you Spanish or at least translate so you don't feel left out?"

Jason shrugged again, then said, "It just feels so different now. I don't like how it keeps changing."

"Neither do I, but we have to do our best."

Jason hoisted his large backpack up onto the table.  He pulled out a book and some notebooks. "Well, I've been working on weapons ideas to keep my mind off of...you know...stuff and to make myself useful."

"Really? Like what?"

Jason opened up a notebook to show her his notes and illustrations. "We really can't use fire in the fort. It's way too dangerous. We could end up setting our own stuff on fire. Burning down the hotel would not be good. But outside the fort, we could make some sort of firetrap. I was looking into making concussion grenades to rip the zombies apart and maybe doing some stuff with shrapnel to rip up their bodies. I noticed the more fucked...um...messed up ones are slower. Easier to kill."

"Yes, yes, they are," Nerit agreed.

"Shelley's little brother came up with a lawnmower-woodchipper-type machine to chew them up." Jason showed Nerit the crayon illustration complete with zombies getting ripped apart by a large lawn mower. "It got me thinking. We could take apart some lawnmowers and use the engines and blades. Not sure how yet, but working on it."

Nerit looked over the drawings and the notes. "Very good ideas."

"Yeah, but not sure how to do some of it."

"Maybe Juan could help you, or Travis."

Jason peered at her from under his bangs. "I guess so. I just don't think they'll listen to me."

Nerit laughed a little. She had forgotten how absolutely moody teenage boys could be. "Oh, I think they will. We need all the clever ideas we can get to survive this."

"Maybe. I just think it's cool that you know what you gotta do. I want to help, but I'm just a kid. I have ideas, but..."

"Jason, I really do think they will listen to you. You're a smart boy with clever ideas. That is better than an old woman who only knows how to shoot a gun."

"Maybe, but you can shoot the eyes out of a fly. I just come up with ideas and don't know how to make them work right." Jason shoved his heavy bangs out of his face and frowned more.

"Well," Nerit said slowly, "that is why you should talk to Juan and Travis. I think they will be able to help you figure it all out."

Jason fidgeted with his notes, then finally agreed. "Yeah, I guess. I'm just used to older guys not listening to me. My Dad never gave a rat's ass what I thought or said."

Nerit took a long sip of her orange juice, pondering her response. "Well, Jason, I think you need to do what your mother is doing. Make this a new life."

Jason stared at her, then ducked his head down. "Yeah. I guess." Shoveling more cereal into his mouth, he looked up at her through his bangs. She could tell he was considering her words.

Nerit stood up, stretching her still stiff body, and picked up her rifle. "I will see you later, Jason. I need to get to work."

"Thanks, Nerit," Jason answered. "You know, for listening."

She nodded and walked on, her dog falling into step behind her. Today she felt stiff and ungainly. Nothing seemed to work just right. It was hard for her to accept her age when most of the time she did not feel her years at all, but today she did. That she had sat down alone and not with the other seniors had been deliberate. This was not a time for her to give into time, but to fight it. With Mike gone, she had a role to play.

Approaching the front desk, she found Peggy typing away on a computer. People still remained on the Internet where there was still service. The Mayor had told her that several servers were up because the workers barricaded themselves into buildings and were trying hard to keep the Internet up and running-so information could be exchanged between the surviving scientists. There were forums to contact other survivors, Peggy often logged onto them to monitor other groups. It was stressful whenever another group vanished off the list. News was hard to come by. No one had any idea if there was any semblance of the government left. The Internet was rife with rumors.

"Do you have the duty roster?"

Peggy started, then laughed. "Gawd, you gave me a fright. Yeah, right there. I updated it like you asked."

Nerit checked it over and noted Jimmy was already on watch where she had assigned him. "Excellent. I'll make sure to get the updated schedule for the next few days to you as soon as possible." With Mike and the others dead, the roster would look very different.

"I can go ahead and take you off kitchen duty, since you took over for Mike," Peggy offered.

Nerit shook her head. "No, no. Cooking is relaxing. Keep me on it."

Peggy shrugged, then cocked her head. "Nerit, I was wondering. Could you show me how to shoot?"

With a grin, Nerit answered, "Of course. I'm thinking about making lessons mandatory, not voluntary."

With a little sigh, Peggy bobbed her head in agreement. "I just don't want to feel so useless or helpless."

"That seems to be the theme of the day," Nerit answered and strolled away. She was halfway across the lobby when she saw Curtis. "Curtis, I have something I need to attend to. Mind joining me?"

Curtis hesitated. "Sure. What are we dealing with?"

"Jimmy."

Curtis frowned. "Yeah. I talked to Travis and Juan about what he pulled yesterday. Juan wants him pulled from anymore excursions."

"We need all the people we can use. He just needs to learn a lesson," Nerit answered coolly.

She entered the elevator and Curtis followed.

"I don't know, Nerit. He's always been twitchy."

"We're all twitchy."

This brought guffaws from Curtis.

She raised an eyebrow at him.

"You're the coldest of us, Nerit, a true killing machine. You're never twitchy."

Nerit shook her head. "I'm just well-trained."

"We don't need cowards," Curtis said in a low voice. "We don't need people who will sacrifice others to protect themselves."

"No, we need well-trained people," Nerit answered in such a way Curtis fell into silence.

Jimmy was up on the second floor, positioned over the front door. He was sitting on the windowsill looking over the street with a bored expression on his face when they entered.

"Jimmy," Nerit said.

He looked up, startled, and quickly slid to his feet. "Hey, Nerit."

"Good morning, Jimmy. How are you?"

"Good...good..." He looked decidedly nervous as his gaze darted between Nerit and Curtis.

"Curtis, can I have the gun you used yesterday to shoot the zombie with the metal plate in his head?"

"Sure," Curtis said, looking confused. He pulled a small .22 from his side holster. "It's my backup weapon."

Nerit nodded, stepped up to the window, and fired down at the zombie still languishing on the street lamp below the window. It took four shots, but the zombie collapsed into final death. Silently, she handed the weapon back to Curtis.

"Sometimes, with small caliber, the bullets glance off hard surfaces. Not just metal plates, but bone. You just have to keep firing. If you shoot them through the eye, the bullet will bounce around their brain and make mush of it. The lesson here, Jimmy, keep firing." Nerit's gaze grew steely. "Never leave anyone behind. If they are bitten shoot them, but if they are alive cover them. Understood?"

Jimmy looked at her sullenly, but nodded. "Yeah, I got it."

"Good." Nerit turned and walked out of the room, her job done.

Curtis shuffled after her. "That's it?"

Nerit turned to face him. "That's it. For now."

Curtis stared at her, then stepped back. "Okay. Fine. Juan and Travis will not like this."

"Then they can talk to me," Nerit answered. She stepped into the elevator and hit the button.

The doors closed on Curtis frustrated features, Nerit sagged against the side of the elevator and sighed.

## 2. Drawing the Tower

The elevators slid open on the sixth floor. Juan and Jenni stepped out, arguing loudly in Spanish. Jenni was limping as she walked down the hall, her face a decoration of purple and green bruises. Waving her hand in frustration, she called Juan a few choice words in Spanish before knocking on Katie's door.

Juan tried to comfort Jenni, but she punched his arm, annoyed beyond words with him. He had ruined a perfectly nice morning by ranting on and on about how he was going to kick Jimmy's ass. All Jenni had wanted to do was strip him naked and have lots of sex once Jason had gone down to breakfast. Juan seemed to only want to devise ways of making Jimmy miserable.

"I just love you, okay, Loca," Juan said, taking hold of her arms and pulling her close.

"Yeah, then show me. Don't talk about something that happened yesterday. I'm alive, okay?" Jenni frowned up at him.

Juan's curls fell around her face as he kissed her. A bit of her anger dissipated. But she pushed him away anyway and stuck out her tongue at him. Juan laughed and kissed her cheek.

Katie opened the bedroom door, clad in a tank top and pajama bottoms. She looked a little flushed and her skin had a light sheen of water on it. Behind her, Travis was in jeans, toweling off his chest, his hair still wet from a shower. Katie's own hair was in wet curls around her face.

"Damn," Juan said in awe.

Jenni took a moment to admire Travis' very impressive chest, then looked at Juan. Lifting her eyebrows, she said, "See? They started off the morning right."

Katie rolled her eyes. "What's up?"

"Juan is having a hissy fit," Jenni answered.

"I am not," Juan protested.

Travis pulled on his shirt and started to button it up. "What's up?"

"The situation with Jimmy," Juan answered.

Travis made a face and sat on the bed. "I thought we talked about this last night?"

"Uh, we came to no conclusion," Juan answered. He walked in and flopped onto a couch.

Jenni slid in and eyeballed Katie. Her friend looked back with an innocent smile that Jenni didn't buy for a moment.

"Didn't we agree that Nerit needed to deal with it?" Travis asked.

"No, we didn't. Curtis was all for finding a way to discipline him."

"I don't know if we have to go that far," Travis answered, his brow furrowing. He tugged on his socks one by one.

Jenni noted how very comfortable he was in Katie's room. Again, she looked at her friend and gave her a sly smile. Katie responded with a wide-eyed innocent look.

"He almost got Jenni killed!" Juan's anger was about to get the best of him again.

Jenni put her hand on his shoulder, but she could feel his Latin temper building up to an explosion. "He just freaked."

"And almost got you killed!"

"Well, it was bizarre with that zombie having that big ol'metal thing in his head!"

"Again, he almost got you killed!"

Travis shook his head. "Juan, we need to drop this."

"I'm not going to, Travis," Juan answered firmly. "What if it had been Katie left alone in a room with three zombies? Huh?"

Travis looked toward Katie and his look said it all.

"Exactly," Juan answered, and stood up. "You know what? I'm going to deal with this man to man. Fuck diplomacy."

"Juan," Travis said softly.

"No, fuck it." Juan walked out, and slammed the door behind him.

"He's having anger issues," Jenni said.

"Obviously," Travis responded. He stood and grabbed his new denim jacket. "I better go after him."

Katie moved to his side. They shared a sweet little kiss that had Jenni grinning. It was good to see Katie and Travis together. She felt a little less guilty about moving on now that Katie had, too. She knew it had been much harder for Katie.

"See you later," Travis said.

"Okay," Katie answered, and walked him to the door.

Another soft kiss, then Travis was gone.

Jenni lifted her eyebrows at Katie as her friend shut the door.

"What?" Katie asked, then broke into a huge grin. Jenni tackled her.

Like schoolgirls, they hugged each other and jumped around laughing until they collapsed into a heap on the bed.

"You have FFG!"

"Do not!"

"Uh huh! Freshly fucked glow!" Jenni howled with laugher, pointing at Katie's flushed countenance.

Katie covered her face and laughed. "Oh, gawd...I do!"

For the first time, laughter filled their time together.

\*\*\*

After missing Juan at the elevator, Travis headed down to the lobby and found him nowhere in sight. Confused, he walked toward the front desk and found Peggy printing out what looked like a map of their area.

"Peggy, have you seen Juan?"

"Uh-mm...no. Not recently."

Travis leaned against the counter and thought for a second. "Can I see the duty roster?"

"Sure," Peggy answered, and handed it to him. She began to use a highlighter to draw circles around areas on the map.

"So Juan didn't just come down to see the roster?"

"No, no."

Travis sighed with relief. Maybe Juan wasn't trying to track down Jimmy.

"Something wrong?" Peggy's big eyes regarded him curiously. "I saw him stalking around earlier this morning before everyone got up bitchin' about Jimmy. He looked at the roster then."

"Shit," Travis exclaimed, and quickly found where Jimmy was supposed to be. Juan's temper was building up to an explosion.

"What's wrong?"

"Nothing," Travis lied, heading back to the elevators.

As he listened to the whir of the elevator rising, he stood in quiet frustration. Couldn't they have just a nice little period of no major drama?

Couldn't they just fucking enjoy the hotel without all of this? Hell, he couldn't even enjoy being with Katie this morning. He was already in work mode.

The doors slid open and he strode out swiftly. Ahead of him, a door was propped open and the early morning rays were filtering into the long hallway in a stream of light. Juan walked out into the hall and stood there, looking angry.

"Juan, you didn't do anything--"

"He's not fucking at his post," Juan answered. "I told you he was a pussy."

Travis lifted an eyebrow. "What do you mean?"

"Not there. We have no coverage in the front of the hotel. The fucker is off picking his ass."

Travis walked into the hotel room and looked around. There was a chair near the window, which was open, and the curtains were pulled back. A table was strewn with soda cans and an ashtray.

Moving toward the window, he looked out. The street had a few of the shambling-type of zombies wandering around.

"I told you he is a fucking pussy that doesn't give a shit about anyone or anything," Juan ranted behind him.

Travis looked directly downward and froze. "Shit, Juan. What did you do?"

"Huh?"

Below him, in a bush, was what remained of Jimmy struggling to get up.

Juan leaned out next to him. "Oh, man."

"Juan," Travis said again, very softly, "What did you do?"

"Nothing! I swear. I got in here and he was not at his post!"

Travis rubbed his brow.

"I did not throw him out of the gawddamn window, Travis!"

"Then who did?" Travis asked. "Then who did?"

## 3. Judgment is Drawn

Travis stood in the corner with his arms folded across his chest. His face was solemn and his gaze intense. The Mayor, Peggy, Curtis, and Juan all sat around the Hotel Manager's office in an uncomfortable silence. Jenni and Katie stood near the door, both of them looking very pensive.

Nerit strode in, her rifle over one shoulder, and looked at Travis. "It's taken care of."

Bill followed her in holding a notepad and looking very official. "Okay, we hooked the body after Nerit put him down and dragged it up to a balcony. I examined it and even though there was extreme damage to the corpse, I was able to conclude that there was no sign of trauma other than some abrasions on his knees and hands. I think he was pushed out the window fully conscious. There was no sign of head injury other than his eyes and parts of his face missing."

Manny fidgeted, then said, "Could he have fallen?"

"I might have considered that a possibility if not for the fact that we already had one murder," Bill answered.

"I didn't do it," Juan said softly.

"I hate to say it, but you are the most likely suspect right now, Juan. Both Ritchie and Jimmy were people you had a beef with," Bill said.

"We all had issues with Ritchie to some extent and Jimmy did piss off a lot of people yesterday," Travis pointed out.

"It could have been me," Jenni said defiantly.

"True. We could have two different murderers on our hands, but the fact remains that two people were pushed out of the safety of our fort and left to die at the hands of the zombies," Bill said in a very serious tone.

"I can deal with this if you want, Manny" Curtis said to the Mayor.

"No offense, Curtis, but I think Bill should deal with this. He has a lot more experience than you and he is an outsider so he isn't biased," the Mayor answered.

"No one is an outsider anymore," Katie spoke up. "We're all intertwined in each others lives. There could be many more people with a beef against both of the victims. We can't just go after the first convenient suspect. You need a solid case before any action is taken to make sure we're not just on a witch hunt. You need a solid case."

"Spoken like a true prosecutor," Bill said with amusement.

"I don't want this getting out," the Mayor said after a beat. "A party is planned for tonight and we need it for morale."

"People are already talking about Jimmy," Nerit cut in. "It is hard to keep things quiet in such a small community."

"She's got a legitimate point. Besides, hiding something from the general population only ends up blowing up," Katie remarked.

"You have to wonder if the government knew what was going on when this whole zombie thing started," Jenni added. "I mean...hell...where did all the zombie movies come from? There had to be something going on that inspired them."

Travis chuckled softly. "I always thought Romero was just sick in the head."

Jenni gave him a dark look, but then shrugged dismissively. "Well, I still think they knew something."

"It doesn't really matter now, does it?" Curtis said darkly. "The government ain't here anymore as far as we know. But we are."

"I'll handle the investigation and keep it on the low down or as low as I can," Bill said. "And I'll start by questioning Juan."

Juan let out an explosive sigh and threw up his hands. "Fine. It's not like I have work to do to make us all safe."

Jenni sat down next to him and took his hand. "I'm staying with him."

Bill nodded. "That's fine, but the rest of you should go."

Manny said, "Okay, but let me know what you find out."

Peggy stood up and headed out the door, Katie following. Travis hesitated then followed them out as Curtis and the Mayor also left with grim expressions on their faces.

The Mayor drew Curtis aside, whispering, "We need damage control, Curtis. We can't let this get out."

Travis sighed and walked on, hands in his pockets. Some things never changed he supposed; once a politician always a politician.

His face brightened when he saw Katie hanging back in the hallway that led from the hotel's offices to the lobby. The fact she was now with him still made him grin and feel a little overwhelmed. Reaching her, he laid his hand on her cheek and leaned down to give her a kiss. Her lips were soft and sweet against his. She slid her arms around his waist and rested against him.

Apart from everyone else, they shared a quiet moment of kisses. "I need to get to work."

"I know. I have to report for lunch duty," Katie murmured against his chest. "I'll see you tonight at the party though."

"Are we going?"

Katie pressed herself up against him and gave him a look he found hard to resist. "I figured we could go and make an appearance, then sneak away."

"How about just sneaking away?" Travis asked with a grin.

"After an appearance at the party," Katie said firmly, but with a wicked gleam in her eye.

"Okay, okay," Travis conceded. "Anything you want."

"Good," she answered, and pressed her lips against his.

Travis slid regretfully out of her grasp and headed out into the construction site. He gave her one last smile, then slipped out through the old janitor's room turned entryway.

With the "civvies" now out of the way and tucked into the hotel, the construction site was being re-organized. The plan now was to set up the third "lock" in the new vehicle entry to add more protection against the undead, then they were going to bust through the wall in the back of the old newspaper building and begin to use it for projects.

Jason was hanging out near Travis' office with Jack. He looked nervous and unsure, his bangs hanging heavily in his face.

"Hey Jason, what's up?"

"I was wondering if I could talk to you about some ideas," Jason answered.

"What kind of ideas?"

Travis opened the doors to the portable office relieved that the civilians were now moved out and that they could once more reclaim it as office space.

"Stuff to kill zombies other than just guns and bows and arrows. No one is really good with the bows and arrows anyway," Jason answered. "Well, except Lenore."

Travis raised an eyebrow. "True. What do you have for me?"

Jason heaved his large backpack up onto a chair and began to unpack it onto a cleared desk. He looked nervous and hesitated a few times before laying down what looked like carefully organized notes. Each small stack was fastened with a paper clip and had notes on yellow notepad paper attached on top. What looked like pages torn out of books and a few printouts from the Internet made up the rest of the stacks along with what looked like drawings with crayons.

Travis sat down and picked up the first one.

"That's for a concussion grenade. It would rip off the zombies' legs, maybe their arms. If we get lucky, their heads. No fire, since fire would maybe end up burning us down," Jason said in a rush of words. "I have the main ingredients written out, but I'd need help finding the stuff to put them together."

Travis reviewed the list and rubbed his chin thoughtfully. "I think these are doable. We may not have everything on the site, but maybe we can figure it out."

Jason pointed to another stack. "This is for a catapult that would toss over really heavy shit. I got that from Lord of the Rings. You know, stuff we don't use to flatten them. We'd have to make sure it was long range so they couldn't crawl up on the stuff and try to get over the wall."

Again, Travis had to admit it was a decent idea.

Soon Jason was talking in a torrent of words, pointing things out to Travis, getting more and more articulate as he went on. Travis found himself smiling at the boy's enthusiasm and impressed with his ideas. In many ways, the adults had been obsessed with just surviving and basic needs. The kids, obviously, had killing on their minds and had come up with some very good ideas.

"Jason, I think I'm going to hook you up with Roger. He used to teach science in junior high before he ended up working construction...if memory serves me."

"Okay, cool. The other kids have ideas, too. They could definitely help out."

"Sounds like a plan," Travis decided.

"Cool!" Jason gathered up his stuff and started stuffing it back into the backpack. He hesitated, then looked at Travis. "Katie's not gay. She's bi. You should go for it."

Travis was surprised and a little taken aback. "What?"

"She told me not to tell anyone. I think cause she thought you'd hook it up with my Mom. But she's with Juan and life is short and stuff so you should go for it."

Travis rubbed his brow, bemused, then nodded. "Okay. I will."

Jason heaved his backpack over his shoulder and headed out the door. "So you'll let Roger know?"

"Definitely. And once we are in the newspaper building, I'll let you kids clear out some space for your projects. You'll have to have Roger with you whenever you are working with chemicals."

"Cool. I can deal," Jason opened the door and stepped out, Jack immediately at his side.

Travis leaned forward, resting his hands on his head and sighed. Why had he been foolish enough to think that once they were in the hotel everything would be fine?

## 4. Enter the Empress

Katie added more water to the instant mashed potatoes she was making and stirred as vigorously as she could. The kitchen was a bustle of activity with the lunch crew working diligently to make a decent meal for those inside the fort from their supplies of boxed and canned food.

After a rigorous run on the treadmill in the very modern gym on the second floor, Katie had enjoyed a long shower before reporting to the kitchen. Rosie, Juan's mother, ran the kitchen with the efficiency of a woman who had overlooked the high school cafeteria staff for over twenty years. Today's lunch menu was chipped beef with mashed potatoes and green beans. Since Katie could barely make a sandwich without a recipe, she was handed the box of potato flakes and put to work.

Rosie's great joy had been the discovery that the grocery store's cold storage had remained cold and that some of the frozen meat could be salvaged. The delicious smell of beef cooking in rich gravy filled the kitchen and big, flaky buttermilk biscuits were being drawn out of the ovens to cool on the counters.

Gretchen, the librarian, had volunteered to make dessert. Big pans of peach cobbler were making Katie's stomach growl with hunger.

Frowning into the bowl, Katie felt pretty sure the potatoes weren't supposed to look so stiff and hard. She added more hot water and really began to put her muscles into stirring.

"Well, Jimmy was a klutz, but I just can't see him falling out of the window," Gretchen said to Stacey.

"But why would anyone push him?" Rosie asked as she began to slide the hot biscuits into a large basket for the buffet in the dining room. "I can understand that puto Ritchie being killed after what he did to all those kids, but Jimmy? He was just a little grumpy man."

Roger carefully poured a large pan of green beans into one of the buffet tins. "He fucked up yesterday. He almost got Jenni killed."

Katie flinched. She had been really hoping that he would keep his mouth shut.

"Really?" Rosie's eyes grew stormy. "My Juan's Jenni?"

"Yeah. He freaked and pushed Curtis out of the hotel room they were in. Left her in there with three zombies. That's why she's all banged up today. I heard she had to jump from one balcony to another to escape," Roger answered with all the fervor of a well-practiced gossip.

And people said women were bad gossips...

Rosie's explosion of Spanish cuss words, though not really understood, impressed Katie. She slammed the lid to one of the skillets down and waved her gravy-covered spoon about like a sword. "Then he deserved to fall out the window!"

"Maybe Juan pushed him," Stacey said softly.

"Oh, he wouldn't do that, would he?" Gretchen looked up from where she was spooning cobbler into little bowls.

Katie looked toward Rosie, almost afraid of her answer.

"He might punch his lights out, but I'd be the one to throw him out the damned window," Rosie responded. Her expression was so intense Katie was pretty sure that the older woman would have shoved Jimmy out the window if she had known that his cowardice had almost killed Jenni.

Then the prosecutor side of her whispered, *Well, how do you know she didn't know? This could be an act.*

"Well, maybe someone did throw him out the window then," Gretchen said in a soft, conspiratorial voice. "Like Ritchie was."

"A vigilante," Roger said to her.

"Yeah. A vigilante." Gretchen took this in and then shook her head. "I don't think I like that."

Stacey leaned across the counter, snagged a biscuit, and began to pull it apart. Rich, fragrant steam rose up from its center, making Katie even hungrier. "So we have to find the vigilante now and do what?"

"Thank him," Rosie said irritably, "or her."

"Or...um...put them on trial?" Gretchen continued to spoon the cobbler out.

Roger looked at Katie. "What do you think?"

"I think we need to finish lunch and not worry about all of this. Let Bill deal with finding out what happened, then we'll go from there," Katie answered as neutrally as possible.

"But aren't you worried?" Gretchen asked. "Aren't you worried that someone is just going to start throwing anyone who upsets them over the wall?"

Katie lifted the spoon and let a huge dollop of mashed potato fall back into the bowl. "Yes. But speculation isn't going to help Bill solve this any faster."

"My son didn't do it," Rosie said firmly. "He may look guilty, but he's just a very fiery Latino who loves his woman."

"Oh, aren't they cute? Juan and Jenni," Gretchen gushed. "They're so cute together."

Stacey continued to eat the biscuit, piece by piece, listening intently.

Roger dumped more green beans and looked over at them. "Well, he's the one who has the most reason to do something about Jimmy being a dumbass."

"I'm her best friend. Maybe I did it," Katie said pointedly.

"Crazed lesbian kills girlfriend's almost killer," a voice said very sarcastically from behind her. "Oh, yeah. I see that."

Katie turned to glare at Shane. He had come in through the side door. His crew had been sent out to bring back more supplies from the grocery store freezer since the hotel freezer was now chilled. They had opened up the loading dock door on the side and were now entering the kitchen with supplies.

Rosie waved her hands at him. "Don't go near the food. You're all sweaty and gross."

Shane just grinned at her. "Yeah, and we smell real funky. Had to kill more of those deadfucks."

Rosie began to put lids over all the food and the others in the kitchen helped her.

Shane turned his gaze back to Katie, the hatred in them cold and furious. "What's up, lesbo."

He had hated her since she had to kill his brother after he was bitten during one of the first major fort battles against the undead. Every chance he got, he harassed her verbally. She tried to avoid him.

"Nothing, dickwad." She moved to dump the potatoes into a serving bin.

"Fuckin' lesbo bitch," Shane hissed.

"Move! Don't mess up my kitchen," Rosie ordered, waving a towel at him.

To avoid Shane, Katie busied herself carrying the big metal bins out to the buffet and dropping them into the slots. Already the water that would keep the food warm was bubbling deep inside the buffet table, steam rising up to greet her.

It was five 'til noon and the old folks, as usual, were already lining up. There were ten officially elderly people who lived in the fort. No one dared group Nerit in with them. Two walked with canes, one with a walker. Old

Man Watson was just deaf as they come. When he saw her, he smiled and waved. She smiled and waved right back at him.

Stacey brought out the big basket of biscuits, which brought a lot of "ooohhs" and "aaaaaahs" from the line. Roger arriving with the big bin of chipped beef made them even more excited. Katie's somewhat pathetic mashed potatoes and the green beans had them positively beaming.

"They're gonna flip over the cobbler," Stacey whispered to Katie with a grin.

Katie laughed. When the cobbler was rolled out it sent little waves of excitement through the now growing line.

It was very rewarding to watch people happily digging into the food they had prepared. The construction workers came in to eat while Stacey was dispatched with lunch boxes for the guards. Mealtime was not the sheer chaos it once was now that they had a decent facility. There was plenty of room to spread out and really enjoy the meal.

Katie was kept busy going back and forth from the kitchen. She kept the food bins full and made sure there were enough clean plates and utensils. Jenni and Juan appeared together. They both looked solemn as they sat in a corner, eating their lunch at a small table. Katie saw one of the tubs, put out for people to bus their own table, was full near their table. She slipped over to pick it up and steal a moment with them.

"How did it go with Bill?" she asked.

"I'm his prime suspect," Juan responded grimly.

"Which is bullshit. I could have killed Jimmy. Easily," Jenni said with a frown. "By the way, the food is great."

"Thanks. I did the potatoes," Katie answered, then said, "Juan, I'm sure Bill realized that it wasn't you."

With a shrug, Juan said, "Yeah, but who else would do it other than Loca? Travis? You? Who?"

Katie sighed and heaved the heavy tub up onto her hip. "I'm sure other people had motives. Or could have motives."

Juan sighed, then shook his head. "It doesn't fucking matter, Katie. Not if they want to blame someone. It will end up me."

Rosie came up just then and Katie hurried off under her stern eye. She glanced back to see Rosie hugging her son tightly and talking to him in a low voice. Katie hated to admit it, but Juan was the most likely suspect. It killed her to think of him doing anything like that. But then again, she had been furious when she had heard about Jenni being left in that room. If she had been there when it happened, who knows what she could have done to Jimmy.

In the kitchen, she helped rinse off the plates and load them up into the enormous industrial dishwasher. In between loads, she managed to eat her lunch in big bites. She was famished and loved every bite. Finally, the crowd thinned out and they were able to finish clearing the tables and wash up the rest of the dishes.

"Did anyone see Travis?" she asked as she began the process of storing the leftovers in Tupperware containers.

"No, can't say I did," Rosie answered.

Stacey glopped some mashed potatoes into a plastic container and shook her head. "Eric said Travis was busy working on something in his office and he said he'd eat later."

Katie frowned a little. "Any idea what he is working on?"

Stacey thought for a second then nodded. "Eric said when he went by with Pepe, Travis was studying some stuff Jason had left off for him to look at. Plans for weapons or something like that."

"Well, since we're pretty much done here, I'm going to take some leftovers to him then," Katie decided.

With a nod of her head, Rosie handed her a clean plate. "Go take care of that boy. If it wasn't for him, none of us would be here right now."

Smiling slightly at this, Katie took the plate and quickly served what she hoped was man-size portions for Travis.

Stacey was eating some cobbler now. She was gaining weight and looking better than she had when she had first arrived at the fort. For being so small, she ate more than someone would expect. "What do you mean, Rosie?"

"Travis is the one that had the trucks made into a wall to protect us. That is why the zombies never got in," Rosie answered.

"Thank God for that or we wouldn't have had anywhere to go," Stacey said thoughtfully. "Weird how things work out."

"Plus, he is very good looking. If only I were younger," Rosie said with a wink.

A secretive smile broke out on Katie's face as she covered the plate with foil.

"Oh, yes!" Gretchen's voice affirmed. "Isn't he handsome? I remember when he moved to town and all the girls would just stare at him. I always thought he had a thing for Brenda." Gretchen's voice got soft, then she said, "Poor Brenda. Did they ever figure out how to get her body down?"

"I think they're gonna use a hook on the end of a broom to drag her off the anti-suicide net," Roger answered. "No one is going to want to see her up there during the party."

"She was always so sweet," Gretchen sighed. "Always checking out romance novels from the library and waiting for Prince Charming to come."

"That's really sad," Stacey said softly.

"Yeah, when Travis came to town, she thought he was the one. She told me all about him when she was checking out her books. It's sad how he found her body." Gretchen shook her head. "It's a sad world."

Stacey picked up another biscuit and slowly pulled it apart. "At least some of us are still alive."

"Thank God for that!" Rosie exclaimed, and yanked open the huge refrigerator to store the leftovers away.

Listening to the conversation, Katie could only feel sad for the young woman who had been so enamored with Travis. It was yet another painful reminder of all the dreams and hopes that had died with so many on the first days.

Katie slipped out of the kitchen and headed out into the construction site. It seemed so empty without all the people milling around. It looked more like a construction site now and less like a refugee camp. She shrugged her shoulders under the thin straps of her tank top and hurried toward the portable building that housed Travis' office. Moving up to the door, she knocked and waited for an answer.

Her smile broadened on her face as she realized how much she was anticipating seeing Travis. Now that she had actually allowed herself to embrace her feelings for him, she was actually getting butterflies in her stomach. She felt girlie and silly, but was enjoying it all the same. She hadn't felt this way since she had first met Lydia. That memory was bittersweet, but too sweet to be denied. After her initial meeting with Lydia, she had been so hyper she had danced around her apartment for an hour. And when Lydia had called to ask her out, she had jumped on her bed with excitement.

Now she felt that way all over again about Travis. It was shocking, yet very good at the same time. He was as much an amazing a man as Lydia had been an amazing woman.

Travis opened the door, looking very serious, but as soon as he rested eyes on her, a smile spread on his lips.

"Lunch?" She lifted the plate for him to see.

"Yeah, sure. Bring it in," he said, stepping back to let her enter. "I was just working on some plans to make the new entry more secure."

Slipping past him, Katie moved toward his office. "How's it going?"

"Okay. I just get real paranoid that those things are going to get in and I start second guessing what we are doing," Travis said following her down the hall.

Laying the plate on a desk, she turned to look at him. "I think we're all a little paranoid about those things."

"Yeah, but after yesterday I admit my paranoia is a little worse," Travis said with a grimace. "I just..." He sighed and sat on the edge of the desk, his hands in his jean pockets. "I just feel like I need to work harder on coming up with good ideas to keep us all safe." He looked toward her. "Keeping you safe."

Katie gave him a soft smile as she moved into his arms and laid her hands on the sides of his neck. His hands were warm against her skin as he slid them under her top to rest on her waist. "Well, you're doing a great job so far keeping us all safe. I know a lot of us are very, very grateful to you."

Travis looked almost sheepish as he looked up at her. "Yeah, well, just trying..."

"And doing a good job," she answered. She stroked the curls on the nape of his neck. She could see the stress lines around his eyes and brow fade as he smiled up at her.

"I look at you and I want to save the world. I can't help it," he answered.

"Are you sweet talking me again?" she lightly kidded.

He laughed and shook his head. "No, no. I mean it. But I always had grandiose dreams." His gaze grew more intense as he looked up at her. "Sometimes I get lucky and they come true."

Katie smiled softly at him and kissed him. He immediately responded and the kiss deepened as the passion rose quickly between them. Katie relished the feel of his lips and tongue against hers. As his hands slid up to unfasten her bra, she drew back long enough to whisper, "What about lunch?"

"Later," Travis whispered huskily, and kissed her again.

It was hard to resist his touch and harder to resist her own desire for him. She felt absolutely intoxicated with him. As their kisses grew more fevered, they struggled to free each other from their clothes. The hunger for each other was so intense, they never made it close to Travis' sofa bed or fully managed to undress.

# Chapter 10

## 1. Past, Present, Future

J enni was annoyed. Up three stories from street level on the fire escape of the hotel, she was on sentry duty overlooking where Main St. intersected Morris Avenue. It was way too hot and windy and the chair she had dragged out to sit on wasn't very comfortable. This, on top of the insinuation that Juan was behind Jimmy joining the ranks of the undead, was really annoying.

Slouching down in her chair, holding her rifle across her lap, and hooking her foot up on railing, she looked over the street as the wind blew her dark hair around her face. She wished a fucking zombie would show up so she could blow its head off. It would make her feel so much better.

When the window opened and Katie slipped out, Jenni was surprised, but relieved.

"Hey girlfriend!"

"Hey," Katie answered. She kissed Jenni's forehead, then sat down on the windowsill and looked over the street. "Quiet, huh?"

"I find myself craving zombies. Isn't that twisted?"

"It's been a weird day," Katie decided.

"But lunch was good."

"Yeah, it was, wasn't it?" Katie grinned, but her expression was odd.

Jenni reached out and tapped her knee. "What's up?"

"Well," Katie started slowly, as if measuring her thoughts before making them into words. "Travis and I just had some really intense, throw you up against the wall, earth-shattering sex."

"All right!" Jenni held out her hand for a high five.

Katie looked at her hand, and added, "Without any protection."

"Oh, shit." Jenni dropped her hand.

"Yeah. We both really spaced it. Completely. I'm not sure he even realizes what happened." Katie sighed softly.

"Um...shit?"

"Yeah. Shit." Katie ran her hands over her face, then looked at Jenni. "Lesbian sex is not this complicated!"

Jenni laughed and shook her head. "Nope, it's not. I mean your girlfriend can't knock you up. It's not like dildos come fully loaded with that baby making stuff."

Katie burst out laughing and covered her face with one hand. "Oh, gawd."

Jenni smiled, but then her expression grew as serious as her thoughts. "You okay?"

With a nod, Katie sighed. "Yeah. I am. Weirdly. I don't really feel panicked at all. I mean, honestly, I had not even thought about it. You know. Babies. But, I guess I have to. Travis...." She smiled at the sound of his name on her lips. "Travis is like Lydia. The one you keep until death parts you. He's in my heart now and I guess I need to think like...uh...."

"A straight woman," Jenni offered.

"A woman who can now have babies biologically with her mate and doesn't have to worry about in vitro-fertilization and the proper donor." Katie smiled at the memories of her and Lydia's discussion about making a family or not. They had opted not to in the end. "Now, right now, this could be it. Babyville."

"I'm sure we could find a pill down in the pharmacy stash," Jenni offered.

"No, no." Katie shook her head. "No. If something happens then it happens. I'll deal with it. We both will."

"You know, I have a feeling that Travis would love a baby with you," Jenni said.

"Me, too. Me, too. But what about you? You and Juan. Being careful?"

"Tubes tied," Jenni said sadly. "Stupid Lloyd didn't want anymore kids. Of course, I had to be the one to face the knife, the bastard."

"Oh, Jenni, I'm so sorry."

"It's okay. I told Juan. He was real quiet then shrugged it off. Said it was kinda cool not to have to worry about condoms. Later on he said something about when people do start having kids that Hillary Clinton will have her wish because it will be a village, literally, raising them. I guess he figures that somehow he'll get in on the kid thing. I mean, if you have a kid, I'm so gonna be Auntie Jenni."

"Oh, yeah, you will be," Katie said with a wide grin. Her smile faded and she looked very thoughtful. "I'm madly in love with him. It's different. Very different. I'm still adjusting. His body, his...smell...the way he touches me...all different, but I love him. I kept wanting to not love him, but I do. And if we have a baby out of our fuck up, I'm okay with that. Because..."

Jenni reached out and hugged her as Katie started to cry. She smoothed her blond curls back, kissed her brow and held her close. Katie clung to her, sobbing, both happy and sad, and Jenni knew she just needed to hold her.

"Hey, lesbos," Shane's voice said from afar. "Can you watch the fucking street instead of making out? We're heading out again."

Jenni looked down to see Shane and three other men getting into a delivery truck. All day, they had been going in and out of the hotel since it appeared to be a slow day in zombieville. Already they had returned twice with truckloads of supplies.

"Fuck off, Shane," Jenni yelled down at him.

"Save your pussy eating for later, bitch," Shane responded.

"Bite me, asshole," Jenni shouted back.

"I have no trouble smacking up a dyke. Trying to be all manly up there like you have a big cock," Shane snapped back.

"Somebody's gotta since you're hung like a light switch," Jenni retorted.

"Fuck you, bitch."

Katie leaned over the rail next to Jenni. "You're just jealous 'cause the girls like me, not you."

Jenni saw such intense rage overwhelm Shane's features that, for the first time, she felt afraid of him.

He merely pointed at them and got into the driver's seat of the truck. It roared down the street.

"He's such a scary fucktard," Jenni said softly.

"Why doesn't someone throw him over the wall?" Katie muttered.

They were both quiet for a while, sitting back down and staring over the streets. The wind was hot and the sky was growing overcast in the distance. Another summer thunderstorm was coming. "I wonder if the heat will make them rot faster," Katie said after a while.

"Yeah, I wish they were like Romero's zombies." Jenni wistfully sighed. "They'd be so much easier to deal with. What the hell?"

A man was coming down the street on a scooter. Its engine was coughing and sputtering and the exhaust was a cloud of dark smoke. He was a tall man dressed in very old jeans and a leather jacket. On top of his head was a beat up, greasy straw cowboy hat that was warped out of its shape so badly it looked like a banana sitting on his head. Even from this great distance he looked dirty and smelly.

"Who the hell is that?" Jenni stood up and tried to get a better view.

Seeing her, the man waved to her and aimed the scooter toward them. Behind him, in the distance were some shambling shapes.

Katie stood up beside Jenni and drew her pistol. "What does he think he's doing?"

The man cruised up to just under the fire escape. "Now, I am a tax paying citizen of not only this country, but the city and county as well and when the Mayor decides to steal my property be sending out rabid CIA clones to try to tear down my fence and get onto my property, I have a God given, constitutional right to defend my property. Now if you think I'm going to just sit back and not complain, you have another thing coming. I fully intend to speak with the police, even if they are a bunch of coke snorting, mafia thugs, about what the Mayor has been doing and I will have justice. I may have had to kill the clones, but I figure since they are clones they really don't count as a life form. Besides, the mixture was bad on that batch and they had all sorts of things wrong with them...."

The man spoke earnestly, in the voice of someone giving an interview with Larry King on a TV show, his hands moving eloquently as he talked.

"Is he for real?" Jenni asked.

"I think so," Katie answered.

"...and even if they are going to sit outside my house and snort up on coke so they don't feel a damn thing, I will defend myself. A good knock to the head seems to do the trick. Took me awhile to figure that one out. But now that I know how the clones have got to be killed, I won't have an issue with them. Now the aliens, well, they don't die so easily..."

Jenni was so fascinated by what the man was saying, she almost didn't see the zombie run around the corner. But her reflexes were fast and sure and she shot a nice hole through its head and sent it sprawling.

"...and that's what I'm talking about. Now they are everywhere! I am going to write to the President of the United States even if he is in league with the aliens to let him know of the blatant abuse of the use of taxes on this cloning program..."

"You need to get the hell off the street right now," Jenni yelled at him.

"The slow ones are closing in," Katie pointed out. She took aim and waited for them to be in range.

"...and I have my video recorder and I will record any meeting that is associated with my complaint because I know that Peggy does alter the minutes to suit her Amazonian agenda..."

"Drive around to the gate," Jenni yelled down at him.

"...and even if you are in cahoots with her, I want you to know that girl's feet stinks. Once in church she came in and took off her shoes and it was the worst smell..."

"Get off the fucking street! Go around the block to the entrance!"

Beside her, Katie fired.

"...and though the aliens have negotiations with the Amazons, I cannot imagine why her feet smelled that bad..."

"Get off the fucking street!"

A zombie came running around the corner and Jenni lifted her weapon and fired.

From the balcony of city hall, Peggy yelled, "Calhoun, you old coot, get your ass in here and file a complaint or I'm locking you out."

"I am a citizen of this great nation and this town and you cannot bar me from a public area during regular visiting hours..." The man whipped away on his scooter down Main Street just in time, for four more zombies came racing up Morris Avenue in pursuit of him.

Jenni and Katie began to fire as the crazy old man disappeared down the side street that would lead him to the gate.

"Just when you thought it couldn't get weirder," Jenni giggled.

"Well, at least you got your zombies," Katie answered, and fired.

## 2. Open the Gate and Let The Insanity In

"Open the gate," came the order over the walkie-talkie from Peggy. "We got a survivor coming in!"

Juan rushed up the stairs to look down from the sentry tower into the street below. Sure enough, stinky old Calhoun was heading down the street on his scooter. Right behind him, and gaining speed, were at least six zombies. As Juan watched, two more came running around the far corner, pumping their legs, running fast, screeching.

"Get ready! Get ready! We have zombies coming," Juan shouted down to the men below. "And they ain't the slow ones!"

The guard beside him took aim and fired. One of the zombies, who was about to grab Calhoun and drag him off the scooter, went down in a spray of blood.

Ahead of Calhoun, the gate opened easily, its mechanism now running smoothly. Guards in the padlock were already raising their guns, aiming toward the widening gap.

Juan lifted his hand, signaling to the man controlling the gate to watch for his mark.

The scooter was making hacking noises, plumes of dark smoke erupting from the back end. A spout of blood and brains erupted from the back of another zombie's head. It went down soundlessly.

Now there were at least three zombies gaining on the old scooter.

"...and now I'm being chased by clones and I hold the Mayor directly responsible..." Crazy Calhoun was shouting as he cruised toward the gates.

Juan actually wasn't surprised the crazy old guy was still alive. If anyone was paranoid enough to survive the zombie apocalypse, it was Calhoun. His property had a huge fence around it with razor wire at the top. It was also well known that Calhoun only ate MRE's and lived in an underground bunker. Why he was venturing into town was a mystery. Juan couldn't imagine why Calhoun was coming into town.

The scooter coughed and sputtered into the padlock. Juan signaled for the gate to be closed. The guard next to him fired more shots and zombies went tumbling to the ground.

Just as the gate was about to close, a female zombie slipped in and screamed before charging after Calhoun. The back of her head exploded in a gush of gore and Calhoun turned around and looked at her sprawled body with contempt.

"...and obviously were not cloned from quality people. They're just insane. And where did all this come from? I do not remember voting on any city agenda to build a fort in the middle of town. I do not approve of my taxes going for this facility when we need to deal with the evil clones epidemic..." Calhoun rattled away.

Juan crossed his arms over his chest and began to laugh. Life was about to get much more interesting now that the town crazy had arrived. Calhoun hated the city government with a passion and always came to every council meeting. He would always sit in the back, talking away non-stop as his video camera whirred and recorded every word said by those on the council. He especially hated Peggy, because she had refused to marry him years before she had married Cody's now deceased father.

"...and I don't know who is going to pay for my scooter, but since it was damaged by me coming all the way into town to file a complaint, I firmly believe it should be paid for by the Mayor out of his personal funds. And I will know if it is out of his personal funds because I can attune my brain to the Internet..."

Juan looked over the gate toward the road and saw more zombies in route. His smile faded as he realized Calhoun had managed to lead more zombies to the fort. With a sigh, he lifted the walkie-talkie.

"Peggy, Calhoun is here."

"Yeah, I know. Feels like old times, huh?" Her voice sounded amused yet weary.

Juan laughed a little. "Yeah. Strangely, yeah."

"...certain I did not vote on this fort being built..."

## 3. Purple Dresses

Nerit walked into the large room used as the "store" of the fort. Everything salvaged from the town's various stores was arranged in boxes and plastic bins. Manny and Peggy had worked hard to organize everything. Every box was labeled. One long table had small boxes full of personal hygiene products. She noted the box with the condoms was steadily diminishing. She had heard Shane mentioning that they were on his shopping list as he had headed out earlier along with cigarettes and booze. The younger people of the fort were finding comfort in each other. She could not blame them.

Snagging a box of Marlboro Lights, she tucked it into the plastic bag she was using as a shopping cart and headed to the far side of the room where gloves, hats and scarves were grouped. She needed a new pair of gloves, preferably leather.

Coming around the corner of the aisle, she found Katie on the floor going through boxes labeled "Women's Dresses". She looked frustrated as she dug down to the bottom of one of the big bins.

"Needing a new dress?" Nerit asked as she began to look through the box of gloves.

"I got it into my head that I need one for the party tonight," Katie confessed. Next to her was a very sexy pair of high heels. "I found the shoes, but no dress."

Nerit pulled out a pair of soft leather gloves and began to try them on. "Nice shoes."

"Yeah, I think they belonged to one of those women that got eaten in the dining room. I asked Peggy about them and she said they were found kicked under a table in a hall. She thinks the woman took them off to run easier. Lucky for me, they fit."

Nerit flexed her hand in the glove and pretended to fire a gun. They were a little stiff, but leather did tend to soften up and mold to fit. "So, what brought on this need for a new dress?"

Katie looked up at her, her expression a little embarrassed, but a glow seeming to emanate from her face. She looked happy.

Nerit grinned. "Oh, Travis."

Katie laughed. "That obvious, huh?"

With a slight nod, Nerit said, "Well, yes, if someone was paying attention. You've played it very low-key. He has been far more obvious."

Yanking another dress out, Katie looked at it, then sighed.

"This town wasn't the hub of fashion," Nerit said.

"Yeah, I noticed." Katie pulled out another box and began to look through it.

Nerit slid the gloves into her bag and walked over to a box filled with Halloween costumes. It had been part of the overstock in the grocery store that had been taken in soon after this had all started. She began to look through the items, her mind twirling ideas around.

"What color do you like to wear?"

"Purple. Lydia always liked me in purple or blue," Katie pulled out a plain navy dress several sizes too large for her frame and sighed.

Drawing a purple sorceress outfit from the box of costumes, she looked at Katie. "Like this color?"

"I am not wearing a Halloween costume."

"If we can locate a sewing kit, I can modify it," Nerit assured her.

Katie stood up and looked at the dress. "Really?"

Nerit nodded. "Oh, yes. It won't be as fancy as anything from Versace, but I can make it work."

"I'm desperate. If you think you can do it, I'm all for it," Katie said with excitement and quickly began to look for sewing supplies.

Nerit laid the dress down on the floor and began to turn it this way and that, thinking hard, ideas flicking in and out of her mind, trying to figure out what she could do.

"I am glad that you are moving on," Nerit said thoughtfully. "Letting go is always hard."

"I wasn't sure I could," Katie confessed as she found some small sewing kits in a basket. "Honestly, I still suffer some guilt over moving on from Lydia."

"I had three husbands. I understand very well," Nerit assured her. She was very happy for Katie and confident that she and Travis being together was a good thing, but she also knew that Lydia would always be a part of Katie and never truly fade away

"I'm doing better than I was," Katie decided. "Accepting it more."

"It's a journey," Nerit agreed. "Just take one step at a time."

Katie walked back to Nerit and knelt beside her with the sewing kits. Nerit looked up into the younger woman's face and could see an unspoken question in her eyes. "Yes?"

"Can you make it a sexy dress?"

Nerit smirked and nodded. "Oh, yes. I can."

## 4. The Stage Is Set

Travis stood up and stretched. His eyes were growing weary and he could no longer concentrate on the plans he was working on for walling in Main Street. It had reached the point where he needed to take a break and not think about it anymore. He stretched again and felt the pleasant burn of scratches on his back. It had been a long time since he had worn any. It felt good.

Pushing the office door open, he moved down the hall, running his hand over his hair. It wasn't until Katie had left that he had realized they had made a major mistake. It had been awhile since he had been with any woman and when he had been, it had been in a monogamous relationship where she had been on the Pill. Since Katie had spent the last decade with a woman....

Of course, it wasn't really an excuse. Their first time together they had both had condoms ready to go.

Stepping into the hot afternoon air, he had to wonder if maybe they hadn't done it subconsciously. His thoughts were definitely in the realm of forever.

He was done looking. Katie was it. And maybe in some sort of Darwinian way, he was trying to secure that relationship with a child.

"Peggy, I am here to protest my treatment as a citizen of this city and the shoddy way that I have been treated since I arrived here in this fort that I did not vote on building. I was kept in that garage for over an hour being checked for bites. No, I do not allow anyone to bite me. I told this vampire once..."

Travis turned to see Crazy Calhoun being escorted to City Hall. Peggy was waiting for the town freak looking weary already. The crazy coot was carrying a video camera at his side and looked ready for an argument.

"Life just keeps getting more interesting," Travis muttered.

Shane moved toward him. "Hey, Travis, keep the lesbos from making out on the job. Seriously, they could have gotten us killed. They were so busy making out with each other they didn't even see us getting ready to leave a while back."

Travis lifted an eyebrow. "What are you talking about?"

"Now, I know you're into the blond and I'm sure you have all sorts of wild fantasies about her. Who doesn't? If that Jewish old hag is going to be running the guards, she better make sure her lesbos don't spend that time making out." Shane was obviously furious and ready for a fight.

"Okay, I'll let her know," Travis said in a calm tone.

"Oh, you better, because I'm not going to get my ass eaten because that blond lesbo chick can't keep her hands off her girlfriend," Shane spat, then stormed off followed, by his buddy, Philip.

Bewildered, Travis walked into the hotel. Some of the older people were gathered in the lobby, playing board games. He smiled and waved at them. Old Man Watson waved and smiled at him happily. Travis felt good about the decision to take the hotel. It definitely had created a real home for the survivors.

Behind him, Calhoun and Peggy entered the hotel.

"...and when did the city take over a privately owned building? This is socialism or communism. I can't remember which. I don't agree with you pushing your Amazonian agenda on the people of this fine town..."

Peggy sighed as she led Calhoun over to the front desk.

Calhoun glanced over and saw Travis. "Now, that young man came here to build the old theater and now he's breaking and entering into hotels. Why hasn't he been arrested? If what people are telling me is true, he is the dangerous ringleader of this new cult..."

Travis winked at a beleaguered Peggy, stepped into the elevator and thankfully watched the doors slide shut.

Reaching Katie's room a few minutes later, he knocked and waited for her to answer. When the door opened just a crack, he saw only Katie's eye staring out at him.

"Hi, uh, can we talk?" he asked.

"Um," Katie hesitated and looked behind her. "Now is really not a good time."

Travis was a little surprised by this. "Oh, I just thought...I guess I'll catch you later."

Katie opened the door a little wider. He caught site of her bare arm and shoulder. Keeping behind the door, she reached out and pulled him close and kissed him. "Later will be perfect."

"Don't move so much," Nerit's voice said from the room.

Travis raised an eyebrow. Katie only gave him an enormous grin.

"It's a secret," she said.

Jenni came down the hall holding a plastic bag. Seeing Travis, she shoved it into her jacket and tried to look innocent.

"Hi, Travis," she said, an impish expression on her face.

"Hey, Jenni," he answered.

As soon as Jenni was close enough, Katie opened the door enough to let her squeeze through, then immediately closed it to a slim crack again.

"Okay, obviously you guys are up to something," he said uneasily.

"Pretty much yeah," Katie answered. "I'll let you know what later."

Frowning just a tad, he backed away from the door. "Okay, then."

As the door closed, he turned and wandered down the hall feeling a little uneasy, but not really sure what was bothering him. He definitely did not give credence to Shane's words. With Nerit there, he was sure nothing that Shane had accused the girls of was happening, but he hated how for a moment, he had felt a twinge of suspicion.

Striding down the hall, he shoved his hands into his jean pockets, his brow furrowed. The elevator doors opened. Shane stood in there with Philip.

"Turned you away, huh?" Shane smirked.

Travis didn't answer and stepped into the elevator. He could literally feel Shane's anger boiling behind his back.

"Things have got to change around here," Shane said to Travis. "Or it's all going to go to hell."

The door opened on Travis' floor and he stepped out. He looked back at Shane. "It already has," he answered.

The elevator doors shut and Travis walked on.

# Chapter 11

## 1. The Characters Enter

The ballroom was alive with music, people, and the rich smell of food. The elderly had arrived first and were settled happily at a table in one corner, their weary bodies nestled into the plush velvet chairs. Rosie's dinner crew had laid out a fabulous buffet of chicken, wild rice, and assorted vegetables with big flaky biscuits and two different kinds of dessert. Someone had gone around collecting CDs. Music now played softly in the background.

Jason and Shelley made their way outside to meet up with the other teenagers and preteens. Gathering in the gazebo, they had hooked up a stereo to play music they wanted to hear and had lugged a cooler of soda out. One of the youngest of the group, Ricky, Shelley's younger brother, was hunched down sipping cola and looking at an old magazine. Jason sat down on a pillow and Shelley sat down beside him.

All together, there were a dozen kids in the fort. They had learned to stick together amidst all the adults. It wasn't easy at times. The adults were always so worried and scared they forgot the kids were just as anxious. They often tried to shield the kids from what was really going on, so the youngest of the survivors often had to find ways to glean information about what was going on.

Melanie, the oldest at eighteen, and Dylan, seventeen, were already smoking the pot they had found on the body of one of the waiters the day before. It had been the big news yesterday amongst the "shorties," as they called themselves. At first, it had just been cool that Melanie, Dylan, Shelley and Jason were allowed to work with the adults, but when there was a discovery of contraband, it had been pretty exciting.

"What's up?" Dylan asked as Jason reached out for the joint.

"Just a bunch of old people listening to country music so far. The food looked good," Jason answered.

"We grabbed munchies," Melanie said, sweeping her red hair out of her face. Handing over a bag of chips to Shelley, she added, "We were thinking about setting off fireworks later. Dylan bought some off that asshole Shane yesterday."

"Sounds like fun," Jason decided. He felt kinda old up here with the kids, smoking dope and swilling cola. He could feel Shelley's hand lying on his leg. It made him nervous. Nerit's talk about taking advantage of the moments of life they had now had really affected him. He was thinking about a lot of things in a different way. He had even made himself scarce when it was obvious in the early evening that Juan and Jenni needed time alone. It was time for him to chill out and try to enjoy life.

"Has your Mom remembered it's your birthday yet?" Melanie asked.

Jason shook his head. "Not yet. I keep waiting, but I'm not sure she even knows what month this is. She's kinda an airhead at times."

Shelley took the joint and inhaled deeply and swatted her brother's hand away when he reached for it. "You're too young."

Ricky frowned. "I'll tell Dad."

"Go ahead," Shelley dared, and thunked him on the head.

"Bitch," Ricky said sullenly, then sipped more cola.

The other kids joined them one by one. Soon, they were all joking and laughing. Drinking way too much soda and candy, the younger kids were soon very hyper, while their older, stoned counterparts just giggled.

Jason was feeling pretty good when Shelly gave him the first kiss of his young life. It wasn't expected so he blew it a little by trying to ask her what she was doing. Her lips pretty much hit his teeth and tongue. She drew back, leaving him startled.

"Sorry," she muttered.

"No, no, try it again," Jason said quickly, and flung his arms around her.

This sent Melanie and Dylan into guffaws of laughter, but Shelley smiled sweetly and kissed him firmly on the lips for about two seconds. It was enough to make him blush and grin.

"Ugh, no making out in front of me," Jenni said from above him.

Jason looked up to see her standing over him wearing a bright red tank top, a knee-length cotton skirt with black abstract designs on it and sandals. Her long hair flowed loose around her face. Juan was lingering at her side, his new cowboy hat looking far too neat on his tussled curls. Jason had seen him earlier trying to get it to look more worn. It had been funny watching Juan throwing it around and smacking it against things to break it in.

"Uh, busted," he decided.

"Yeah, you are."

"Oh, gawd," Jason moaned.

"I'm sorry," Shelley said quickly. "It's his birthday so..."

Jenni laughed. "Yeah, yeah, I know." She hugged Jason tightly and kissed his cheek, embarrassing him as only a mother could. She handed him a small brown bag as Juan sat down across from them. "Open it."

Jason smiled and opened up the bag to find a copy of "Ender's Game," his favorite book.

"I grabbed it a few weeks ago when scavenging the library," Juan explained.

Hugging his Mom, he kissed her cheek. "Thanks, Mom." To Juan's surprise, he hugged Juan, too. "Thanks, Dude."

Juan nodded. "No problem. Hope you enjoy it."

Jenni leaned over and snagged the joint from Dylan, who was trying to hide it. "What's this?"

"Look, I...uh...found it on a waiter. I think it's a cigarette..." Dylan mumbled.

"Sure you do," Jenni answered. She inhaled deeply and handed it to Juan.

"I'll pass," Juan said, and handed it back to Dylan.

"Shit," Dylan whispered in awe, staring at the doorway to the ballroom.

Jason looked up to see Katie in the doorway. She was wearing a very slinky purple halter dress with high heels. She looked absolutely hot. He must have been staring, because Shelley smacked his arm.

Katie walked over to join them, her heels clicking on the patio. Dylan was openly gawking. Juan looked over and whistled. With a grin, Katie sat next to Jenni and tucked her legs to one side.

"Katie, you're totally hot," Dylan said in awe.

"Thank you!" Katie beamed.

Jason noted she was actually wearing makeup and had let her hair fall free and curly to her shoulders. "Yeah, totally." Shelley smacked him again and he looked at her and said, "Well, you are, too. Seriously, you are." He kissed her cheek. Her smile was a relief.

"Yeah, I put on her makeup and fixed her hair. She has a hot date tonight," Jenni said.

"Yeah, who?" Melanie looked very curious. "I didn't think there were other gay girls."

"Travis, actually. I'm..." she faltered, "open-minded."

Jason knew this wasn't the case at all, but figured Katie didn't feel like going into the details of it all. He was glad Katie was looking happy. For a long time, she had looked rather sad.

"Cool," Dylan said with a wide grin that had Melanie glaring at him. "Wanna smoke?"

Katie took the joint and arched an eyebrow. "You do realize I was a prosecutor before the zombies."

Dylan blinked. "Oh."

Katie shrugged. "Oh, well. I haven't done any since college." She took a drag and handed it back.

Jason couldn't help, but stare as the smoke unfurled from her lips. She was really, really hot tonight.

Ricky, again, reached for the joint. Shelley smacked his hand. There was a brother/sister tussle and lots of giggling over it. The world on top of the hotel was full of laughter. Jason found himself smiling more than he had for a long time.

When his Mom and Juan helped Katie to her feet so they could go join the other adults inside, he stood up and hugged them all again.

"Travis is pretty lucky," he said to Katie.

"So is Shelley," Katie answered back.

Jason blushed and sat back down as the adults left.

"Super damn hot," Dylan said, watching Katie leave.

Jason laughed as Melanie smacked him. He turned to Shelley and kissed her very firmly on the lips.

It was an okay birthday after all.

## 2. Hell Erupts

Katie felt a little embarrassed as she entered the ballroom. Nerit's amazing work on the Halloween costume had resulted in a slinky dress that made her slim, athletic build look very womanly. It tied behind her neck and revealed her strong shoulders before gliding down over her hips and ending in a slanted hemline that accentuated the curve of her legs. Despite all her bruises, she looked amazing.

She felt very much like a girl and it made her a little nervous. No one would have ever called her a dyke before, but she was most comfortable when dressed in her running clothes or a good pair of jeans and a tank top. Dressing up was what Lydia had been good at while she had just tried her best to look presentable when they went out. But tonight, she felt that she had achieved a level of femininity that was new territory for her. She felt like a bombshell.

Feeling a bit lightheaded and giddy from the pot, she moved to the bar where Felix was playing bartender.

"A glass of wine," she said and blushed under his awed stare.

Sipping the chilled white wine, she began to make her rounds around the ballroom, greeting people, and trying not to look too anxiously for Travis.

Juan and Jenni were out on the dance floor laughing and hoofing it up to some country music. They were both pretty good and their moves were fluid and graceful. A few older people were on the floor as well, moving slower, but obviously enjoying themselves.

Peggy was trying hard to get away from a tall, older man who smelled so badly Katie winced. She recognized him as the crazy old guy who had arrived on the scooter. He was talking rapidly and waving a video camera around.

"...so you can tell the Mayor that I don't believe he has the flu and I think he is avoiding me as he always does, because I alone know the real truth of what he is planning to do. And I plan to write letters to the media and report to them how he has blocked their transmissions from this town so he can..."

Peggy walked by Katie and whispered, "Nice dress" then kept walking with the crazy man right behind her.

Finishing up her glass of wine, she went back for another and found Bill at the bar, drinking a beer.

"Nice dress, Katie," he said with an appreciative smile.

"Thanks, Bill. I'm trying to impress someone tonight."

"Well, I'm impressed, if that counts."

She laughed and nodded. "Yes, it does. How are you doing?"

"Still trying to figure out this vigilante business, but letting it go for now. We have a lot of other stuff to worry about."

"That we do," Katie admitted. She was now feeling very lightheaded and a bit tipsy and her shoes suddenly seemed way too high to walk in, but she gave Bill a soft smile and turned to watch Jenni and Juan tearing up the dance floor.

Among all the fond memories of her life, one of them was when Lydia saw her for the first time in her wedding dress. The look of awe and love in her lover's eyes would stay with Katie forever. It was only matched by the look on Travis face when he finally entered the ballroom looking very handsome in a dark blue shirt, jeans, his leather jacket with his freshly washed hair curling slightly over his brow. She finally knew what it looked like to see someone struck speechless.

Walking across the room toward him, she enjoyed his look of absolute adoration and awe. She set her wineglass down on a table and held out her hand to him and he took it, blinking slowly. His hand was slightly trembling and sweaty in hers.

"Damn," was all he managed.

"You like?"

"Damn," he said again.

"This is what Nerit was helping me with earlier," she went on.

"I'll thank Nerit later," Travis decided.

"Want to dance?" she asked.

Travis got the goofiest look on his face. It made her laugh.

"I have other things in mind, but dancing is good for now," he responded.

Taking her hand, he guided her out onto the dance floor and drew her close. They danced slowly to a ballad sung by Patsy Kline, slipping across the highly-polished floor gracefully. Staring into each other's eyes, they were oblivious to all the looks of approval they were receiving. Old Man Watson even applauded as they danced past his table. At last, to everyone in the room, it was clear that Travis and Katie were in love with each other.

When the song finished, and Travis kissed Katie softly, the room erupted into applause.

Giggling, a little too tipsy and stoned for her own good, Katie clung to Travis, embarrassed. Travis just looked dazed and happy and did a little bow to those in the room. The laughter that followed was heartfelt and warming. He turned and kissed her again. Katie was absolutely happy.

A few glasses of wine later, she found it harder to stand in her shoes. Plus, she was having issues keeping her hands off Travis. She was sure they were making a spectacle of themselves. When they sat down to eat some dinner, she had sat on his lap.

"Disgusting," Jenni decided. "You two are disgustingly happy together."

Old Man Watson sat nearby, nodding, pointing at them, and smiling. Peggy had finally ditched Calhoun onto Old Man Watson and she grinned at Katie and Travis.

"I always knew those rumors about you liking women was bullshit," Peggy said with a wink.

Katie opened her mouth to correct her, but Travis lightly pinched her leg. She thought better of it.

Finally, she knew the wine had gotten the best of her and she excused herself to the restroom. Walking out of the ballroom, she felt even more lightheaded and giddy and was cursing herself for drinking too much and the hit of pot she had taken.

The foyer was empty when she entered it and she hesitated to fix her shoe. The elevator doors opened. Philip and Shane came into view.

"Fuck," Philip said staring at her.

Katie looked up, saw their expressions, and her blood turned to ice. Ignoring them, she moved quickly to the restroom and slipped in. The last thing she needed was a confrontation with Shane and his sidekick when she was drunk and a little stoned.

Splashing cold water on her face, she took a deep breath and felt a little better. Realizing she had smudged her makeup, she picked up a hand towel and started to dab at her eyeliner. When she looked up into the mirror, she saw Shane staring at her.

Twisting around, she fell back against the counter top. "Get out."

"It's a damn shame that a fine piece of ass like you is a carpet muncher," he said in a low, dangerous voice.

"Get out!"

"Look at those titties," he said, and reached out and grabbed one of her breasts.

She thrust his hand away and repeated in a low voice, "Get out now."

"And that ass," he said. His gaze was dangerous and feral.

Katie felt horrifyingly sober at all at once. She knew this wasn't another one of the stupid confrontations they had when they threw insults back and forth. This was damn serious. He had already touched her and it would now be easier for him.

"Get out now!"

He moved fast and she tried to duck away. His hand gripped the straps of her dress and he yanked hard. Her breasts fell free from her dress and she picked up a decorative candle holder from the marble counter top and swung it at his head.

Blood sprayed over her as she managed to hit his nose. Enraged, he tackled her full force, sending both of them sprawling across the long marble counter. Gripping her hair, he shoved her hard up against the wall and pushed himself between her legs. She beat on him with her fists, and began to claw at him.

"I'll teach you to cock tease me, bitch," he hissed.

Fumbling with her dress, he tried to grab hold of her panties.

It was then Katie started to scream.

***

Travis felt too happy for words. He now knew what it meant to be beaming with happiness. After Katie sashayed out in that damn hot dress, many of his friends had come to congratulate and wish him the best.

"You're damn lucky." Bill winked.

"I would say you have the hottest girlfriend in town, but Stacey would kill me," Eric added as he got drinks for him and his girlfriend at the bar.

Travis laughed and flushed a little.

Jack, Pepe, and Nerit's old dog, Tucker, scampered past him, dancing around with doggy delight. The party was in full swing now and everyone was having fun. Travis smiled as he saw Lenore and her best friend, Ken, dancing away in one corner and Katarina and Peggy line dancing to one side. Even Belinda had come out and sat at a table with Rosie and Linda, Juan's cousin. Belinda's eyes were red from crying. Travis couldn't blame her mourning Mike's death. If Katie had died yesterday, he didn't think he would even be able to function.

He was so grateful they were both alive and together.

A minute or two later when Curtis approached he assumed the younger man was coming up to him to make some comment about what a lucky man he was. But then it became obvious that Curtis was really upset about something.

"Travis, I found contraband on the kids," Curtis said in a low voice. "They were smoking pot out in the gazebo. I confiscated what they had, but there may be more."

"Pot, huh?" Travis considered this. "Well, they are kids..."

"We are rebuilding this society. We do not need drugs to worm their way back into it and destroy our youth!"

"Well, Curtis, look around. Half the adults in here are pretty damn drunk. Hell, I'm on my way, too. A little pot isn't going to hurt them."

"Pot is a gateway drug!"

"To what? The drug war is over, Curtis. The kids found some pot. Big deal. Once they smoke it, it's gone. It's over. I smoked it myself back in the day. And I'm a fine outstanding citizen," Travis said in a voice he hoped wasn't too condescending. He was really annoyed with Curtis ruining the kids' party. Yeah, he wasn't fond of the idea of the kids smoking, but it wasn't going to kill them.

"I thought you would be a little more understanding," Curtis said in a tone that was half-hurt, half-angry. "I really did."

"Well, I am understanding, but I don't think it's such a big deal in the grand scheme of things." Travis sighed. "Sorry, Curtis, but I don't. I'm going to go check on Katie. She's a little blitzed."

Curtis sighed, then nodded. "Okay...okay. I guess I'll drop it."

Travis squeezed Curtis shoulder and walked out into the foyer. He noticed Philip standing near the women's bathroom the second he was in the hall and he paused in his steps. Rubbing his chin, he moved toward Philip slowly.

"Have you seen Katie?" he asked.

Philip turned, startled. "Oh, um, yeah. She went into the ladies room with someone."

"What?"

Philip looked a little flustered. "Yeah, she, uh, she, uh...you know. She's trying out the other side of the fence."

"What the fuck are you talking about?"

Philip stepped away from the door, looking vastly uncomfortable. "She came on to Shane, all slutty-like, saying she wanted to know what it felt like to have a man."

Travis didn't even respond. He burst through the bathroom door and took in the scene.

Katie was fighting Shane as he tried to push himself into her. Katie had one hand planted hard into his throat, but the other was twisted behind her back. Shane was exposed and the sight enraged Travis.

"Get off my girlfriend," Travis shouted. He grabbed Shane by the shoulders and sent him flying across the room.

"Travis," Katie sobbed.

"Baby, I'm here," Travis said, wiping away her tears. His heart was thudding so hard in his chest it hurt. The anger he felt was so intense it was pulsing in his temples. He was torn between comforting her and beating the shit out of Shane.

Shane resolved that dilemma by punching him in the kidneys and knocking him forward into Katie.

"Leave us alone!" Katie slammed her fists against Shane.

Travis twisted around and nailed Shane with a hard left to the jaw. He tackled him to the ground and began to slam his fist into his opponent's face over and over again.

Philip appeared, grabbed Travis and swung him around into the wall.

"Run, Katie," Travis grunted, turned, and swung at Philip.

To his relief, she managed to evade Shane and run out the door. It slammed shut with a resounding boom and left him trapped with Shane and Philip bearing down on him.

## 3. Descending into Chaos

The foyer seemed to swirl around her, then Katie found her bearings and backed away from the bathroom. She could hear the men inside fighting with each other and tears streamed down her face. Nearly falling, a she walked to the doorway to the ballroom. She pulled the top of her dress up around her breasts.

Already the self-incrimination was starting.

*...how could she drink so much...*

*...why had she worn such a sexy dress...*

*...why hadn't she just gone back into the ballroom, not the bathroom when she had seen Shane...*

Stumbling to the doorway, she called out in a hoarse voice, "Can someone help Travis?"

Nerit saw her first and immediately walked toward her. She caught Jenni's arm as she passed her on the dance floor and Jenni looked startled until she saw Katie. She immediately ran to her.

Katie flung her arms around Jenni and held onto her tightly. "Someone needs to help Travis."

"What happened? Where is he?"

Juan ran up just as Katie pointed toward the bathroom. "Shane...Shane...he...he..."

"Shit!" Juan cursed and ran for the bathroom.

He was almost to the door when it was flung open. Travis came stumbling out backwards with Shane right on him. Juan was in the fray immediately, shoving Shane off his feet and into a planter. He was sucker punched by Philip as the older man barreled through the door.

"Break it up!" Bill shouted as he ran out of the ballroom. Curtis was right behind him and they ran toward the brawlers.

Shane recovered enough to kick out at Travis and trip him. Travis stumbled, but regained his feet. He whirled around and slammed his fist into Shane's jaw. The men began to exchange a flurry of blows as Juan struggled with Philip.

"Break it up!" Bill managed to hook his arm around Shane's neck and haul him backward away from Travis.

Travis lunged forward for one last punch, but Curtis caught him. "That's enough, Travis."

"Did you see what he did to Katie?"

Katie clung to Jenni, sobbing. The sight of her made Travis even more upset and Curtis had to put extra pressure on his arm to keep him under control.

Juan and Philip were still grappling with each other. Finally, Juan managed to get him down to the ground. Roger and a few other men hurried to help subdue Phillip.

"He fuckin' attacked me out of nowhere! I demand you arrest him!" Shane was still struggling to get free, his angry gaze on Travis.

"You were hurting Katie!"

"The bitch wanted to try out a man. Yer just jealous she didn't pick you!"

Nerit very calmly said, "If you hadn't been late to the party tonight, Shane, you would realize how foolish your words sound to everyone. Katie and Travis made it very clear tonight that they are a couple."

Shane turned his bloodied face toward her and said, "Back off, Jewbitch. I don't give a fuck what you say."

"It's true, Shane," Bill said pulling him away from Travis. "You better come up with a better story."

"The lesbo wanted to try out a man," Shane hissed through his bloodied teeth.

"You sonnofabitch," Katie said in an angry voice. "You tried to rape me!"

"You can't rape the willing," Shane spat back.

"That's it," Jenni said.

She launched herself at Shane and managed to get in a few good slugs before she was yanked off of him by Roger and carried away to a safe distance.

Nerit slid her sweater around Katie's shoulders and drew it close over her breasts. Katie was trembling, but was looking more in control of herself.

"Let me go," Travis ordered Curtis. "I want to go to Katie."

Curtis hesitated, then let go of Travis.

Travis was walking to Katie when Shane managed to slip free of Bill and landed a solid punch to Travis' jaw. They went down in a jumble, fists, flying once more.

Nerit let go of Katie and picked up a candleholder from a nearby corner table. Bill and Curtis once more tried to draw the two fighters apart. It was hard going with both men determined to kill each other. Nerit finally managed to squeeze in between the two cops and clocked Shane across the back of the head. He collapsed over Travis. Bill and Curtis immediately dragged him off.

Travis struggled to his feet and reached for Katie. She took his hand and pulled him up and into her arms. Clinging to him, she stared angrily at Shane.

Bill and Curtis finally got Shane and Philip handcuffed and managed to get the crowd in the foyer to step back.

"We didn't do nothing wrong!" Philip was shouting. Next to him, Shane was slumped over unconscious.

"I want to know what is going on right now," Bill said in a loud voice that sent most of the people in the room into silence.

"That bitch lead Shane on then Travis busted in on them--" Philip began in an almost shrill voice.

"From Katie, I want to know from Katie," Bill said.

Travis gently rubbed her back as she took a deep breath. "I went into the bathroom to splash water on my face and Shane followed me in. Then he...he...attacked me...and...I fought him...until Travis came..."

"I'm going to kick his ass!" Jenni started across the foyer again and Juan grabbed her right before she reached Shane. She was cussing away in Spanish with impressive dramatic flair.

"Jenni, back off," Curtis ordered.

Travis looked ready to beat the hell out of Shane again, but Katie clinging to him forced him to calm down. He wrapped his arms tightly around her and held her close, laying his cheek on the top of her head.

"That bitch asked Shane into the bathroom with her and said she wanted to try out a man," Philip protested. "They asked me to stay outside and not let anyone interrupt. Shane was more than willing to the turn the lesbo straight."

"Oh, please," Peggy said, rolling her eyes. "She's with Travis. She's obviously not gay."

"And if she was, it wouldn't make no difference if Shane was trying to rape her," Bill said firmly.

Shane managed to open one swollen eye and slurred, "She fuckin' begged me."

Jenni shouted something about Shane being a puto and tried kicking him. Juan dragged her a little further away from Shane.

"Let's get them down into the holding cell," Bill said to Curtis. "We're not going to get anything settled like this."

Curtis nodded and motioned for Roger and a few other men to help him. Philip and Shane were then half-dragged, half-carried into the elevator and disappeared from view.

"What are you going to do with them?" Jenni asked angrily.

"Nothing yet. Need to get the story down and process it. Then we'll decide," Bill answered.

"Throw them over the wall," someone shouted from the back of the crowd. There were murmurs of agreement.

"I think the clones would enjoy playing with them," Calhoun said from somewhere in the crowd. "Obviously, those two men have no protection against the alien overlords and are controlled by evil forces."

Bill walked up to Katie and Travis and said softly, "Katie, want to sit down with me and give a short statement."

She nodded and pulled Nerit's sweater tighter around her shoulders. "Yeah. I would." She seemed to be gathering her strength and her jaw was set determinedly.

Bill motioned to those standing around. "Go back into the party now. Clear this area out. There's been enough drama."

People began to slowly walk away, talking to each other in hushed voices. Juan had pulled Jenni aside and was talking to her softly in Spanish, obviously trying to calm her down. Nerit stood stoically next to Travis and Katie.

At last, Bill guided Katie into the elevator, Travis right beside her. Nerit, Juan, and Jenni followed along with Peggy. They all rode down in silence to the lobby, where Bill sat Katie down in one of the comfortable chairs and very gently questioned her on all that had happened.

When the statement was finished, Bill pulled Travis aside and whispered, "I'm going to get the Mayor down here and we'll need to have a meeting about this."

Travis nodded, his jaw set grimly.

"I need you to be calm though," Bill added.

Travis sighed then said, "I know. But she's...she's...my everything..."

"I know. But still, we need to decide what is best for all of us."

Travis rubbed his brow then nodded again. "Okay. I'll be back down in an hour. I want to get her settled."

"Okay, then we'll meet at midnight in the hotel manager's office."

"I'll be there, Bill." Travis moved toward Katie. It hurt him to see her looking so traumatized. He could see how hard she was trying to not give into her emotions. He felt proud of her for that.

How this was all going to end was beyond him, but it felt as if they were quickly descending into chaos.

## 4. The Casting of Lots

Katie could hear Juan and Jenni talking swiftly in Spanish in her bedroom as she gently eased her way out of her once sexy purple dress, that was now only tatters, as she stood in the bathroom. Jenni was still in full-blown "Shane must die" mode and Juan was trying to get her calmed down.

"Let me help." He sat on the counter watching her with the saddest eyes.

She was hurting. She was sure the bruises would be showing up soon to add to all her other bruises. Shane had not actually hit her, but he had wrestled her with brutal intensity.

"My arm hurts where he twisted it," she admitted.

Travis sighed and fought down his anger. He drew her close and gently helped her out of the rest of her clothes. The water was already running hot in the shower. He stood up and pulled the curtain aside.

Stepping into the shower, Katie looked back at his battered face. Reaching out, she touched it lightly. "Come in with me?"

"If it won't upset you," he answered.

She shook her head. "No. It won't. You make me feel safe."

He smiled and undressed. Stepping in behind her, he tenderly rubbed her back. They silently helped each other wash away the blood and grime from their battle. It hurt Katie to see Travis' bruises, but at the same time, it made her feel protected. She knew he would defend her with his life if he had to. Finally, she just rested in his arms until the water ran cold and they were forced to get out.

Travis helped Katie into her pajamas and dressed himself in his old clothes. They hadn't discussed it yet, but Katie was sure he would be moving in with her soon. Before they stepped back into her bedroom, she drew him close. They shared several soft, tender kisses. He held her gently against him for a few precious seconds.

Jenni looked less agitated when they finally emerged from the bathroom.

"How are you feeling?" Juan asked.

"Okay, I think," Katie answered, and crawled onto the bed and lay down.

Travis hovered over her, gently stroking her hair. "She's a fighter."

Jenni sighed and moved to sit with Katie. "Yeah, but that puto should never have been released after the first time he beat up on her."

Travis nodded. "Can't say I don't agree with that." Leaning over, he kissed Katie's cheek.

"What do you think will happen next?" Katie reached out to hold Travis' battered hand.

"Not sure. I'm sure something has to be done, but we don't really have anything in place to deal with this. It's not like any of us are elected officials." Travis rubbed his brow. "There is no easy way to deal with this. And I better get down stairs and see what's up."

Juan stood up as well. "I'm going with you. Shane's had run-ins with Jenni. It could have easily have been her in there with him, or any woman, really."

Travis nodded. "He's dangerous. And we have to accept that."

Katie pulled lightly on his battered and bruised hand. He leaned over and kissed her. "I trust you to do what is right."

Travis smiled. "I wish I trusted myself."

Katie reluctantly let go. Jenni snuggled up next to her, spooning her, her body a comforting presence. The men shut the door behind them and left them in the comforting glow of a lamp.

"I punched him pretty hard," Jenni said after a long pause.

Katie couldn't help, but laugh. "I noticed. Thank you." She turned and kissed Jenni's cheek. "You're a very good friend."

"The absolute best," Jenni said with a wink.

Snuggling back down, Katie pushed thoughts of Shane out of her mind and slowly relaxed in Jenni's arms until she finally found sleep.

\*\*\*

The elevator doors opened onto a lobby full of people. None of them were speaking in anything close to calm tones. Voices ricocheted off the marble floor and pink granite columns to fill the room with chaos.

As Travis and Juan stepped into the chaos, Rosie grabbed onto Juan's arm. His mother's brow was furrowed with worry and her lips were tight with agitation. "Is she okay?"

"Yeah, resting," Travis answered in a low, terse voice.

"What's up with all this, Mama?" Juan looked around in confusion.

"People are very upset," Rosie answered. Her expression was just as strained as those gathered in the lobby. "About what happened..."

Juan heard Travis let out a low sigh and understood his agitation. He could feel the tension in the lobby building around them. Everyone was voicing his or her own vehement opinion about the events of the night.

Bill stood in the middle of the chaos looking amazingly calm. Curtis, on the other hand, looked overwhelmed. Juan couldn't blame him. The rookie cop was the only survivor of the small police department that had once patrolled the small town that now was a wasteland surrounding the fort. It was a good thing Bill was able to keep an unruffled, steady demeanor. Juan wasn't so composed. He wanted to go drag Shane and Philip out of the fort and feed them to the zombies.

"This is ridiculous," Travis muttered. "This a mob."

"You cannot allow him to stay in the fort. He is a danger," Eric said to Bill in a loud voice. He shoved his glasses further up his nose and gave Bill the sternest look he could muster. Stacey stood at his side clutching his arm as their small dog, Pepe, tap-danced around their feet, excited by all the noise.

"You just can't turn him out," Steven Mann protested nearby. He was dressed in his very expensive clothes and standing apart with his wife away from the rest of the people in the lobby.

"Why not? He is a danger to the women of this fort." Stacey put her hands on her slim hips and glared at Steven. "You should worry about your wife."

Blanche Mann rolled her eyes. "Please. I wouldn't lead him on like that blond slut did."

Travis took a step forward, but Juan grabbed his arm. "Dude, keep focused."

Travis took another deep breath.

"What a man and woman do is their own business," Ed said from nearby. His grizzled features were emotionless.

"Ed, you can't believe that Katie allowed Shane to-" Peggy started.

Ed cut her off by saying, "I wasn't there. Can't say what did or didn't happen. But whatever did go down, it's between them."

"So you won't mind if Katie shoves Shane over the wall?" Juan asked. He folded his arms over his chest to keep from punching someone. He was close to losing his temper, but knew he had to keep it in check. He was already under suspicion for what had happened to Ritchie and Jimmy.

Travis was silent beside Juan, but he was fuming. Juan could see him clenching his hands at his sides.

"Now, I didn't say that," Ed answered. "Just sayin' that it's a personal thing between them."

"She was leading him on," Blanche said. "We all saw it."

"Actually, we all saw her getting cozy with Travis," Peggy drawled. She gave Blanche a look of disgust.

More voices chimed in. Frustration and anger made them harsh with emotion. People began to argue with each other in small groups. It was becoming raucous.

"All I know is that man is nasty and he shouldn't be allowed to stay!" This was from Lenore. The black girl stomped her foot and put her hands on her ample hips as she glared at Blanche.

"We gotta do something," Curtis said to Bill. "We can't let Shane go around assaulting women."

"What do you we suggest we do? Due process isn't around no more," Bill reminded him.

"Then we find a new way," Juan interjected.

People murmured in agreement.

"A fair and just way to deal with situations like this," Rosie added, supporting her son.

"Because this won't be the last time someone breaks the law," Curtis said in a morose tone.

"We are civilized people. We need to remember that," Travis finally said.

The arguing people around them fell into silence at the sound of his voice. Travis rubbed his chin slowly and thoughtfully. He looked up at all the faces surrounding him.

"What do you want, Travis?" Juan's voice had a hard edge to it, but he couldn't help it. He was pissed off. He couldn't imagine how Travis was feeling. The need to protect the women they loved was a trait they shared.

"Yeah, Travis," Peggy said. "What do you want to do?"

Travis lowered his hand, and sighed. "My inclination is to feed both of them to the zombies, but that isn't the right thing to do."

"Hey, I'm fine with feeding them to the zombies," Lenore answered.

"Me, too," Ken chimed in next to her.

"He is a danger to this fort as a whole," Eric said firmly. "He can't be trusted."

"I think this discussion should be handled in a more discreet setting," Manny, the Mayor, said as he joined the group.

People fell silent as he moved to the center of the crowd. The Mayor had been sick for days and his health was waning. He had suffered a heart attack a few years back and he was without his medication now. He was a fading figure in the politics of the fort, but he had the respect of many in the town. He was known for being amiable, good-natured, and a peacemaker. All the things that had helped him keep the peace with a cantankerous city council and opinionated townsfolk worked against him in the new world. He was not a fighter, he was not a firm hand; he was the kindly uncle who just wanted everyone to get along. Despite the anger in the lobby, people still respected him.

Juan thought Manny was right. The discussion needed to be taken elsewhere before the crowd became a mob, but the Mayor's breed of leadership wasn't going to help in this situation. Manny would look for a compromise. Juan didn't have the desire to throw down with the Mayor in front of everyone, so he shrugged and looked at Travis.

"I'm willing to discuss this in a more calm setting," his friend finally said.

"Good. Bill, Curtis, Juan, Peggy, and Travis, please join me in my office." The crowd murmured, but seemed somewhat satisfied. Smiling like a true politician, Manny shook the hands of a few people as he made his way back through the crowd.

Juan followed, his agitation settling into his shoulders. He felt tense and angry and he glanced over toward Travis. If he felt wired up, he was sure Travis was worse. But, regardless of the situation, his friend looked surprisingly calm. Only the tension in his neck gave away his internal turmoil.

"It's going to be okay, man," Juan assured him.

"I keep telling myself that," Travis answered grimly.

A few people patted Travis on the shoulder as he passed by them.

"We're behind you on this, Travis," Eric said.

"I say we throw him over the wall!" Lenore said loudly again.

Juan sighed and shoved his hands into the pockets of his jeans as he walked toward the office. Tonight was a bitch and only bound to get worse.

***

Travis entered the office and looked around the room. The Mayor, looking very ill, was already hunched down in a chair in the corner while Peggy spritzed the air with Lysol. Bill and Curtis took their places in deep leather chairs. Juan flopped onto a couch while Travis leaned against the wall.

"So, are we throwing them over the wall?" Juan asked.

Bill looked up and shook his head. "Phillip and Shane are both sticking to their story that Katie asked Shane for sex and Travis assaulted them."

"That's bullshit," Travis muttered.

"Yeah. But they are corroborating each others stories," Bill answered.

"And I'm corroborating Katie's. I saw what Shane was trying to do!" Travis felt his temper rising. "She was fighting him!"

Manny coughed and wheezed, then said, "Shane and Phillip have been invaluable to this community with their salvaging expeditions. We need to take that into consideration."

"They also tried to rape Katie," Travis snapped.

"And Shane beat her up that day for shooting his brother when he got chewed up by a zombie," Peggy added. "She was doing us all a favor before he turned."

"He's shit on our heels," Curtis said in a low voice.

"He deserves some sort of due process," Bill said firmly.

"He deserves to be chunked over the wall!" Juan exclaimed. "There is no fucking due process anymore. You even said that! The world ended. All that is in the past!"

"C'mon now, Juan. We can't be going off all half-cocked and pissed off and start chunking people over the wall. You know that," Bill said sternly.

Peggy sighed heavily. "Yet, we're the ones that everyone looks at to make it better. Bill, those people out there expect us to do something. You especially."

"That doesn't give us the right to choose the fate of these men." Bill shook his head. "I don't want that kinda of power. Do you?"

"Chunk them over the damn wall," Juan repeated. "I'm willing to take that power."

Bill gave Juan a sharp, thoughtful look. Travis reached out to calm his friend down. The last thing Juan needed to do was draw even more suspicion on himself.

"They do expect us to do something," Peggy said. "All those people out in the lobby expect you-" she pointed to the Mayor, and then Bill "-to do something."

"They think he's guilty," Manny said in a soft voice. "I can't condemn a man just because there is a consensus by a lot of angry people that he did something wrong."

"You have to believe Katie," Travis protested. "You have to believe us. You know those guys are trouble."

"They are entitled to some sort of due process, Travis," Bill said determinedly. "Whatever the hell that is. I'm not even sure anymore, but we gotta come up with something."

Curtis snorted. "They gave that up when they attacked Katie."

"And who makes that choice?" Bill looked around the room. "When did we decide that? And by 'we,' I mean the whole damn fort. I thought we were trying to make a new civilization for ourselves, not chaos. I do not want that much power. The power to put a man over the wall because a bunch of people believe he did something wrong."

Travis winced at his words and rubbed his hands over his face trying to focus himself and not let his deep anger overwhelm him.

Peggy sighed and fumbled with her collar nervously. "I won't feel comfortable if they stay here."

"But they do contribute to our society as a whole," Manny interjected. "They've brought us many supplies. We have food to eat because they risked their lives to bring it back into the fort. They are not bad men. Maybe stupid, but not ba-"

"Manny, rape is bad! Okay! It's bad. Stop being an idiot," Peggy snapped.

The Mayor winced and drew back in his chair. Before he could answer, the door opened unexpectedly.

Calhoun shuffled in with his camera. "I am now filming a top secret city council meeting that was not announced in the public notices. I am filming all conspirators--"

"Gawddammit, Calhoun," Curtis exclaimed. "This is not a city council meeting."

"And it's not top secret," Peggy added. "The Mayor announced it in the lobby."

"The city secretary speaks. She is devious and the secret power of this town. She controls the Mayors as they come in and out of office. She is the one that sets the true agenda. Now Peggy, the Amazonian who controls all we see, speaks-"

"Gawddammit, Calhoun, anyone worth their salt knows the true power in small town Texas is the city secretary," Peggy responded. "Shit, it's the big joke when I go to Austin with all the city secretaries for election school. Most of them don't even see the Mayor except for when they phone 'em up to sign paperwork. Manny wasn't in the office but for a few hours each damn day. So stop jabbering about what everyone knows!"

Calhoun looked speechless, then turned the camera toward himself. "I now have her full confession of an Amazonian take over of all the small towns in Texas...except the messed up clones did it first."

"I so give up on him," Peggy drawled out and threw out one hand. "Someone else deal with the ol' coot."

"Calhoun, we're just discussing what happened tonight," Travis said. "Why don't you just sit down, film it, and keep quiet?"

Calhoun turned and aimed the camera at his face. "...is the man who beat the alien-possessed men into submission. I have yet to determine if he is human or not...As this top secret meeting continues-"

"It's not top secret!" Peggy looked ready to bust a blood vessel.

"Then if it is not top secret, you won't mind us attending," Steven Mann said from behind Calhoun, dragging his wife Blanche with him. "We do have a say in these proceedings."

Blanche drew away from her husband and took a chair far away from Calhoun. She smoothed out her silk dress and crossed her legs. "We have always had a say in the town's politics. My sister is a state senator."

"And we feel Shane and Phillip are valuable resources to our community," Steven added.

"So the rumors that they went out to ya'll's place and snagged some of ya'll's goodies is true, huh?" Curtis' eyes were very cold and fierce.

"What?" Travis blinked.

"We need essentials to survive." Blanche waved her hand as if to dismiss any argument. "They were kind enough to secure them." She frowned as Calhoun zoomed in on her face and shoved him away with one foot.

Manny looked shocked. "But we said that all the runs into town were for supplies, not for personal reasons. We swore that to everyone who wanted to go home and get their things."

"We're not just anyone, Manny," Blanche said with a light laugh.

"I paid them for their time," Steven added.

"...a full confession is caught on tape..." Calhoun muttered, circling Steven.

Travis felt his anger growing once more. He turned toward Steven and said in a harsh voice, "People die on the supply runs. We've lost good people to the zombies. Going all the way out to your fucking ranch for your personal stuff-"

"It was necessary," Blanche cut him off.

"We can't go around risking people's lives just so you can sit pretty," Juan retorted.

Travis shook his head. "Look, this is tough enough without you coming in here and spouting off about what good goons Phil and Shane are. Lord knows how many lives they put at risk going out there into the deadlands to get your fancy shit."

Manny rubbed his face with one hand. "This is not acceptable."

"No, what is not acceptable was that Katie woman obviously acting like a complete tart in the ballroom and it was obvious to all she was intoxicated," Steven said in a tight, controlled voice. "I'm sure she did lead Shane on."

"What?" Travis stood up sharply. He was close to losing his temper.

Calhoun whipped around to zoom in on Travis. Travis forced himself not to shove the old man away.

"I mean that dress...that awful dress...with such nice shoes," Blanche sniffed.

Juan moved to Travis' side. "Look, bitch, you have no right to say-"

"Shane is a good man and she is smearing his name in an effort to get him thrown over the wall," Steven said, cutting off Juan's comment.

Travis took a step forward and Juan grabbed his arm. He was sure he was looking furious if Juan felt the need to rein him in. And he was furious, beyond furious. He had been trying to be rational, but he was not going to be able to keep from punching Steven in the mouth if the man kept it up.

Manny looked at Bill and said, "There are conflicting stories."

"Yes, there are, but we should consider-" Bill started to answer.

"Just do a vote," Peggy said simply.

"...the Amazonian speaks her words..." Calhoun narrated. "All fall silent to listen."

Blanche snorted.

"A vote?" Bill blinked.

"Just type up their statements and let everyone in the fort read them, then vote." Peggy looked determined, tired, and pissed off. "Let the people of the fort decide what to do. You're saying you don't want us with all the power. Fine. Give it back to the people. Let them decide."

"And what are the options for punishment?" Juan demanded.

"We could give them a car, weapons, ammo and food and set them on their way if guilty," Bill offered.

Curtis shook his head. "Why waste our supplies on criminals?"

"Because it's humane," Bill retorted.

"And what is the other option? Letting them go?" Travis could feel Juan's grip tightening on his arm. Travis was so overwhelmed with emotion, he wasn't sure what the hell he wanted other than Katie safe.

"Of course," Steven and Blanche chorused.

"With a restraining order against him to steer clear of Katie," Bill added.

"So basically Katie's safety is dependent on how people vote," Travis said with frustration. He wasn't sure if he liked that idea or not. It made him feel helpless.

"I say we dump them over the wall," Juan said firmly.

"Let our vigilante do it," Peggy said with a sigh. "I'm sure Shane is on his list now."

"I have round the clock guards on that holding cell," Bill said. "They are not going over the wall."

"So we vote," Peggy said again.

Manny nodded. "That sounds fair to me."

"Well, I'm not certain we want all sorts of people voting on this, Manny," Steven said sharply.

"I think everyone old enough to understand should vote," Peggy retorted. "You can't count people out because they are not your version of the right sort of people."

Blanche rolled her eyes.

"You know what? Do whatever. But you better be damn well sure you are setting a precedent you can live with," Travis said, and stormed out.

"...may be human after all as he exits the top secret meeting..."

Juan followed Travis down the hall and into the lobby. Travis tried hard not to let his temper get the best of him.

"Travis," Eric called out from nearby, and rushed over to him.

Travis took several deep breaths as he looked back and forth between Juan and Eric. Both of the men looked concerned and maybe a little fearful. Travis could feel the heat of his anger burning in his eyes. He rubbed them with his fingertips.

"What's going to happen?" Eric asked.

"A vote. The fort will vote on what to do," Travis answered.

"Okay. That seems fair," Eric said. "Are you okay with that?"

"Just scared," Travis confessed.

"Why?" Juan folded his arms over his chest. "This is a good thing."

"But what if people vote to keep them?" Travis shook his head. "I hate this feeling. Voting out a person into the deadlands. It doesn't feel right."

"We don't want them here, that's for damn sure," Eric reminded him. "I know you want them gone."

"Yeah, but what if we start voting out people for the wrong reasons?" Travis shook his head. He felt compromised by his own beliefs in this moment. He wanted Shane and Phillip gone, but the thought of people voting out someone from the safety of the fort was terrifying.

"It's the right thing to do, man. It's the right thing. You know it," Juan assured him.

Travis set his hands on his hips as he considered this, then sighed. "Nothing feels right anymore. Nothing." And with that, he walked to the elevator to go up to be with Katie.

When Travis finally entered Katie's room, he found her fast asleep with Jenni holding her close. He walked over and gently smoothed Katie's hair back from her face, then sighed. Sitting in a chair next to the bed, he sat in silence, deep in his thoughts

# Chapter 12

## 1. Justice

The next week was sheer hell.

The idea to vote on what to do with Shane and Philip had seemed like a good idea at first. Nicely printed copies of the depositions of those involved were handed out to anyone over the age of seventeen who were willing to vote. It became the most popular reading material in the fort. It also became the most talked about and scandalous.

Philip and Shane were tucked away in one of the guardrooms where they could be constantly monitored and put to work keeping an eye out for marauders or zombies. They weren't allowed to touch weapons during their watches, but their duty did allow them enough time to flap their jaws to spread rumors. Roger had become so disgusted by their tales, he had asked Nerit not to assign him to their guard duty anymore. Nerit had made sure Roger understood that he needed to keep his spot to limit the damage they were doing.

Rumor was rife throughout the fort and Katie's sexuality became the focus of a lot of discussions. Some people staunchly refused to believe she was anything other than a good ol' straight girl. Others suspected that she was a lesbian in hiding. That it was even considered part of the decision making process made Katie angry and feel hurt all at the same time.

"Yeah, someone asked me if I was your mustache," Travis said with a wry smile one night.

"Huh? Oh! My beard!" Katie rolled her eyes. "I'm surprised they even knew the term."

"Yeah, I'm the mustache for you and Jenni." Travis shook his head and laughed.

"Of course. What else would you be," she said with a laugh. The words hurt more than she cared to admit.

It was painful reminder of all she and Lydia had gone through. The furtive looks, the guarded questions, the gossip: all of it had been hell. Somehow, it had been easier with Lydia because they had each other to help them through the hard times. They understood what the other woman was going through. Katie remembered one woman screaming at her and Lydia at a gay pride parade that there was no way they loved each other like a straight man and woman loved each other. Lydia had just laughed and said, "Yeah, true. Less beard burn!" Katie had nearly fallen over laughing and Lydia had waltzed her around, then kissed her.

Travis was trying so hard, but he didn't really know what it was like to know that a good portion of the old world population hated you simply because you looked at your own sex and saw no issue with loving them. As a bisexual woman, Katie had struggled with both the gay and straight community at times, when they had been trying to force her to decide. She let her heart decide when it came to both Lydia and Travis. She was very aware, as was Travis, that if not for the zombie holocaust, she would still be with Lydia.

Loving Travis was the same, yet different. How she could explain that to any of the people giving her strange looks? So she didn't say anything except, "Travis and I are together and I would never cheat on him with Shane or anyone else." She was torn between feeling like she was betraying her relationship with Lydia and feeling that she was preserving its sanctity by not going into details about her past.

But the rumors continued and Blanche dragged her name through the dirt. She heard the woman's mocking words ringing in her ears. She saw the condemning stares from a few. The scary old Southern Baptist woman named Mary especially took to saying nasty things around Katie. She just tried to ignore it all.

Yet at the same time, she had the sweet hugs of her supporters. Old Man Watson went out of his way to stand up and hug her tight. Nerit, of course, was unwavering. Jenni was almost psychotic in her defense.

Every night, she went to bed with Travis' arms around her waist as his chest fit snuggly against her back. He had surprised her with a cell phone charger he had found somewhere and plugged in her cell phone when she wasn't looking. One night, she had slipped into bed and looked over to see Lydia's picture smiling out at her. She had almost cried at the sight and looked up to see Travis smiling sheepishly from the bathroom. Running across the room, she had flung her arms around his neck and clung to him while clasping the phone in her hand.

He understood more than she gave him credit for, perhaps.

"It scares me sometimes," he whispered in her ear one night, "to realize that, if not for all this shit going down, I would never have found you. And I know you would be happy without me, since you would be with her, but I don't know what would have happened to me. Would I have found happiness somewhere else?"

Katie had held him close and stroked his hair. "We have to live with what is, not what could have been."

He reached out and snagged the cell phone. "She was really beautiful, Katie. I like her smile and her eyes. She looks really kind."

"She was amazing. I loved her," Katie said in a soft voice. "And you are amazing and I love you."

Travis smiled. "Oh, I know. I'm not afraid of Lydia's memory. I just want her to know I'm going to take good care of you."

Katie gave him a loving smile and kissed him. "She knows. I know it."

A day before the vote, the little pink stick said she wasn't pregnant. Katie was relieved, considering what an idiot she had been drinking the night of the party. But at the same time, she had felt a pang of disappointment. When she showed Travis, he had sighed. She could see he shared the same feelings. They had stood in silence, pondering it for a long moment, then he had kissed her lips lightly and said, "Eh, one day."

"I'm thirty-six," Katie had said.

"I'm thirty-two," Travis answered. Then he had mussed her hair. "No fair looking younger than me."

But her point was made. That night they returned all the condoms to the supply store. Bringing a baby into the world was a scary thought, but the reality was that they had to keep living their lives or the dead would truly win.

The day of the vote, Travis held Katie tight as the ballots were counted and announced. When she closed her eyes and sank back against him, he had kissed her neck and cuddled her close.

That night, Shane and Phillip were given a sedan with a full tank of gas, two rifles with ammo, and a week's supply of MREs.

"The bitch will pay," Shane said to Travis and Juan as he climbed into the driver's seat.

The gates opened and the two men, who had caused so much pain, were gone.

"Good riddance," Nerit said as the sedan drove away.

"I hope the zombies eat them," Jenni said with a fierce look.

"I'm just glad it's over," Katie sighed.

Travis just stood in silence and had a terrible feeling that it was not yet over.

## 2. Vigilante Justice

Five hours later, Phillip stumbled up to the far corner of the fort. It was an isolated point, one that was always manned. Breathless and terrified, he called up to the guard on watch.

"Help me! They are right behind me," he cried out frantically.

"Where's your friend?" the guard asked.

"Shane? I don't know. Our car broke down and we tried to make it back here. We got separated when zombies attacked us. Our guns didn't work. I barely escaped and ran here. Let me in for god's sake," Phillip said in breathless desperation.

The guard's head tilted. "I don't think so."

Philip looked up at the guard in shock. "You can't do this. You have no right. You know me. You know I didn't do anything. It was all Shane!"

The guard's head shook from side to side. "Sorry, but it ends here for you."

Slowly, the truth dawned on Philip. "It's you! You set it up! You killed Jimmy and Ritchie! You rigged our guns so they wouldn't work."

With a slow sigh, the guard nodded. "Yeah, I did. You should have died out there with Shane. Good thing you came to my post." Then the guard's gun barked and Phillip toppled over, screaming and clutching his leg. With satisfaction, the guard watched as the zombies finally caught up with Shane's sidekick and began to pull him apart, feasting with ravenous hunger.

## 3. The Aftermath of the Verdict

The next morning when Katie came on duty, she looked down to see Philip staring up at her with one eye.

"Shit," she said, and pondered putting a bullet through it. "Ah, dammit. Seriously, dammit."

Phillip's horribly mutilated form moaned low in its throat as one badly chewed arm lifted toward the fort. He was torn in half and his torso was propped up by one arm. His legs lay nearby. The zombies that had eaten him wandered around in the street below, not aware of Katie on top of the wall. As always, the zombies seemed listless and confused unless they saw their prey.

The Phillip zombie let out another anguished cry and his undead brethren slowly moved to where he stood. As Katie lifted her walkie-talkie to her mouth, a few looked up, saw her, and began to moan.

"I've got Philip outside the wall," she said.

"He came back?" Peggy's voice answered in disbelief.

"Yeah. But not alive," Katie responded and sighed.

There was a burst of static, then, "Shit. I'll let her know."

Jenni bounced up the wood steps to the platform with two breakfast tacos wrapped in foil in her hands. "Hey, girlfriend, what's up?" Her hair was up in a ponytail and she wore a T-shirt that read "Zombie Killah" in red puff paint. The women of the fort had a t-shirt-decorating party a few nights back. While most of the T-shirts were decorated with flowers, animals, or cowboy paraphernalia, Jenni's had fake bullet holes and a nice slogan.

Katie pointed down into the street.

"Whoa. It's like Ritchie, Part Two," Jenni said, her eyes widening. "But like, grosser. It looks like he was a big ol' wishbone."

"Nice way to put it," Katie said, and rubbed her nose. The fragrance of the tacos mixing with the decaying reek of the zombies was not very palatable.

"He is seriously chewed up," Jenni set the tacos down and leaned against the wall. This made the zombies howl and began to beat against the concrete bricks. "Gnawed down to the bone in some places. Wow."

Katie slid the new crossbow Jason had made into position and aimed it downward. It was a huge contraption that slid on a track along the side of the wall. It was loaded and ready. The crossbow was already aimed downward. A small lever let the person firing it adjust the angle. The trigger always remained in the same position. The sight was rigged up with mirrors and was very accurate. It was an easy way to kill the zombies without wasting ammunition. Katie personally thought the thing was monstrous in size, but it was effective. And it made Jason very proud that he had designed and built it.

The zombies below were banging against the wall with their decaying hands, or in some cases, gnawed stumps. One was moving its arms and legs up and down, as if it was trying to swim or climb up the concrete wall.

"Don't kill the Phillip one. Nerit and Bill are going to want to see that one," Jenni said as she ate her taco.

Katie nodded and began to fire down at the other dead creatures. It was hard to look into those once-human faces and feel anything other than stark fear. The gapping maws, pale eyes, and decaying flesh were the stuff of her nightmares. As the crossbow fired, there was a satisfying *thwank!* as the bolts slammed through the skulls of the undead beasts below. Katie gave in to her grim duty and pushed away thoughts of who the zombies had once been.

"Let me see, Katie-girl," Bill said as he lumbered up onto the platform.

Katie slid the crossbow away and stepped to one side.

Bill looked down at the dead man in the street below surrounded by his now truly-dead brethren. "Yep. That's Phil."

"I like him better this way," a voice called out from a nearby sentry platform. It was Lenore.

Jenni gave her the thumbs up.

Lenore nodded.

"Zombies definitely had a field day with him," Katie sighed. "Any ideas of what may have gone wrong?"

"Maybe Shane ditched him to lessen his load," Bill said in a low voice.

"I would not put that past him. He is such a total shit," Jenni said, and continued munching on her breakfast taco.

The sight of Jenni eating with that awful smell wafting up from below made Katie nauseous, but Jenni had a better defense mechanism built into her brain than most of them. It was probably because she was an abused wife. Katie knew from experience that abused women developed extraordinary coping skills to survive their abusive situations. Jenni was quite adept at disassociating herself. It was probably both a blessing and a curse at times like these.

Nerit joined their small group, her sniper rifle held lightly in the crook of her arm. She glanced over the wall and studied the scene. "I want a closer look at him."

"Me, too," Bill said.

"Why?" Katie arched an eyebrow at them. "He's obviously undead now."

Nerit pointed to one of the legs. "I want to see that one. Something is wrong with it."

"Well, it is chewed down like a chicken leg," Jenni commented.

"The way the bone is shattered doesn't sit right with me either," Bill said.

"Put him down and let's drag him up," Nerit ordered.

Katie dragged the crossbow back into position. It felt strange to put Phil down one last time, but somehow right. She fired once and watched his torso flop backwards.

"He so deserved that," Jenni said with satisfaction, and shoved the rest of the taco into her mouth.

# 4. Ghosts of the Past

Jenni landed feet first on the street below Katie's sentry post and raised her pistol quickly. Bill scrambled down the ladder behind her, his big belly giving him a little bit of trouble as he went.

The bodies of the dead zombies were scattered around them, the deadly bolts from the crossbow having done their job. Jenni knew they were finally, truly dead, but she couldn't but be afraid. Every time she was outside the walls, she was terribly aware of her vulnerability.

Bill set his booted feet down on the street and heaved his belly upwards as he tried to get his belt hoisted up on its girth. His keen eyes looked around the street from beneath his cowboy hat.

Felix easily climbed down the ladder. Nerit followed more slowly. Jenni and Felix took up positions to the left and the right, watching the road while Nerit and Bill moved over to the pieces of Phillip's body.

"That smell is enough to make me puke my tacos up," Felix grumbled, and kicked a dead body in irritation.

Jenni looked down at the gray, decaying carcass at her feet. It could have been a woman at one point, but it was so badly eaten, it was hard to tell gender. There were no clothes on it and most of its hair had been pulled out. It wasn't the smell that got to her. It was seeing their empty eyes, like Mikey's as he snarled and clawed at the window of the white truck on the first day. She blinked hard and shoved that thought away.

"Mighty chewed up," Bill said to Nerit. "Can't tell much about what happened before he got ate."

Jenni rubbed her nose and narrowed her eyes as a few shambling figures appeared in the far distance.

"Look at his leg," Nerit said from nearby.

Jenni glanced over to see the older woman squatting down by one of the torn off limbs. The skin was shredded and muscle and tendons were ripped from the bone.

"Shattered," Bill said after a moment.

"Human teeth couldn't do that," Nerit agreed.

"What does that mean?" Felix's voice was tight with his fear.

"I'm thinking bullet," Bill answered. "I think someone shot him in the leg."

"I betcha Shane did it," Jenni offered, and watched as one of the far away shambling creatures tumbled to the ground. It struggled to get back up resulting in an almost comical series of pratfalls.

"Maybe," was all Bill said. "We better go see if we can find Shane."

Nerit continued to stare at the shattered bone thoughtfully. She prodded the limb with the edge of her gun, then began to look around on the ground around her.

Bill called in to the fort for a vehicle to be brought around while Felix began yanking the bolts out of the zombie heads to be cleaned up and recycled for use later. Jenni kept her eyes on the figures in the distance.

"What's going on?" Katie's voice sounded worried.

"Heading out to see if we can find out what happened to Shane!" Bill gave her a thumbs up.

Jenni could see the worry in Katie's expression and knew that her friend was probably feeling some sort of misplaced guilt. Jenni didn't mind Phillip being in pieces. She kind of wished Shane was out here, too. She returned her gaze to the figures wading through the shimmering heat. The one that had fallen was still not able to get back up on its feet. They were still some distance away. Jenni wasn't too worried.

Nerit continued to look around, shoving the decaying bodies out of her way, obviously intent on finding something. Bill pulled up on his belt again and stared down the road where the zombies were moving relentlessly toward them.

"Helluva day," he said at last.

The school bus roared around the corner, Ed behind the wheel.

Felix said, "Thank God."

Jenni understood his relief far too well. She was keeping a cautious eye on the walking dead slowly approaching their position. She liked them slow like this. It was easier to kill them and it was more like the old zombies movies. She hated it when they were fresh and fast.

She was the last one on the bus and gave Katie a little wave. The worry in Katie's expression was touching. It was a good feeling to know that people actually gave a damn about what happened to her.

"Another day. Another dollar," Felix muttered as he slung his long body onto a seat.

"We don't get paid," Jenni reminded him.

"Oh, yeah. This job sucks." Felix grinned, and winked.

Jenni winked back and grabbed hold of the bar over her head. Ed shifted gears and the mini-bus roared forward. She watched the approaching zombies with irritation. She didn't feel like dealing with them today. The dead would only complicate things as they tried to figure out what happened.

Nerit sat across from Jenni, her rifle on her knees. Her hand was gripping the back of Felix's seat as the mini-bus bounced down the road. She looked eerily calm, as usual. Jenni envied her.

"Nothing is ever simple," Bill decided. He let out a weary sigh.

"Never is," Felix agreed.

"We just do our best," Nerit said. "Do our best and hope."

"Do you think we're it? The only ones left other than those little pockets out there that Peggy talks to?" Felix was staring out at the dead town and his voice sounded weary.

Jenni didn't want to think or talk about other people trapped out there. She didn't want to think about anything their own little world.

"Does it matter?" Nerit finally said. "Does it really matter if we are the last ones or not?"

"Puts a helluvalot of pressure on us if we are," Felix answered.

Bill nodded. "That it does."

Ed plowed over the slow moving zombies and the bus bounded on down the road. He was taking the route Shane and Phillip had taken the day before.

"It don't matter if we are or are not the last. We just gotta not mess it up. We gotta do what we have to and hope that anyone out there still alive is doing okay, too. My boys are still somewhere out there and I just gotta trust that they are alive and doing their best to survive. I didn't raise no fools."

"Where are your boys, Ed?" Nerit asked.

Jenni didn't want to talk about this, but she was stuck. She didn't want to think about families destroyed in the first days. She didn't want to think about her own dead children still out there seeking out the flesh of the living. She just wanted to get this job done and get back to Juan and the safety of the fort.

"Got two sons up in College Station going to A&M."

"Aggies," Felix muttered with the disdain only a Longhorn from the University of Texas could muster.

Ed ignored him. "The youngest is in military school up near Fort Worth."

Jenni gazed out at the abandoned buildings of the town and frowned as several zombies shambled into view to watch the bus pass.

"If they are anything like you, Ed, I'm sure they are fine," Jenni said, and hoped that would finish the conversation.

"I raised them good. They're smart boys. I know they are fine."

"They're country boys. They got a better chance than most city folk," Bill agreed.

Felix and Jenni, the only city folk in the bus, both protested the same time. "Hey!"

Nerit just chuckled.

"There it is," Ed called out. "There's their car."

The sedan the fort had provided the outcasts, far too generously in Jenni's mind, was listing on the side of the road. Its front tire was tucked down in a drainage ditch next to the road. There were a few old buildings and houses in the area and nothing stirred except the wind in the tall grasses.

"Let's get this done." Nerit slid to her feet.

"Same drill as always," Ed added.

Jenni picked up her ax and double checked her pistol. The ax felt good in her hands. Her anger against the zombies and the terror they had brought into her life was a hot furnace inside her.

The bus doors opened. She was the first one out. Her boot heels kicked up dust as she jumped down. She quickly took up her position, covering the others as they disembarked. Felix moved to cover the other side of the road while the others moved to examine the car.

From where Jenni stood, she could see one side of the car was smeared with zombie gunk. Nerit picked up a discarded weapon and looked it over thoughtfully. Bill squatted down to pick up a box of ammunition tossed nearby.

"All shots fired," Nerit said.

"This box is filled with gravel. I'm not liking how this is looking." Bill stood and adjusted his belt. It was a common gesture for him. He had a pretty big gut, but he was losing it now. It meant he was always hiking up his belt. Jenni found it an endearing, but amusing action.

"Got six zombies dead on this side of the car," Ed called out. "And another box of gravel."

"Someone sabotaged them," Felix exclaimed.

"Why is the car abandoned? Why did Phillip head back to the fort?" Bill stood back a few feet from the car and peered in, while Ed hunkered down to look under it.

Jenni saw the zombie lunge for Ed out of the corner of her eye. "Ed!"

The older man scrambled backwards quickly as the zombie reached for him. It was terribly mutilated and missing a good chunk of its torso. It's feet scrabbled at the ground, trying to find purchase to push it toward the grizzled old man. Ed got to his feet and kicked it in the face, knocking its head back. Yanking his hatchet off his belt, he motioned to the others he had it under control.

"Hurry up and kill it," Jenni exclaimed, trying not to yell and draw more zombies to them.

Ed slammed the hatchet down on the fearsome growling face lunging toward him. The zombie shuddered. Its skinless fingers clawed at Ed's boots.

*...like those tiny fingers pressed under the door on the first day...those tiny little fingers...*

Jenni shook her head to break the memory.

Ed slammed the hatchet down one more time. The thing's fingers finally stilled.

"And here we go," Felix sighed as two badly decomposing zombies appeared from around a nearby building.

"I hate company," Jenni grumbled. Her head was throbbing. She felt off kilter. Seeing the zombies' fingers straining to reach Ed had sickened her. She tried hard not to think of Benji.

"Especially the kind of company that wants you for dinner," Felix agreed. "I hate zombies. I hate them. I really, really hate them. I wish they would just go away."

Bill popped the hood behind them while Nerit walked slowly around the car. Ed joined her. They studied the area together.

"No one likes zombies." Jenni frowned as more staggered into view. "But at least they're slow now."

The shambling dead were a strangely reassuring sight. Jenni preferred them slow and relentless to fast and relentless. The zombies were a mess now, often indistinguishable as male or female. Not only were the zombies mutilated from the attack that killed them, but from wandering around looking for the living.

Four months of rot, the elements, and wear and tear had the walking dead in bad shape. Their skin was dry, cracked and shredded. Their limbs were mangled and twisted. The zombies felt no pain, so they had no concern for their bodies. They struggled through brambles, bushes, and low fences, wandered off elevated areas, tripped down inclines, and, sometimes, rammed themselves repeatedly against obstacles. On her trips outside the walls, Jenni had seen the undead do extraordinary damage to themselves trying to get the living.

"They're getting closer," Felix called out.

"Almost done," Bill answered.

Jenni felt uneasy despite the slow advancement of the zombies. Her rage had dissipated at some point to be replaced with a low pulse of fear. But she couldn't let it get to her now. One of the zombies, a female in a truly tacky pink tracksuit, was drawing too close.

"Ax time!" Jenni moved toward the female zombie reaching for her, moaning that terrible sound, and forced back her fear.

The zombie snapped and lunged forward. Jenni slammed the flat of the ax head hard into the sternum of the creature and knocked her flat on her back. She quickly pinned the creature down with one foot placed solidly on the dead thing's chest and heaved the ax over her head. As the zombie grabbed at her boot, Jenni brought down the ax as hard as she could and cleaved its head in two.

"One down!" Jenni yanked her ax out of the zombie's head and took a few steps back.

"I got visitors," Felix yelled. He used almost the exact same moves to take down a zombie near him with his double-bladed spear. He miscalculated how far away the second zombie was, and it lunged at him from behind. Felix shoved the spear back hard behind him and impaled it before it could grab him. Jenni moved to help him. The zombie began to push its body down the spear to grab Felix, but the young man turned and shot it in the face.

"I got it, Jenni, I got it," he said, and grinned.

Jenni nodded. "Good job." She held the ax at the ready, her eyes scanning the approaching dead, trying to figure out her next moves.

"I would really like to go now," Felix called out as more dead stepped into view around them.

Bill motioned to Ed. The two men talked in soft tones.

"C'mon, guys! Hurry up!" Jenni's voice was full of exasperation.

The limping, gruesome dead were drawing ever closer. They were too clustered together to take down individually.

Ed got down on the ground and slid under the sedan.

"Guys, seriously! Seriously, this is not good!" Felix wailed.

"I'll thin them out," Nerit assured Felix. She raised her rifle and began to fire at the less mutilated, more dangerous zombies.

Jenni watched with fascination as the zombies went down one by one. A plume of blood, brains and bone would erupt out the back of their skulls, then they would crumple to the ground.

Felix also began to fire at the growing crowd of zombies. The reality of the new world was that a small group of zombies was manageable, but too many swarming together was hard to survive.

Jenni pulled out her handgun from its holster and aimed at the remains of a mechanic shambling toward her. It didn't have much of a face left, but its tongue flicked out between its stained, broken teeth.

*Mikey's torn face flashed across her vision...*

Jenni shook her head, trying to shake the memory away.

"Kill it Jenni!"

She forced herself to focus and looked back at the zombie. It was Lloyd, her dead abusive husband , lurching toward her. His mouth was open to utter that terrible zombie moan and his shirt was covered in the blood of her children.

*Join us, Jenni,* Lloyd's voice whispered.

"Jenni!"

"Fuck you, Lloyd," Jenni growled. She fired. The bullet sheared off the top of his head.

Lloyd swayed on his feet for a second, then collapsed at her feet. Jenni lifted her foot and slammed it down on the zombie's head for good measure a few times.

"Who the hell is Lloyd? Did you know that zombie?" Felix yelled.

Jenni ignored him and looked down at the zombie that was no longer her husband, but some pathetic mechanic. She raised her gaze and lifted her gun to fire into the group of zombies nearing her.

"Let's go! Done here!" Bill called out.

Jenni and Felix began to draw back toward the mini-bus. Nerit disappeared into it, only to reappear at a window. She slid it down so she could provide cover.

Bill jogged around the back of the mini-bus and headed toward the open door. More zombies were appearing now. They were being drawn by the gunfire. Jenni reloaded her weapon as Felix backed toward her. Ed fired up the engine.

"You first," Jenni told Felix.

"I'd say ladies first, but-" Felix ducked into the bus.

Jenni slowly backed up toward the open door. She was almost to safety.

A little boy around Benji's age walked into view. He trailed behind the other zombies, then spotted Jenni. With a small cry, he lifted his hands. His small fingers reached for her.

*Let him bite you. Die and join us.*

An uncomfortable tightness gripped her throat. She wanted to scream. She stumbled backwards and gasped. The little boy wasn't just Benji's age, he *was* Benji! He had found her. He was coming for her. His fingers were reaching for her so he could claim her.

*His tiny fingers reached for her...strained for her...*

Bill grabbed Jenni around the waist and dragged her up into the bus. Jenni didn't fight him as she stared transfixed at Benji. The doors snapped shut.

"It's Benji," Jenni gasped.

"No, it's not," Nerit said sharply. "It's not him."

"Who's Benji?" Felix was completely bewildered.

Bill set Jenni down firmly in a seat. "Jenni, it's not him. It's not Benji."

"But..." She couldn't look away from Benji's tiny zombified form and his searching fingers. He was reaching toward her, wanting her to go to him. "He's coming for me."

*Yes, he is. Get off the bus. Embrace him. Join us,* Lloyd's voice urged.

Nerit grabbed Jenni's chin and forced her to look away. "It's not him, Jenni. It's not him. Look away. Close your eyes. Don't look, because it's not him."

She finally tore her gaze away from the small dead boy and squeezed her eyes shut. She felt the terrible fear that had gripped her slowly begin to release. She took in a shuddering breath. Finally, she looked back out the window.

The zombie wasn't Benji. It wasn't even a little boy. It was a tween girl in a torn nightgown.

Lloyd had tricked her. Anger flashed through her and she felt it burn away the last vestiges of her paralysis.

"Sorry," she murmured.

Ed shifted gears and the min-bus lurched forward.

"It's okay," Nerit assured her. She gently rubbed Jenni's back. "It's okay. It was just a bad moment."

"What just happened? 'cause I'm very confused."

"Felix, it's over. That's all that matters," Bill said calmly.

The bus rumbled on. Ed would take an indirect route back to the fort to avoid leading the zombies to their safe haven.

Jenni felt reality slipping back into place around her and the morning of the first day began to recede into her memories. Her children were gone. Maybe their bodies sill roamed the earth, but the spark that had made them human was gone.

Jenni looked up at Nerit, who was still gently rubbing her back trying to calm her. "I'm sorry I'm crazy."

"Honey, we are all crazy," Nerit assured her.

"That's the truth," Felix agreed.

"I ain't been sane in a long time," Ed said in a grim tone.

"Ya'll speak for yourselves." Bill grinned. "I'm as sane as they come in a zombie infested world."

Nerit smacked him upside the head. "Liar."

Bill laughed. He was obviously trying to break the somber mood.

Jenni lowered her head into her hands. Concentrating on the rocking of the bus, she slowly regained her composure. "I'm so embarrassed," she said at last.

"It's all right. We're all fine. That is what teamwork is for. We take care of each other." Nerit touched Jenni's cheek lightly. "Besides, how many times have you saved our lives? We just returned the favor."

"And no need to tell anyone about this," Ed said. His tone implied something the others had not even considered.

"The Vigilante?" Jenni queried.

"Shit," Felix swore. "He killed Jimmy for freaking out."

"She didn't get anyone killed or even nearly killed," Bill pointed out.

"But whoever the Vigilante is has a distorted perception of reality and who deserves to live or die," Nerit reminded him.

"We keep it quiet," Ed said firmly as he drove on.

"Agreed," Bill said.

Felix nodded. "Gotta put up with zombies and crazies."

Jenni sighed heavily. She hated feeling weak.

"It will be okay," Nerit assured her.

Jenni wasn't too sure she agreed.

"What did you find out anyway?" Felix asked.

Nerit looked at Bill. He shrugged.

"We learned that the Vigilante is still at work," she answered.

Felix stared at her for a few seconds, then shook his head. "Great. Just great."

Jenni rested her head against the cool window and gazed out at the dead town. The world still didn't feel right to her. It wasn't just the Vigilante. It was Lloyd. She felt him, somewhere, nearby, watching her.

She was afraid.

# Chapter 13

## 1. When Plans Go Awry

t was quickly apparent that something grim had been discovered by the expressions on the team returning to the fort. Travis was with Katie at her sentry post when they returned.

"I better go find out what is going on," he said.

"You better tell me everything later." It was obvious that she was annoyed at having to stay at her post while the fate of Shane and Phillip was discussed.

"Do I have a choice?"

"Absolutely not." Katie grinned.

Travis kissed her and left her to her duty. He made his way across the old construction site to city hall. Juan was also on his way. They met up at the back entry.

"It's not going to be good, is it?" Juan pushed his cowboy hat back on his dark curls.

"Nerit had her poker face, but Jenni's expression said it all."

"That's my girl. Always destined to lose every game of strip poker we ever play." Juan smirked and wagged an eyebrow.

Travis just laughed and headed inside. Peggy and Manny were already in their old office with the team and Curtis. Juan and Travis were the last two to join the group. Jenni looked pale and a little spacey. Juan quickly moved to her side and asked her something in Spanish. She shook her head and looked away. Juan looked a little surprised and stood awkwardly at her side.

"So what happened out there?" Travis sat down in an ancient wooden office chair.

"Other than lots of zombies?" Felix asked. "Because there were lots of those."

Nerit sighed and looked at Bill, obviously deferring to him as the person of authority on the issue.

"To put it simply, the Vigilante."

"What?" Juan's expression of disbelief was mirrored in Travis'.

"The boxes of ammunition we gave them were full of gravel. Once Shane and Philip spent the ammunition in their guns, they were done. To make it worse for them, the fuel line of the car was cut and rigged with cheap tape that would give way pretty quickly. They were dead in the water very quickly. I actually don't think the Vigilante meant for them to break down so close to the Fort." Bill shrugged. "The Vigilante couldn't get them in here, so he or she got them out there."

"Damn," Travis said in a stunned voice.

Manny calmly folded his hands on his desk. "We need to find this person and stop them. This is not acceptable behavior."

"Manny, don't you think Curtis and Bill are doing everything they can?" Peggy arched her brows.

Curtis sighed and sat on the edge of the desk. "The Vigilante is not stupid."

Bill laid a reassuring hand on the younger man's shoulder. "We'll find him, son."

"Does anyone really disagree with the ones he has punished? It's not like he's killing innocent people." Juan's temper was getting the best of him again, Travis gave him a warning look.

"Maybe not, but how he or she is going about this isn't right. No one should hold so much power of the lives of others," Nerit answered.

Curtis looked very tired and overwhelmed. "He's doing what the rest of us don't want to do."

"We're all in this together," Peggy pointed out. "One person can't decide who lives and who dies. Or who stays and who leaves."

"Was there any sign of Shane?" Travis asked.

"From the foot prints around the car and in the nearby field, we think they broke down, encountered zombies, used up their ammunition, tried to reload, realized what was happening, and that they both ran for it. It looks like Shane ran across the field. Phillip ran in the opposite direction. He eventually made it back to the fort," Bill explained.

"We looked around for Shane, but didn't find him," Ed added.

"He is probably already dead and wandering around," Jenni decided. "And I can't say I feel sorry about that."

It was the first thing she had said since the meeting had started. Travis noted the rawness in her voice. Jenni seemed unsettled. That bothered him. Juan placed a hand on Jenni's shoulder to comfort her, but she didn't seem to notice.

"We need to keep this quiet," Manny decided.

"We can't keep this quiet," Travis protested.

"C'mon, Manny. People need to know what is going on," Peggy caste an exasperate look toward the Mayor.

"People are already figuring it out." Felix shook his head. "They ain't stupid. Phillip showed up eaten up something fierce."

"In pieces," Jenni pointed out.

"We can't have people panicking," Manny stated firmly. "They are scared enough as it is."

"People need to know so they will be on the alert and report anything suspicious." Bill shifted in his chair and studied his notebook. "The Vigilante isn't going to stop."

"How do you know that?" Curtis wore an expression of curiosity.

"Because people like the Vigilante don't stop." Nerit answered. "They believe they are right and they alone can deal with what is wrong."

Travis rubbed his chin, deep in thought. "I think we should have full disclosure and let everyone know what the real dangers of this world are. This hotel already has us in a different mindset from when we were roughing it. Rose told me people aren't showing up for duty like they were when we were in the construction site. Yeah, we're safer when it comes to the zombies, but we still have food, water, energy, and sanitation concerns. We don't even have a doctor on hand. People need to understand we are still at risk."

"Don't forget the bandits," Nerit added. Her voice was tinged with pain.

"Or winter approaching." Peggy sighed.

"We just don't need them riled up. You know how people get when they feel the city officials or the authorities can't do their job." Manny rubbed his broad forehead to wipe away beads of sweat.

"Don't matter," Ed said. "They're gonna be unhappy anyway if you don't tell them. Sorry, Mr. Mayor, but the old ways are bullshit now. This ain't about reelections no more, but 'bout keeping alive."

"Everyone who voted to eject those two men deserve to know what happened to them." Travis' tone was firm.

"Why? They shouldn't feel guilty for doing the right thing," Juan said sharply.

"People's actions-and votes- have consequences. We all need to be aware of this." Travis stood and looked around the room. "As far as we know, we are the biggest and best off of the survivors in this area. Hell, maybe the whole state."

"Or country," Jenni sighed.

"Maybe the world," Nerit added.

"So we need to have our shit together. People have got to realize that every damn choice we make has consequences that not only affects our lives, but the lives of everyone around us." Travis sighed deeply. "We need to let everyone know what happened. We need them to understand the situation with the Vigilante. And they need to understand that just because we are now in this amazing hotel, we are not necessarily safe. Call a fort meeting and lay it out, Manny."

"The political fallout from this-" Manny started to say.

"Fuck politics, Manny." Travis hated how harsh his voice sounded, but he knew he was right.

Manny put his head down, his hand rubbing the back of his neck. "It's what I know." Manny looked up at them, his eyes stricken. "I don't know how to do anything but be who I was before all this happened."

"This world is messed up," Jenni grumbled.

"Voting those assholes out was the right thing to do," Juan declared firmly. "The Vigilante killed them, not the rest of us. Not the ones who voted."

"We all knew they would probably die out there." Nerit shrugged. "We made the choice."

"God help us do the right thing. From now on this is the kinda shit we gotta take deadly serious." Bill flipped his notebook shut. "If this is our new brand of justice, then we all better be damn sure we can live with it."

"Agreed." Travis folded his arms across his chest.

"We're getting close to mob rule," Manny said in a soft voice. "People need leaders . Order. Law."

"If we-the people in this room-try to dictate to everyone out there how it should be, we're gonna fail. Yeah, we need officials of some sort to handle every day administration, the planning of the fort defenses, things like that, but the big issues need to be in the hands of the people." Travis faced the silent people in the room. "We have to do this together or we'll fail."

## 2. Turned Upside

The first official fort-wide meeting was held in the dining room. It started right after dinner. Only the people on patrol didn't attend.

It stared off calm and ended up strained. Guilt ate at some, while others vehemently defended their choice to evict Shane and Phillip.

There was a mixture of reactions at the news of the Vigilante striking again. Some obviously saw him as a person willing to do what the authorities would not. Others were terrified for their safety. No one wanted to end up on the wrong side of the wall.

The Mayor lost control of the meeting after half an hour and Peggy and Bill took over. Manny looked sickly. Rosie and Felix helped him out of the room.

Kate and Travis sat in the back of the room, listening to the other survivors. The strain and terror of the last four months was spilling out. It slowly became apparent that people were very aware of the fragility of their new existence and wanted assurance that life would safely continue. Making new societal rules was something most didn't even want to deal with.

When they finally decided to vote in a new mayor and fort council, Travis wasn't surprised. When the town nominated names for the position of mayor, he was shocked.

Katie's fingers slid over his hand. She gave him a reassuring smile.

"Well, shit," he muttered.

## 3. The Camera Doesn't Lie

"...as it dawns on them what they have done, the ramifications of their Romanesque gladiator games continue to reverberate throughout the fort," Calhoun's voice narrates as the camera focuses in on four people lounging in plastic chairs, having a drink.

"Here we see the beautiful, yet psychotic Amazon named Jenni. Sources tell me her real name is Genevieve Maria de la Lourdes Blakely. I'm sure that is some sort of top secret Catholic Church code..."

The camera zooms in on Jenni who promptly sticks out her tongue and crosses her eyes.

"...this bizarre secret salute once more appears on her face. Whenever I approach her, she immediately signals the other Amazons. But little does she know that with the use of some foil and toothpicks, I have eliminated her secret signal..."

The camera zips around to show Juan looking annoyed as he lounges next to Jenni.

"...as I once more document their top secret meetings..."

Juan looks toward the camera and scowls. "This is not a top secret meeting, Calhoun. We're chilling out together as friends."

"...is Mr. Juan De La Torre. He's Mexican-American and, as usual, he is issuing denials of his secret activities..."

Juan rolls his eyes and waves the camera away.

"Next is Travis Marcus Buchanan. Now, he used to live in England so I strongly suspect he is a spy for the Queen..."

The picture zooms in on the curly-headed man sitting in a chair looking grim. He sighs and pushes the camera out of his face. "Calhoun, give it a rest."

"...then his ladylove. The center of this debacle, Kathleen Mathilde Kiel. Her code name is Katie..."

The blond woman looks up into the camera; the light illuminating her golden locks, making her pale face look even whiter. "Calhoun, I know you think you should document all of this, but please aim the camera away from my face."

"...this one eludes me to her origins..."

Katie sighs and covers her face with her hands.

"...but the truth remains that they sent two men into the wilderness...and one came back...or actually it was his clone...and not a very well done one...It was kinda chewed up and in pieces..."

"Calhoun, put the fucking camera away," Juan's voice demands.

The camera turns to show the wizened face of a man wearing a cowboy hat. Calhoun is obviously holding the camera on himself. "I alone seek the truth as the others cower before the powers that be. I will unearth their secrets and reveal in my camera's light...oomph..."

The camera suddenly swings crazily and there is obviously a scuffle. When it's over, the camera is on Calhoun. He looks very uncomfortable.

"...and this is Crazy Calhoun," Jenni's voice narrates. "Rumor is that he is an overgrown leprechaun on steroids..."

"Am not!"

"...and that he is spying for the Wicked Witch of the West..."

"I am a proud citizen of these United States and I have never consorted with witches!"

There is another scuffle, then the camera reveals Travis looking at the camera, obviously trying to figure it out. Finally, he adjusts it and says into the camera, "We're going to vote in a mayor and city council. They nominated me."

Juan's voice says, "And he's gonna freaking win."

Travis looks annoyed at this. "So, yeah, I'm chilling with my friends and hoping to God I don't get elected." He hesitates, then adds, " And I do not spy for the Queen of England."

The screen goes black.

# 4. Haunted

It took some finesse escaping Calhoun and his camera. It took a little luck avoiding the little packets of survivors who wanted to talk to Travis about his nomination, but at last, they made it into the elevator.

"You're gonna get elected," Juan repeated for the umpteenth time.

"You say that one more time and I'm going to deck you." Travis scowled.

"Play nice, boys." Katie ran a hand over Travis' curls to soothe him.

"Just tellin' him the truth." Juan shrugged.

"Which he obviously doesn't want to hear," Katie answered.

Travis continued to look out of sorts as the elevator dinged its way up.

Juan thought his buddy was being a big baby about the whole thing. It was amusing as hell though. Besides, giving Travis shit was alleviating the tension he felt from Jenni's silence and distant expression. Juan watched the numbers over the door light up. Just a few more floors and he could find out what was wrong with Jenni. She had been putting him off all night. He was tired of it.

The elevator arrived at the next floor and chimed. Travis slid his arm around Katie's waist as the doors opened. Juan took hold of his shoulder.

"You'll win because you're the best man for the job, Travis."

Travis sighed and opted not to punch Juan's lights out. "We'll see."

With that, the couple walked away and the elevator doors shut.

Juan looked toward Jenni and smiled. She either didn't see him, or she ignored him. She continued to stare into nothingness, her arms folded over her breasts. He loved her, but at times he felt powerless and incompetent. He could feel her emotions churning just beneath the surface of her eerily-detached expression.

Tentatively, Juan reached out and touched her arm. She glanced at him. Her focus appeared to return to the here and now. She stepped closer and he slung an arm over her shoulders. Her body was very tense. He kissed her cheek, trying to soothe her.

It didn't seem to work.

She continued to stare ahead.

At their floor, Jenni briskly walked out of the elevator and out of his reach. With a sigh, Juan followed, his tired, battered fingers searching for their key in his pocket. She stood impatiently at the door as he unlocked it. Unlike other times, when she was flirting and anxious to get him alone, she avoided looking at him and was silent. He had a feeling her lack of patience had nothing to do with sex, but something unpleasant.

When they entered the small suite, Juan quickly looked around for the kid. A closed door with music loudly thumping behind it, let Juan know where Jason was hanging out. The dog was probably in there, too. The kid and the dog were pretty much inseparable.

"I'm going to bed," Jenni stated.

"You don't want to talk about whatever it is that is making you like this?" He already knew the answer, but he had to ask.

"No."

"Why not?" He couldn't help himself. He wanted to know what was wrong.

"It's not important."

"If it wasn't important you shouldn't be flipping out."

"I'm just tired."

"You're lying."

"Fuck you!"

"Whoa! Where did that come from?"

"I told you it's not important!" Jenni's dark eyes were full of indignation.

"Then why are you acting loca, Loca? Juan felt his temper rising. He loved her madly, but she was getting on his last nerve.

"Maybe because I am! You knew that when we go together!" Hands on her hips, her jaw set in a defiant line, she seemed to dare him to push the topic further.

He hated himself , but he couldn't help it. "Something happened out there. I have a right to know what is going on in that loca head of yours. I love you."

She stared at him for a few beatings of his worried heart, then simply walked out the door.

"Hey! Hey! Hey!"

He rushed after her, but the door slammed firmly behind her. Flinging the door open, he looked out to see her getting back onto the elevator. His anger told him to follow her, confront her and make her tell him what was going on, but his love for her told him to not be a selfish bastard. Struggling to rein in his emotions, he stepped back into the suite they shared.

Taking off his cowboy hat, he ran his hand over his long curls. Loca was nuts, but she wasn't stupid. She wouldn't rush off and do anything stupid; well, stupid as in going zombie hunting alone or anything like that.

Arching an eyebrow, he suddenly knew exactly where she was going. Snatching up the phone on the table beside the door, he dialed Katie's room. It took a few rings before she answered.

"Hello?"

"Katie, Loca just blew out of here."

"What do you mean?"

"She was acting all weird-"

"I noticed."

"-and was not telling me what was up-"

"She tends to do that."

"-and I basically ordered her to tell me-"

"A very stupid move on your part."

"-and out the door she went. I think she's heading your way. You're not naked and doing anything sweaty with Travis right now, are you? Cause Loca will need you to calm her ass down."

"I'm not naked or doing anything sweaty with Travis. He's actually about to head out and meet with Eric to work on some plans for Main Street." Katie sounded worried and bemused all at the same time.

"Okay, so you will take care of my girl?"

"Absolutely," Katie answered.

Juan sighed. "Take care of her, Katie. Please."

"I will."

Hanging up, Juan closed his eyes to rub his eyelids. He was weary. His eyes felt like salt had been poured into them. Jenni not being with him was disconcerting. He felt lost without her. Surprised to feel tears in his eyes, he slid onto a stool tucked beside a small bar next to the kitchenette.

The music in Jason's room was still pounding away and it did nothing to calm his nerves. Letting out another weary sigh, he swept a tear away with his rough fingers.

Loca would be okay. He knew it. She was too tough to let anything drag her down. He just had to wait for her to come back to their little home.

It would be okay.

He hoped.

***

Katie hung up the phone and stared at it, deep in thought.

"What's wrong?" Travis emerged from the bathroom, his face and hair a little damp. He was feeling tired, but still had a few more hours of work. A splash of cold water on his face had him looking more alert.

"Jenni is on her way. Juan says she walked out on an argument." Katie folded her arms over her breasts. "I noticed she was abnormally quiet tonight, but I thought she was just tired."

Travis walked over and kissed her cheek. "If anyone can calm her down, it's you. It'll be fine."

"If she talks to me," Katie grumbled. "She's been evasive on a lot of stuff lately."

"She's haunted. Maybe a little more than a lot of us." Travis rubbed Katie's shoulders. "I better go before she lands on our doorstep."

Katie's fingers brushed over his hand and she gave him a worried smile. She was sincerely worried about Jenni. She remembered the near catatonic woman in her truck. No one else in the Fort had ever seen Jenni that way, but Katie knew how fragile Jenni's condition had been on that first day.

Travis pressed a kiss to her lips, then moved toward the door. "See you at breakfast."

"I'll miss you," Katie said with a slight smile.

There was a sharp rap on the door.

"I think she's here. Take care of her, Katie." Travis smiled ruefully, then opened the door.

Jenni stood there, hands on her hips, her head down. Her face was obscured by her hair.

"Hey, Jenni," Travis said, and brushed past her quickly.

Katie could tell he did not want to upset Jenni anymore than she already was. Another reason why she adored him so. He always was considerate of others.

Jenni stepped into the room and slammed the door behind her.

"Jenni?"

Her friend looked up, her face streaked with tears. With a small cry of despair, Jenni launched herself into Katie's arms and clung to her.

"Oh, Jenni! What is it? What's wrong?"

"He can't see me like this! He can't! He doesn't know how I used to be!"

Katie held her tightly and could feel her friend trembling violently. "Jenni, what is it? What is it?" Jenni's tears were soaking her neck and shoulder. Katie stroked Jenni's dark hair soothingly with one hand.

There was no answer for a minute or two as Jenni wept. Then, at last, she raised her head and wiped at her soaked cheeks with irritated hands. Jenni struggled to get her breath, then regained some of her composure. "I think Lloyd is haunting me."

Katie blinked and ran Jenni's words through her mind one more time. "Huh?"

"I think Lloyd is haunting me and trying to kill me." Jenni's dark lashes glittered with tears and she fastened her red eyes on Katie defiantly. "And I'm not joking!"

Katie could see the anger, desperation, and fear in Jenni's face. She was not about to argue with her. She had suffered her own struggles with the past and couldn't judge her. "Why do you think that? What happened?"

In a voice that trembled with emotion, Jenni explained the events of the day. Katie listened in silence, taking in the words, watching Jenni's expression. It was obvious that the seal Jenni so painstakingly kept clamped over her past had been ripped off. She was trembling and afraid. Instead of looking like her usual rough and tough self, she appeared emotionally shattered. She resembled the woman standing on the front porch of her home in her pink bathrobe watching tiny dead fingers pressed under the door.

"And Juan cannot see me like this! He can't! He loves the new Jenni. Not the old one. I hate being the old Jenni! I hate it! I don't like feeling this way! I don't like being weak! I thought I was past this!" Jenni flung herself onto Katie's bed in a dramatic finish.

Katie slid onto the bed and gently rubbed Jenni's back. "It's okay, Jenni. It's okay to have a bad day. We all have them. It doesn't mean you're the old Jenni. It just means that something happened today that really upset you. I told you about the dreams I used to have about Lydia. I still struggle with that guilt. I struggle with the knowledge that I did not kill the thing she became. Hell, I struggle with the guilt that I did not put your children and Lloyd out of their misery."

Jenni gave her a fierce look over her shoulder. "I don't give a shit if Lloyd wanders out there forever. I hope he rots slowly. I hope his soul is still in his body! I hope he's aware of what he is! Fuck him!"

Katie slightly smiled at this tirade. It sounded more like the Jenni she knew now. "Okay. So if you feel that way, why let his memory-"

"His ghost," Jenni corrected.

"Okay, his ghost. Why let his ghost upset you like this? Why let him make you weak and scared? You know that..." Katie hesitated, then plunged on. "You know Benji can't get out of the house. He couldn't be there today. As for Lloyd and Mikey, they are hundreds of miles away. Even if his ghost is here, he can't hurt you."

Jenni sat up and looked at Katie fiercely, her dark eyes burning with raw emotion. "He wants me to die so I will be in his power again. That is what it is."

Taking Jenni's hand gently in hers, Katie said softly, "Then don't let him. You have a life here with Juan. We're about as safe as we can be in this world. You have Jason and Jack. You have friends. You have so much."

"He wants to take it away," Jenni whispered, and fresh tears fell.

"You can't let him, Jenni. You can't let him have power over you from beyond death. You're more than he ever imagined. You know that, right?"

"He said I should die and be with the boys," Jenni said in a low voice.

Katie could feel the terrible pain in Jenni's voice mingled with an even more terrible guilt. "It's not your fault, Jenni, that they died."

Jenni turned her head away, deep in thought. Katie could almost see the invisible walls sliding back up around that train of thought. Jenni couldn't deal with that right now. Katie could see it. It would wait for another time.

"Fuck, Lloyd," Jenni said at last. "Fuck him. I'm not going down without a fight. Whether it's fighting zombies or bandits or ghosts, I'm not going down without a fight."

Katie smiled and kissed her cheek. "That's my girl."

Jenni's lips slightly quirked upwards and she raised a trembling hand to wipe away her tears. "But I don't want Juan to see me like this."

"He doesn't have to," Katie assured her. "Stay here tonight. He called me. He knew you would come here."

"I'm that predictable, huh?" Jenni laughed.

"He knows we're tight. He knows that if you're not with him, you're gonna be here with me. We're kinda like Thelma and Louise."

"Meets the zombies," Jenni added with a soggy grin.

Katie laughed. "Yeah."

"I'm not driving off a cliff with you though," Jenni said firmly.

Katie embraced the morbid humor that kept them from falling into the darkest of emotions. "But we can run over zombies together."

"Totally," Jenni agreed. She fell over on her side and tucked her head on a pillow. She stared at Katie thoughtfully, her tears finally abating. "I'm not crazy. It really is Lloyd's ghost trying to kill me."

Katie lay down and tucked one hand under the pillow Travis' usually slept on. His scent comforted her. "As long as you don't give into him, you'll be fine."

Jenni rubbed her reddened nose. "Sometimes the first day feels like a hundred years ago. Today it feels like...today."

Katie gently smoothed Jenni's hair back from her face. "I know."

Rolling over, Jenni hid her swollen eyes and tear-stained face as she fought to recover herself. Katie draped one arm over her waist. They lay in silence for a few minutes. It was not a strained silence, but a comforting one as Jenni regained her composure and her shoulders relaxed.

Katie reached over her and switched off the lamp. Jenni sighed in a way that was reassuring. Katie could feel her friend letting go and sinking into the drained weakness that came after an emotional storm. Katie snuggled down behind Jenni again, holding her close.

"You're the best friend in the world. The best I've ever had," Jenni whispered.

"I love you, Jenni. You're my best friend. I'll always be here for you."

Closing their eyes, the two friends held each other until, at last, sleep carried them away.

# Chapter 14

## 1. The Dead in the Night

We have a problem. Let's go!"

Travis and Eric looked up to see Curtis rushing toward them. They were standing in the lobby, studying a map of the town. It was an antique and kept under glass, but it was surprisingly accurate. The town had not changed much in seventy years.

"We have to go! We have to go!" Curtis' young face was flushed under his blond hair. He was agitated and motioning with both hands.

"What's going on?" Travis lifted an eyebrow.

"The Hackleburg survivors are under attack!"

"Shit! Get Nerit!" Travis headed toward the communication center.

"What does that mean? Is that zombies? Bandits? What?" Eric was flustered as he rushed after Travis. He shoved his glasses up on his nose and looked as alarmed as Travis felt.

"In this crazy world, who knows?"

They burst into the center at the same time. Bill was perched over an array of radios.

"Repeat! Repeat! I can't make out what you're saying!" Bill looked up, his expression one of despair.

"...got through...we are fight-...please hur..." The sounds of gunshots peppered the woman's voice. She sounded terrified and static kept overwhelming her voice. "...please hurry! Please hurry! They're...repeat...got in!"

"Zombies?" Travis asked in a soft voice.

"I don't know. I can't make it all out," Bill said in a surprisingly composed voice.

Travis was always impressed by Bill's ability to handle stressful situations in a calm manner.

Eric cocked his head, listening to the frantic woman's garbled message. "Are we really going out there?"

Bill looked at Travis.

"Hey, I'm not the mayor."

"Not yet," Bill answered.

Nerit entered the room, her yellowed silver hair in a braid over one shoulder and her bathrobe tied tightly at her waist. "What is the situation?"

"Hackleburg is under attack. I can't make out if its zombies or bandits. Sue just keeps screaming into the microphone that someone got in." Bill rubbed his broad forehead. "It don't sound good."

Peggy rushed in with Curtis behind her. She was in her pajamas and her son clung to her like a monkey. "Hackleburg? Shit! They have kids in there! That's the one where they are in the church community center. They had enough food to make it through another week!" She tried to dislodge Cody, but he wouldn't let go. She ended up snatching up her map and heaving him onto one hip.

"Show me," Nerit said to her.

"They're here. On the outside of town. They holed up in a church community center. Twenty-two people are in there. Mostly old folks, women, and kids. All, but four of the men went back into town to fight the zombies. They didn't come back alive. Anyway, they didn't have any vehicles to escape in and they ended up with zombies banging on their doors. They've held them off by barricading the doors and windows. They even managed to thin them out a little by dropping things down on the zombie's heads from the roof. They were saving the ammo just in case the zombies got in."

"There have been gunshots going off," Bill said quietly.

Through the static, they could still hear the woman crying and begging for them to come.

"We gotta go get them! Save them!" Curtis looked desperately at Nerit. "We gotta go."

Travis sighed. It was decisions like this he did not like making. Did they sacrifice resources to save other survivors, or did they stay safe within their walls? His humanity told him one thing, his fear for those he cared about told him another. He felt conflicted, yet he knew what he wanted to do. What he felt was truly right.

"How far away, Peggy?" Travis asked.

"Twenty-one miles going southeast." Peggy was trying to sound calm for the sake of her son and her own nerves, but her eyes were wide with fright.

"We have to get them," Eric said. "We have to. If we can, we have to go get the survivors. We have room and food. We can't let them just...die." His voice shook with emotion. It had not been that long ago that Eric had been trapped outside the fort and under siege by zombies.

Travis rubbed his jaw and looked at Nerit, waiting for her to say something. He wanted to rush out and save the people, but he knew Nerit understood the actual dynamics of the situation better than he did. Nerit finally turned her gaze to Travis. Her expression said it all. Travis was glad for her in that moment. She was quick to decide and quick to action.

"We take two trucks and the bus. We leave immediately. I need you to get Felix, Ed, Jenni, Katie, Roger, and Juan down here, Bill. Have them meet me in the Panama Canal," Nerit said in a firm, authoritative voice.

"Gotcha, Nerit."

The older woman patted Travis' arm and headed out the door. He immediately followed.

"What are the chances we'll find survivors?" Travis had to hurry to keep up with her.

"Slim to none. But we need to know for sure if it's the zombies or the bandits attacking them," Nerit responded.

Travis blinked. He hadn't thought of that. "Which is worse?"

"I haven't figured that out yet," Nerit answered with a grim look on her face. "Let's get moving."

Travis took a deep breath, then followed her. He tried to push back his fear, but his stomach kept coiling into a tight knot . As he walked away from the communication center, he heard the woman's screams distorted by the static.

## 2. Into the Darkness

Jenni and Katie were asleep when Bill called.

"Will this day ever fuckin' end?" Jenni groused at him.

But once they heard what was up, they had scrambled out the door as fast as they could. Strapping on their holsters and making sure they were fully armed as they went, they were both struggling to shake off sleep and get focused.

"I hate shit like this," Jenni grumbled.

"You and me both."

Katie shoved the wrought iron gate door open to let them out into the old construction site. It squealed open and they stepped out into the humid night.

"I'm so ready to stomp some zombie ass. I'm so sick of this shit. So sick of people dying," Jenni bitched. She braided her hair as she walked.

"We're going to need to try to get all those survivors in here soon," Katie answered. "Now that we have room and food."

Jenni shoved pins into her braid to keep it on top of her head. "Fuckin' zombies." She wanted them all dead. Chopped up, mashed up, dead.

They climbed up the ladder and over to the padlock. Juan stood near the ladder talking to a few of his men as they prepared to let the vehicles out of the fort. The sight of him made Jenni's heart beat a little faster. He glanced over at her from under his cowboy hat and winked. She smiled back at him. Just like that, their fight was forgotten.

"Hey, Loca," he said, and they shared a soft kiss.

Her arms felt good around his waist and she rested her head against his shoulder. "I'm heading out."

"Yeah, I heard. My own little zombie killin' loca." Juan ruffled the fine strands of hair at the base of her neck and kissed her forehead. "Come back."

"I will. Katie's driving and she's a psycho bitch behind the wheel."

Katie grinned at this.

"Yeah, but you get all loca, Loca."

"Only in a good way," Jenni answered flirtatiously.

Juan laughed and kissed her again.

Jenni felt better now. Everything felt more solid. Lloyd's specter seemed like a bad dream.

Ed drove the small bus out of the newspaper building garage. The bright lights blinded Jenni for a second. She raised her hand to shield her eyes. She could make out Nerit and Felix already tucked inside.

Bill motioned for Katie to grab Nerit's red Ram 1500 truck. Katie looked like a badass. She had her rifle slung over her shoulder, a bowie knife tucked into a sheath at her waist and her pistol in its holster on her hip.

"I better get my ass in gear. We got people to save and zombies to kill," Jenni said.

Juan touched her cheek and kissed her one last time. "Hurry back."

Jenni smiled. "If Jason wakes up before I'm back, tell him I love him." She hurried past Roger and Katarina as they climbed into another truck. Travis was already there, sharing a moment with Katie. Travis would take care of Katie no matter what. That made Jenni feel secure. Her own mortality felt fragile. It made her think about the ones she loved and who would take care of them if she was gone. Katie would be safe with Travis. But Juan...

She looked back toward the tall Mexican-American with the gorgeous green eyes and knew she would never leave him. Even if she died, she would watch over him. She couldn't imagine their love ending even with death.

"Let's go, children!" Nerit's voice was a hard bark in the night.

Jenni slung herself up into her old seat and strapped herself in. Slamming the door shut, she gave Juan the thumbs up.

Katie shared a few more soft kisses with Travis then slid into the driver's seat.

"Take care, you two," Travis said, his worry puckering the flesh between his eyebrows.

"We're Wonder Woman and Super Girl," Jenni chided him. "Sheesh."

"We'll be back for breakfast," Katie assured him.

Travis forced a smile and shut the door.

"Men are such worriers," Jenni grumbled.

Katie laughed. "Yeah. We're just heading out into the deadlands. No reason to worry." She turned on the truck and it roared to life.

"Piece of freakin' cake," Jenni declared.

"Of course. Absolutely!" Katie placed her slightly-shaking hands on the steering wheel, guiding the truck out of the garage.

Jenni could feel the adrenaline rush. It had her trembling, but she embraced it. That surge reminded her that she was alive. Heading out into the dead world was always terrifying, but she trusted the people she was with. It would be okay.

Katarina and Ralph were in another big truck, this one black. They were the first into the lock system. The bus followed. Jenni and Katie followed last in Nerit's red truck.

It felt strangely good to be back in the old truck. Anxious to get out there and see who they could save, Jenni drummed her hands on the dashboard. Jenni missed Jack sitting in the back seat like he had during the first days after the outbreak.

"You're so wired," Katie remarked.

"I just want to get going." Jenni pouted.

"Obviously."

The big gates slid open. Katie drove the truck into the first lock. Jenni looked out the window at the tall cement block wall beside her. She craned her head to look up and waved at a sentry standing post.

Nerit's voice cackled over the CB. "Katarina knows the way. She's leading. Watch out for deer and cows. Some of the fences are down now. Don't drive too closely together in case anything happens. The town is heavily infested, so we are keeping to the outskirts and heading straight for the church. We don't stay around any longer than we have to."

"Gotcha," Roger's voice said through the static.

Jenni snatched up the mouthpiece. "We're good."

The final gate opened up. The silent, dark street opened up before them. Only the lights from the fort illuminated the night. The darkened world seemed bleak and forlorn.

"Here we go," Katie said.

"Yeah. Again."

The two vehicles were waiting for them. Now that the red truck was clear, Katarina took off at top speed in the black truck. The bus followed. Katie shifted gears. The red truck followed last in line.

The drive through the countryside was strangely exhilarating. The cold stars in the velvet darkness above were brilliant. The waning moon was a glowing a Cheshire Cat smile. In the dark fields, washed with moonlight, cows slumbered and deer wandered. Occasionally, birds took flight from the tall trees as they were startled awake by the passing vehicles.

Jenni glanced over at Katie, studying her friend's features in the glow of the dashboard. "You scared?"

"Yeah. You?"

"Shitless. Not of the zombies though. I'm scared those people are all dead." Bill's debrief over the phone had been quick, simple and to the point.

"Me, too." Katie swept her hand over her hair. "There's no rest from this stuff. Just when we start to feel a little comfortable, something goes down again."

Jenni propped her feet up on the dashboard and glowered at the bus in front of them. "Seriously, zombies should take a vacation from eating us. Let us unwind. Refresh ourselves before we have to shoot their heads off in the next round."

"If only life were that simple," Katie commiserated.

"And if it's the bandits, I'm shooting their balls off."

The CB cackled to life. "We're getting close. Katarina, you and Roger cover the north end of the parking lot. Katie, you and Jenni cover the south. Ed will pull up in the center and we'll see how the situation is going down. Everyone be alert," Nerit's voice ordered.

Jenni slid her gun out of its holster and rested it on her thigh. She could feel her heartbeat speeding up. She took a deep breath.

"This isn't good," Katarina's voice said a minute later.

Katie drove the red truck after the others and followed a curve in the road. A building tucked behind an old whitewashed church came into view. It was a rectangular building made with aluminum siding. It had only a few windows set high on the walls. The gravel parking lot was empty except for the walking dead feasting on the freshly dead or dying.

"Dammit!" Jenni slammed her fist into the dashboard.

Katie grabbed up the CB mouthpiece. "Nerit, what do we do?"

Katarina's voice cackled through. "If we start firing, the zombies will come from the town."

"That's too many to kill by hand," Jenni whispered. "We have to shoot them."

Before them, the feast continued. The zombies did not seem to even notice the three vehicles-idling just a short distance away.

Nerit's voice finally sounded through the static. "We're going to make sure that if anyone is still alive in there that they have a chance. Kill the ones eating and on the ground dying. Make it fast." Nerit continued with her instructions, her voice calm and steady.

Jenni listened to the directions, her finger flicking on and off the safety on her gun. Katie exhaled slowly and gripped the steering wheel even tighter with her hands.

"This really fuckin' sucks," Jenni said under her breath.

"We do what we can and let the rest of it go. Otherwise, we'll go batshit crazy," Katie answered.

Jenni nodded.

Nerit's voice gave the word and Katie followed the other vehicles into the parking lot. Using the big metal beasts as weapons, they ran over the zombies devouring the people they had come to rescue. The big bus did a good job of flattening the disgusting creatures that were so greedily consuming the dying. Katie aimed for any it missed.

After four rotations through the parking lot, if anything was still moving, it was doing so feebly. Jenni shoved her door open and jumped out. She pulled her ax out of the truck and headed toward the nearest twitching zombie. Heaving the ax over her head, she brought it down hard on its skull. Katie followed behind, holding a spear and doing the same duties. The squashed and mangled zombies were barely mobile now and basically lay on the ground, their spasm obvious in the glow of the headlights.

Jenni dispatched the still-moving zombies swiftly. She had no time to deal with them and had no desire to see Lloyd try to make an appearance. She felt back to her new, normal self. She wasn't going to let his ghost fuck with her anymore. Of that, she was certain.

Once their grisly task was done, the group from the fort stood stoically among the dead. Jenni tried not to notice the old people and children among the bodies.

"Ed, Felix, Bill and I are going in. Roger, Katarina, Jenni and Katie, you stay out here and keep watch. If we call for you, come quick," Nerit ordered.

Jenni began to protest, not wanting to be left out of the mission inside, but one look at Katie's expression and she clamped her mouth shut. Jenni could not easily define what she saw in Katie's eyes, but it made her bond to her best friend feel tighter. Maybe Katie needed her.

Katarina stood nearby, her red hair coiled on top of her head, staring toward the town. The grisly remains at her feet were ignored. Jenni didn't know the quiet woman very well, but in that moment, she reminded her of Nerit. There was a calm coldness to her that Jenni admired. She felt hot and emotional inside in contrast. She couldn't bear to look down and see the twisted remains of the dead and know that they were too late.

The smell was terrible. Jenni's eyes watered as she stepped away from a cluster of bodies. A group of zombies had been greedily eating one of the larger women when they arrived. Jenni had briefly wondered if the woman had been fat or pregnant, but the thought made her feel unbalanced, so she shoved it away.

"I hate this shit," Roger said in a low voice. "I really, really do."

"Something is going on over there," Katarina said suddenly. "I see headlights. I think a vehicle went down in a ditch over there."

"Binoculars are in the bus," Roger said, and hurried to retrieve them.

Katie stood nearby, watching the road and their surroundings. "Is anyone alive?"

Katarina shrugged. "Can't tell. Something is moving. I can see a shape moving in front of the lights."

Jenni strained to see down the road, but from where she stood it wasn't clear what Katarina was looking at.

Roger returned and handed off the binoculars to Katarina.

She immediately raised them and studied the scene.

"Zombies. Trying to get into a truck that is definitely nose down in a ditch."

Jenni took a few steps toward the road.

"Jenni! We can't leave," Katie called out.

Jenni made a face and stomped her foot. "C'mon. Someone is probably alive over there."

"We have to provide Nerit and the others backup," Katarina reminded her.

"Ugh!" Jenni felt frustrated by her inability to act and go rescue whoever was stranded down the road. She stomped her foot again for good measure.

Gunshots sounded from inside. Everyone froze. There was a long silence, then Nerit and the others emerged with a young woman and a small boy. Seeing the carnage in the parking lot, the woman grabbed up the boy and pressed his face against her neck to hide his view.

"They were in a bathroom with the door barricaded. They are the only survivors," Nerit said to the others.

Felix quickly escorted the woman to the bus while Bill took the time to examine the double doors leading into the community center.

"Nerit, we got a vehicle up the road with zombies around it. I count six zombies," Katarina explained quickly. "Could be survivors in the truck. But we're gonna have to shoot the zombies."

"That'll get the town zombies moving our way," Nerit said thoughtfully.

"We gotta go save them," Jenni protested.

"I'm with Jenni. We have to save anyone we can," Katie agreed.

Bill walked toward them, his expression dark. "I agree. Let's do it."

"The road is narrow. Take one of the trucks, but make sure you are facing away from the town. We'll stay here and provide as much cover as we can, but make it quick," Nerit said firmly. "The longer we are here, the more dangerous it is."

Katie headed toward the red truck. "C'mon, Jenni. We'll do this."

Bill jogged after Jenni as she headed back to join Katie. "I'm coming with you. There weren't no vehicles left with the survivors. We don't know who is in that truck."

Jenni slid into the back seat, while Bill got into the passenger seat. Katie shifted gears and slowly drove up the road.

"Maybe they'll rush the truck so we can run them over," Katie mused.

"We're never that lucky," Bill answered.

As they drew closer to the stranded vehicle, they could see that it was lodged firmly in deep ditch nose first. The hood was smashed up against the cracked windshield on the right side and only the left headlight remained shining into the night. The zombies were pounding on the windows, obviously trying to get into the cab. Inside, two young girls were screaming in terror.

"I'll take the two on the left." Bill said, gripping his rifle tightly.

"I can get the ones on the other side. The two on the windshield are not going to be easy. We'll have to get all the way out for those," Katie decided.

"We need to make this fast," Jenni agreed.

Katie stopped the truck, Bill did a silent countdown with his fingers. At three, they both flung open their doors. Jenni scrambled over Bill's seat and dropped into the road. She darted past Bill and aimed at one of the zombies rearing back off the windshield to screech at the new flesh. She fired. The zombie jerked back and fell into the tall grass. Bill and Katie picked off the other zombies as the remaining zombie, trying to pry its way through the shattered windshield, ignored the attack. The two girls screaming inside disappeared from view as they took cover. Jenni aimed and fired again. The last zombie tumbled over the hood and disappeared from view.

"Get them fast," Katie shouted at Bill. "We've got company coming!"

Jenni looked up the road to see zombies materializing out of the darkness of the trees onto the moon drenched road. "Fuck!"

Bill waded into the tall grass, his form illuminated by the red truck's headlights, his gun and gaze aimed downward, wary of anything lurking there. Jenni kept him covered as Katie stood ready to jump into the truck and drive them out of here.

One of the girls popped up and shoved the truck door open. Bill reached for her and she jumped into his arms. Another girl, younger than the first, also dove into his arms. He clutched them tightly.

Jenni watched the terrain around him. "Hurry, Bill. Hurry!"

Bill hurried out of the grass and onto the road. He glanced over his shoulder at the moaning forms drawing ever closer. Katie rushed over to him and grabbed one of the girls. Together, they hustled them into the truck as Jenni continued to keep her gun trained on the zombies closing in.

Katie slammed the driver's door shut as Jenni and Bill squeezed in beside her. Bill yanked the door shut as Jenni scrambled into the back with the two girls.

"Are either of you bit?" she asked, and felt like a bitch doing it.

"No! No!"

One girl was blond with huge blue eyes. The younger one was Hispanic with the darkest eyes Jenni had ever seen.

The zombies were closer now. Their mutilated forms were slow, but relentless as they stumbled down the country road.

"What drew them here?" Bill wondered. "Couldn't be the gunfire this fast."

"Don't know. Don't care," Katie answered, and shifted the truck into reverse. Looking over her shoulder, she began to drive backwards toward the church parking lot. The other two vehicles waited for them.

Suddenly, a man ran into the glare of the headlights. Waving his arms, he was covered in sweat and breathing hard.

"I have a feeling we now know what is drawing them here," Jenni said. "I think they're chasing him!"

One of the girls peeked around Bill's chair. "That's the bad man! That's the one that opened up the door and took us away!"

"A bandit!" Katie slammed on the brakes.

"No, leave him. Fuck him!" Jenni said.

"We can't leave him," Bill protested.

Katie looked at Bill. "He did this! He did this!"

Bill looked torn for a second, then said, "We can't risk it. Leave him."

Katie looked like she wanted to run him over, but instead hit the accelerator and the truck roared backwards. The man screamed in anguish as the truck roared away, leaving him to the zombies.

Once Katie cleared the other vehicles, she turned the truck around, switched gears, and headed back down the road.

Jenni looked at the two girls huddled beside her. They were both trembling and staring at her with wide eyes.

"Tell me what happened," she said in a gentle voice.

## 3. The Devils in the Darkness

"So then the fuckers show up saying they're there to rescue the people, that they were there to evacuate them to a safe place," Jenni explained to the group gathered in the city council room in city hall. It was all the usual suspects; Nerit, Juan, Travis, Manny, Peggy, Katie, Bill, and Curtis.

"How many were there?" Travis asked.

"Four," Nerit responded. "They cleared out some of the zombies when they arrived, then forced their way inside. They used a crowbar to get the doors open."

"The bandits didn't even wait for the people inside to let them in. They just immediately broke in," Katie added. "Said they were on a tight schedule or some horseshit like that."

"When Esmerelda, the woman that was in charge, said she would call Peggy at the fort for confirmation, they shot her," Jenni continued. "They grabbed some of the girls and held them hostage while they ransacked the place. Every time a zombie wandered in, the guys would shoot the zombie. But it was getting crazier. They loaded the young women and girls into their vehicles and left the older women, elderly and the boys. The vehicle we found went off the road when one of the remaining survivors opened fire on it. A tire was blown out and it went into the ditch. The bandits took off on foot, but left the girls behind for the zombies."

Nerit shook her head and lit another cigarette. "Animals."

"Bastards don't deserve to live," Curtis growled.

Nerit sighed and finished the story. "Since the survivors had limited ammunition and the doors were wrecked, it was only a matter of time before they were over run. Lily had hid in the bathroom with her little boy when the bandits first arrived. She barricaded the bathroom door when she heard the screams starting as the zombies got in. From inside the facility, they were the only survivors. We found them because two zombies were still beating on the bathroom door."

"So four people survived out of all the people who had been living there safely," Travis said at last.

Peggy sat nearby, her face drained of blood. Travis felt for her. He knew she considered all the survivors she spoke to via the radio her friends. Manny had his head down and was rubbing the top of his head. Juan looked pissed off. Curtis looked sick and Bill looked weary.

"Yes," Nerit finally said. "But at least six females were taken from there. And their fates are unknown."

"Bandits," Travis decided.

"Yes. The bandits," Nerit said.

"Let's start bringing them in," Travis decided. "Any survivors we can reach now safely, let's bring them in."

"You're not Mayor yet," Manny said in a low, tired voice.

"Then what do you want to do?" Travis asked pointedly.

"Bring them in," Manny said with a weak smile. "Bring them in."

"I will get with Peggy and figure out which ones are viable to bring in now. Some are a distance away. Others are heavily surrounded by the zombie infestation." Nerit's expression was grim.

"We can only do what we can," Travis said. It was something all of them said at times like these, but it was the truth. Katie lay her hand over his. He held it tightly. "Bring in as many as you can. We'll plan for the rest. We need to be careful." He hesitated. "I don't think the bandits knew we were here before, but Esmeralda mentioned us. The bandits may come looking for us now."

The somber expressions at the table said it all. Life had just got a lot more complicated.

# Chapter 15

## 1. The Others

Three weeks slid by. The fort was kept busy as they prepared to take in more survivors. But as plans were drawn up to bring in more people, Travis found himself consumed with making sure any new additions were secure. This meant meetings with Juan and Eric as they poured over every option before them.

Groups headed out to hunt, salvage, and bring back any supplies they could lay their hands on. Construction workers made sure they had enough building supplies as new expansions were planned and repairs were made.

They brought in many of the small groups closest to the town. Nerit made plans to recover the ones at farther distances. All the groups were warned that when the fort people came for them, they would be notified well in advance and to be on the lookout for the bandits.

Things seemed calm out on the deadlands except for the wandering zombies, until one day...

***

Jenni walked briskly across the roof of the old newspaper-building with a rifle in her hand. Wearing a red tank top, cowboy hat, and jeans, her shoulders and arms were deeply tanned. She had suffered a nasty sunburn the week before, but some aloe vera had done the trick and now she had a great tan.

Nearby Jason and his crew of teenagers, along with Roger, practiced with their new enormous slingshot. They were firing off coffee cans filled with earth at a bundle of zombies staggering on the street out in front of the hotel. Every time they managed to nail one, they would cheer.

So far the slingshot and concussion grenades had been their best creations. Now they were trying to combine the two. Jenni thought it looked like more fun than she was having, but then again, being on guard duty meant she was able to hang out with her hot man.

Jenni's cheeks were reddened and her eyes bright as she walked up to Juan and handed him a thermos of ice tea. He smiled at her and pressed a kiss to her lips, then took several painful gulps of the cold brew.

"It's hot here," he complained, wiping his brow with the back of his hand.

She laughed and kissed him again. "Wussy. We can always strip naked to cool off."

"On duty," he said regretfully. "Later though..." With a smile, he kissed her quickly and settled back into his chair.

She took her place in the chair next to him. They both stared out over the town toward the hills. It was almost like sitting out on a porch on a nice lazy Sunday, except for the intense heat, the gusts of wind, and the zombies.

"They are so going to vote in Travis as mayor," Jenni decided.

"He's gonna be pissed," Juan responded.

"They love his calm demeanor and peacemaking skills. Plus, they know you got his back and won't let him be too soft. Your hard-line stance has everyone cheering."

"The 'do your damn work or take a hike' stance? I'm an asshole." Juan shrugged.

"Yeah, but it kinda makes sense. Except for the really old people like Old Man Watson and the disabled and kids."

"I just liked it when people were doing stuff to help out and nobody had to yell at them." Juan drank more tea and grimaced. "We got into this damn hotel and it was like everyone went soft and stupid. Travis complains about it all the damn time. I don't blame him."

"Well, nobody is going to vote for Mr. Mann, that's for damn sure. His bitch-wife pisses everyone off." Jenni lifted her rifle and began to survey the town through the scope.

"They're both flaming assholes." Juan watched the teenagers lob another coffee can down the street. It flattened a zombie.

"I was surprised that the Manns just didn't back Manny for mayor again."

Juan snorted. "They want the direct power now, babe, instead of pulling someone else's string. They want to be able to tell everyone what to do for their 'own good' and make sure that the social classes are restored. Must be hell for them to be forced to work."

"Yeah, Blanche tends to just stand there and pretend to be doing something when she's on duty." Jenni slowly scanned the section of town they were watching over. "It's so damn annoying. She told Katie that she was too delicate for hard work."

Juan shook his head and looked toward the towering hotel. "Yeah, my ass she's too delicate. She teeters around in those high heels all the damn time. I'm sure that takes some work balancing on them. And her helmet head hair? How long does that take to shellac?"

Jenni rolled her eyes and squinted. Catching a glimpse of something suspicious, she froze, swinging the rifle back along the line of trees she'd been scanning. She caught sight of a figure standing under the shade of some trees, watching the fort through a pair of binoculars.

"What are the chances of a zombie knowing how to use binoculars?"

"Those shit for brains?" Juan realized it wasn't a joking question and leaped to his feet. "Damn! Where?"

"Two blocks down, near the front porch of the blue house. Under the trees."

Juan lifted his binoculars. "Can't see-shit! Yeah...that's someone alive."

Jenni tried hard not to blink as she tried to adjust the scope and make out the person. It looked like it was probably a man. As she watched, the person lifted what looked like a walkie-talkie.

"Bandits?"

"Maybe, Loca. Or someone trying to figure out if we're alive in here."

"Well, obviously we are," Jenni said. "I mean listen to the sound of the machinery working on the new extension."

"True," Juan said. "So bandits it is. Shit. Anyone else would come up and knock."

Jenni snatched up her walkie-talkie. "Nerit, we have a situation. I've spotted what appears to be a man observing us with binoculars."

There was a pause, then, "I'm on my way."

Within minutes, Nerit was on the roof with Travis right behind her. "Where?"

Jenni pointed.

Nerit grabbed the binoculars and peered through them. "Near the blue house?"

"Yep."

Nerit's lips pressed tightly together.

Beside her, Travis squinted, trying to see through Jenni's rifle scope.

"See them, Travis?"

"Them? I see one."

"I have three. Three men. And a van with fresh mud on the tires. We're definitely being studied." Nerit quickly pointed to the other two locations. 'How many teams do we have out, Travis?"

"One. They're picking up that Reverend and a family out in Summerville," Travis answered.

"Pull them back in. Tell them to waste no time," Nerit said sharply. "That contingency plan we drew up is now activated."

"Shit," Travis muttered, and ran for the stairs.

Jenni took a deep breath. "Think it's the bandits?"

Nerit handed the binoculars to Jenni. "Possibly. Keep an eye on them and keep me informed. Juan, we'll need you down below. I'll send someone else up to help Jenni."

Jenni looked at Juan worriedly as Nerit strode away. He kissed her cheek. "It's gonna be okay, Loca. I gotta get down to the gate."

She kissed him firmly on the lips. "Love you."

"Love you, Loca."

He hurried away and she couldn't help but admire his taunt ass. To steady her nerves, she took a deep breath.

"Kids, Roger, stop doing that. We have a situation," Jenni called out. "You better get back inside."

Down below her, she heard Travis on the bullhorn calling a Code Red. Her palms sweating, she raised the rifle and looked through the scope at the man down the street.

"Who the hell are you?"

## 2. Code Red

"Bring 'em in," Travis said firmly to Curtis as he entered their communication hub.

Peggy was at a small computer station on the Internet per the usual. Curtis was perched in front of all the radio equipment.

"Are we really Code Red?" Peggy asked worriedly.

"Yeah. Unidentifieds in the neighborhood. And they're the living kind," Travis responded as he listened to Curtis calling the team that was out rescuing survivors.

Peggy frowned. "This worries me. Another survivor group didn't contact us today."

Travis rubbed his chin. "I had heard that."

"Not a good thing to hear," Peggy exclaimed, throwing up her hands. "When they have lasted this long and then one day nothing..."

"Could be zombies," Travis reminded her.

Curtis snorted. "Fuck, we're worse than them half the time. Humans are shits when it comes to survival of the fittest."

"Gee, Curtis, bitter?" Peggy asked.

"They killed Nerit's husband," Curtis said.

Katie walked into the hub just then. Her hair was up in a ponytail and her face was reddened from being outdoors. She had been helping build a new wall. "I hear there's trouble."

"Yeah. We're calling a Code Red," Travis answered solemnly. He reached out and touched her warm skin.

Katie swallowed a little. "Okay. That doesn't sound good."

"We knew it was a matter of time." Travis lightly rubbed her shoulder.

"It's been almost a month. A girl can hope they dropped dead or got eaten or something." She forced a smile.

Travis kissed her. "We ain't that lucky."

She sighed. "Yeah. I'll see you up at the post then."

"Give me a few minutes and I'll be there," he answered.

Peggy sighed as Katie left. "You two...I swear..." She slid into Curtis chair as he stood up. Sliding on the headphones, she looked down at Curtis' notes.

Travis blushed a little, then looked toward Curtis. "How far out are they?"

"Twenty minutes. Bill's flooring it."

"Okay, let us know when he gets in, Peggy. I'll be in position over the gate with Katie and Juan."

Peggy gave him the thumbs up. Travis and Curtis hurried out.

## 3. Nowhere is Safe

In the van, Katarina scrambled between the front seats. She scooted past the family and minister filling the back seats and made her way to the back window. She held her rifle tightly in one hand as she peered out at the receding road.

"Anything?" Bill's voice was terse.

"Nothing." Katarina glanced toward him. "Are you sure you saw a truck?"

"Positive. Out of the corner of my eye as we passed that billboard back there." Bill was frowning at the road ahead of them. He glanced warily toward the steadily setting sun. They had maybe thirty minutes before sunset. His palms were sweating and he knew in his gut things were going bad fast. A cop's instinct never faded.

The family, haggard, thin, and smelly, huddled together in the seats behind him. They were an intact family: young father and wife with three small children, a rarity in these terrible days.

The Reverend sat in the very last seat. He was a very poised older black gentleman with sad amber eyes.

It had taken almost two hours to get the family out of their home. The Reverend had to talk them into leaving. The older man had been holed up alone in the church, living off of the donated canned goods and the water in the baptismal. He had kept in contact with the fort during the last few months via his ham radio. It was the Reverend, just a month before, who spotted one of the young kids squatting over the edge of the roof of their family home to defecate. He had thought he was the sole survivor of his town up to that point. It was the Reverend who had directed Katarina and Bill to the family's boarded-up home.

The rescue had not been easy. It had taken nearly two hours to lure the zombies away from the church and down a back road by driving the van very slowly. Finally, Bill had floored it and double backed to rescue the survivors.

"Are you sure this is safe?" the father asked for the millionth time. "This fort you are taking us to. Is it safe? Yer looking mighty afraid right now."

"It's safe. Getting there is another story," Katarina answered.

"Nothing is safe in this world, but it's safer than where you were," Bill added truthfully.

The family clung together. They were terrified. It was the father's sheer determination that had kept them alive. A long time survivalist, his house had withstood the attacks of the zombies in the first days. For awhile, they had lived in the basement, but then the plumbing had failed and they had carried everything up into the attic. Bill had to respect their tenacity.

Katarina stared out the back window, her long red braid curling over one shoulder. "Shit! We have company!"

The Reverend twisted around in his chair and saw a truck racing toward them from behind. "Why are you afraid of them? Aren't they also survivors?"

"Not everyone in this world is a good guy, Reverend," Bill tersely answered. His hands tightened on the steering wheel.

As the truck raced to catch up with them, Katarina could see two men in the cab. There was a camper attached to the bed of the truck. It looked ominous to her.

"I see only two guys," she called out to Bill.

Bill kept the van moving at a quick pace and dared to look in his rear view mirror. The men looked scraggly and rough. The truck was gaining fast.

Katarina scrambled back to the passenger seat and let out a deep breath. "This feels bad."

"I agree," Bill answered in a low voice.

"Who are those men?" the father asked.

"We think they are bandits," Bill answered. "I want all of you to get down on the floor right now. Keep your heads down and keep as close to the floor as possible."

"I thought you said my family would be safe!" The young father with his scraggly black hair looked both frightened and angry.

"They will be. Just get down!"

The pursuing truck was moving in fast.

Katarina looked back to see that their passengers were nervously obeying. She usually loved rescue missions. The expressions on people's faces as they finally saw other humans, their sense of relief at being safe and the exclamations of thanks made it all worth the risk. Usually on rescue missions, they had to fight zombies, but this felt worse somehow. Fighting other humans in a dead world was just wrong.

The truck was now pulling up beside them. Katarina could clearly see the mud and gore spatters over its roughened side. What appeared to be bullet holes pockmarked the truck bed. She flicked the safety off on her rifle and took a breath.

Bill glanced over into the cab of the truck as it pulled up close and began to pace them. A scruffy man with lots of wild blond hair rolled down the window and began to shout at them. It didn't take a lip reader to see he was yelling at them to pull over.

Bill shook his head and pressed his foot down.

Again, the truck pulled up. The scruffy guy leaned out of the window and literally knocked on Bill's window. His voice was barely heard above the whine of the road and the wind.

"We want to be friends with you," he was yelling. "We want to be friends!" But his look was too wild and he looked at Katarina in a way that made Bill want to bash his teeth out with his rifle butt.

Glancing over at the unkempt man, Bill said, "Sorry. Gotta keep moving." And he floored the mini-van.

The children were now crying and their parents were trying to shush them. The Reverend was praying softly.

Katarina made sure her seat belt was on tight and watched the truck anxiously. The guy who was banging on the window had crawled back into the cab and was talking with the driver.

"We're almost to the bridge," Bill said to her. "We have to beat them there." The van had pulled ahead enough for Bill to swerve in front of the truck. He wasn't sure who had souped up the min-van, but he felt like hugging them at this moment. The engine was roaring. So far, it was handling fine.

The truck gunned it, then swerved sharply in front of them.

"Shit," Katarina whispered.

"They plan to trap us at the bridge," Bill said grimly.

The children were crying louder now. Bill didn't even want to think about what these men may do to the kids, their mother, or Katarina.

Katarina took a deep breath, then said, "We need to do something now."

"Can you pull a Nerit and shoot out the tire?" Bill knew that Katarina had been training faithfully with the former Israeli sniper.

Katarina furrowed her brow, then said, "I'll try." She immediately began to roll down the window.

Bill concentrated on the road and kept the van steady. The truck was speeding ahead of them, kicking up dirt, heading straight into the sunset.

Katarina slid out and perched herself in the window. The Reverend scrambled forward and grabbed hold of her legs to keep her steady and provide a human safety line. Trying to balance herself, Katarina took aim at a tire.

"Don't swerve," she yelled at Bill.

There was a long pause, then Katarina fired. The shot hit the camper and shattered the back window.

"Shit!"

She aimed again, trying to adjust for the speed, and the bumpiness of the road. A face appeared in the shattered window. It was a young girl, maybe thirteen. Her face was badly bruised and caked with blood. Her hands were tied in front of her and her mouth was gagged. She tried to wave at them.

"Sweet Jesus," the Reverend whispered.

Bill felt his gut coil as he stared at the captive in the back of the truck. He couldn't let her fate fall on any of those in his care.

Katarina saw the girl as well and hesitated, but the cries of the children behind her were a reminder of what they had to lose.

"Do it," Bill said in a ragged voice.

She fired.

The truck tire unrolled like a ribbon and vehicle careened wildly. The girl fell back out of sight. The driver fought the wheel, which tipped the truck. The camper went flying off the back and into the gorge that bordered the road. The truck slammed onto its side and went sliding off the road in a shower of sparks.

Directly ahead was the bridge.

Katarina struggled back into her seat and said thanks to the Reverend. She looked sick to her stomach, but took a deep breath to steady herself.

"You had to," Bill said, and tried not to think of the girl's face.

"I know," Katarina whispered. "I know."

The mini-van roared over the bridge, then sped around a hill. The hotel in all its lighted glory came into view. He sighed with relief.

"Almost home," Bill assured the people clustered behind him.

Katarina picked up the CB. "We're almost home. We had some issues, so please keep us covered."

"I copy that and am passing on the word," Peggy's voice answered, then said more softly, "What kind of issues?"

"Bandits" Katarina answered. "It's the bandits."

## 4. Watching the Board

The gates closed behind the mini-van. The newcomers were quickly ushered into the hotel. Just like that, the excitement was over.

Jenni watched through the binoculars as the man who had been watching the fort turned and vanished into the darkness. She never saw the stranger's vehicle leave town.

She dutifully reported in to Nerit, then settled in to wait.

She waited...and waited.

They all waited.

Everyone in the fort, on pins and needles, waited.

The minutes, full of tension, full of fear, ticked by, right until they turned into hours.

"What do you think is going on" Travis asked Nerit at around four AM in the morning. His eyes were bloodshot. He was gulping coffee.

Nerit was taking slow, luxurious drags off her cigarette. "I have been thinking about it and I have a theory."

"What is it?" Bill asked.

They stood on a sentry platform near the gate.

"Their plans went awry," Nerit said simply.

"And?" Travis arched an eyebrow.

"That is all for now," Nerit answered. "They're done for now."

Morning came.

The shifts rotated. Travis and Katie fell asleep in their clothes, guns nearby, a tangle of limbs as they held tightly to each other.

Jenni slept fitfully and woke up to prowl the roof again with Katarina.

Still, there was nothing.

And the day slipped away without incident.

Then another.

Followed by another, then another.

"Time to see if my theory is right," Nerit said after another day passed. "We leave in the morning. Bill, Travis, and Jenni are coming with me."

The next day, the gates slid open and Nerit's new pride and joy, the Mann's H2, roared out into the town. The Manns had been furious when they were told in no uncertain terms they needed to relinquish the vehicle to assist in the security of the fort. Nerit had fastened her steely gaze on them and said, "Do you really think you can just jump in it and go shopping? Because you can't." Finally, they had handed over the keys.

Nerit drove, Travis at her side, Bill and Jenni in the back. It was far too luxurious for Nerit's taste, but it drove well and would get them to where they needed to be. If the bandits did arrive, Nerit's crew had a vehicle they could take off the road with relative ease. She was glad that the Mann's had bought the top-of-the-line H2. It would survive off-roading with ease.

"I could so get used to driving something like this." Jenni grinned. She was happy to be out of the fort and doing something and not just sitting around waiting for something to happen.

"Up ahead is where they went off the road, Nerit," Bill said solemnly.

Travis sat in the front seat, rubbing his brow. He looked haggard, the stress eating away at him.

"Keep a look out," Nerit said. "We don't need them sneaking up on us."

"Who? Zombies or bandits?" Jenni turned and looked out the back window.

"Both," Nerit answered.

As the Hummer glided over the bridge, Travis looked down into the river to see a zombie, in fishing gear, wading through the water still clutching its fishing pole.

The skid marks on the asphalt told where the truck lost control and gone off the road. Nerit pulled over. They all cautiously disembarked. There was a deep gorge on one side of the road. It appeared the truck had slid right down into it. As they drew near the edge of the road, they saw that both the camper and truck were logged firmly in the trees that grew up out of the deep crevasse in the earth.

"It fuckin' stinks of the dead," Jenni moaned.

"Let's check it out," Nerit said, and started downward.

Bill was already poised to respond quickly to every threat. He slowly rotated as he walked, taking in all that was around him.

Nerit reached the camper first. She walked slowly, each step carefully measured. Travis was right behind her, looking far more at ease with a gun in his hands than anyone had ever seen him before. He looked alert and ready.

Gazing into the back of the camper, Nerit said, "One dead. Young female. Broken neck."

Bill sighed sadly behind them. "Probably the best thing for the poor kid."

Nerit began to slowly descend toward the truck, the roots of the trees providing a natural staircase for her to use. She hesitated, then slowly squatted down where she stood.

"Two male bodies at the bottom of the gorge. Both bound, gagged, appeared to have been raped, then shot execution style in the back of the head," her voice said with no emotion.

Bill frowned and motioned to Jenni. "Follow me down. I want to get a closer look."

Nerit held her position as the other two made their way to the bodies. Travis kept a watch on the road with a troubled expression on his face.

Bill took his time examining the bodies and moving around the crime scene. Scrutinizing every detail, he slowly came to some terrible conclusions. With a sigh, he motioned to Jenni and they both struggled to get back up to the road.

"What do you think?"

"Honestly, Nerit, I think they were punished for failing. It's very methodical. Very intense. It feels...angry."

Nerit nodded. "The young girl, the loss of an asset: the loss of the truck, another asset. But worse, I think they weren't supposed to attack anyone from the fort. They were watching us. Probably trying to determine our strengths and our weaknesses. Maybe even determining their approach. Either they would have attempted to deceive us into letting them in or would have just launched a surprise attack. But now the element of surprise is gone."

"This is what you were thinking the first night," Travis said after a beat.

Nerit nodded. "I just needed the proof."

"So now what?" Bill followed the others toward the truck.

"We return to waiting. Keep alert. They will wait now. Wait until they feel we are vulnerable. We are at stalemate." Nerit opened up the door to the Hummer and slid in.

Jenni looked back down the road at figures lumbering toward them. The zombies were far off, but coming. She slid in as well. "Great. This sucks. One more thing to worry about."

Bill slammed his door shut as Travis climbed into the front seat. "Nothing is easy now, is it?"

"No, not at all," Travis answered grimly. "Not at all."

# Chapter 16

## 1. And a Move is Made

Awave of zombies hit the fort two days later. One of the guards explained that she had been leaning over to pick up her thermos when she heard a growl. Looking down, she saw a zombie turn the corner and began to beat on the trucks making up the first perimeter. She had raised her gun to pick him off when suddenly thirty zombies rounded the corner and began to rabidly attack the perimeter.

"Good for sniper practice," Nerit said when she was informed. She lit a cigarette and walked out to view the newcomers.

Travis and Curtis stood side by side on a guard platform watching the crowd.

"Not from this town," Curtis told Nerit. "I don't recognize them."

"Think they are migrating?" Travis asked.

"Maybe following food," Nerit said thoughtfully.

Bill yawned as he joined them and looked out. "Well...shit."

"Understatement," Travis said with a smile. Katie slipped up behind him and slid her arm around his waist. Turning, he kissed her forehead.

"Gawd, the reek of them," Katie murmured.

"Looks like farm workers," Bill decided. "Clothes are pretty screwed up, but looks like farm workers."

"Could be from anywhere," Curtis added.

Nerit pointed to one of the male zombies. "A WalMart worker. Where is the nearest WalMart?"

"Lemme think. About an hour south of here," Curtis answered.

"Migrating," Travis sighed.

"Maybe someone corralled them toward us," Nerit said in a thoughtful tone.

"When Jenni and I were on the road, a crowd of zombies chased us and just kept following the road we escaped on. When we came back, they were still pursuing us on that road," Katie said to Nerit. "Someone would just have to give them a little lure in the right direction."

"In our direction," Curtis snorted. "Great."

"Think the bandits are that smart?" Travis wondered aloud.

Bill shook his head. "Who knows? There are different breeds out in this area. It's remote. Country mentality is strong outside the towns. A lot of hardheaded, old-time mindsets."

"Women are property?" Katie was thinking of the girl Katarina and Bill had seen tied up in the back of the truck that had nearly run them down.

"You can beat your wife as long as it's on the county courthouse steps with a stick no thicker than her thumb," Curtis said softly. "Old country law that never got erased from the books."

Bill nodded. "Assholes live everywhere. Just in the countryside, they got more privacy and more leeway. Makes a lot of stuff easier."

"We still have some pockets of survivors to pick up, right?" Katie put her hands on her hips and tilted her head toward Travis.

"At least eight. We've been picking them up in order of proximity or if their supplies are low. We're also trying to send in double teams. Ones to rescue, others to get supplies from the stores. Winter is still months away, but we have to be ready." Travis stared down at the rabid crowd below. "We got a few groups that got bad infestations around them, too."

"I think we need to bring them in as soon as we can,"Nerit said. "Each time out, change tactics. They're watching us. Let them stay confused."

"I hate to be the devil's advocate, but maybe we should sit tight," Curtis said softly. "We got our own to take care of."

Nerit gave him a long look. "They are our own. We've been in contact with them for quite some time."

Curtis sighed and nodded. "I just feel like we should be trying to be safe inside and not going out there."

Travis shook his head. "We may not want to admit it, but we are building a new world here. We need good, solid people to help us continue it. We need some of those people out there. One is an RN, another is an electrician."

"We have no choice, but to get them," Katie said firmly.

Curtis was staring at Travis intently. "What if people die going out there?"

"We are all taking risks," Bill answered for Travis. "To do what is right."

"Protecting the good of society is what we are trained to do. It is what comes first to our minds. Protecting our own should be a priority." Curtis shook his head.

"We bring them in," Travis said. "Because they are our own."

There was an uncomfortable silence. Curtis just sighed.

Nerit waved to the zombies rabidly growling and jostling each other below. "Target practice for Jason and his crew. Don't they have some new weapons to try out?"

"Herding zombies," Curtis chuckled to himself. "What will those dumb fuck bandits think of next?"

Katie turned to Nerit. "Well, it was nice of the bandits to send us targets."

Nerit gave Katie a sly smile. "Oh, yes. It gives me a little more insight into their leaders mind." She slipped past Katie and down the stairs.

"Okay, is it just me, or is she one scary old woman?" Bill blinked his eyes rapidly, his hands on his hips.

"The scariest," Curtis said somberly. "She scares me shitless." He followed Nerit down the stairs.

"Glad she's on our side," Katie added, and followed.

Bill looked over at the zombies. "Yeah, me, too."

## 2. And So It Begins Again

Peggy studied her little map with all its highlighted spots she had laid out on the front desk in the lobby. She drew an x through one of the bright yellow circles. They had lost contact with one of the survivor groups. She had finally given up hope this morning after a third day of no response. It could be the zombies, or it could be the bandits. There was no way of truly knowing.

Looking up, she saw the newest additions to the fort, three little kids, running around the lobby with her son, playing what looked like a superhero game. The new family had broken her heart when they had arrived, reeking to high heaven and absolutely terrified. When the wife had seen their new suite in the hotel, she had burst into tears. At their first meal, the children had kept stuffing their faces until the youngest had thrown up. It had grown too easy to forget just how good those in the fort had it compared to those stuck in tiny pockets out in the hostile world.

Nerit glanced over at the children, then back down at the map. "Five locations. Which is the most desperate?"

Travis was at her side, staring down at the map as well. He was certain to be the new mayor, despite Steven Mann's dirty politicking. Manny was a fading leader as he struggled with health problems. People automatically deferred to Travis now. The vote was the last step to making his ascension to the fort leader official.

"Sadler Farm. It's a family and a few workers. They've been holed up in the main house since the second day of the outbreak. It's an old stone house with storm windows, shutters and doors. Originally, they declined joining us. They felt they had it under control. Considering how far out they are, you would think they would be safe, but a wave of the dead arrived about ten days ago. They're just about out of ammo now and they are low on food. For awhile, they told me they had come and gone from the house to the garden and the chicken coops with no issue. Then one day the zombies hit in force and they lost two men and ended up barely holding them off."

Nerit nodded stoically. "The RN is where?"

"Bowie High School in Raymond," Peggy answered. "She has two teachers and four kids with her. Two are hers. She was at the school giving flu shots on the first day. The school was evacuated, but they remained behind deliberately."

"Why?" Nerit's gaze was curious.

Peggy laughed a little. "She watches horror movies and saw one of the walking dead and was pretty sure it was a zombie. Then she noticed bites on some of the people being put on the buses. So she and the others hid and waited until everyone had been shipped off to a rescue center, then barricaded themselves inside the school. It's a very small school, so it wasn't that hard."

Nerit smiled wryly. "Horror movies...odd how they became a guideline for survival."

Katie joined them, dressed in hunting gear. She leaned into Travis and he slung an arm around her shoulders. A tender kiss followed, Peggy grinned.

Peggy loved seeing them together. Her own marriage had been rocky and never very romantic. She knew she was a sucker for country love songs and soap operas. She couldn't help it. But this was the real thing. She could see it. Feel it. Travis and Katie had found real, true love. She was happy for them. She just wished it would one day happen to her. Of course, in this dead world, what were the chances of that?

"So these are the last two groups?" Travis pondered over the map.

"One more. A family trapped in a trailer. Again, doing okay until a recent mob of zombies arrived a few days ago. They were also holdouts, but they have not been doing so well. They're just bullheaded country folk, but they now need us to go get them." Peggy tapped the map and stared up at Nerit and Travis.

Nerit was deep in thought, her finger tracing over the various points on the map.

"Who is out there right now?" Travis leaned against the counter and stared up at Peggy.

She really liked his style. He always gave his full attention to her and valued her opinion. It wasn't like how she had to bust heads with Manny constantly.

"Ed is out with his group protecting the harvesting of his peach groves right now," Peggy answered. "He took Lenore with him."

"Lenore?" Travis blinked.

"I felt she was ready," Nerit muttered as she studied the map.

"Jenni is out on a scavenging run with Curtis, Katarina, Felix and Dylan," Katie added. "They're due back soon."

"Dylan? We sent Dylan out? Isn't he a bit young?" Travis arched an eyebrow.

"He just turned eighteen. We have men in the military that age...or at least we did," Nerit pointed out.

"And no one out on the field is reporting anything odd? No bandits?" Travis lifted his eyebrows.

"No, just those waves of zombies showing up. Kinda like they do here. I think that's the bandits," Peggy answered.

"I agree with that assessment." Nerit began to write notes down on a pad of paper.

"You don't think they've decided maybe we're too big to take on?" Katie asked.

"I think they're trying to figure out what to do with us," Travis answered.

"Agreed." Nerit leaned over the map and studied it. "Waiting for a time to strike."

Ken rushed down the hall from the communication center and leaped behind the counter. Hugging Peggy, he startled her.

"Oh, my gawd! You will not believe my news!"

Travis slightly smiled. "Oh, yeah?"

"Yeah! Ed called in from where they are getting all those delicious peaches!"

"So the good news is we're having peach cobbler?" Katie queried teasingly.

Ken gave her a dark look. "I'm building this up. You're cramping my style! Shush, you!"

"Spill it, Ken." Peggy was about to smack him upside the head.

"My girl, Lenore, my bestest girl, is safe and on her way back with mission numero uno under her belt. That's the first part. Second part, Ed's boys were there!"

"No shit?" Peggy was stunned. Ed rarely spoke of the three sons that were somewhere out on the deadlands. When he did, it was often when he was drunk. The boys were all Ed had left in the world after his wife, Edna, had died. All three had been away at school on the first day. Peggy knew Ed had hopes they were still alive, but this was amazing news. "Seriously. The boys were all alive?"

"Yep! They fought their way back to Ed's farm and holed up there! They thought their Daddy was dead until they saw him in the peach groves with the team!" Ken danced around. "Lenore is trying to find out if any of them are gay."

"I swear to God, all you think about is finding a boyfriend," Peggy groused.

"Like you don't?"

"Hey, my sex life, or lack thereof, ain't your business." Peggy shook her pen in his face.

"Hard up, aren't you?"

"I'm gonna kick your ass, Ken."

Katie smirked. "My money is on Peggy if they throw down."

Travis shook his head as he laughed. "Ken looks kinda vicious."

Ken playfully snarled at him. "Okay, good news time is over! Back to the communication center!" He bounced back down the hall.

"I'm gonna choke him. I swear to God, I will," Peggy muttered.

Nerit looked up from her map, seeming impervious to Ken's exploits. "I think I see how we need to handle this. What we need to do. They're after resources: food, guns, drugs, and women. We're going to need to lure them out. I think I know how." She tapped the map with one finger.

Peggy leaned over and looked at where she was pointing. "Nerit, that's where you're from. No one is there."

"The gun store is there," Nerit said calmly.

Travis shifted uncomfortably on his feet. "You said the weapons are in the safe. They can't get in there."

"Nope. They can't. But we're going to need those weapons. That ammunition. We've put off going out there." Nerit looked very pale, but calm. "We should have gone before." She pulled out her keys and handed them to Travis. "It's the round gold key and silver square one to get into the store. I will give you the safe combination."

Everyone gathering around the map looked uncomfortable. An excursion to the gun store to reclaim the last of the gun stock and ammunition had long been on the list of things to do, but they had found other stockpiles to keep them well armed.

Peggy shifted on her feet, feeling uncomfortable with where this was going.

Travis slid the keys into his pocket. "We didn't really need to go until now, you know. "

"We didn't go because of Ralph," Nerit said simply. "And we have no time for such sentimentality anymore."

Travis reached out and rubbed her shoulder gently. "We'll be respectful."

"I know," Nerit answered.

Katie slipped an arm around the older woman's waist. Nerit, surprisingly, leaned against her for comfort.

"If we head to the store and make a production of it, that will pull them out. And we can use it as a diversion to get the last of our survivors in," Nerit said in a slightly quavering voice. "We need to pull them out. Get them to confront us."

"So we can get into a fight with the bandits?" Peggy looked at her incredulously.

"No, so we can show them they can't beat us," Nerit answered grimly.

Travis looked at Nerit long and hard, then slowly nodded. "I get where you are going with this."

"We'll work out the details, but I have the general plan already in my head," Nerit answered.

Jenni exploded into the lobby of the hotel. Her fury was livid in her eyes and her skin was flushed. "Where the hell is Bill?"

"Communication center," Peggy said, and pointed down the hall. "He's training Ken."

"What's going on?" Katie stepped toward Jenni.

"Fucktard got Dylan killed!" She pointed behind her, trembling with rage.

Curtis came into view, his head down, looking pale. "Jenni, I didn't mean to-"

"Oh, shut up!"

Katarina and Felix appeared behind Curtis. Katarina laid a gentle hand on the younger man's shoulder.

"Let it go, Jenni," she said in a soft voice.

"No! I won't! He's the gawddamn Vigilante! He told Dylan to go into that storeroom and it had a fuckin' zombie inside! He did it on purpose cause he was mad at him for smoking weed!"

Curtis was trembling with emotion and looked up at Jenni, tears streaming down his face. "I thought it was clear!"

"You liar!"

"Get Bill," Travis said in a soft voice to Katie. "And Juan."

Katie gave him a quick nod and hurried down the hall.

Travis pushed off from the counter and walked slowly toward Jenni. "Jenni, things go wrong out there. You know it."

Jenni whirled around, toward Travis. "Dylan was a boy! He's just a boy! Curtis got him killed."

"I thought it was clear!" Curtis' face was red, his hands clenched at his side.

Katarina held onto Curtis shoulder, partially to comfort him, partially to keep him back from Jenni.

"It was not an easy ride back with these two going at it," Felix grumbled.

"I want him locked up!" Jenni stomped her foot.

"Jenni, calm down. We need to take care of this in a calm manner."

Peggy slowly walked up behind Travis, glad for his gentle demeanor. She, personally, wanted to slap Jenni and shake Curtis, but she also felt sick at the thought of someone so young dying so horribly. Poor Dylan.

Bill appeared with Katie, hoisting up his belt and looking slightly annoyed. "What's going on?"

Jenni and Curtis started talking at the same time. Katarina and Felix kept trying to interject, but the noise was unbelievable. Peggy felt like screaming at them to shut up.

Bill raised a hand. Everyone fell silent.

"Curtis, talk to me. What happened?" Bill looked at the younger man with a fatherly compassion that Peggy admired.

"We were in the Walgreen's. We made a sweep through. I checked the storeroom. Didn't see nothing. Told Dylan to go in and start organizing what we needed to take. I went to get a dolley. I heard him screaming and ran in. I guess the zombie came off a shelf or something. I don't know. I shot both of them." Tears were streaming down Curtis' face. He rubbed at his flushed cheeks furiously.

Bill looked at Katarina and Felix. "Is that what you saw?"

"I didn't see anything, but I heard Curtis telling Dylan to take care of things in the storeroom," Katarina answered.

"I didn't check the storeroom myself, but I heard Curtis call it as clear." Felix shrugged.

"He sent him in there to die!" Jenni couldn't hold her tongue anymore. "He did it on purpose!"

Juan came running into view just then. His boot heels rang out in the huge lobby. He skidded to a stop near Jenni. "Babe?"

"Curtis did it on purpose," Jenni shouted again, tears streaming down her face. "He did it on purpose. He's the fuckin' Vigilante! It could have been Jason! He could have killed my son!"

The minute the words left Jenni's lips, the atmosphere in the room changed significantly. Peggy could feel it. The accusation against Curtis suddenly felt impotent. Bill reached out and snagged the younger man's shoulder in a firm, comforting grip.

Juan grabbed Jenni's arm and twirled her into his arms. She clung to him, crying violently.

"Curtis, go to your room. Clean up. Rest up. We'll talk later," Bill ordered.

Katarina and Felix both sighed as Bill shooed them off as well.

Katie smoothed Jenni's hair back from her face as Juan whispered in her ear.

"You two, calm her down?"

Juan nodded to Bill. He helped Katie lead Jenni away.

Travis stood beside Peggy. "What do you think?" He looked at Bill pointedly.

"Shit happens out there. People die. And it ain't easy," Bill answered.

"Can't disagree with ya there." Slowly, Travis turned back to where Nerit was still studying the map. "C'mon, Peggy. We got work to do."

Peggy looked back at Curtis one more time before the elevator doors shut. Her stomach clutched tightly. Her nerves were getting the best of her. It was a fucked up world and she hated it. But at least Bill and Travis were there to make it better.

Trying to hide the trembling of her hands, she followed after Travis.

"What's the plan?" Travis asked Nerit, leaning his elbows on the counter.

"I heard there was a disturbance! I fully intend to reveal the truth behind the matter to all who will listen! I will not allow the truth of the conspiracies of this illegal fort to go unreported to the-" Calhoun burst into the lobby with his video camera already filming.

"I'll get rid of him, "Peggy said with a sigh.

"Actually," Nerit said with a wicked little smile. "We're going to need him for our plan."

Peggy looked at the smelly old man and then Nerit. "Him?" She was incredulous."

Travis looked back at Calhoun and then Nerit. "You sure?"

"Oh, yes," Nerit said. "I'm sure."

Calhoun spotted them and headed toward them, his foil hat looking about to fly off his head his was coming so fast.

"Just the man I am looking for," Nerit said.

Calhoun looked shocked, then a little afraid. "I will not assist you in your nefarious plans, Amazonian Queen!"

"Yes, you will," Nerit assured him. "Because it will help defeat the marauding aliens attempting land grabs and abductions."

Calhoun looked at her suspiciously from beneath his scraggly eyebrows, then slowly tilted his head. "Okay. I'm listening."

As Peggy listened to Nerit's plan slowly unfurl, she felt her fear began to subside. Perhaps, it would all work out okay after all.

# 3. When Nothing is Clear

Travis handed Katie a beer and slid into the chair next to her. She was sitting with her feet hooked up on the balcony rail, her lean legs looking tan and fit in the waning sunlight. Dinner was sitting nice and filling in their bellies. Sitting out on their balcony seemed like the right way to end an evening.

Travis stretched out his legs in front of him and stared at his bare feet. They ached, just like the rest of him.

Katie tapped her beer against his and took a swig. "Jenni's okay now. I called Juan while you were in the shower."

He looked toward her. "She took it hard, huh?"

Katie pulled on her shorts a little, still trying to get comfortable. "Yeah. Once she saw Jason, it was a little better. I think she understood why she flipped out so bad after awhile."

"She's still not talking about the boys, huh?"

"Sometimes I wonder if she ever will. I feel so bad for her. She says she sees Lloyd every day now, out of the corner of her eye, or standing in the shadows. She's ignoring those visions. That's good, but she's not dealing with any of it."

"We're all fucked in the head cause of all this," Travis decided. "I've been hearing a few things around the fort."

"Like what?"

"People seeing ghosts, for one. Or hearing their voices."

Katie nodded. "Me, too."

"You dream of Lydia."

"I miss Lydia," Katie reminded him, then slightly shrugged. "But I do have to admit that, sometimes, in my dreams, I feel her presence. Or at least I think I do. Most of my dreams about her are just like flashes of memory or something along those lines. But, sometimes, I dream about her and she feels...real."

Travis' brow puckered as he considered this. "I can't say I do believe in ghosts exactly. But considering that we got the living dead running around, I can't really discount stuff either. Maybe Jenni's asshole husband really is haunting her, trying to finish what he started. I don't know. But I do know that until she deals with what happened with those boys, he's gonna be able to get to her. Ghost or not."

Katie sighed and ran a hand over her blond curls. "Yep. I agree. Do you see ghosts? Dream them?"

Travis shook his head. "No. But I wasn't exactly close to anyone when it went down. My parents died in a car crash a few years back. I don't have siblings. My fiancée and I were over. Being in Ashley Oaks to help with the restoration was my new beginning in life. Juan was the one who got me out here. He was the one person in my life giving me any sort of grounding, I guess you could say."

"You're kinda like Jenni that way. This whole thing going down gave you a new lease on life, too."

"It gave me you," Travis answered, taking her hand. He looked at her. His emotions were very close to the surface. It was never easy at the fort. There was always hard work to be done and problems to sort out. He spent long hours planning with Eric and Juan on the fort expansion, long hours with Nerit on fort defenses, long hours with Peggy and Bill on the internal workings of the fort. He wasn't officially mayor yet, but everyone was acting like he was. Some nights he was so exhausted all he wanted to do was lay in Katie's arms and listen to her breathe.

She ran her fingers over his. "Did you know that today is the first day of August?"

Travis laughed and shook his head. "No. No, I didn't. Hell, we missed the Fourth of July, didn't we?"

"Uh huh." Katie looked toward the Texas flag in the distance, most likely over the library. There was a huge one that flew over city hall.

"We can't miss out on other holidays. That's not right," Travis decided. He held her hand as he lifted his beer with his other.

"Halloween, Thanksgiving, Christmas, New Years. Once we handle the bandits, maybe we can start looking forward to those."

"We should have enough food to get through the winter and beyond. The hunters are bringing in plenty of venison and beef right now. We got that garden planted. Things should be okay. The well is good, got generators the ready for back up, firewood in case of power outages-"

"Travis."

"Huh?"

"Stop."

He blinked.

"Stop. It's okay. Just let it go. Just relax." She motioned toward the hills and the approaching night. "Enjoy the view, enjoy the moment, the here and now. You've done all you can for today."

Travis nodded. He tried to shove it all away. It took about a minute for his pulse rate to drop and for his tense body to relax. When he finally opened his eyes, he saw the first stars appearing. It was beautiful.

"What would I do without you?"

"Let's not find out," Katie answered.

She slid out of her chair and snuggled onto his lap. He wrapped his arms around her and relaxed even more as she stretched her legs over his and got comfortable. Travis kissed her brow and relished the feel of her in his arms. All he wanted to do was protect her and their home, but he had to remember that he needed to just relax and enjoy the fact that she was safe.

*I'm going to marry you,* he thought, and pressed his lips against her cheek. When the time was right, he was going to marry her. And it would be the happiest moment of his life.

All they had to do was get through the next few days, defeat the bandits, and buckle down for the coming fall and winter.

"Stop thinking about work," she chided.

"What?"

"You got all tense again." Katie laughed.

"Dammit," Travis muttered.

"Okay. There is only one thing that will get your mind off work. I'm going to have to get naked," Katie said, and slid off his lap.

Travis grinned. "Can I come along?"

"You better." Katie slipped into their bedroom.

Travis scrambled after her.

# Chapter 17

## 1. The Countdown Begins

The morning of the big day arrived. They were done waiting for the bandits to come to them. They were going to lure them out.

Nerit was standing with Peggy when Travis and Katie walked through the lobby together. They were dressed and ready to go. Holding hands, they looked pensive, but ready.

"We're heading out to the shop, Nerit," Travis said.

Nerit nodded tersely. "And you have the vault combination?"

Travis bobbed his head and said, "Yeah. I have it." He looked at Nerit with compassion, but seemed reluctant to say much.

Peggy marveled at Nerit's way of dealing with things. With her husband dead of a gunshot, Nerit had collected all the ammunition and stuffed it into an old bank vault in the shop. Next, she had stacked the better firepower in as well until she could fit no more, then shoved the door shut and twirled the combination lock. What she had left in the cases were .22's with no ammunition. Peggy would have just run, terrified of the bandits. Nerit's straight thinking in the midst of her personal tragedy had made things a little safer for them all.

Nerit looked down for a long moment, then finally said, "Please, don't disturb him."

"We won't," Katie responded, and kissed Nerit's cheek.

Nerit gave her a small smile, then it slipped away as she looked determined once more. "Thank you," she said.

"We'll see you when we get back," Travis said to both of them.

Katie gave a little wave, then they walked off, hand in hand.

Peggy sighed wistfully and Nerit raised an eyebrow.

"I can't help it. Young love!" Peggy blushed and pretended to scrutinize her map.

"And soon a baby," Nerit sighed.

"She's pregnant?" Peggy blinked rapidly with surprise.

"I don't think she knows yet," Nerit answered. She leaned over the map and studied it.

"Really?" Peggy thought about how long it took her to realize her own pregnancy. Cody had sneaked up on her. "She has the glow, huh?"

Nerit gave a curt nod.

"But she shouldn't be going out if--"

"We all take risks. All of us," Nerit answered coolly. "Even living here is a risk. We never know what tomorrow may bring or the next hour or minute."

Peggy started to protest, then looked at the bricked-up windows and doors. Nerit was right. Nothing was really safe. It was all just varying degrees of it.

In the beginning of all of it, she had really thought the army would come and save everyone, that big trucks would drive up and everyone would get on board, that they would go off to some top secret underground fortress. But it had never happened. She remembered how silly she had thought their truck perimeter was in the beginning and how she had rolled her eyes at the wall. *The army will come soon*, she had thought over and over again. Now she realized the wisdom of them defending themselves and making it safe for everyone taking refuge in the construction site.

"Contact the survivor groups and let them know we are coming today," Nerit ordered.

Peggy chewed on her bottom lip, her nervousness growing. Behind Nerit, there were children, squealing with delight and running around with the little Jack Russell terrier named Pepe. It was hard when their people traveled out into the deadlands. It was too horrible when you had to wait and see if they all made it back and if not, who hadn't made it. Dylan wasn't their only loss in the last few months. The children running around were who they were doing this for.

Nerit slid the paper across the counter to Peggy.

Looking over it, Peggy scratched behind one ear. "Okay, I'm on it. I'll start contacting the groups."

Nerit gave her a nod then walked off slowly, slightly favoring one leg. If she knew Peggy noticed, she'd probably be annoyed.

Peggy sighed and hurried to the communication center.

## 2. The Countdown Begins

Katie watched the gates glide open, her stomach knotting. The gates to the inner courtyard were already closed behind the two vehicles leaving the fort. Katie and Travis were in the Hummer. Four others were in the souped up mini-van behind them.

In the distance, two zombies moved toward the opening gates, but the fort snipers took them down with eerie efficiency. Nerit had meticulously trained the most gifted of the fort's people in her art and Katie heard that Katarina had risen to be her star pupil.

Katie pushed down the accelerator and started down the road. Glancing into the review mirror, she saw the mini-van following closely. Felix was driving with a new guy, Bob, sitting beside him. She was hoped the new people would be able to handle the stress of entering the deadlands.

"This is pretty nice," Travis decided, looking around the interior.

"Should be, for how much it costs," Katie answered.

"I hear it's actually Blanche's. She used it to go shopping." Travis looked amused.

Katie shook her head. "Amazing, isn't it? And I felt guilt over the convertible Lydia gave me."

"You would look cute in a convertible," Travis decided.

"Yeah, but I think I have a fetish for big 4x4 trucks now." Katie winked. "They smash up zombies better."

"Oh, you better watch yourself. You're starting to sound like a redneck and not a big bad prosecuting attorney," Travis teased.

"Oh, I am still the big bad prosecuting attorney," Katie assured him, and gave him her coldest courtroom glare.

"Damn," he laughed. "I hope I never get that look for real."

"Just watch yourself and you'll be okay. Otherwise, you're screwed." She turned her gaze fully to the road as the Hummer sped out of town.

"Ruthless, huh?"

"And I still am."

A zombie staggered out into the road, clawing at the air in their direction. Katie didn't flinch. The truck hit it straight on, flinging it off the road. The van behind them swerved to avoid its flying body.

"Ummmm...I noticed," Travis said with a wry smile, settling back into his seat.

Katie was comfortably settled into the leather seat. There were less and less zombies in town as the snipers picked them off from afar. The idea of systematically clearing the town had been considered, but without a sufficient way to keep the zombies out, it was a waste of man and firepower. It had finally been determined they would aim to slowly take over the entire downtown area with a wall encircling them, then concentrate on keeping that area secure. Even controlled burning of the rest of the town had been discussed. What would happen to the parts of town that they would no longer use was still up for debate, but Katie had seen Travis' plans for what could become of their little fortress. She knew that he had definitive ideas that could work very well and keep them safe.

If they could only keep safe while they built it...

"Do you think Nerit is right?" Travis asked after a stretch of silence.

Katie was so wrapped up in watching the road, his voice startled her. "Probably."

"She does have a lot more experience with this type of thing I guess," Travis said thoughtfully.

"And she has trained and briefed all of us," Katie added. Her gaze swept over the road in front of them.

No zombies.

No bandits.

So far so good.

Travis looked back at the mini-van, then returned his gaze to the scenery quickly flying by the windows. The scorching heat of the late summer had crisped the trees leaves, and the grass was so dry and brown it merely resembled the world they had grown used to. It was hot and dead. He couldn't help but feel a sense of foreboding.

"Having to deal with the bandits on top of the zombies is bull shit. It's hard to understand why they just didn't try to help out instead of...you know...killing, raping, stealing."

Katie sighed a little. "Trust me, I've pondered that many times during my career. But then again, maybe it's just human nature to try to survive. And some people have a twisted nature and a twisted way of surviving."

Three zombies were standing in the road when they rounded the bend. Katie didn't swerve, but hit them straight on. One managed to cling to the deer guard on the front of the Hummer for a few seconds, then slid off and bounced down the road. The zombies didn't look very human anymore. Their shrunken features and mottled bodies just didn't seem quite as terrifyingly human as they had been in the first days. It was easier and easier to see them just as monsters.

Travis reached out and rested his hand on her thigh. "You be careful, okay?"

Katie ran her hand over his. "And you be careful, too."

***

Jenni sat in the front seat behind Ed, the driver of the short bus. Bill sat across from her, looking grim and anxious. Four more people sat scattered throughout the bus. There was sparse conversation, but mostly silence. Behind the bus was a large moving truck that carried another team. Jenni's would pick up any survivors; the other team would look for supplies.

The bus was even more tricked out than before. Now it had heavy mesh over all the windows and a heavy deer guard in the front. Jenni thought it was almost like being in a prison bus.

They were bringing the last of the survivors in their area today. It was a big moment for the fort. After today their population would basically be complete.

Running her hand over her rifle, she sighed. She was very hot and the air conditioner was barely working. Outside the windows, the world was brown and dead. Occasionally, they would see a zombie staggering down the road or through a field. It didn't take much imagination to know that the cities were probably crammed with the creatures, but out here, they were seemingly sparse these days. She had a feeling they should never get too comfortable with that thought.

Jenni had come a long way in these stressful long months since that first day. It was as if her life before that morning was just a dim memory of another world. The days on the road seemed stark and vivid in her mind. The crazed sense of liberation, the fear, the adrenaline, the passionate desire to live; she had felt stripped of all her boundaries and free to be herself, whatever that was, at last.

Despite all that she had lost, she was happy, happy to have Katie and Jason as her family, happy to love and be loved by Juan, happy with her role as the psycho zombie killer. She felt free to speak Spanish to Juan and not fear someone's disapproving gaze. That was an enormous relief.

She still had nightmares about her children. It hurt to think of Benji and Mikey. She missed them horribly. At times, she would weep uncontrollably when no one else was around. It hurt to think of them out there, decaying slowly as they prowled for flesh. Those tiny fingers still reached for her in her nightmares. Lloyd's damn ghost lingered on the corners of her life. She ignored his taunts and tried not to listen to him. His words only stirred her guilt at surviving. He reminded her of that other time, that other life, that other home.

The fort was far away from her old house and old life. She loved it, but she was terribly afraid that they could lose it all.

If Nerit was right, this would be a decisive day for all of them. It would be a day none of them would forget one way or the other.

Today would decide if they all lived and died if Nerit was right.

Jenni lowered her head and sighed.

Those tiny fingers seemed oddly closer today...

# 3. Ten, Nine, Eight

When the Hummer drew up to the old hunting store, it was immediately obvious the bandits had not only returned, but had broken into the store. Decaying bodies littered the street. A van with its tires blown out and all the windows shattered listed to one side of the street.

"Nerit's handiwork," Travis decided.

The bars of one of the windows were twisted to one side. Katie stared at the damage and could only imagine that the bandits had pulled the bars loose by using a chain and a truck.

"Move with extreme caution," Travis said into the CB.

"Understood," came the answer over a cackle of static.

Katie drew up to the front of the store and looked around. The bandits had gone nuts in this small town. All the windows of the main street were shattered and merchandise from the store littered the street. The body of a woman was tied to the lamppost nearby.

Correction.

A zombie woman was tied to the lamppost. She was mostly eaten, but her eyes were moving, watching them, her mouth opening and closing on slender sinews.

"I really hate these guys," Katie whispered.

"Yeah," Travis agreed grimly.

Turning off the Hummer, Katie drew her rifle onto her lap. "Ready?"

Travis gave her a quick nod. He drew Nerit's keys from his pocket and moved toward the front door. The people from the min-van also slid out into the street and followed, guns drawn, looking alert.

As Travis moved past the gaping hole that was once a window, a face appeared snarling and growling. Its hands reached desperately through the hole toward him.

"Wait! Don't kill it yet!"

Katie moved toward the opening and stared intently at the zombie's face. The long scraggly hair and beard fit the description both Bill and Nerit had given of the bandits. "One of their own, I think." She drew her revolver and shot it point blank in the face.

"You're scary sometimes," Travis said with surprise, but also with admiration. He peered into the store, his gun raised to cover the interior. "Hello! Hey zombies! Hey, come here!"

Katie stood behind him, giving him cover. Nothing stirred within the store.

"Let's go in," Travis said to his team. He moved to the front door and slowly unlocked it.

Two members of the team stood guard. One was the new guy, Bob. The other was Lenore. She stood with her hunting bow at the ready staring at the tied up zombie woman with a somber expression. Lifting the hunting bow, she drew back her arm, then let the arrow fly. It pierced the zombie woman's eye and silenced her growls.

"No point in leaving her like that," Lenore shrugged.

Pushing the door open, Travis  stood at the ready, waiting to see if anymore of the dead lurked inside. Katie walked past him and into the store, Travis following close behind.

Bob followed, his face sweating profusely. Travis was worried about him. Bob had been rescued in the last few weeks and had yet to really prove himself at the fort. This was his first big chance. Travis hoped that Nerit's training would pay off.

They made a sweep of the first floor, checking behind every counter and behind tables. Most of the merchandise remaining in the store was littered across the floor. As Katie passed one pile of canvas bags, she was disgusted to see someone had urinated and defecated on the pile.

"They're animals," she grunted.

"Let's find the vault." Travis tried to ignore the stench and kept moving.

To their relief, the old bank vault was still locked. There were signs that the bandits had tried to get into it, but it had remained impervious to their attempts to open it.

"Okay, this is a good sign," Travis said with relief. He pulled out a piece of paper and began to twirl the knob, his brow burrowed with concentration.

Katie glanced toward the stairwell that lead up to Nerit and Ralph's apartment. This place had felt so safe in those first horrible days. Now it was desecrated. It made her angry, sad, and filled her with other emotions she could not quite define. She wished she could walk up those stairs and find Nerit and Ralph in the kitchen, sipping coffee and talking in their strange shorthand version of a conversation.

Something upstairs moved.

Katie looked toward Travis as he grinned and yanked the door open. Inside the vault, she saw weapons and boxes of ammo piled high.

""We're in business," Travis declared. "Let's get this stuff loaded up."

"Travis, I heard a noise upstairs," Katie informed him.

"Shit," Travis sighed. "Okay, let's check it out. Bob, you and Felix get the stuff into the van. Have Lenore and Ken cover the road."

Bob nodded. "Gotcha."

Moving slowly, cautiously, and as quietly as possible, Katie and Travis moved up the stairs into Nerit and Ralph's old apartment. The stench of death filled their nostrils when they reached the landing. They stood in horror at the destruction that had been wrought on the apartment.

The furniture was destroyed and tossed in pieces into corners. Mementos, photos, and personal possessions were strewn about. Some of the photos were deliberately defaced. Porn magazines were also mixed in with the debris.

"They're animals," Katie gasped.

"Yeah," Travis said, and felt a chill sweep over him. He looked at her and felt fear. If these monsters ever got a hold of Katie...

He couldn't bear the thought.

Moving down the hall, they entered the dining room and found the source of the noise Katie had heard.

A woman lay on the floor, spread eagle, naked. Her wrists and ankles were shackled and chained to huge spikes driven into the floor. Her mouth was duct taped shut. The silver tape went around her head so many times, only her eyes were visible.

There was a nasty bite on her shoulder and her undead condition explained her fate. She was trying to growl and was thrashing about. What looked like a tongue lay on the floor nearby. Travis had a feeling it was hers.

She had been brutally raped over and over again. That much was too clear. He grabbed a sheet off the floor and threw it over the zombie's body. It was too much to bear to see her like that.

"Why do I have a feeling the rapes took place before and after her death?" Katie's expression was grim.

Travis raised his gun and put the woman out of her misery. He then called downstairs to explain the shot and told the others to keep working.

Katie moved cautiously into the kitchen and looked around in shock. It was a mess. "They built their own meth lab."

Travis shook his head. "Damn. These guys are fucked up."

"Running around, strung out on meth, while zombies eat the living...what a nightmare."

Together, Travis and Katie swept the rest of the apartment, finding it in utter shambles. The bandits had used photos as toilet paper and thrown them against the bathroom wall. It looked like they had squatted here for some time before moving on.

In silence, they pushed open the ajar bedroom door. Ralph's remains lay in a jumble in a corner. It looked like someone had just ripped off the quilt with him in it and tossed it aside. To make matters even more disgusting, it appeared the bed had been used. Cigarettes, drug paraphernalia, and beer bottles littered the bed. But it was a relief to see that Ralph was still very truly dead. Travis moved to the body's side and drew the blanket over its decomposing features.

"I hate these guys. Maybe even more than the zombies," Katie gasped. Tears filled her eyes, but she fought not to spill them.

"Let's go," Travis said in a tortured voice. "Let's get these bastards."

Together they moved back downstairs and began to help load the rest of the boxes into the van.

"We're being watched," Lenore said after around twenty minutes of packing. "I saw the glint of glass through those trees over there. I've seen it three times now. I'm sure it's binoculars."

"Nerit was right," Travis said, working as though they didn't know they were being watched. "Call it in, Ken."

The younger man nodded. He calmly climbed into the van and pretended to do something other than call the fort.

Lenore raised her hunting bow and let another arrow rip. A zombie just coming around a far corner dropped. "So I guess this is it."

"Can't be sure yet, but my money is on yes," Travis answered.

Katie shoved more ammunition boxes into the back of the Hummer. "I say we go now."

Felix heaved a huge box in. "I'm with her. Let's roll."

Ken slid back out of the van. Walking calmly to pick up a box, he said, "The scary old woman says we keep to the plan. No deviations."

"How many do you think there are?" Travis asked Lenore.

"I've seen at least one set of binoculars. I'm guessing one vehicle. Otherwise more guys would be staring at us."

"Good point," Katie said, lifting another box into the Hummer. "Are we done?"

"Last box here," Bob answered.

"Then we go," Travis said, and moved to the passenger door of the Hummer. "Felix, keep to the plan and don't panic."

"Dude, I have more experience out here than you do," Felix griped.

Travis shrugged. "Yeah, but I gotta sound like the condescending leader. It's my job."

Felix slightly laughed, shaking his head and climbed into the van. This time Lenore and Ken climbed into the backseat of the Hummer.

Katie turned on the Hummer and began to u-turn slowly. For a second, she too saw the glint of glass up in the tree line. Silently, she prayed that they would survive whatever came next. As the Hummer picked up speed, she reached out and took Travis' hand in her own.

Up behind the tree line, a truck started.

# Chapter 18

## 1. Seven, Six, Five

Jenni rubbed her trembling hands together and glanced out the window toward the dead town in the distance. It was just a few buildings. She could see the zombies milling around in the street, aimless without human prey to chase. They were far enough away that the zombies did not see or hear them, but the tiny outlines of their forms still made her stomach clench.

"We're getting close," Bill said. He looked tired and a little anxious. She knew he had been up many nights talking and planning with Nerit and Travis. "We'll deal with this and keep to the initial plan unless things change."

Jenni began to pull her long dark hair up into a knot on top of her head. She liked to wear it long and flowing, but that could be far too dangerous with zombies around. "I'm really sick and tired of these fuckers scaring us shitless."

"Truer words were never spoken." Bill chortled. "And I feel exactly the same way."

Jenni finished with her hair and looked at him curiously. "You got a bad feeling, huh?"

"Woke up with it in my gut," Bill admitted. "You too, huh?"

"Yeah. Things feel off," Jenni answered. She thought of the long, sweet kisses she had shared with Juan before she had left. It was as if they were sharing their last kisses. The thought of him made her stomach twist a little more. She missed him and just wanted to crawl into bed with him and feel his warm, strong arms around her.

"We're coming up on it," Ed announced.

Jenni steadied herself by holding onto the back of her seat. Her rifle held tightly in one hand, she looked ahead with intense scrutiny.

They were rescuing what remained of a family; three teenagers; one boy, two girls, and their mother. Their father had died after the first day of a bite. The kids had put his zombified remains down. Their grandparents had passed away recently from natural causes. The grandfather stopped eating so the rest of the family could have more rations and had died of a heart attack. His wife had followed soon after. The surviving family was holed up in a trailer house. Jenni was told they had been living off the grandmother's preserves the entire time. According to the briefing, the family's truck was broke down. They had no way to escape their small town. They had tried to walk to the neighbors for supplies, but had been chased back by zombies. The rescue team expected at least half a dozen zombies to be in the area.

"This isn't good," Bill decided.

The narrow dirt road unwound to reveal the trailer tucked in a clearing a ways back from the road. It had at least two additions built onto it. All the windows appeared to be boarded up, but the front door was hanging from its hinges. The muddied driveway revealed tire tracks. A group of zombies was gathered beneath a tree, growling and clawing at the trunk.

"Damn," Jenni said.

Behind her, the rest of the team were standing and releasing the safety on their weapons.

"Jenni, go up top," Bill said.

Half the zombies, around six, turned and rushed the bus.

Climbing up onto the back of the seat, Jenni shoved the hatch on top of the bus open. Bill helped raise her all the way up. Hot, grainy wind greeted her as the bus slowed down. She sat on the scorching metal roof as Bill handed up her rifle.

The zombies were closing fast, screeching, growling, clawed hands outstretched. They were more inhuman looking than ever before. The elements definitely were having an impact on them. Their skin was dark gray, their hair matted and wild, their faces shrunken. But the fresher ones that were nearly whole were startling fast, while their more mutilated counterparts staggered along behind them.

Jenni took down the front runner of the pack. The momentum of its run carried it forward and it skidded into the side of the bus with a wet sound. She fired at another zombie. It tumbled to the ground in a jumble of skirts.

*Ah, damn. It was a bride.*

Jenni wiped that thought away. She took aim at another zombie, a male. It reached the bus and began to bang on the driver's window. It startled Ed and he jerked the wheel. The bus swerved sharply. Jenni found herself pitched to one side and her hair unfurled as she clung to the roof. Peering down over the edge, she saw a zombie look up at her. She knew before it happened what it would do.

It grabbed her hair and began to yank.

She managed to hook her feet on the edge of the hatch and held onto the edge of the roof.

"Gawddammit, Ed," Bill shouted from inside the bus.

Jenni pushed back from the edge of the bus with her hands, the pain from her hair being pulled making her gasp. She tried hard to wrestle free, but the zombie was holding tight.

She heard a window slide open beneath her, then a shout, followed by two gunshots. Her hair came free and she fell back onto the roof of the bus. Grabbing up her rifle, she steadied herself as the bus came to a stop. She immediately aimed at the other zombies heading toward them.

More gunfire from those within the bus chorused with her shots. One by one, the zombies fell to the ground. A few persistent ones kept jumping up and down, reaching up toward the branches of the tree. Now that they were close enough, Jenni saw an emaciated young woman and a boy hardly older than Jason clinging to the high branches.

Jenni efficiently took out the zombies at the base of the tree and then looked down into the bus. "We need to move fast." She blinked as she saw blood splatter all over one side of the interior of the bus, then saw the body of a woman whose name she kept forgetting. She had been shot in the head. It took Jenni another moment to realize the woman's hand was bitten. It was more like a graze, but it looked like a zombie bite.

"She was trying to shoot the one that had your hair through the window. She fell against the grill and it bit her," Bill answered her unspoken question.

In this world, a bite was an instant death sentence. They all knew it, but it didn't make it any easier to deal with. Besides Ashley in the hotel, the fort had witnessed two other people turn into zombies before actual death. No one was sure why this sometimes happened, but they could take no chances.

Jenni blinked back tears, then nodded. "We need to get the kids out of the tree."

Ed pulled the bus up close to the tree, trying not to get cornered up against the trailer or the trees. The boy scrambled out onto a limb, clutching precariously to it.

"Jump down!" Jenni motioned to him.

"They got my sister and mom," he yelled down to her.

"The zombies?"

"No, some guys! They came and kicked in our door and grabbed my Mom and sister. I was in the back room with Annie and we went through the window."

"Jump down!"

The boy motioned to his sister, who shook her head, still clinging to the trunk of the tree.

"Annie, c'mon," the boy said.

She shook her head again.

"Jump down," Jenni ordered.

"Annie, please come with me," the boy insisted.

The girl once more shook her head, terror in her eyes.

Jenni fastened her gaze on the girl and felt sick to her stomach. Was this the way she looked when Katie had first seen her, shell-shocked and dazed? If so, too damn bad. "Annie, get your fuckin' ass down here now! Otherwise, you're gonna have to sit in that damn tree until the zombies figure out how to climb or you get so weak and fall. Now, if you want to die that way, be my guest, but I am taking your brother and we're getting the hell outta here."

Annie blinked, then began to cry. Trembling, she slowly crawled out onto the thick limb to her brother. With infinite care, her younger sibling helped lower her down to the top of the bus, then dropped down beside her.

Jenni blinked at the utter reek of them, but shoved that out of her mind. "The men who came here...why did they leave you in the tree?"

The girl disappeared through the hatch into the bus, Bill carefully lifting her down.

The boy rubbed his nose and shook his head. "I don't know. They kept trying to get us down, saying all sorts of sick shit. But we kept climbing higher. I knew we couldn't make a run for it with the zombies around. Anyway, they were even telling me stuff...about...you know...doing me in the..." The boy took a breath. "Anyway, one of the guys in a truck started yelling about a gun store and they all just went crazy. They told me and Annie that they would come back for us later if the zombies didn't get us first."

"Shit," Jenni whispered. "Bill, did you hear?"

"I heard," Bill answered, gazing up at them through the hatch.

Jenni and the boy scooted down into the bus as the back door slammed shut. The woman who had tried to save her now lay with the zombies on the cold, muddied ground.

"How many trucks?" Bill asked.

"Four," the boy answered. "And those guys were really fucking sick and scary."

His sister sat in a seat nearby, wrapped in a light blanket, shaking uncontrollably. "You need to get our Mom and sister."

"Ed, call it in," Bill ordered. "Nerit was right. It's going down today."

Jenni sighed. They had come up back roads to this place deliberately. In all likelihood, they had just missed the bandits on the main roads.

"How long ago did they leave?" Bill asked.

"Thirty minutes ago maybe," the boy answered.

"Let them know, Ed," Bill said.

"Taking care of it," Ed answered, turning the bus around and heading back down the road.

Jenni held tight to the pole near the front door and took a deep breath. It was time.

## 2. Four, Three

Nerit's eyes narrowed when the first report came in from Ken. He was part of the team at her old hunting store. The sound of his voice made her go cold inside as she tucked away all her emotions.

"Everything going as planned here at the gun store. But, you know, you can't help but feel the ghosts," his voice said.

Katarina lifted an eyebrow.

"You know what to do," Nerit said.

Katarina nodded and strode out of the communication hub.

Peggy chewed on her bottom lip, her hands trembling.

Thirty minutes later...

"We reached our target and all is quiet except for the undead. They're making some noise. We have two missing. Maybe carried off by the baddies. Two remaining, but lunch meat. We saw four zombies running on down the road. I swear one of them had a shopping bag," Ed's voice said.

Curtis looked up. He was seated in the corner, listening to the reports coming in.

"Nerit?"

"The bandits got two of the people we were rescuing. We rescued two others and four of the bandits' vehicles are heading toward Katie and Travis," Nerit translated.

"Can we do this?"

"Of course," Nerit answered.

There was a coldness in her voice that terrified Curtis. She could see it in his eyes. Sometimes, she wondered if he understood what it meant to protect the fort. Certain things had to be done that not everyone would agree with, but opinions did not matter. Safety did; the protection of the all. The individual be damned.

"Peggy, make sure everyone is in position," Nerit said firmly.

"Nerit? Old Man Watson wants a gun. He says, and I quote, he fought in WW2 and that if he took out the Japs, he can take out some punks." She sounded annoyed and amused at the same time.

"Give him one then. Put him on the third floor," Nerit answered.

"Nerit, he's an old guy," Curtis said in protest. "You can't expect him--"

"Why not?" Nerit looked at him intently. "I'm no spring chicken."

Curtis broke down with a weary laugh. "Yeah, true, but--"

"Give him a gun and plenty of ammunition, Curtis. Make sure he understands to stay behind the curtains."

Nerit gave him a look that silenced his protests and only reinforced his fear of her.

Good.

He needed to be afraid.

She briskly walked out of the room, ignoring her hip. The dull ache was bothersome, but she wouldn't let it slow her down. She could be extraordinarily strong when she had to be. It wasn't uncommon for her to ignore all her pain and push her body to get things done. Only later would she let her body hurt, once she was done and behind closed doors.

Calhoun emerged from the shadows, flipping on his video camera and aiming it at her face. The tiny red light blinked at her.

"The queen of the amazons is in full battle mode. There is a look of death in her eyes and she is..." he faltered as she stared into the camera.

Nerit tilted her head.

"...kinda hot."

Nerit burst out laughing and patted Calhoun's shoulder as she passed him.

"...and she walks confidently to amass the defenders of this illegally built fort. The mayor has yet to explain himself and release an accurate accounting of how much of the taxpayer money was used in its construction. Meanwhile..."

Nerit turned and gave Calhoun a look. He stared, silenced by her look.

"Yes, your majesty?"

"It's time for you to turn off the camera and do what you're supposed to," Nerit said.

Calhoun dramatically sighed, then tucked it away in his backpack. "You're a mean old bitch."

"I haven't pitched you over the wall yet," Nerit reminded him.

"Are you the one pitching people over the wall?"

"Would you be surprised?"

Calhoun considered this, rubbing his grizzled chin. "Nope."

Nerit shrugged. "Just get to your position."

"Wanna go on a date?'

"No."

"Have sex?"

"Definitely not."

"Lesbian, huh?"

Nerit smirked and walked away.

"Damn Amazons."

***

Jenni hit the ground running. Already the humidity was filling her lungs, making her feel slow and sluggish. Behind her the bus was idling, waiting. Beyond the bus, about half a mile away, a large crowd of zombies was coming.

The high school was very small, very modern, and locked up tight as a drum. There had been no response when they had tried to contact the school by the CB. But they had seen someone alive standing on the roof watching their approach. Jenni was taking a chance it was their people. It was a small comfort that Bill, Ed and the others were covering her.

Running up the steep slope to the back of the school, she headed for a set of double doors. Reaching them, she banged hard on the doors.

"Open up! It's the rescue team from the fort!"

She kicked and pounded on the door relentlessly.

A woman's voice said from the other side, "We're not opening up unless we know you're not with the assholes from earlier."

"Look. I'm from the gawddamn fort and there is a crowd of your very dead townspeople on its way so get the fuck out of there or we are leaving you!"

The door opened slightly, a thick chain still keeping it partially locked. A large woman with mousy brown hair looked at her for a long second.

"There were these guys--"

"No freaking time. We're gonna leave now," Jenni said firmly.

"...and said they were going to rape us."

"Bye."

Jenni turned and ran down the hill, her lungs burning, her eyes on the swiftly-approaching undead. To her relief, she heard the door open behind her and footsteps.

"But we need to get our--" someone started to protest.

"No time!" Jenni waved at the zombies.

There were no more protests.

She clambered onto the bus. The nurse, her kids, and the surviving students and teachers climbed on as well. They were amazingly clean and looked well fed. For a moment, they stared in shock at the two scraggly, skinny survivors the team had rescued from the tree.

"Sit down," Jenni ordered.

They obeyed.

Ed shifted gears. The bus lurched forward.

"Where were you?" Jenni asked, picking up the thread of their earlier conversation.

"Oh, yeah, so on the third day, the lady walks by the parrot in the doorway to the pet shop and it says again, 'Hey Lady!' And she says, 'What?' all angry, because she knows what is coming." Ed drove swiftly down the drive as the zombies rounded the corner behind them. "And the bird says, 'You're damn ugly.' And the woman marches into the shop and says to the owner, 'I'm going to kill your bird and sue your pants off. Your parrot tells me that I'm damn ugly every day.' And the owner says, 'Lady, I'll take care of the parrot. You don't have to do anything crazy.' So she leaves and the bird just laughs." Ed swung the bus around the front of the building and creamed a zombie loitering in the road. "Fourth day comes along. The lady passes the parrot and it says, 'Hey, Lady!' And she is righteously pissed off and says, 'What?' And it says., 'You know.'" Ed grinned at Jenni.

"You're so lame, Ed." Jenni rolled her eyes.

Ed shrugged and the mini-bus lurched back onto the country road, the zombies in hot pursuit.

*** 

Travis pressed the button on the mouthpiece, "Is it just me or are the shadows longer in the summer?"

Peggy's voice cackled back. "I hate the damn bad weather."

"It's putting us in a bad mood, too," Travis sighed as he understood her code.

More trouble was coming.

"Still pacing us," Lenore said from the backseat. "I keep seeing flashes of light off the windshield."

"Town is in sight," Katie said as they crested a hill. The towering hotel loomed in the distance.

"If they are gonna make their move, it should be now," Ken decided. He was looking as strained as they all felt.

The mini-van passed them as planned. Katie watched the vehicle take the lead with a mixture of relief and fear. Now their job was to protect the ammunition and guns.

"They're making their move!" Lenore exclaimed.

Katie glanced into the review mirror to see the vehicle that had been tailing them suddenly come roaring into view.

The CB radio cackled again. "About those shadows," Peggy's voice was trembling. "Four more are heading in from the north."

Katie's hands gripped the steering wheel even more tightly as the mini-van and Hummer accelerated to top speed.

Behind her, a mud-covered truck came barreling down the road.

# 3. Two

From her bird's eye view on top of the hotel, Nerit watched it all happen with a strange sense of pride.

The mini-van and Hummer split up the second they hit town. The mini-van took a predetermined course that would lead it straight down Main Street. As expected, the bandits followed the mini-van. To the north, the four trucks racing into the town also changed course.

"Find their frequency. They're talking to each other," Nerit said into her head set. She adored Calhoun for rigging up a system where she didn't have to constantly be dealing with the walkie-talkie. He was insane, but a wizard with electronics.

"On it," Peggy answered.

Next to her, Juan was crouched down, fidgeting with his gun. He was rigged up to the speaker system Calhoun had created. He kept messing around with the microphone, looking nervous and worried.

The Hummer whipped around a block, now heading directly toward the incoming trucks on the north end of town.

Meanwhile, the mini-van took another turn, just keeping ahead of the truck pursuing it. Below, the gate was already yawning open slowly, guards watching to make sure no zombies slipped in.

The battered, mud-covered truck accelerated as the gate came into view. The mini-van was starting to slow.

"Nerit?" Juan asked.

"She's on it," Nerit assured him.

Then through her binoculars, she saw the windshield of the bandit truck explode into shards of glass. The vehicle veered off into a building, busting through the storefront and plowing into the building out of sight.

"Shit."

Nerit smiled proudly. "I trained Katarina well."

Juan nodded, clearly impressed.

The mini-van safely slid into the first lock of the entrance. The gate slid closed behind it.

"Objective one accomplished," Nerit said with satisfaction.

She watched as the Hummer continued on its mission.

***

Katie listened to Peggy's voice, her stomach tightening. "Turn on Madison, Nerit says."

Travis was gripping the dashboard with both hands, watching the road anxiously. Behind him, Lenore and Ken were armed and ready.

Katie twirled the steering wheel and the Hummer ripped around the corner, nearly cutting off the first bandit truck as it headed down Madison. There was a great crash behind them as one truck barreled into the back of another. Glancing into the rearview mirror, she watched the last two bandit trucks veer around the fender bender and keep coming.

"Just like Dallas traffic," Travis decided with a lopsided grin.

Katie laughed, then turned sharply down another side street. The town wasn't very large and a lot of the downtown streets were narrow red-bricked affairs that ran in all sorts of weird directions. Some were diagonal and others looped around. Nerit had sat with Katie for hours going over a map of the town. It was paying off in a big way now. Katie knew where she was going. The bandits did not.

The two battered trucks from the fender bender appeared distantly behind the other pursuing vehicles.

Lenore sat silently, watching out the back window. Her jaw was set and her dark eyes were blazing. "All ugly crazy white men."

Ken glanced back into the truck right on their tail. "I was praying for a man, but those guys are so not the answer. I may be hard up for a man, but not *that* hard up."

Lenore high-fived Ken. "Amen, sistah."

Katie didn't have time to study the men behind them and make any judgments. She was busy trying to make sure they didn't die as they distracted the bandits from the mini-van going into the fort. She whipped the Hummer around another corner. The mini-van needed to get into the second lock before the Hummer could make its run for safety.

Peggy's voice came through the static. "Hate to say this, but shadow number five has arrived. It's a huge ass 4 x 4 truck."

"Where is it?" Travis asked.

"Heading straight up Main Street," Peggy answered.

"Let's go play chicken," Katie said with an evil grin.

"Damn," Ken sighed. "I'm going to die without ever getting laid again."

\*\*\*

Katarina lay perfectly still on top of the newspaper building's roof. Covered in a bed sheet spray-painted to look like the roof, she blended in perfectly. Her sniper rifle was poised, ready, and warm in her grip. Her eye was just as cold and just as deadly. Her long hair was braided down her back. The wind whistled in her ears.

"We have a change in plans. Another truck has arrived," Nerit's voice said in her ear piece.

"Same dance as before?" Katarina asked.

"No. Let Katie play with them, and then we're going to drop our surprise on them. Then we continue as planned."

"My dance card has empty slots," Katarina answered into her headset.

"I have a feeling they'll be filled."

Katarina smiled and watched the spread of road before the gates.

\*\*\*

Katie led the four trucks straight down Main Street, toward the new truck. It didn't see the Hummer until it crested the hill. Katie didn't swerve an inch.

"Shit," Travis muttered.

The oncoming truck did a sharp swerve to the left and clipped a street lamp. It shimmied, then came to a sharp stop. Meanwhile, the four bandit trucks slammed on their brakes and nearly piled up.

Wrenching the wheel to the left, Katie turned down a side street then hit Morris St. "Fuck the gate. Let's ditch the Hummer."

"I am all for that," Lenore agreed.

"We're taking the side door," Travis said into the mouthpiece as the Hummer roared up to the hotel.

"Understood," Peggy answered. "I'll let them know you have a delivery."

Travis was sure that Peggy's years as a dispatcher was coming in handy today.

The Hummer drew up to the service entrance. The heavy iron door slid open. Jumping out, the four of them made a run for it. Two guards emerged from inside and watched the road.

"Hurry up!" Bill was just inside, waving at them.

After scrambling up onto the dock, Travis reached back and pulled Katie up. She spun around her heel, looking back to make sure Ken and Lenore were following.

Ken easily pulled himself up onto the dock and turned around. He promptly began to wave and urge on his best friend.

"I'm coming. I'm coming. Hold on!" Lenore, being quite large for her height, huffed behind the rest. She was almost to the loading dock when a truck came squealing into view.

"Lenore!" Ken sounded frantic and almost jumped back into the street. Travis barely caught him in time.

The young woman turned and fired with seamless grace. The arrow drilled into the front tire, blowing it out. The driver lost control and slammed into the Hummer. The screech of metal and the smell of burnt rubber filled the air. The Hummer groaned as it was shoved a few feet over. Lenore jumped out of the way with more agility than one would think.

A huge man, disgustingly dirty, staggered out of the truck, bleeding fiercely from a wound on his forehead. Lenore seemed to use this as a target. The man fell back, the end of the arrow protruding from between his eyes.

Two more men were still in the truck, but they ducked down.

For their guns, Travis thought.

Katie shouted, "Hurry, Lenore!"

Lenore shrugged and hauled herself up onto the loading dock.

"White people," she muttered slipping past Katie. "Always screaming about something."

Ken threw his arms around her and dragged her inside. "Girlfriend, you scared me shitless!"

"Get inside!" Travis ordered. "Let's not wait for them to find their guns."

As soon as they were all inside the doors were sealed shut.

Together, both Travis and Katie made a mad dash for the elevator.

***

Nerit watched as the last four bandit trucks finally found their way down the road. They were moving a little more cautiously than they had been. Their leader was wising up. Peggy couldn't find their frequency. Nerit was sure her opponent had ordered radio silence. She could see someone in the second truck motioning to the others.

The trucks were about ten feet from the gate when Juan gave the signal. The crane overhead dropped a small storage unit. Nerit smiled with satisfaction as it crashed down, clipping the front end of the first truck. It sent the hood flying and the truck jackknifing.

All went silent below.

Juan looked at her, holding his binoculars tight. "We're winning right?

Nerit shook her head. "We're not planning to win."

Juan frowned. "I don't understand."

"We're going to make them fear us," Nerit answered with a cold smile. "And that is far more effective."

## 4. One

"It's the Boyds," Curtis said to Nerit and Juan. He was watching the video feed from the cameras Calhoun had rigged up on the walls. Four tiny black and white TVs were serving as monitors. "Drug smuggling, raping, murdering assholes. The whole family has been the bane of this county for more than a century. Half of them are in jail. Or at least they were."

The three of them were hidden by a false front Juan had built. They could see quite well, but it was hard to see them from below. Nerit was watching the street through the scope of her sniper rifle.

With Nerit and Katarina on watch, Juan felt a helluva lot safer.

283

"I bet they went and busted Martin out," Curtis went on. "He was up for murdering his ex-girlfriend and her husband. He didn't take to her dumping him when he was in jail and marrying someone else."

Juan took a deep breath. "Nerit, I don't know if I can--"

"You're a strong man, Juan De La Torre. You just have never faced this sort of situation before. I have faced similar situations. I will guide you. You will learn. They will not respond to an old woman with an Israeli accent, but they will listen to a strong male voice with a good West Texas accent."

Juan rubbed his face. "Okay, you have a point."

"What are they doing?" Travis asked as he joined them.

"Sitting there," Nerit answered.

"Trying to figure out what to do next?" Katie wondered.

"They came this far," Nerit said. "They will not want to leave empty handed. Juan, say what I say." She spoke swiftly never letting her gaze leave the view below.

Juan pressed down on the button Calhoun had showed him on the microphone. "Attention trespassers. You are to leave immediately."

On the small monitors set up in the "eagle's nest" Curtis watched a man in one of the trucks flip off the fort. "Nice answer. I hate these guys."

"Say this," Nerit said to Juan.

He listened then said, "We know of your acts of violence against others and will not tolerate your presence. You must leave immediately."

He hesitated then ad-libbed, "Because your shit doesn't fly around here."

Katie laughed and Nerit smiled.

Curtis frowned as the men inside the trucks began to talk to each other. A few flipped off the fort again.

Calhoun slid into the now cramped eagle's nest and began to fiddle with the equipment he had set up. "If I had more time I could have gotten the sound perfect. The equipment I had to work with was ridiculous. Do you realize how hard it was to-"

Nerit put her hand over his mouth.

Faintly, the microphones hidden along the wall picked up the bandits' voices shouting out insults.

Finally, a large bald man stepped out of one of the trucks with a camper on the back. Cupping his hands to his mouth, he shouted, "We're here for food and supplies. You're the ones who attacked us."

"Tell him you want to speak to their leader," Nerit said to Juan.

"That's bullshit," Juan answered through the microphone, resorting to talking his normal way and dropping the pretense. "I want to talk to your leader."

"I am the leader," the bald man answered.

"Katarina," Nerit said softly into her mouthpiece.

The man went down, screaming, gripping his shattered knee.

Juan blinked.

"He's not the leader," Nerit explained.

"Oh." Juan hesitated, pushed the button, and then said, "I said your leader, not his girlfriend."

Curtis laughed at this.

Calhoun snorted and said, "Yeah, damn aliens. They have ugly ass women."

There was more discussion on the video feed. Finally, a door opened on the opposite side of the truck, facing away from the fort, and figures were slipped out and moved to the back the truck. At last, a tall, almost handsome man stepped into view, dragging a girl with a gun firmly pressed to her temple. The girl looked to be around sixteen. Her features were badly distorted and her arms and legs were covered in bruises and cuts.

"Enough of the bullshitting. We want guns, ammo and enough food to get us through the winter, or I'm going to kill this little girl," the man shouted.

"That's Martin. Gawddammit. They busted him out of prison. He'll do it. He'll kill her," Curtis said.

"No, he won't," Nerit answered and said into her mouthpiece. "Katarina."

"High or low," Katarina's voice said, small and tinny and barely heard by those around Nerit.

"Low," Nerit said after a pause. "It will be merciful. We can't save her anyway."

On the monitor, the tall, gruff, charismatic man was jerking the girl about by her hair, making a good show. Her head jerked back and blood splattered his face. He found himself holding a very dead young woman. Her blood dripped from his startled features. With a wordless exclamation, he dropped her and stepped back in shock.

Curtis jerked his head toward Nerit. "What the fuck?"

Katie covered her face with her hands and turned away.

"It's a better fate than the one they would have dished out," Travis said in an agonized voice.

"We just don't kill innocent people," Juan protested, then hesitated, before adding, "do we?"

Katie looked back at the monitor to see the leader had recovered.

"Oh, so you'll kill someone who doesn't mean shit to you, huh? Then what about one of your own?"

Travis later thought he shouldn't have been surprised when a large burly man dragged Shane out of the back of the camper. He should have known that Shane was too mean to die at the hands of the zombies like Philip had. It shouldn't have been a shock that he would find a way to the bandits. But the once arrogant sonofabitch was dressed in a ragged dress and had makeup smeared all over his face. He looked battered and abused with his mouth gagged and his hands tied with rope. It bothered Travis to no end to see tear marks streaking Shane's face.

Beside him, Katie put her head down, and whispered, "Oh, God."

Shane was struggling, trying to get free. Maybe he had not told the bandits why he was out of the fort, but it didn't matter.

"I got one of your boys from a patrol right here! He's a pretty thing, don't you think?" Martin grinned and patted Shane's cheek.

"What did they do to him? What the fuck? That ain't right!" Curtis was horrified.

"They're beasts. They don't need a reason to do what they are doing," Nerit answered. "Katarina," she said into her headpiece. "Take care of it."

Shane was struggling, reaching toward the fort with bloodied hands, screaming behind his gag. The big guy cuffed him hard and Shane staggered. He fell to his knees and his head snapped back as Katarina put him down.

Travis was surprised that he felt remorse. No one deserved what Shane had endured.

The monitors showed that the leader was startled and a bit confused by this turn of events.

"This is what you need to say now," Nerit said to Juan. "Tell him that we have much more to lose than he does, that we have no problem fighting to the death. We have fought zombies and we can fight them. Tell him that we will sacrifice our own to protect the fort. Tell him that we have no problem with killing him or his people. Tell him that we are relentless and cannot be intimidated. Tell him that we have contingencies on contingencies. Tell him that right now, my sniper can blow his fucking head off without blinking, that she just did it to two innocent people and that right now she's not aiming at his head, but his dick."

Juan laughed. "I'm gonna love saying that." And he did...with his own flair, but almost verbatim to what Nerit had said.

On the tiny black and white monitors, they watched the leader take a step back, his bravado completely faded away. Beneath all the grime, the arrogance, and the wild eyes, was a man strung out on drugs and booze and living at the edge of the abyss. For once, he was not in control and he shifted uneasily on his feet.

"Now, let's put cherry on top," Nerit said. "Signal Jason."

On top of city hall, a camouflage's sheet was thrown off. The teenagers and Roger quickly unfurled the long slingshot and loaded it up with a nice homemade Molotov cocktail. The kids had been practicing for weeks, so when their first shot hit the last bandit truck and sent it bursting into flames, no one was really surprised. Cheers erupted all over the fort.

Below, the bandits panicked. Through the smoke, they could be seen scrambling to get back into their trucks.

It was then that the mini-bus flew down Main Street, zombies flowing behind it. Ed was leading the zombie horde like a pied piper for the undead.

Through the smoke, the bandits did not see the mini-van or the zombies, until the mini-bus turned into the quickly opening gate.

The zombies, finding fresh bodies, were immediately on the bandit trucks. They ripped at Shane's body, the guy Katarina had shot in the knee, and the body of the dead girl. They lay siege to the trucks, beating on them, desperate to feast on those within.

Meanwhile, the gates closed quietly behind the mini-bus, not one zombie slipping in with it. They were too intent on the bandits.

The bandit trucks slammed into each other as they tried to escape, then finally the remaining trucks roared off, the fresher, stronger zombies running along behind them.

In the street was the burning truck, a few straggling zombies, and the dead.

***

Silence filled the eagle's nest. They knew they had won. They felt it and it was glorious. But they had gone to a place that was not quite pleasant. No one could seem to make themselves look at Nerit.

Finally, she stood, and shouldered her sniper rifle.

"That'll teach them to mess with the Amazons," Calhoun decided.

"They're afraid now," Nerit said. She looked at Katie and Travis, then at Juan and Curtis. They were all quiet and overwhelmed. Only Calhoun was grinning and dancing a weird jig.

Katie finally looked up. "We did the right thing."

Nerit shrugged slightly, then said, "I need a smoke." and walked away. She could hear the cheers of the people in the fort as she made her way to a quiet corner. Calhoun jigged away to the music in his head as Curtis sit in sad silence, his hands over his face, weeping. Katie rested her hand on Travis' shoulder and he kissed her forehead soothingly.

The cigarette was lit and dangling from her fingers when Katarina sat down across from her a few minutes later. In silence, Nerit offered her a cigarette. The younger woman took it. Katarina lit up and slowly exhaled.

They looked at each other and said absolutely nothing, but they exchanged something powerful in their gaze. They would always be the ones to do what was right and hard.

After two cigarettes, Katarina finally said, "I should have shot his dick off."

They both laughed.

# Chapter 19

## 1. Alone Time

Bill was weary, bone weary. Every muscle in his back was cramping. If it was possible, his eyes were even cramped. Rubbing his grainy eyes, he sat on top of the city hall roof. Since the hotel had opened, that roof with its gazebo, pool and nice patio furniture had become the place to hang out. The wind could be brutal up there, but the building had been angled to break down the wind. Personally, he preferred the city hall roof. He sat in a plastic chair, staring out over the fort.

He could hear sounds of the party in full swing up on the top of the hotel. The music and laughter were loud. People were ecstatic at their victory. He wished he was.

Popping open another beer, he exhaled slowly. Nearby Katarina was on patrol. She was so silent he barely noticed her. Well, he did notice her. She was pretty in a sort of rough way. Her face was very lean, her cheek bones high. Her eyes were very keen and had fine lines around them. Of course, what was truly beautiful about her was her long, thick red hair that was now always braided down her back. He had considered asking her out, but when he wasn't sure what that meant in this dead world, he just gave up. One thing for sure, she was Nerit's star pupil, and scary as hell when on the job.

He sighed.

Right now, he hated his job.

A lot of people had thought it was all over when the bandits high-tailed it out of town. Of course, that wasn't the end of it, but the civvies had thought it was. While they celebrated, Bill and Curtis, with a small group of armed guards, had exited out the loading dock door and grabbed one of the surviving bandits. Actually, it had been easy to grab him since he was crying hysterically and banging on the door. The two survivors from the vehicle that had chased Travis' team had tried to shoot their way out of town. Out of ammo and his partner being eaten by the zombies, the last man standing had run back to the fort.

It had been Clyde Otis. Bill knew him. Clyde was the youngest of a family of crooks that hung out with the Boyds. The Otis Auto Repair Shop was nefarious for underhanded dealings and the scamming of unlucky travelers who broke down in the county. But the family was also in the center of other illegal dealings that went back a century. Though the Boyds were the main crime family in a three county spread, the Otis family was tied into it by marriage and association.

Clyde, all of twenty-two, had cried like a baby the second Bill had hauled him into the fort. He reeked of alcohol and body odor. His red-rimmed eyes and haggard expression spoke of hardcore drug use. Unfortunately for Clyde, he was on his way back down from a high and completely overwhelmed. He had not struggled one bit. As a precaution they had tied him to a chair, but all Clyde did in response was cry more. He was unshaven and pale. His pupils were dilated and his nose raw.

"Lots of drugs, huh," Curtis had said coldly.

Clyde had cried harder.

It had taken nearly an hour for him to calm down. The story came out in angry, then desperate answers to their questions.

The story was simple.

When the zombie plague hit, the Boyds rounded up their buddies and went on a crime spree. The first few days were full of looting, raping, revenge murders, and zombie hunting. The Boyds took full advantage of the situation. Clyde, unmarried, cried when he said his Mama and girlfriend had been eaten, but admitted that the gang had not attempted to protect their family other than the boy children. The wives, who had often sported broken noses, blackened eyes, and had a terrible lack of teeth, had been left to fend for themselves. The men gathered up the boys and took off in a caravan of death.

They picked up women survivors along the way, used them until they were lost to the zombies or died. Sometimes they played games with the women, dangling them off a rooftop over crazed zombies. Sometimes the women were bitten and they tied them down until they died. Clyde swore up and down he had nothing to do with it, but Bill had seen all the classic symptoms of a man who was lying.

The bandits lived in a blur of violence, drugs, and alcohol. The new violent, deadly world was to their liking at first. They would listen to the fort's contact with survivors until they figured out where the survivor's were located, then swoop in if there was any indication of women or food.

Clyde admitted that the ruse that had often worked was to hold one of the women or young girls they had kidnapped at gun point and threaten her life if they were not given supplies. It was a ruse to get the survivors to open up their safe haven. The false promise to let the girl go was often believed, much to the bandits' amusement.

Moving from one place to the next, the bandits had slowly dwindled in numbers. In fighting among the bandits, zombies, and armed survivors had an impact on them. From the sound of it, most of them had been inebriated or high as a kite through most of the first months. The bandits had avoided the fort out of fear of a military presence. It was only later that they realized the fort was just civilians.

Then the hot weather blew in and their steady diet of drugs, junk food, and alcohol began to have an impact. The need for food sent them scavenging. It was then they realized that the fort they had been ignoring had salvaged the food before they arrived. They had done some drunken hunting to sustain themselves, but eventually, their desire for guns and food had pushed them toward the fort.

Bill took a long drink and stared out toward the hills.

How long the bandits had watched, Clyde wasn't sure. But their leader, Martin, had been smart and sober enough to herd some zombies down to the fort to see how the survivors reacted. He had put the gun store under constant watch. Martin had been sure that the people in the fort would return to the hunting store when they felt threatened enough by the bandits and zombies. He had monitored enough of the conversations between the fort and Ralph to know of its importance. Clyde did admit the truck that attacked the rescue mission Bill had been on had not been planned. Martin had a sense of prison justice and the men who had screwed up so royally were given a fate similar to Shane's.

Bill rubbed his brow and sighed.

The survivors in the fort had been so terrified of the bandits. The precautions taken had been extraordinary. Every inch of the fort had been scrutinized. Extra spears had been made. They had tried to attach barbwire along the tops of the walls. Contingency plans were made for every possibility they could think of. Everyone had been gripped with paranoia. Even the children had been instructed in protecting themselves. One of the worst images in his mind was of Peggy's son wielding one of their makeshift spears. Peggy had to take it away from him before he stabbed someone through.

Taking a long swig of his beer, Bill sat back in the plastic chair and let the warm breeze flow over him.

The bandits had been routed and were not anything more than drug addled hoodlums. But that did not mean that more dangerous and clever people were not out there. That thought terrified him. Could they truly be that thorough? Truly make the fort as safe enough to withstand anything? Hell, they had actually bricked up all the windows on the second floor. The basements of all the buildings were secured. The wall was being reinforced...

He looked over the street and sighed softly. There were no lights to be seen anywhere but the fort. The world was so black and empty, the stars shone with unequaled brilliance above.

How long the fort's lights would stay on was anyone's guess. So far it was good, but there were plenty of generators on standby. Hopefully things would remain as they were for the fall and winter.

He was glad that his deceased wife, Doreen, had not lived to see this day. She had fought the cancer so diligently as it slowly ate her away, but now he was glad she had lost that battle. It would have been sheer hell to see her endure this. He was very lonely, but it was better than seeing her suffer. Besides, if she had been in a clinic or hospital when it all went to hell, she could have very well ended up one of the undead.

Glancing over at Katarina, Bill sighed. When they let Clyde out the side door, he had been sobbing, begging to be allowed to stay. Curtis had handed him a spear and sent him on his way. Clyde had only made it a few steps before Katarina ended his life. Even though Bill had seen it coming, he had flinched.

He lifted the beer to his lips and took another long drink. He was thinner now, but his beer belly persisted. Rosie was working on brewing her own beer, so chances were it was not going away once the local supply was used up.

Katarina slowly walked up to him and stood over him, her sniper rifle cradled in her arms. "Shouldn't you go sleep? Or maybe go up to the party?"

"Ever think we missed something? Something important?"

She lifted an eyebrow, then shrugged. "No."

Bill frowned. "How can you be so sure?"

"Well," Katarina said, kneeling down. "We have all worked pretty damn hard to do everything we can do. At this point, we have covered everything possible. But..." she shrugged again "Something impossible may happen. We just have to do what we can. So I don't worry about it."

With a slow sigh, Bill reached down to his side for another beer. "The bandits sure weren't what we thought, eh?"

"Always go with the worse case scenario," Katarina answered.

"Nerit's advice?"

Katarina nodded.

Bill popped open the can, then said, "Well, then, I guess we're doing okay considering what has gone down."

"We're alive," she agreed. "That's saying a lot."

With a laugh, Bill nodded. "Yeah. Yeah, it is." He stood up, his knees creaking. "I'm going to take this and go to bed now."

"Good night, Bill." Katarina moved on, her gaze returning to the perimeter.

He trudged down the stairs, anxious all at once to sleep and not deal with reality. Maybe...maybe...if he was lucky...he would dream of Doreen and their wonderful day in Venice...

And maybe, just this once time, he wouldn't dream of everyone around him turning into zombies chasing him and Doreen into the ocean.

*It would be nice*, he thought. Very nice.

## 2. Together Time

Jenni sat in her bed, the covers pooling around her waist, her long hair falling over her bare breasts. Beside her, Juan was sleeping soundly, one arm thrown over his head. She had woken up after a particularly bad nightmare. She could feel its terrible tendrils still infecting her mind. Staring out the window at the stars, she tried to reclaim her mind and her life from the ghosts of her nightmares.

Rubbing her nose, she took a deep breath.

The bandits were beaten. The zombies were beyond the walls of the fort. Juan was her lover. Jason was alive and safe. Katie and Travis were happy together. Life as a whole was good...until she slept.

Sliding out of the bed, she walked naked to the window and laid her hands on the warm glass. Down in the street, Lloyd was staring up at her. His torn face was twisted into a deadly smile.

Jenni took a deep breath, then let it slip from between her full lips. She reached deep down inside and pulled on her strength and love. Her anger was useless against Lloyd.

"Lloyd," she whispered.

*Come die with us,.*

"You are not the beginning or the end of me."

His smile faded.

"I'll die when I choose. And I know one thing for sure, I'm not going where you are."

His smile disappeared.

"Fuck you, Lloyd. I don't need you to be afraid of anymore. You're not the biggest or the baddest monster in my world." Jenni flipped him off and turned away from the window.

There were worse things in this world to fear than the stupid ghost of her dead, asshole husband, and there were wonderful things to enjoy and love. Jenni didn't have the patience to be afraid anymore and ruin her new life.

Sliding into the bed, she ran her hand over Juan's chest. He stirred slightly. Taking her hand, he drew her into his arms and she settled down against his body.

"What's wrong?" he asked.

Jenni slung her arm over his waist and draped one leg over his. "Nothing," she answered truthfully. "It just took me awhile to figure that out."

Juan was too sleepy to understand so he just kissed her forehead.

When Jenni fell asleep, she wasn't afraid anymore. She wouldn't give Lloyd anymore of her life.

She was done with him.

## 3. The Time of Beginnings

Katie stared at the little stick, squinting in disbelief. She checked the box again, then sat back on the edge of the bathtub and exhaled slowly.

Despite all the insanity of their life, despite the dead world, despite all the terror, this was a choice they had made together. They had decided to live a new life and embrace it fully. In their strangely accelerated world where there was really no time to mourn, but only time to fight to live, this had been a distinct possibility they had embraced.

"Travis!" She pulled the rayon robe tighter around her body and held the stick in one hand as she crossed her legs.

The door opened and he peered in at her. He must have fallen asleep while she showered. He looked a little bleary-eyed. He was clad in his pajama bottoms only and his hair was mussed.

She held up her announcement and he padded into the bathroom to squint at it. It took a few seconds for it to register in his mind.

"For real?"

Katie lifted her eyebrows and nodded. "Oh, yeah."

Travis let out a wild laugh and dragged her to her feet. "Amazing!"

Katie began to laugh and tossed the stick into the trash. "Yeah! We are! We've just made our life a helluvalot more complicated."

"I'll take it!" Travis gathered her close and kissed her.

Happiness and fear were jumbled up inside of her mind, but Katie embraced those feelings. In a world full of death, life was something to embrace.

She kissed Travis and felt the first of her tears on her cheeks.

Joyously, Travis clutched her tightly. And together they laughed with delight.

## 4. Time of the Dead

Katarina watched the zombies beating against the wall with cold eyes. She knew there were plans in the morning to destroy them and clear the area around the fort. She would be sleeping at that time. She was fine with that. She had done enough killing to last her for awhile.

The deadlands beyond the fort were dark and full of mystery. She had no idea what lurked out there and she wasn't sure she wanted to know. There was enough weirdness in her world as it was. Zombies and the ghost of her mother were enough to make her on edge.

She wasn't too sure what to think of the ghost. It didn't speak to her, just stared at her with disapproval. At first she thought she was dreaming, but she was seeing her mother's stern angry face more and more often. She had overhead other people talking about dreaming of dead ones or thinking they saw them in darkened corners of their room. Maybe it was just paranoia. Or maybe there were ghosts.

The dead now outnumbered the living. How did that affect the world beyond the obvious? Maybe the dead weren't just walking and hunting the living, but haunting them.

Katarina rubbed her eyes and looked over her shoulder. Her mother stood in the shadows, near the doorway.

"You're not really here," Katarina said.

The ghost remained.

Shaking her head, Katarina looked back toward the street and the zombies.

"So, if hell is full and the dead are walking the earth, Mr. Romero, where are their souls?" Maybe she should ask the Reverend.

In silence, Katarina watched the moaning dead and ignored the ghost of her mother lingering over her shoulder.

She had too much work to do to bother with the dead anymore than she had to.

"Fuck the dead," she whispered. "This is our world."

# Chapter 20

## 1. The Seasons

Fall lived up to its reputation as a time of harvest as the occupants of the fort loaded up on as much supplies as possible. With the area around the fort pretty much clear of zombies, they worked as hard as they could preparing their winter stores. The hunters brought back venison, fowl and beef to fill the hotel freezer. Every bit of food was carefully cataloged and menus were prepared well in advance of the cold weather.

Halloween came and went. Despite the obvious reality of monsters in the world, the handful of kids in the fort had fun dressing up and trick or treating through the hotel. Everyone stuffed themselves on candy and a pumpkin patch that Ed knew about allowed Jack-o'-lanterns to be placed on the fort walls. These seemed to disturb the few zombies that did appear during the holiday. The teenagers had fun pelting the dead with them.

Thanksgiving was surprisingly joyful. Wild turkeys ended up on the menu and pumpkin pie was a wonderful delicacy that everyone enjoyed. As December approached, the world seemed remarkably peaceful, despite the occasional zombie.

It began to feel like the fort was truly secure, that a true victory had been won over the dead.

## 2. The Good Things in Life

Jack, the German Shepherd, wanted a cookie.

Lying on the floor, watching Jason on the phone, he wondered if the boy could see the sheer hunger that loomed in his eyes, hunger for a cookie.

Jason was talking and talking and talking...

Jack yawned, his sharp teeth flashing in the early morning light. He couldn't understand why his boy was always talking on that stupid phone with Shelley. Shelley lived just a few doors down. In fact, Jack could hear her voice quite well from her room without the phone.

Girls were loud.

Jack whimpered a little and was rewarded, not with a cookie, but a pat on the head.

Jason finally hung up and walked out of their very untidy bedroom, into the small living room. Jack followed, head down and tail limp, trying to show Jason how desperately he needed a cookie. He could hear Jenni and Juan snoring in the other room. They had been wrestling a lot last night and despite his doggy whimpers and his scratching on the door, they had not let him in to play.

Jason leaned down and hugged him tight, kissing his head and nuzzling him. Jack forgot his cookie for a moment, enjoying the love he received from his boy. He loved his boy very much, but sometimes it was hard taking care of him.

They left their rooms in the big house and went down to the weird room Jack wasn't too sure about. For one thing, there were never cookies inside, but also, it did a weird thing where when the doors shut they always opened to a different room. He also didn't like the way it moved. It made his head swim. With a doggy sigh, he walked into the small room, head down and endured the strange noises.

Happily, after they left the nasty little room, they made their way to the dining room. Jack inhaled the rich fragrance of food and felt much better. As he walked through the room, many people gave him pats on the head and a few nibbles of bacon. He gave them his biggest grin and wagged his tail extra hard. Certainly someone had a cookie.

But, alas, no one did.

With a certain amount of grumpiness, he wandered over to his dish and was happy to see someone had put a few pieces of bacon and some of that good yellow stuff on top of his kibble. Tucker was already at his bowl, eating slowly since he was an older dog. Jack knew Tucker was very old and very tired. He liked to sleep a lot, but he enjoyed Jack's occasional companionship. Tucker swung his head toward Jack and they touched noses briefly in greeting, then went back to eating.

Jack gulped down his food, then drank a bit of water. Tucker rubbed against him as he ambled away and they sniffed each other briefly, mostly as a courtesy. Licking his muzzle, Jack trotted away, searching out someone to give him a cookie.

Glancing back one last time at Jason, he noticed the boy was holding Shelley's hand under the table. Ah, his human puppy was wanting to mate. Oh, well. That was okay, but he really needed to be better about cookies.

Jack strolled down the hallway, looking around for one of his many human friends to greet and see if they would understand his need for the sweet goodness that was a cookie. He had loved Halloween when the human puppies had sneaked him lots of treats. But that was a little while back and yesterday's turkey was just a memory. He had gotten lots of hugs with people telling him they were 'thankful' for him.

Again, humans were kinda weird at times, but he loved their hugs!

"...and they took my Hummer and make me scrub floors and toilets! My nails are broken and there is not a decent manicurist around here! And you are doing nothing about this," a woman's voice was shrieking from the stairwell. "And now Travis is mayor and you're nothing!"

Jack kept walking. He didn't like the woman who smelled too clean and always kicked him when no one was looking. He wanted a cookie not a kick.

The very stinky man was standing in another hall. He was holding up what he called a camera and talking to himself. Jack thought the man smelled great. He smelled of chickens, dogs, and yucky stuff. Jack wondered if he could roll around on top of Calhoun while he slept and get that great scent on him. But Jenni would probably throw him in the bathtub and give him a bath like she had when he had managed to roll around on a dead squirrel before she caught him.

Jack pushed past Calhoun and looked into the room. Travis was there talking to Pepe's man. Pepe's man had nice leather shoes that Jack wanted to chew on, but never got the chance. Peggy was there, too, and Jack looked around for her puppy. The puppy usually had cookies or candies. But to his disappointment, there was no human puppy with goodies in his pockets.

"... had just received a grant for community development. We were trying very hard to improve the city," Peggy was saying.

"So," Pepe's man said thoughtfully. "Most of the city is on septic tanks or rudimentary sewer systems."

"Exactly. We didn't start actually zoning of the city until a year ago. It pissed off a lot of people, that's for sure. And we just started passing ordinances for new construction."

Jack stared at Peggy as she talked. She must realize he needed a cookie.

Travis sighed. "We're dealing with an archaic system for the hotel and city hall. We'll have to come up with something soon. This isn't like a big city with a network of underground systems. Sewer will become an issue."

Pepe's man frowned as he studied something on the desk. "It's better to start planning now before it is an issue. Now that we have most of the fort construction mapped out, we need to think long term."

Jack decided to concentrate on Travis.

*I need a cookie,* Jack thought intently.

Instead, Travis patted his head and scratched him under his chin.

"Okay, so how we are going to make the fort sanitary and functional in the future? I would suggest that we began immediate inspection of any buildings we absorb into the fort so we..."

Jack gave up and left the office.

Walking into the lobby, he saw the human puppies playing hard. They were running around and screaming, but none of them even smelled like cookies.

Jack sat down, yawned, and looked around.

Katie walked up to him and leaned down to give him kisses. She wasn't smelly like the old man, but she smelled like a mother. He kinda liked it. Smothering him with kisses, she hugged him tight, then wandered off.

Still, there was no cookie.

Jack flopped down and began to chew on one paw, studying his surroundings. The human puppies may not smell like cookies, but maybe one of them would go get some. Yes, this was his best bet.

Nerit walked up to him, knelt down carefully, and patted his head. "You're a good boy, Jack." She smiled and rubbed his ears.

As she reached into her pocket, his ears perked up and he thumped his tail.

With a smile, she slipped him an Oreo cookie and walked off.

Jack chewed it up, grinning to himself, then gulped it down.

Ah, now he could enjoy his day.

He stood up, stretched and headed out into the construction site. Maybe if he was lucky, they'd let him sit up next to the guard so he could bark at the loud, stinky dead things.

Yes, yes, that sounded good.

Too bad he couldn't roll around on them though...

## 3. Silent Night

What had once been dubbed the "zombie corral" was now a very nice, walled-in courtyard decorated in a thin film of fresh snow that glimmered with the reflections of the Christmas lights strung all over the fort.

Katie leaned against the rail of the guard post, looking down over the wall where children were being hustled back in after an impromptu snow fight. The tiny snowflakes were still falling, but she knew that by morning the snow would already be melting away. Snow never lasted long in these parts.

November had been a hard month. Construction had gone into over drive. It had felt like it had been non-stop until December 16th. They had reclaimed Main Street, the former zombie corral, and moved the trucks out to a new perimeter. Bit by bit they were spreading out, making things more secure.

Travis was working long hours with Eric to map out their future expanded fort. At times, Travis looked overwhelmed as he sat deep in thought. It was a lot to worry about. At times, it consumed him. But every night, when he held her, she could see that he was happy and at peace with her.

Katie looked up. More flakes touched her lips and cheeks. The sky was clear and beautiful. She sighed at the wonder of it.

Nearby, down in the street, Bill and Katarina were trying to build a snowman with Peggy and her son, Cody. It was a peaceful scene. It made Katie smile. In a few years, Katie and Travis would have a little one to build a snowman with. If things didn't go to hell...

No, she couldn't think like that.

A few weeks ago, the bulldozing of the old buildings across from the hotel had brought many people up onto the roof to watch. Zombies had rushed the bulldozers and the snipers had picked them off. The bulldozer drivers also seemed to have fun running the zombies over. The cabs had been encased in a protective mesh, so no one was lost, though there had been a scare when one zombie had dragged a sniper down off a truck. The sniper had shoved the tip of his rifle through the zombie's eye and had been rewarded by cheers from the onlookers.

This was definitely a strange new world.

And thinking of strange...

Below her, Calhoun was running around in the snow, his arms outstretched, his mouth open to catch the snow. Nearby, Eric and Stacey were running around playing with their little dog, Pepe.

The survivors in the fort were extending the wall and claiming long abandoned buildings. Some would be destroyed, others renovated. But it would take time, and time was a strange, strange beast that did very weird things.

Lenore and Ken slipped out of the city hall front doors to join Calhoun in the snow. They immediately began pelting each other with snowballs.

Nearby, a sniper took aim and Katie heard the soft pffft sound of it being fired. She knew that beyond the wall a zombie lay in the snow truly dead at last.

Travis joined her, wrapping her tight in his embrace. She snuggled into his warmth and smiled.

"Love you," he whispered, and kissed the top of her head.

"Love you," she answered.

Behind her, the hotel was illuminated. People were still celebrating the turning of the year. Christmas lights were strung in many of the windows. A huge, fake Christmas tree, dragged up from the city hall basement twinkled in the night on the roof of city hall.

Christmas had been good. The Santa Patrol, made up of all volunteers, had successfully brought back all the gifts the kids had asked for. Calhoun had explained that Santa had to rendezvous with the crew away from the fort due to the messed up clones and aliens. The kids had bought this hook line and sinker. It had been nerve-wracking to watch the volunteers leaving just to get stuff for a good Christmas for the fort's children. The Reverend had prayed over the group before they left. When all had returned safely, there had been many tears.

Christmas Eve had been lovely with caroling and a midnight service in the makeshift church in one of the old conference halls. Katie and Travis had squeezed in with everyone else and sang all the old carols. It was at the service that the Reverend announced to everyone that Katie and Travis were with child. And it was at the service that Travis had shown her what the Santa Patrol had brought back for her. It was a silver ring with a cubic zircon, but she didn't care. She had sobbed like it was a diamond. Clad in jeans and sweaters, they had said their vows in front of everyone, including Baby Jesus and the Holy Family tucked into a manger scene in the corner.

"Couldn't show it for years in city hall cause of the supreme court," Peggy had said as it had been set up in the makeshift church. "I guess all that is done with now."

Now, snuggled into her husband's arms, Katie watched the serene scene in the street with a small smile on her face.

"A new year," Travis sighed.

"A new year," Katie echoed.

"Couldn't be much weirder than last year," Travis decided.

"No, probably not."

Had it only been nine months since the first day? It didn't seem possible. It felt like a lifetime ago. At times, her serene life with Lydia in their beautiful home felt like a dream. She still missed Lydia terribly, but the truth was that time was now gone. It was lost like the rest of the world. This was her new reality, her new life, her new world.

She tilted her head to look up at Travis. The stress was showing between his eyes. She reached up with her cold red fingers to brush them over the grooves. He relaxed and smiled at her.

"It'll be the best year we can make it," Katie decided. "We have the baby coming and so much to do with the fort."

"I just want to make things safe for you and the baby and everyone else."

Katie pulled him down and kissed him as she snuggled against his chest.

The snowball caught them smack dab in the middle of their kiss. Sputtering, they both looked down over the old wall to see Jenni and Juan wrestling in the snow, shoving handfuls of the white stuff down each other's clothes.

Then they saw who the guilty party was. Nerit was fashioning another snowball with a grin on her face. With unequaled accuracy, she nailed Jenni.

Calhoun ran past, whirling around as he went, laughing hysterically.

Jenni snagged up a hand full of snow and tossed it at Nerit, who couldn't duck fast enough.

Meanwhile, Jack ran around barking as Jason hurled snowballs at his girlfriend, Shelley.

"Let's get down there, Katie."

Scooping up the snow off the rail next to her, Katie tossed it at Travis' face, then ducked around him shouting, "Beat you down there!"

Beyond the walls, a lone zombie stood staring at the twinkling Christmas tree in the distance, fixated and confused, just staring...and staring...as the snow fell all around it.

# Epilogue

The man with the binoculars watched the snow fight from beneath a tree. Clad in Army fatigues, he shivered in the cold and wiped snow from his face. Behind him was another solider, a woman, was sitting in the jeep that would carry them back to the waiting helicopter.

"What do you think?"

Lieutenant Kevin Reynolds lowered the binoculars and turned toward his companion. "It's perfect. It's exactly what we need," he answered.

He slid into the passenger seat and settled in as the private drove the jeep back toward the edge of town.

From the darkened sky above, the snow continued to fall.

The new year had arrived in the dead world as the fort celebrated. The terrors of the new year were yet to be discovered and for one night there was peace among the living.

# About the Author

Rhiannon Frater works and lives in Austin, Texas. She became an Independent Author at the urging of her husband.

She loves reading, movies, gaming, and hanging out with friends and family when she's not tapping away at her computer on her latest story. She also loves hearing from her fans and tries to respond to everyone who emails her.

To contact the author directly, email her at:
**gothgoddessrhia@gmail.com.**

# Other Books By Rhiannon Frater

### As The World Dies: The First Days
### A Zombie Trilogy
### Book One

*Two very different women flee into the Texas Hill Country on the first day of the zombie rising. Together they struggle to rescue loved ones, find other survivors, and avoid the hungry undead.*

### Pretty When She Dies:
### A Vampire Novel.

*In East Texas, a young woman awakens buried under the forest floor. After struggling out of her grave, she not only faces her terrible new existence but her sadistic creator, The Summoner. Abandoning her old life, she travels across Texas hoping to find answers to her new nature and find a way to defeat the most powerful Necromancer of all time.*

# As The World Dies: Siege
## will be released in 2009.

All  novels are available in both paperback and Kindle on Amazon.com.

eBook versions are available at smashwords.com

For more information on the author, her upcoming appearances, and her writing projects, check out her blog at:
**http://rhiannonfrater.blogspot.com/**

# DYING TO LIVE
# LIFE SENTENCE
## by Kim Paffenroth

At the end of the world a handful of survivors banded together in a museum-turned-compound surrounded by the living dead. The community established rituals and rites of passage, customs to keep themselves sane, to help them integrate into their new existence. In a battle against a kingdom of savage prisoners, the survivors lost loved ones, they lost innocence, but still they coped and grew. They even found a strange peace with the undead.

Twelve years later the community has reclaimed more of the city and has settled into a fairly secure life in their compound. Zoey is a girl coming of age in this undead world, learning new roles—new sacrifices. But even bigger surprises lie in wait, for some of the walking dead are beginning to remember who they are, whom they've lost, and, even worse, what they've done.

As the dead struggle to reclaim their lives, as the survivors combat an intruding force, the two groups accelerate toward a collision that could drastically alter both of their worlds.

**ISBN: 978-1934861110**

# AFTER TWILIGHT
# WALKING WITH THE DEAD
## by Travis Adkins

At the start of the apocalypse, a small resort town on the coast of Rhode Island fortified itself to withstand the millions of flesh-eating zombies conquering the world. With its high walls and self-contained power plant, Eastpointe was a safe haven for the lucky few who managed to arrive.

Trained specifically to outmaneuver the undead, Black Berets performed scavenging missions in outlying towns in order to stock Eastpointe with materials vital for long-term survival. But the town leaders took the Black Berets for granted, on a whim sending them out into the cannibalistic wilderness. Most did not survive.

Now the most cunning, most brutal, most efficient Black Beret will return to Eastpointe after narrowly surviving the doomed mission and unleash his anger upon the town in one bloody night of retribution.

After twilight,
> when the morning comes and the sun rises,
> will anyone be left alive?

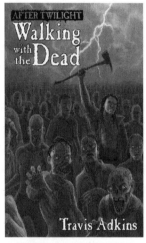

**ISBN: 978-1934861035**

# Permuted Press
## The formula has been changed...
## Shifted... Altered... *Twisted.*™
# www.permutedpress.com

Book One of the *Undead World Trilogy*

# BLOOD
## OF THE
# DEAD

A Shoot 'Em Up Zombie Novel by A.P. Fuchs

"*Blood of the Dead* . . . is the stuff of nightmares . . . with some unnerving and frightening action scenes that will have you on the edge of your seat."

- Rick Hautala
author of *The Wildman*

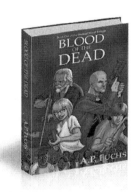

Joe Bailey prowls the Haven's streets, taking them back from the undead, each kill one step closer to reclaiming a life once stolen from him.

As the dead push into the Haven, he and a couple others are forced into the one place where folks fear to tread: the heart of the city, a place overrun with flesh-eating zombies.

Welcome to the end of all things.

**Ask for it at your local bookstore.**
**Also available from your favorite on-line retailer.**

ISBN-10   1-897217-80-3 / ISBN-13   978-1-897217-80-1

**www.undeadworldtrilogy.com**

4316441

Made in the USA
Lexington, KY
14 January 2010